Rafe's heartbeat surged.

"No, I've never been in love."

Rafe drew Viv toward the darkened doorway. She held back for a second, and his hand gave a small tug, urging her. Cupping her face, he kissed her, not roughly as he had this morning, but softly. His lips barely touched hers before they withdrew, then brushed again, again, their touch warm and soft as his breath. Then his mouth pressed more firmly, lush and hot, and his moist tongue tip flicked at the seam of her lips. Desire erupted, flaring out from her core. His arms tightened around her, lifting her against him.

For a moment, the danger of where they were vanished. The walk home to a wide bed and clean sheets was too long. Viv wanted him here and now. The hard heat of his body pressed against her. She felt the solid muscle of chest and thigh. Abruptly he tensed, then drew away. His eyes looked wary, but there was a breathless edge to his voice as he whispered, "This is not safe."

"You knew that when you started," Viv said, still not caring. She wrapped her arms around his neck. "You don't like things that are safe."

"A superlative read. . . . Clear the decks and unplug the phone, because you won't want to be interrupted."

—Susan Wiggs, author of *The Charm School*

"Highly recommended for those who are looking for something new and absorbing."

—Anne Stuart, author of *Shadow Lover*

Heart of
DECEPTION

TAYLOR CHASE

HarperPaperbacks
A Division of HarperCollinsPublishers

▣ HarperPaperbacks

A Division of HarperCollins*Publishers*
10 East 53rd Street, New York, NY 10022-5299

ISBN 0-06-101289-0

HarperCollins®, ▣®, and HarperPaperbacks™ are trademarks of HarperCollins Publishers Inc.

Cover illustration by Jon Paul

First printing: October 1999

Printed in the United States of America

Visit HarperPaperbacks on the World Wide Web at
http://www.harpercollins.com

❖ 10 9 8 7 6 5 4 3 2 1

To Sue Yuen—

For angelic patience and demonic laughter

O Tiger's heart wrapp'd in a woman's hide!

—Shakespeare

Heart of
DECEPTION

1

London, 1586

Treason ... The word was a soft incessant hiss in Raphael Fletcher's mind.

Rage, fear, and exhaustion waged war in his limbs, stringing his sinews taut then slack as he waited for the gangplank to be lowered on the Southwark side of the Thames. The August morning dawned chill and bleak as February, and Rafe felt a week's rough, dark stubble of beard as he wiped the gray misery of rain from his face. At last he slung his pack over his shoulder and descended to the dock, pushing through the throngs clustered along the bank of the river. At every corner, smoky bonfires struggled against the growing jabber of the rain. Despite the early hour and the damp weather, a frenzied clamor spilled from the taverns into the streets. A plot to assassinate Queen Elizabeth and place Mary Queen of Scots on the throne had been discovered. A seminary priest had been arrested, and a wellborn Catholic named Babington seized yesterday, skulking in St. John's wood, his skin stained dark with the rind of green walnuts. All the conspirators were being hunted down, and rumor whispered Mary herself was implicated. The whole of London seethed with a volatile mix of jubilation and rage.

"God save the Queen! God save good Queen Bess!"

A passing drunk careened into Rafe, drenching his

cloak with ale, then staggered back. Rafe grabbed the inebriated fool before he fell in the Thames. The drunk
glared up at him, affronted and eager for a fight.
Exasperated, Rafe stepped closer, towering over him. The
man had swallowed enough ale to fill the six-inch dispar-
ity in their height. They weighed the same, though Rafe
was hard muscle to the man's fat. Puffing his cheeks, the
drunk fumbled with his sword. He would likely get himself drowned or skewered before nightfall, but it would
not be Rafe who did it.

"God save the Queen," Rafe echoed with as much
vigor as he could muster.

The drunk's belligerent scowl became a broad grin. He
raised his empty tankard in a toast. "Hang 'em all!" he
cried. "Quarter 'em! Rip their guts out!"

Rafe watched the man reel away through the crowds,
then continued on his way toward London Bridge. The
thin rain became a downpour, extinguishing the scattered
bonfires. Through the streaming curtain, the twenty
arches of the Bridge wavered, a glazed blur. The waters of
the Thames rushed fiercely through the narrow portals.
Rafe paused by the gatehouse tower, gazing up at the
spiked ramparts where a half dozen heads rotted atop the
spears. The odor of corrupt flesh mingled with the reek
of wet ashes.

Treason . . . Sabotage . . .

Rafe shuddered. He closed his eyes against the ghastly
visages, but the image of his grandfather's severed head
glowed, lurid in the darkness of his mind. In another
month that vision might be reality—his grandfather and

cousin hung, then drawn and quartered, their heads left to feed the carrion birds circling the Tower Gate.

Fury at the injustice of it twisted with fear and guilt. Silently, he prayed that Gabriel had received the letter announcing his return—prayed that his best friend was not abroad on some spying mission for the Crown. Rafe would fight the charges against his family alone if he must, but Gabriel knew London best. He prowled its alleys, a tawny gentleman cat with spotless white ruff. Sir Gabriel Darren knew secrets, and men who knew more secrets. And Rafe was convinced the secret of the deception lay hidden here in London.

Turning away from the Thames, Rafe crossed a dozen small bridges arched over ditches of murky tidewater as he threaded his way through the Liberty of the Clink. All the old outlaw liberties of Southwark were now officially under London's rule. The ward was growing ever more respectable and prosperous, but those who lived within the old walls of the great city across the river still eyed the bawdy upstart askance. The Clink was the richest of the boroughs, fine new inns and handsome residences crowding cheek by jowl with ugly tenements. Brothels, gambling dens, the savage bear-baiting pit—the Clink was infamous for them all. Infamous, too, for the vile prison that gave it its name. The Liberty of the Clink was the very heart of Southwark—a dark and vicious heart, Rafe warned himself, but he felt its vitality throbbing around him.

Like fat black and white magpies, shops lined the busy streets of the mercantile district. Their upper stories jutted out, the top floors almost touching, forming staggered canopies against the rain. Gabe's lodgings were not far from the Thames. The youngest son of the Earl of Brightsea, Gabriel was rich in wit, but relatively poor in purse. He kept two rooms above his favorite inn, not far from the newly completed theatre, the Comet. Rafe climbed the stairs and knocked, first to silence, then to muffled noise within.

"It's Rafe," he called out, and the door swung wide. Gabriel gazed at him, linen shirt and fair hair equally rumpled, hose tugged on hastily. Then Gabe's arms were around him, slender and strong. Rafe returned the embrace fiercely. It had been a year, and they held each other in a long hard grip.

"I have your letter," Gabe said. "I've been hunting since I heard of the arrest."

Weary, riddled with frustration and fear, Rafe thought the rush of tenderness and relief would overcome him. He scrubbed the rising tears on the back of his hand, then drew back, giving Gabe's shoulders a last quick squeeze.

His friend's eyes were bright as well, but his smile was warm and easy, making light of desperate troubles. "You look a much-gnawed thing to me, and smell worse. Sleep and a bath would serve you well."

Rafe smiled in answer. For a moment, they might have been students at the Inns of Court once more. Even then, the others had dubbed them the Avenging Angels for their habit of interfering in quarrels they deemed unjust. The women had called them angels, too, one dark, one golden, their blue eyes the shades of winter and summer skies. However different in looks, they were brothers in heart.

"No time for sleep." Grimed with travel and splotched with ale, Rafe had no doubt he looked as haggard as he felt, with only a fistful of hours' sleep in a week. "I admit soap and water would be of good use."

Gabriel took Rafe's elbow, tugging him into the chamber. "There's a pitcher of cold water on the cupboard, and clothes that might fit in the chest."

Rafe nodded. Gabe was his height and broad-shouldered, though not so solidly muscled.

"Food?" Gabe asked.

"Something without weevils."

"I'll order a meal from the tavern."

Rafe stayed him at the door. "Gabe, have my grandfather and cousin been brought to London?"

"Not yet. They were being held in Exeter, but they are now under escort here. Most likely they'll be imprisoned in the Fleet."

Rafe nodded, thinking how terrible the journey would be for the proud old man. Gabriel hesitated, then left on his errand. Alone for a minute, Rafe succumbed to the tide of weariness. A wave rose suddenly, darkness closing over him. He pitched forward, asleep on his feet, waking to catch himself from falling. Gritting his teeth, he went to the chest by the bed, poured water from pitcher to basin and splashed his face. The sudden douse of cold revived him a little. Stripping naked, he washed vigorously, then dried himself with a rough cloth hung on a hook. In Gabe's chest he found hose and a loose shirt of fine Holland linen. The leather breeches were snug, but would do. He combed his fingers through the thick mass of his hair, smoothing it as if the gesture might order his thoughts.

For the last year Rafe had been in the Netherlands, where Protestant and Catholic alike had taken arms against the oppressor Spain to fight for their freedom. Only England had remained a faithful ally to the lowlands. When the Queen had called for volunteers, Rafe joined other English yeomen and nobles inspired to fight for their cause. But once there, he'd found himself fighting his own war against the incompetence and corruption of the very men who led them into battle, men who piled up gain and glory at the cost of others' lives.

Now, charges of treason called him back—home to an England already crazed by a conspiracy against the Queen.

Gabriel returned, nodding that his errand was successful. He sat on the bench beside the table, regarding Rafe seriously. "You didn't desert your post?"

"No, Gabe, I didn't desert," Rafe answered, glad he had not had to make the choice. "My captain is from Exeter, and knows my family. He gave me leave."

"We may have a month or less before they come to trial, and it could not happen at a worse time," Gabriel warned. "The shadow of Babington's treason falls long and dark. It obscures your family from immediate scrutiny, yet that same darkness may consume them."

"Scapegoats are poor slaughter when there are wolves circling. What good will their deaths bring, if the real saboteur walks free?" Anger grated in his voice.

"The populace is hungry for revenge, and will feast happily on scapegoat," Gabe replied.

"And will your masters feed them such tainted meat?" The man who recruited Gabriel was still a mystery, but Rafe knew they both must answer to Sir Francis Walsingham, the Queen's spymaster.

Gabriel regarded him solemnly. Rafe knew full well the question was naïve, but he had little stomach for injustice. "So they slaughter the goat and leave the wolves to ravage the flock?"

Finally, Gabe answered. "My masters want the truth. But if they don't find it, they may believe what is most convenient. If your family is executed, it will become most inconvenient to question the verdict."

"My grandfather is innocent," Rafe insisted.

"Indeed, he is positively grim in his integrity." Gabriel gave him a slightly bitter smile, for Rafe's Puritan grandfather had disapproved of their friendship, castigating the fine clothes Gabe wore, blaming him for the impious books he discovered Rafe now avidly read, and for the worst sin of all, taking Rafe to the theatre. They exchanged a silent look of affection and regret. Pursuing the main question, Gabriel lifted his fine brows and asked, "Your cousin?"

Peter was twenty-five, three years younger than Rafe, and always the more obedient grandson. Like Rafe, he had been called home from college when their grandmother had been taken ill. That same year highwaymen had killed his parents, Rafe's aunt and uncle. Son of the eldest son, it was Peter who would inherit Easton Arms.

"My cousin had a heavy burden to shoulder which he has borne admirably," Rafe said. "He has little facility with design, but has proved skillful at managing the money. He would not dream of treason. My family is loyal—to the Queen and to the Protestant cause."

"You suspect papist meddling?"

Rafe had not seen Gabe for over a year, but the affinity was the same as always. Their thoughts circled like sword tips in a friendly duel, testing, even now, when it was not a game for either. "I'm certain—as I'm certain the sabotage was committed here in London. Now I must find the proof of it."

"As soon as I heard the charges, I went to the docks and licked a few palms with silver." Gabriel crossed to the desk and removed a wrapped bundle, unfolding it to reveal a pistol. "It bought me this."

Rafe took the gun, studying the weight and balance, the fine engraving coiled with the Easton mark. He ran his thumb over the snaphance mechanism, superior to both wheel and matchlock. "There is nothing wrong with this."

"It is perfection," Gabriel agreed. "Perhaps the incidents are separate, but I doubt such a coincidence—this gun in perfect condition, the ones meant for the war marred."

Rafe's grandfather owned Easton Arms, manufacturers of the finest swords, guns, and cannon in England. The weapons his family had donated when their own Exeter company embarked were proof of it, faultless in every respect. The weapons purchased by the Crown should have been the same. But, a month ago, accusations began

flying that the guns made by Easton Arms were worthless
metal. Irate soldiers had showed him the jammed and
ruined weapons to prove it. Examining the most recent
shipment to Ostend, Rafe discovered that the weapons
had been tampered with, the screws of snaphance pistols
and muskets deliberately removed and exchanged. After
one shot the guns were useless. Because of them English
troops had died. Knowing that neither his grandfather
nor his cousin would commit such an atrocity, Rafe had
reported the sabotage.

A week ago word came that they had been arrested,
and Rafe had sailed for home filled with apprehension.
Now his heartbeat quickened with excitement. It seemed
a miracle to have a clue in hand so soon. "Who gave it to
you, Gabriel?"

"A scabby wharf rat named Scratch Jones. Yesterday he
brought me this, with a tale of seeing some crates, great
and small, transported in the small hours to a house
between the bridge and the Tower. It was guarded, but he
managed to sneak in through an unlocked window. This
gun was in one of the small crates. Most likely the others
were filled as well."

"Where is the house? Who does it belong to?"

"He would not tell me where without more coin in
hand. But that territory is controlled by the Swifts."

The name of Swift was only vaguely familiar, part of
the colorful lore of the criminal underworld that students
gathered piecemeal. "Nick Swift?"

"Yes. Nicholas and Vivian. They've risen in power
since you left London."

"Brothers?"

"Brother and sister. I've not seen Mistress Vivian—but if the tales can be believed, she is a virago."

"A woman?" Rafe shook his head, feeling the old mix of fascination and aversion for the underworld.

Gabe leaned forward, intent. "We cannot be certain of the Swifts' involvement. They've snatched that piece of London, but Jake Rivett's borders hem them close round."

"Snatched from Rivett?" That name conjured dark tales of smuggling and assassination. "A dangerous thing to do."

"Possibly lethal," Gabe agreed. "They call him Smelly Jakes—but never to his face. It's said Rivett detests the noisesome nickname so much, he shoved the man who first said it headfirst down the nearest privy."

Rafe shuddered at the ugly image of a man drowning in the shithole of a jakes.

"Rivett controls most of London's crime, as Nick Swift now controls the Clink. Kings ruling the lesser barons' domains—prostitution, gambling, thievery, beggary— what you will. And smuggling pays best of all."

"So one of them is most likely involved."

"In the smuggling, if not the treason. They control the docks."

"It is worse treason for no motive other than profit." Rafe handed back the pistol. "Have you shown this to Walsingham?"

"Not yet. There is nothing in this to prove your family innocent."

Rafe insisted. "If we go to him—"

"No." Gabriel's reply was sharp. "Not we. You must stay here."

Rafe regarded him in silence for a moment, then said quietly, "I do not think they will arrest me, too. For a year I've not been directly involved with Easton Arms— except for discovering the exact method of sabotage."

Gabe leaned toward him, his expression grim. "It is fortunate you wrote to me, Rafe. When the Earl of Leicester reported the tampering, he claimed credit for the discovery."

"You showed your masters the letter—that is why I was not named in warrant," Rafe deduced.

"Yes." Gabe sighed and nodded. "Leicester used your discovery to deflect attention from his military blunders in the Netherlands."

"More than blunders," Rafe said savagely. "There is no worse jackal fattening himself on the offal of death."

"Leicester is the Queen's favorite," Gabriel warned, laying a hand on his shoulder. "Your tongue will slice your head off, Rafe, if you do not take care how you wield it. You can be crafty enough, when you see cause for it."

"I am glutted with ugliness till I am like to vomit." Rafe clenched his fists, slammed one on the table. "The Netherlands is a bloody chaos of incompetence and corruption. Captains pocket the wages while their men starve. Worse, they send their soldiers to die, but keep their names alive to claim their pay."

"And you fought it, of course. I am surprised you lived to return."

"It was like battling an avalanche of mud," Rafe said bleakly. His gaze met Gabriel's. "Nothing will stop me from finding out the truth behind this conspiracy."

"'Courage stands halfway between cowardice and rashness,'" Gabe quoted Plutarch.

"'Yield not to evil, but attack all the more boldly,'" Rafe answered from Virgil.

There was a knock at the door, though it offered nothing more sinister than a hot breakfast. Ever cautious, Gabriel nodded Rafe to conceal himself in the next room while he took the tray. He could smell the food, and hoped the servant could not hear his stomach growl. When Gabriel summoned him, Rafe found a feast waiting on the table—a bubbling, crusty pie with beef, leeks, and cabbage, a slab of cheddar, and summer peaches with clotted cream. He sat down at the bench and ate ravenously, washing the food down with good brown ale.

They talked of better days. Rafe asked after Gabriel's family, and was assured that his father's latest alchemy experiments had caused only a small explosion, that his mother was beautiful as ever, his elder brother prosperous, and his beloved sister was recovering from her boating accident. When the last crumb of crust was gone, Rafe heaved a deep sigh. His eyelids shuttered and he forced himself to stand, fighting off the heavy weariness of satiation.

"Sleep." Gabriel gave him a push into the bed chamber, another onto the bed.

Rafe sprawled facedown, then rolled over, shaking his head to try and clear it. "We should go to the docks."

"First I must burn my path to Walsingham," Gabe said with a curious smile, tugging on a doublet of buff suede. Rafe frowned, sensing some hidden meaning in the words but too groggy to decipher it. Gabriel draped a dark cape over his shoulder and put on his hat. Rafe smiled at the dragon of enameled gold and amber glinting on its brim. He had given the brooch to Gabriel the day they met, after Gabe had supported his battle with the Midas Men, three golden popinjays of noble birth and envious disposition. Smiling in answer, Gabe laid his hand over Rafe's, where his ring still circled Rafe's finger. "Don't worry. I'll look for Scratch Jones tonight."

"We'll look." When Gabriel did not answer, Rafe insisted. "Together. Wake me."

"Tonight," Gabe replied. "We'll go out together tonight."

When the next wave of sleep rolled over him, Rafe surrendered.

Rafe started awake to a thud. A harsh clarion of alarm rang in his blood. Throwing aside the covers, he leapt from the bed and groped for his sword, his eyes sorting unfamiliar shapes in the gloom. Gabriel's room. Night. But Gabriel had promised to come back for him. Anger fired the fear that had awakened him. He grabbed the tinderbox from the bedside table, flint and steel rasping as he struck them. He lit the candle, then held it aloft as he moved into the front room. His ears caught the rough scratching of the key in the lock.

"Gabriel . . ." It came out a whisper, and Rafe felt no relief, only a deeper apprehension as the lock clicked and the door swung open.

For a moment Gabriel leaned against the threshold. His hat was gone, and his pale hair obscured his features. Then he lifted his head, staring at Rafe, his face livid above the dark folds of his cape, a knowledge beyond fear in his eyes. Death. Rafe felt its presence even as he cried out in denial.

Gabriel shoved himself from the portal, staggering across the room, falling as Rafe reached out to him. Half catching him, half stumbling with the sudden weight, Rafe sank to his knees with his burden. The metallic scent of blood clouded the air. Rafe had smelled it before he felt it, felt the wetness before the dark cape opened, revealing the soaked doublet, pale buff drenched red in the flickering candlelight. Gabriel gazed up at him, pupils wide, the blackness of the abyss into which he fell lit only by the faintest spark of life. Rafe pressed his hand to the slash of the wound, willing it closed. Gloved scarlet with blood, Gabriel's hand closed over his, so tight he could feel the grip of each bone.

"Rafe. Guns . . ." The whisper scraped, harsh as metal against bone. "Find Topaz . . ."

"Topaz?"

Gabe sucked another breath, willed it out in a long hiss. "Topaz, Silver, and . . ."

Gabriel choked as blood spilled over lips, silencing him.

"Gabriel!" Rafe called his name, holding him by it. He stared into Gabriel's eyes, watching the terrible falling away, further and further. The darkness rose, swarming around Rafe as the last fragment of light extinguished.

"No." He choked on the word. Weeping, he held Gabriel, rocked him. Emptiness opened inside his gut, an endless abyss. Gabe was dead because he had tried to help him. Dead because Rafe had come begging, then fallen asleep. He cursed himself for that, cursed Gabe for setting forth without him.

The sparks of anger ignited into flares of rage. They burned in the dark of his grief and guilt, lighting his way. This was not chance. Gabriel's death and the sabotage were linked, and Rafe would discover how. All he knew was the little he had learned from Gabe this morning. But it could not be so little, if the knowledge led Gabe to his death.

"I will avenge you," he whispered, lowering Gabriel to the floor. "I swear it."

There was a faint sound in the doorway. Releasing Gabe's body, Rafe gripped his rapier and whirled into a crouch. Tall and thin, a man stood in the open portal. The pistol in his hand was leveled at Rafe's chest. Waiting for the fatal shot, he recognized the snaphance, and wondered if it was too much to hope that the gun might be one of the tampered ones. Perhaps, even if the man shot him, he would be able to thrust home. Slowly, Rafe stood, his sword still extended.

The muzzle did not waver, but neither did the man fire, only assessed him coldly. Rafe studied the stranger in turn. Approaching forty, with an oval face, small even features, light brown hair with a thin tracery of beard and mustache—the intruder was unremarkable except for his attenuated height and his strange glistening eyes, the pale green of peeled grapes.

Gabriel's blood plastered the linen shirt to Rafe's skin. The stranger's clothes were unstained, though Gabe would not have fallen to one attacker. The man had neither shot Rafe, nor attempted to question him. Gabriel's killer would likely have done one or the other, so Rafe asked, "Who are you?"

"I am Sir Nigel Burne." He gave a nod toward Gabriel's body. "Sir Gabriel came to me this afternoon. I was to meet him again tonight in the tavern—with you, I believe. You are Raphael Fletcher?"

"Yes." A pang of guilt twisted Rafe's guts. Gabriel's voice echoed in his mind. *First I must burn my path to Walsingham.* "Burne. You work for Walsingham."

Perhaps this was the very man who had recruited Gabe to work for the Queen's spymaster.

If so, it meant little to him, for Burne frowned at Gabriel's corpse. "He said he did not tell you my name."

"He didn't. I guessed from a twist of words." Rafe confronted the pale green gaze, icy with suspicion and censure. If this man burned, it was with the acid fire of poison. Rafe knew his own face was still streaked with tears, but made no move to wipe them away, only let the anger sear through the grief, brighter and harder. They were at an impasse. Already he disliked Burne, but he doubted the man had killed Gabriel. Slowly Rafe lowered his sword. If he was wrong, he was dead.

After a moment, Burne slipped the pistol into a scabbard under his cloak. "Yes, I serve Walsingham. And from now on, so do you."

Rafe drew a harsh breath of relief, sure his own plea to join forces would have been denied. Instead Burne had chosen him. "That would suit my purpose."

⤮

Keeping his face well shaded, Rafe leaned against the doorjamb of the Lightning Bolt and surveyed the interior of the inn. He located his quarry near the back door, blond hair bright in the lamplight, fancy red boots propped on a table. London's underworld was a realm unto itself, carefully guarded. But among the criminals known to be working for the Swifts, Burne had named Garrin Garnet. Topaz, Gabriel had said. Topaz, Silver, and—Garnet? Another gemstone glinting. The first surge of excitement dissipated when they found Garnet had been locked in the Clink prison that night, after a drunken brawl. He could not have been the third of the triad. Nonetheless, they must choose between the Swifts and Rivett. Rafe took the name not as coincidence or clue, but as an omen. Garnet was another marker pointing him toward Nick Swift. Scratch Jones had told Gabriel the guns were hidden somewhere in the Swifts' territory—and yesterday Scratch Jones' body had been found in an alleyway there, his belly gutted.

So, he would play his game against the Swifts. Yesterday, discussing their opening move, Burne had dismissed Garnet as useless. "He has a reputation for a strutting cock—no friends, only rivals. Choose someone lower in the ranks and have them bring you into the fold."

If time did not press, it would have been the best approach. Rafe had rejected it. "No, I want them to take notice of me. I'll take the pawn—then take his place on the board."

Garnet was sometime bodyguard, sometime collector, sometime thief. Rafe couldn't pretend to the deftness of the nips and foists who trained from childhood to learn their illicit trade, but he knew how to fight. Guard or courier were positions he could fill. Tonight he'd let himself be robbed. Tomorrow he'd take both purse and job from the robber.

Ordering a tankard of ale, Rafe settled down at the darkest table he could find near Garrin Garnet and mimicked a sullen stupor. Though he made an easy target, at first not one nip tried to cut his purse. There was no guarantee his quarry would take the bait. Rafe lolled his head on his shoulder, eyes half-closed, watching only the customers' feet as he considered an alternate plan. At last he saw the red boots approach him stealthily. The thief hovered beside him, and Rafe remained motionless till he felt the subtle touch at his belt. Lifting his head, he gazed a bleary accusation at Garnet and grasped clumsily at his cloak. With a quick jerk, the thief eluded him, moving for the back door. Muttering curses, Rafe rose and stumbled after him. Two patrons quickly rose and bumped Rafe backward. Feigning surprise and confusion, he let them shove him toward the front door and out into street, where they melted into the night.

Still muttering, Rafe made his way along the street. "Robbed," he muttered as he passed Burne, who waited in the shadows of the nearest alley. "Dog-hearted whoreson robbed me."

Mission completed, Rafe kept up his drunken façade till he returned to the rat-hole of a room he'd rented. Brimming with an uneasy brew of excitement and anxiety, he stripped and lay in bed, staring at the ceiling till the dawn lightened the windows, then slept fitfully till noon. It was just as well, for there were still three hours till the rendezvous.

After a quick wash, and a meal of stale bread and cheese, Rafe dressed in clean linen and laid out doublet and trunk hose of dark green fustian and a slightly bedraggled ruff. The attire had been supplied by Burne, who was meticulous in such details. The garments were all such worn, serviceable clothes an unemployed fencing master might retain, after he'd sold off his most dashing finery for food and lodging. With his knowledge, it was a role Rafe could play easily enough. His grandfather had traded weapons for Rafe's tutelage in fencing, and the skill was in his blood. Rafe's father had been a fine swordsman as well as a fine actor, studying with the best fencing masters to improve his performance on stage. His mother had fallen in love with his father the day he came to purchase a sword from Easton Arms, and had been disowned when she married him against her parents' wishes.

Sliding the narrow chain over his head, Rafe studied the miniature his mother had once worn over her heart.

Rafe had the strong bones and powerful muscle of Easton masculine stock. Their bold visage—high cheekbones, lean nose, adamant jaw—underlay the sensuous features of his father's portrait. Those matched his own in form and color. Heavy brows framed large eyes, thick lashes shadowing their pale sky blue. The full curve of the lower lip was offset by the upper, long and narrow, its edge sharply sculptured. The only difference was a small mole marking the summit of his own. Rafe ran a hand through the thick mass of his own dark hair, remembering his mother smoothing back the wayward forelock, first from his father's forehead, then from his own.

The brightest joys of his youth were watching his father on stage in his magnificent duels, and nestling in the warm lap of his mother, fragrant with rosemary and lavender, as she read Bible stories to him—stories his grandfather had taught her. His father was all laughing, nonchalant charm, his mother sweet tenderness when Rafe was good, rigid aloofness when he was bad. Rafe remembered the telltale crumbs that trapped him in the lie about the pilfered gingerbread. Shaking his head, his father dusted off the crumbs and said with appreciative envy, "Raphael, that wide-eyed gaze could make the angels believe your innocence. Perform so on stage and you will be a god." He was whipped, but not as if his father meant it. Rafe was proud of the theft, his lie, his beating, until he faced his mother's accusing eyes. It was her shame, her icy reproach, that secured his repentance.

A week later they were dead of the sweating sickness. Rafe's grandparents claimed him and took him to Exeter.

He had been wretched at first, drowning in strange waters. But while his grandparents were stern in their judgments, still they offered refuge, a stability he had never known in his vagabond life. Craving their affection, he learned to hide the wildness they feared. Slowly, his life flowed into the narrower channel they set. He learned to swim more deftly, seldom colliding with the hard walls of their faith. But like sunken treasure, the memories of his childhood glittered just below the surface.

The ache of the loss echoed through him once again. Carefully, Rafe folded the miniature within a handkerchief and tucked it among his few belongings. He dressed in the clothes, then picked up the ruff and fastened it about his neck, detesting the discomfort of the thing. His grandfather approved of virtuous discomfort, but thought ruffs immoral and condemned starch as the Devil's liquor. After strapping on sword and dagger, Rafe picked up the leather purse that was his third weapon, dense and heavy with the weight of sand, and tied it to his belt. He set a cap on his head, swung his cape over his shoulders, and left the grubby room behind.

Rafe made his way past the gruesome Tower Gate and up the road to St. Savior's parish where he secluded himself inside the portal of the great Gothic cathedral. Close by, the air was tainted with the odor of the weed Raleigh had brought back with him from the New World. Overnight, tobacco had become the latest fashion. A cluster of young gallants gathered together in the churchyard, puffing on slender pipes and sending up wreaths of blue smoke as they argued whether Babington should be drawn and quartered while still alive, or allowed the relative mercy of slow throttling on the rope. Rage simmered, a hot cauldron ready to boil over. Rafe's own anger at the treason was subdued beneath the fear of how this rabid mood would affect his family.

When the great bells of St. Savior's pealed three, Rafe scanned the perimeter of the churchyard and saw Burne make his arrival. Rafe subdued his flash of antipathy. He still distrusted Burne, with his chill reserve and devious calculation, and knew himself distrusted in turn. He had not been permitted to meet even one of Burne's intelligencers. No doubt Sir Nigel wanted to keep his other agents hidden, but Rafe sensed the man held some other piece of the puzzle. Nonetheless, Burne's sanction and help were invaluable—if Burne could be trusted to keep his part of the bargain and use his influence with Walsingham, and through Walsingham with the Queen. In return, Rafe would attempt to infiltrate the underworld, and try to discover the links to the sabotage.

On the edge of the churchyard, Burne adjusted his hat and set off down the street, signaling Garrin Garnet's arrival. Rafe felt a jolt of cold excitement. He drew deeper into the shadow of the doorway as Garnet and his guards appeared on their appointed rounds. He let them pass, then followed well behind, keeping the thief's blond hair in sight as they wove through the crowd and made their collections. Merchants, both honest and dishonest, handed over a portion of their profits for protection. Righteous anger grew as Rafe watched the tribute gathered. At best, he would uncover a vile treason. And whatever information he discovered would help destroy the current infestation of human rats in Southwark—creatures of the same ilk as the highwaymen who'd butchered his aunt and uncle.

Rafe smiled grimly. At worst he'd be gutted in an alleyway. So he'd best take care.

As soon as Garnet separated from his men, Rafe walked swiftly through the crowded mercantile area into the suburban lushness of open fields, walled orchards, and tree-shaded streets that bordered the Clink and led to the borough of Paris Gardens beyond. While the guards took the larger collection back to the Swifts' townhouse, Garnet would make the last round through the brothels on his own. It was a prize route, for after the courier collected the tribute, he could linger and have his pick of the women if he chose. Rafe did not know how long he'd have to wait for Garnet, but he had already chosen the best spot for an ambush, a crisscross of narrow lanes between the walled gardens of two wealthy brothels not far from the Swifts' great townhouse. Rafe waited an hour before Burne passed ahead of him, signaling that Garnet was not far behind, and alone. Burne turned up at the next corner, waiting out of sight in case there was trouble.

Rafe untied his purse, feeling the compact weight of sand dangling from his hand. He wanted minimal struggle. Footsteps approached, and he tensed for action. As Garnet passed, Rafe grabbed him by the shoulder and whirled him round, swinging the weapon hard against his temple. Garnet sagged unconscious at the blow. Rafe

quickly hauled him out of sight into the narrower crossing lane. He bound Garnet, gagged him, then unbuckled
sword and knife and dropped them over the nearest wall.
He poured the sand from the purse and discarded it, then
untied the heavy, red leather pouch fastened to Garnet's
belt. Opening it, Rafe saw the gleam of gold sovereigns,
angels, double crowns, and rose nobles mingled with silver farthings, shillings, and pennies. After tying the heavy
purse onto his own belt, Rafe adjusted the angle of hat
and cape, then made his way back to the street. He gave
Burne a discreet hand signal as he passed.

There was no help, no protection from now on.
Excitement rushed hot over a colder current of fear as
Rafe went to face the enemy.

2

$\mathcal{T}$he Swifts' townhouse was among the richest and most elaborate in the Clink. High walls surrounded the house and grounds. Glimpses of fruit ripening on trees hinted at lush green gardens within. Looking through the gate, Rafe saw a great house of dazzling white plaster and elaborate black half-timbering. Bold rectangles delineated the walls of the ground floor. On the second story, crosses quartered the rectangles, and on the third, diamond diagonals radiated out from the center of the crosses. Despite extravagant displays of mullioned glass, the elegant townhouse retained aspects of a solid fortress, with guard houses branching off from the gatehouse and wrapping the courtyard. The Swifts would be well prepared for any raid against them.

Rafe approached the two guards blocking the gateway, both dressed in fancy red and black livery, both well armed. He assessed them carefully even as he nodded a civil greeting. "I have money to deliver to Nick Swift."

They inspected him in turn, taking stock of his obvious weapons and calculating what others might be hidden. They signaled a third man-at-arms, who emerged from the guard house and escorted Rafe through the gates. Within, a marble fountain babbled placidly in the center of the courtyard. Sunlight sparkled in the trickling streams of water and gleamed on the brass trim and mullioned glass of the house. Gallery windows flanked a central door of carved oak. Above the door, a projecting bay overlooked the court below. The guard told him to wait, and Rafe moved to stand beside the fountain, tracking the progress of the guard as he crossed the flagstones and entered the house. Since there was nothing suspicious in his curiosity, Rafe indulged it to the full, carefully examining the plan of the buildings, taking stock of the guards and servants moving about. He shifted his position a little, so he could keep watch on the gate. There was no telling when Garrin Garnet would turn up again. *Later better than sooner.*

A slim man dressed in moderate garb emerged from beneath the house and ambled toward him. Rafe glanced at him curiously, wondering what his importance in the scheme of things might be. Pausing, the fellow returned the look with equal curiosity, a little smile quirking the corners of his lips. He reminded Rafe of a squirrel, alert and quick, with bright brown eyes and reddish-brown hair.

"Wanting your money back, are you?" the man asked. "No need to pad your codpiece—whoever it is that you are."

Surprised, Rafe studied him intently. The man must have been at the Lightning Bolt when Garnet robbed him. Rafe did not recognize him, though he'd have sworn he memorized every face. At last he placed someone with a nebulous resemblance at a table toward the back. Seeing that uncertain spark of recognition, the man smiled. "Remember me?"

"Maybe," Rafe conceded, playing the uncertainty. "I was very drunk."

"A beslubbering, folly-fallen malt-worm," the man agreed. "And I wasn't at my most noticeable myself." Even as Rafe watched, the man lowered his gaze a fraction, and let himself slump just a little. Small as the changes were, the man seemed to shrink, his color fade and brightness dim. Everything about him suggested that Rafe had better things to look at. *If I blink, he'll vanish,* Rafe thought, realizing the man wove a spell of utter ordinariness to cloak himself. His hair and beard were trimmed to the simplest style. His garments were humble shades of dun and dust, and of a quality to insure respect without garnering admiration. A small touch of trim suggested modest means as opposed to Puritan austerity. Everything about him was mild, neat, and nondescript. Then, in a single blink, the man's eyes were gleaming with humor and intelligence, making him very present.

Rafe shook his head ruefully, acknowledging the fellow's skill. He gave his name and got Ezekial Cockayne in return. "Izzy's what everyone calls me."

"Izzy, then." For all his impudence, the fellow's manner was disarming. Deciding to play out the game, Rafe slid a hand under his cloak to jingle the coins in the purse. "As for my money—I took it back myself."

Izzy whistled softly. "From Garnet?"

"From whoever," Rafe affirmed. "A point of pride— for all I was stupid enough to get drunk in the Clink."

"Not just *your* money," Izzy reminded him with a roll of the eyes at the Swifts' house.

"True. But it's not just my pride, either. Necessity has a bit to do with it. I thought returning this might buy me a job, if it doesn't get my throat slit."

"Your throat slit?" Izzy clucked his tongue. "Only if you'd kept what you stole. But you still might get all the bran beaten from your peascod."

Rafe shrugged, all arrogance and indifference. "I'll take my chances."

"You've proven that already." Izzy nodded. "Come to think of it, Garrin will want to slit your throat. Unless you slit his already?"

"No."

"No?"

"Just a little tap to the head."

"More's the pity."

"Is it?" Rafe asked, realizing at least some of Izzy's amiability arose from a dislike of Garnet. "Then I'm sorry I didn't oblige, though I'd hardly be here now if I had."

"True. And there's still a chance he'll cut his own throat. The spleeny pignut shouldn't have been slitting strings in the Lightning Bolt." Izzy gave him a quick look, rubbing his nose to display the cutpurse's sharpened sliver of horn set along the edge of his thumb. "Can't be fouling your own nest."

Rafe nodded, tucking that interesting piece of information away, too.

"You're right to try and hook up with us," the nip went on his confidential tone. "Territory's too well guarded for private enterprise. Best to find favor with the ruling class—and the Swifts are King and Queen o' the Clink."

Prickling with the awareness of being watched, Rafe looked up to the house, his search stopping at a shadowy form behind the great bow window. He stared up at the window until the shadow moved forward. Circular panes sparkled in the sun as the central casements opened to reveal a woman watching. Dark and slender, she looked clothed in flame, her velvet gown a blaze of scarlet slashed with black. A shock went through Rafe as her glittering gaze met his own, then slowly browsed him from head to toe.

Used to seductive appraisal, flirtatious or serious, still he flushed at the flagrant assessment, and the heat that flashed through him seemed to ignite in her eyes, bright within their dark. Rafe had never seen a lady with so bold a glance, which mocked as it weighed, invited as it challenged. But no true lady would be here among these criminals, though the woman gazing down at him knew how to dress the part. Rubies burned at her throat, and ropes of sparkling jet draped her vivid scarlet bodice. The distinctive garb, the total presumptuousness of the woman, made him tense with suspicion. Slowly, her gaze swept his body, scanning the breadth of his shoulders and assessing the strong muscles of his thighs. Her appraisal lingered at his crotch, and a smile curled her lips, as if she knew the quick stirring of his cock. The black eyes sought his again, and he stared back defiantly, icy anger running in cold currents against his hot arousal. Rafe felt more than provoked—he felt deliberately tested to see how long he could stand in the fire.

As long as you dare, he defied her silently.

Suddenly, the woman canted toward him. Taut with wariness and arousal, Rafe braced himself as if she might leap over the casement and into his arms. But she did no more than lean across the wooden ledge. Her lips pursed to blow him a kiss—playful, taunting—then she laughed and pulled the windows closed with a bright flash of sunlight. Freed from the brazen assault of the woman's presence, Rafe drew a deep breath and eased his stance. He glanced at Izzy, who grinned at him gleefully.

"Vivian Swift." Rafe wondered why he was so certain. This woman might be nothing more than a wealthy courtesan flaunting her erotic power. But for all her blatant sexuality, he doubted she was a whore. Under that assessing gaze, he felt like the one weighed for purchase. It rankled.

"Seems you've caught her eye. I thought you might." Izzy gave him a lecherous smile. He seemed so pleased, he might have procured Rafe himself.

Rafe bristled. "Easy enough—with a wanton eye."

"Don't get your coxcomb in a waggle," Izzy chided. "Her eye may be lusty, but 'tis hard enough to please. Viv Swift likes her men fierce as she is."

"Perhaps I like my women gentler than I am."

"Perhaps you've yet to meet your match." Izzy's quirking smile was followed swiftly by a warning. "If she offers you a tupping, take care. You'll have the pleasure of her bed, but you'll be out alone on the streets again if you can't control your head and balls better than most. She'll have no master."

"Perhaps she's yet to meet him," Rafe retorted.

"No." Izzy shook his head. "Our Queen may take a consort, but not a ruler."

Scarlet flashed as Vivian Swift moved behind the windows of the ground floor gallery, and Rafe realized he'd been waiting for her to appear. The front door flung wide and she stepped outside. As her gaze honed on Rafe, he tensed, willing ice to chill his simmering heat. They took each other's measure for a heartbeat, then she crossed the courtyard toward him.

Rafe wondered if Cockayne would reveal their conversation, but it seemed Izzy preferred to watch the game unfold. With a wink, he slipped away sideways, whispering with salacious delight, "They say she's a tigress who can take a man to shreds."

The tigress halted a few feet away, then began circling slowly, studying him from various angles, her carnal interest bordering on carnivorous. This was not what Rafe had anticipated. He did not want to play the whore. He had hoped his audacity, his strength, his skill in weapons, would win him a place with the Swifts. But how quickly could a stranger's steel cut to the dark heart of this world? It seemed a fleshy dagger might pierce its core. If this woman's brother had implicated his family in treason and murdered Gabriel, it was likely she knew of it. The bitter chill of those thoughts darkened the fire Vivian Swift ignited, but did not smother it. Animosity, curiosity, shame, and hot lust collided within him.

Rafe faced straight forward as she prowled around, meeting her gaze only when she passed in front of him. She wore a tiger brooch, he saw. Gold and black enamel with ruby eyes, it caught up the strands of jet that fell over her bodice, the striped arch of its back pressing against the creamy skin of her breasts. The tight bodice lifted them, the rounded swells rising and falling with her rapid breathing. He could sense the radiant heat of her body, and smell the exotic musk of her perfume as she circled. Each encounter set his groin glowing like a coal and magnified his anger, at her and himself. Viv Swift might not be able to read his reasons, but she was well aware of his turmoil. She savored his response with obvious relish, her lascivious scrutiny of his body mingling amusement and rapacity. But under that unsubtle assessment, Rafe sensed a keener one that gauged his strength and tested his will. He couldn't quell his reaction, not with her eyes on him like a touch, so he used its heat to stoke his defiance. Throwing her arrogance back, Rafe folded his arms across his chest and studied her in turn.

Dark against the pale olive of her skin, sable hair flowed smoothly down her back. The narrow oval of her face curved into a small pointed chin, and the inquisitive tilt of her nose emphasized her impertinence. A thin scar like a knife cut incised a crescent along one cheek. *Not beautiful,* he thought. *Not fair. Not tall.* But he could not deny her magnetism, the seething energy that enlivened every feature. Her lips were not full, but sensuous in their mobility—the upper like the fluid ripple of a wave, the lower a tender, supple thrust of flesh. Her gaze compelled him. Fine dark eyebrows sketched a deft arch. Beneath them, iris fused with pupil in eyes black as night and as opaque—yet the flame within them leapt and flared.

Desire danced there now, alight with mockery. It was impossible not to imagine her in bed.

She faced him directly, tilting her head back to look up at him. "No," she said, as if it was *yes* to everything his mind was conjuring. Not denial at all, but invitation.

"No?" he challenged.

Maybe this game of glance and verbal pricks was only caprice, but the possibility of more was palpable. Part of him coldly weighed the opportunity, even as another rebelled at the insolence of her appraisal. Both heat and ice told him if Viv Swift was fool enough to invite an enemy to her bed, then join her there. Heat demanded far more, its hot fierce whisper urged him to shred his garments and hers, to take Viv Swift there on the flagstones of the courtyard.

"No," she repeated with a little smile. "I've never seen you before." Light yet husky, her voice licked like a cat's rough-napped tongue, teasing his senses.

"I'm sure we would both remember," he answered in kind.

"Mmmmmm?" The husky purr encompassed agreement and question. "Such surety needs a name."

"Fletcher." He swept his threadbare cape over one shoulder like a gallant. "Rafe Fletcher."

She tensed slightly, and he wondered if he had misjudged his anonymity. He was not heir to Easton Arms, and had worked only in the background. He'd thought his own name safe to use.

"And I, as you must know, am Vivian Swift."

Another chill touched him. Was it arrogance or suspicion that cooled her voice? "Mistress Swift," he acknowledged.

She began circling him again, and he watched her warily. Small, slender, there was nothing fragile about Viv Swift. Her body had the fine density of feline muscle, and she moved like a stalking cat. It seemed that any second she might spring away or attack, all taut nerves and lissome sinew. She smiled at him, the same sly curl of her lips. But now her eyes were cold. Danger prickled the hair on the back of his neck. What was wrong?

Abruptly, she stopped, and the direction of her glance drew Rafe's attention to the gallery. Dark and fair, a richly garbed couple descended the stairs into the courtyard. Watching their approach, Rafe noticed the woman was tall and beautiful, but he kept his attention on the man, certain he was Vivian's brother. Though Rafe could not match feature to feature, their coloring was almost identical, and some subtler link resonated between them. Swift's straight black hair was elegantly trimmed. His features were ordinary, yet odd in sum. Thin, curving brows punctuated restless brown eyes. Angled cheekbones sharpened a round face, while mustache and beard made an elegant tracery about a small, vulnerable mouth. Like his sister, he wore rich garments, his black velvet slashed with scarlet and embroidered with gold and pearls.

Rafe stood straight and unyielding as the couple approached. The woman paused, idling by the fountain as Nick Swift made his way to Vivian's side. Cold shock spiked through Rafe as the man raised a languid hand to stroke his ruff. On his middle finger a massive ring gleamed like a pale yellow eye. A topaz. Rafe knew it could mean nothing—or everything. Had that ring been what Gabe saw, looking down at the hand that thrust the knife into him?

Some wordless exchange passed between brother and sister, and when Swift looked back at Rafe his eyes seemed chillier. His gaze did not shift, though when he spoke it was to Vivian, drawling a little. "He's large. Does he have a name?"

"Rafe Fletcher, so he says." Vivian Swift's dark eyes measured him coldly—for a shroud instead of her bed sheets. "He's carrying Garrin's purse."

Clothed in his armor of arrogance, Rafe hardly blinked. Apprehension increased, but relief leapt beside it. At least he knew now why the fire in her eyes burned cold instead of hot. He untied the purse from his belt and tossed it lightly from hand to hand. The color was a deep red, embossed around the bottom edge. There were many purses plainer, and many far more elaborate. It was not particularly distinctive, but she had recognized it. He meant to reveal it himself, so nothing was lost except the element of surprise.

"So, Rafe Fletcher, I am Nicholas Swift. And the money you have for me seems to be mine already." His voice drawled, but the brown eyes were hard and cold as river pebbles. Vivian Swift watched them both intently.

Rafe unknotted the cord and counted out two shillings and sixpence. "These are mine." He slid the coins into his breeches pocket and tossed the purse at their feet. "And that is yours. I thought delivery might buy me a job."

Vivian scooped it up, tossing it from hand to hand in mimicry. Her gestures were quick, graceful for all their abruptness. "It seems a weighty payment. But it cost you nothing and gains us less."

"It cost me effort and you nothing."

"Nothing?" Nick Swift's voice affected indifference as he asked, "And just where is Garnet?"

"Bound in an alleyway. He should be able to wriggle free, if he works at it."

"And you want his job." Swift's small mouth stretched to a narrow-lipped, derisive smile. Giving his pretty companion a brief glance, he adopted a languid pose, but one hand toyed continuously with the scarlet plume of his hat. Unlike the feral energy which animated every atom of his sister, his restiveness seemed more the result of a nervous temper, as though some continuous subtle vibration quivered beneath his skin. His humors were ill-mingled, Rafe judged—caustic, vacillating, and moody.

Rafe shrugged. "Or one like it."

"And just why is that?" Swift asked sharply.

"Why?" Rafe snorted. "Because I've learned earning an honest living costs too much."

"Then you are well educated," Vivian said.

He glanced at her, relieved the warmth had returned to her gaze. "Yes, but my education has left me impoverished."

"And what were you exactly, when you were honest?" Swift asked, stroking his plume.

"I was fencing master to a young nobleman. . . ." Rafe paused, then set his jaw belligerently. "He was a friend of Anthony Babington."

"A most expensive choice," was all Swift said.

"It cost me dear." Rafe waited another breath and went on. "My employer may have shared no interests with him save gaming and whoring, but just before Babington's arrest he decided that France would be healthier for him than England. He left in a hurry, quite short of funds." All of that, save Rafe's employment, was true and conveniently difficult to trace, as a number of Babington's cohorts had fled to Catholic countries. He doubted they would bother to check—it was not uncommon for a man to fall from debt into thievery.

"And neglected to pay you?" Nicholas Swift mocked.

"He did not pay what he still owed me—and he stole what I had saved." Feeling the shadow of these invented emotions darkening his own, Rafe let bitterness seep into his voice. "When I inquired for new service, I found I was tainted by association, though I care not for such matters."

"Are you Catholic?" Nick Swift asked.

The question was casual enough, but either yes or no could be hazardous. Rafe shrugged. "I belong to the Devil either way, so it makes no matter."

"And he has no employment for you?"

"It remains to be seen." Rafe smiled, chancing Swift was villain enough to relish the insinuation.

Vivian laughed, and Nick Swift gave him a narrow smile. The woman hovering by the fountain gave a little snort of laughter. When Rafe glanced at her, she smiled with malicious sweetness and tugged at a curl of red-gold hair lolling over a shoulder. He felt a shock as he noticed the hands. They were well-tended, slender, and graceful, but there was no mistaking their length and breadth for a woman's. Shocked, Rafe looked him over quickly but saw no other clue to masculine sex, except perhaps the tenor of the laugh which first caught his attention. The willowy being before him was seraphic and sensuous in lavender silks, with great, heavy-lidded hazel eyes and tawny hair hazed with pale red. No beard was visible beneath the dusting of powder, and coral rouge painted a mouth of rounded curves. Any breadth of shoulder was disguised by the winged flare of the bodice over the sleeves. Tight corseting forced a mock cleavage and the slight curve of a waist. Youthful, still this fellow was older than the boys who normally played women in the theatre. An actor, or a male whore? His garments were lavish without a hint of lewdness. Swift might dress a valued mistress so, in sumptuous fabric and strands of amethyst.

Noting the direction of Rafe's gaze, Swift glanced at his companion. "What say you, Rosy, has the Devil use for such a knave?"

"He hasn't the finesse to cut purses." Rosy's scoffing voice was as androgynous as the rest of him. "He's too big and clumsy to do much but bash heads."

Stepping forward, Viv surveyed Rafe with feigned criticality. "I'll wager he's graceful with a sword . . . and skillful," she murmured, playing the double edge.

"If his weapon measures to the rest of him, he's like to need two hands to wield it," Rosy responded, contemptuous and lewd.

"Oh, Rosy, would you not wish to wield such a splendid weight?" Viv laughed softly at Rafe's discomfort at being the subject of the ribaldry. But her eyes were alight and he found himself laughing in answer, embarrassed, annoyed, and aroused.

"A supple blade may fit better in the hand than a club," Rosy declared, smiling coyly at his companion.

"You're good with a sword, then?" Nick Swift asked Rafe, ignoring the innuendo.

"Do you have anyone to test me against?"

"One, at least." A sarcastic smile thinned Swift's lips again. The smile, and the movement he caught in the corner of the courtyard, warned Rafe. He turned, drawing his sword from its sheath. Garrin Garnet stood near the gateway. Rafe felt the hot spur of anticipation even as he groped for a way to avert the confrontation. Garnet had no weapons, and Rafe deliberately sheathed his blade. Despite his boast to Swift, Rafe wanted to keep this fight hand to hand. He'd made an enemy. Even if the Swifts decided to shun Rafe, Garnet had still been bested at his own game. The man could not afford the humiliation. The question was if the thief would be satisfied with a brawl or if only steel would settle matters. For all that Rafe relished fighting, killing made him queasy. This fight could easily turn lethal.

Still holding Rafe's gaze, Garnet held out his hand to the guard standing by the gate. "Give me your sword."

"No," Viv Swift ordered. "No swords."

Nick Swift frowned but did not countermand Vivian. Glad of an excuse to avoid a duel, Rafe unfastened his sword and laid it by the fountain. The blond thief cast Vivian a look of disbelief, then crossed the courtyard and stopped in front of Rafe, glaring antagonism. The garnet earring he wore seemed even more sinister after seeing the topaz on Nicholas Swift's hand, as if the gems were indeed a secret code.

"You're too late, Garrin." Rosy's voice was honeyed malice. He tilted his hips, swaying his satin skirts provocatively. "Vivian's already found someone to fill your place."

Garnet's gaze was venomous.

So, the thief was a discarded lover. Rafe wanted no place between Viv Swift's sheets, but he could not help assessing Garnet as a rival as well as a fighter. If Vivian Swift liked her men fierce, Garnet would please her. Hawk-handsome, compactly built, he looked like a hard and experienced fighter—quick on his feet and fearless.

"You can forget working here," Garnet snarled at him, face mottled with rage. "You can forget Southwark—permanently."

"You've enough trouble as it is, Garrin." Izzy appeared soundlessly, perching on the edge of the fountain.

"Enough to share," Garnet said.

"Generous, for once," Izzy remarked to the air. The very placidness of his tone goaded. That the Swifts countenanced his interruption showed he had more power than was apparent on the surface. It was obvious Izzy wanted Garnet dismissed. It was equally obvious Rosy just wanted trouble. Rafe was the means to their ends. But what did the Swifts want? To test Rafe's mettle, perhaps? They had no use for a coward, but changing one troublemaker for another gained them little. Rafe backed off slightly, gave a shrug. "I say we're even. You robbed me first, last night at the Lightning Bolt."

Peripherally, he saw both Swifts turn toward Garnet, and hoped the information Izzy gave him had done some damage.

"We'll be even when I knock off your head." Garnet crouched, balling his hands into fists.

The man was already over the edge. Forestalling his attack was impossible, provoking it, easy. Eventually Rafe could overpower Garnet with sheer force. But the thief was tough, fast, and infuriated. There was a danger the smaller man could wear him down, striking quickly, then leaping out of range. Rafe smiled lazily and shifted back a step, planting his feet for balance. Lifting his hands, he flexed his fingers, beckoning Garnet to him. His tone echoed Izzy's, mild and infuriating. "You can try."

Rafe snapped his hands into fists as Garnet snarled and attacked. Stepping aside, Rafe dodged the rain of blows to his head, but the blond thief sprang on him again. Concentrating on keeping his wits and his temper, Rafe deflected three blows. He only avoided the next by twisting his head to the side, taking a glancing cut over his eye. Another punch flew, but Rafe shifted away, blocked it solidly, feeling the bone-on-bone impact as his forearm knocked Garnet's fist to the side. Hurt, the thief changed direction once, twice, and danced just beyond Rafe's reach, shaking off the pain in his arm.

Blood ran down from the cut over Rafe's eye, obscuring his vision. Rafe reached up a hand to wipe away the blood. Garnet saw it, and tensed to attack. Anticipating just when Garnet would strike, Rafe quickly slid to the left, keeping ahead of the lighter man's speed as Garnet came at him again. Letting calculation and anger fuse, Rafe whipped his fist backward into the thief's face, staggering him. Rafe grabbed for him and Garnet dove to the ground, tucking and rolling away. Rafe plunged forward, seizing him as he rose. The thief had his feet under him quickly and tried to punch again. Rafe jerked him off balance and the blow went wide. He punched Garnet hard, once, twice, driving him back against a column. Rafe caught hold of his doublet, yanking him forward, then slamming him against the stone. Garnet groaned, slumping in his grip, and Rafe let him collapse to the pavement.

Looking down, Rafe nudged Garnet lightly with his toe, then asked, "Are we done?"

He received a heavy groan in answer. Garnet struggled to draw himself up on his hands and knees, then sagged limply to the stones. Rafe turned and went to the fountain, drawing cool water to splash on his bloody hands and face. As he leaned forward on the rim, he heard the metallic slide of metal on stone as Garnet snatched up Rafe's discarded sword. He whirled.

"No, you're done," the thief growled.

"Enough!" Instantly, Viv Swift was beside Garnet, twisting his free arm with one hand as the other pressed a dagger across his throat. Rafe watched, amazed by her skill and audacity. The glaze of fury faded from Garnet's eyes, fear giving them clarity. He dropped the sword and Rafe retrieved it. Viv Swift eased the pressure of the blade only a fraction. "There's no place for you here any more. Understand me?"

A spasm of hatred marred Garnet's features. "Maybe Jacob Rivett will want my sword arm."

"If he gets it, the rest of you goes in the Thames." Viv's black eyes glittered, not hot but cold with anger. Utterly fearless. A quick gesture summoned the two guards from the gateway. Taking hold of Garnet, they led him back to the street. Rafe knew Burne or his men would track him from there.

Then Viv Swift spun and glared at Rafe, as if he should be dragged after Garnet. He saw his chance evaporating. He'd disrupted their organization too much. Instinct warned that Nick Swift would dismiss him with a shrug and a smirk. His one chance was with Vivian. The fire between them was banked beneath her anger. Rafe did not want to ignite the coals, caught between the fear that it would either aggravate her anger, or drag him into an incendiary lust that was the last thing he had planned or wanted. Exasperated, he flung up his weaponless hands. His gesture proclaimed that he'd done just as she ordered.

Viv set her shoulders and tilted her head skeptically, her stance arguing that Rafe had started the trouble. Breathing hard, he held that dark gaze, acknowledging and challenging in turn, refusing to look away. He'd only reclaimed his due. After a moment her lips curled in a little smile. The black-eyed gaze swept over Rafe and he felt another surge of arousal and antagonism. Yet the mocking eyes invited him to laugh as well, and suddenly, unable to help himself, he did.

"It seems we have need of a new guard," Viv remarked to her brother as she tied Garnet's purse to her girdle. Nick Swift did not reply, only turned and walked off with Rosy flowing alongside. Facing Rafe, Vivian studied him a moment, then said, "You're a bold one. I like that." Her dark eyes issued both dare and warning. "We'll see if you know the difference between boldness and insolence."

Rafe subdued his demeanor, murmuring his gratitude. "My lady."

"Izzy will show you the guard house. Go get yourself fitted for my livery. From now on you're working for me."

3

Stealthy footsteps moved up the stairs. A single soft knock sounded at the door, followed by three quick taps. Then came a whisper. "Silver?"

Sliding his knife back into its sheath, Silver unbarred the door. "Topaz."

Topaz crossed quickly to the window, looking out over the jagged crests of rooftops to the ramparts of the Tower beyond. He checked the street, giving a quick hand signal to one of the guards waiting below. Silver waited beside a stack of guns, the smaller wooden boxes of snaphances piled atop the one great crate holding the cannon. Set atop them, a tallow candle emitted feeble light. Leaving the window, Topaz moved into the dim circle and flipped back his hood. Fragments of shadow carved the corners of his nose and mouth, but his eyes caught the yellow flame with hard, fervent glitter. The disguise was good, Silver thought: mud-spattered cape, doublet and trunk hose of rough brown wool, aged doeskin gauntlets to hide the well-tended hands. His height was exceptional, and his arrogant posture proclaimed him a gentleman to the practiced eye. What matter? Gentlemen often disguised themselves when frequenting Silver's territory. He slipped the edge of his own black velvet cape over his shoulder, displaying oyster brocade, maroon velvet, a lace ruff. Always his garments were rich as any worn at court. Such men were no better than he.

Topaz paced to the window again. Silver studied the other man closely. Usually, Topaz' smooth face wore an expression of chill disdain, but tonight small twitches plucked at eye and mouth, and his body was stretched tight as catgut. "Trouble?"

"Yes—and no." Topaz glanced around. "Where is Agate?"

Best get it over with, Silver thought. "I've had trouble as well. Agate's nerve broke. He had to be silenced."

"You killed him? Why?" Topaz regarded him with suspicion.

"You saw yourself, killing Gabriel Darren made him queasy. Even before that, he was looking over his shoulder, claiming he was being followed." That was true enough, and would give credence to the rest. "Word reached him the Eastons had been arrested. The sabotage was discovered sooner than we expected and he panicked."

"Such decisions are mine," Topaz claimed. "There was no need for such a drastic action. We planned for this eventuality."

Silver stepped face to face, looking up at him. "I could hardly consult you."

Most men would have been afraid of him. Topaz was not. Foolish, but at least he was no coward. "He was committed to our cause," Topaz said. "We had an escape route planned, believers in France who promised to shelter him."

"No longer. I went to see him late at night, and found him sweating wine and fear." Silver held his gaze. "He claimed Walsingham's dogs were following him again."

Topaz did not blink. "Agate had a brain for schemes, but no stomach for blood, it's true."

"He threatened to confess." The last was a lie. They'd hoped the weapons sent to the Netherlands would be dispersed, the sabotage blamed on malfunction. But despite his apprehension, Agate had been reluctant to leave England even after Scratch Jones had set Darren on the scent of treason. Agate was the direct link between Silver, Topaz, and the weapons from Easton Arms. Entirely too risky. Darren and Jones were safely dead, and Silver had seen to it Agate followed swiftly. "Agate's weakness threatened to betray us both—to betray all your plans."

"Nothing must jeopardize our success, though it costs our own lives," Topaz asserted.

Topaz, no doubt, awaited the day when he could proclaim his true identity. Whether he received reward or punishment seemed to matter little. But Silver had no intention of dancing an air jig for the crowds. He nodded as if he believed such zealous drivel, then buttressed his lie with an attack. "If there is more trouble, then I acted wisely."

"Trouble, indeed," Topaz said. "They have arrested the Queen of Scots. Walsingham is a deadly chess master. He has taken our Queen with Babington, that prattling, mewling pawn."

"May God protect her." Silver raised one hand and made the sign of the cross. Raised Catholic, he remembered enough of such flotsam to pass as a believer when it helped his business. Beneath his cape, the other hand went to his knife handle.

"He has sent her deliverers." Topaz crossed himself as well.

Silver's hand curled tightly about the handle of his dagger, one breath from striking.

Gun tampering was one thing, but he had never intended to commit himself to Topaz' greater folly. Believing him ardent in the Catholic faith, Agate had brought Silver to Topaz. Though they were both involved in smuggling, Silver had resources Agate did not possess. Topaz had wealth enough to pursue the obsession he shared with Agate, and direct access to information at court. They used code names always. Ignorance was safety, Agate had said. Though they both knew Agate was Edward Chettle, customs official, Topaz and Silver were not to reveal their true identities until the conspiracy succeeded—an eventuality Silver did not expect to arrive. True to his word, Agate had refused to yield Topaz' name. Silver had to ferret it out himself—as he suspected Topaz had done with him. The code names were feeble protection. Only the grave ensured silence.

The scales quivered as Silver measured the growing risk against the heavy weight of Topaz' gold. Next time, he thought, the scale would dip too low. For now he would take the gold. "These untampered weapons were always meant to arm the true queen's rescuers."

"Yes. But now timing is crucial. We must rescue the Queen of Scots or Elizabeth will have her head." Topaz began to pace. "If she is being brought to the Tower, it will be to our advantage. The rescue will be easier to organize close at hand. If there are loyal Catholics among your men, they too will gain a pardon if they help in the raid."

"Few will act out of pure faith." Topaz had paid him richly in metal, and extravagantly in promises. Silver was to have not only a pardon, but a knighthood. The thought teased the corners of his mind, sweet as bird song. He listened for a moment, then closed his ears. Such pretty schemes of glory would make him pluckings for kites and crows. He himself would remain the predator. For now, he would take Topaz' money. When the risk grew too great, he would take Topaz' life. Finally, he would claim the guns for himself.

"When I know where the Queen of Scots is to be taken for trial, I will arrange a hiding place for our weapons," Topaz went on. "We must be ready beforehand, the guns secreted, then dispensed to men we can trust."

"I will arrange for the wagons, and buy the necessary passports for the roads from London north." Easy enough. Silver's jarkman kept him supplied with forged documents. And producing such flimsy paper would convince Topaz of his allegiance

"The rescue will insure the true Queen's survival," Topaz said, then turned to face him. The fervid glow was back in his eyes. "But I believe I have found the means to do far more than that. I believe I can place her on the throne."

Silver did not show his skepticism. "To place her there, you must topple Elizabeth."

"I will topple her into her grave," Topaz said fiercely. "With the bastard gone and Queen Mary safe, the Catholic monarchs will rally to her cause. If King James dares leave his heretic warren in Scotland, he will crumble before such opposition. With your help, Silver, England will be Catholic once more."

"I like your plan—but how do you intend to achieve it?"

"Next time." Topaz shook his head, refusing any further revelations. He drew forth a heavy purse. "This for the passports. Another when the guns leave London."

"Look for the same markers to signal our meeting." Silver took the purse, feeling the hard weight of the coin beneath the leather. For payments like this, he would play Topaz' game a little longer.

4

*B*eelzebub's balls!" Vivian pushed aside the gold tray, leaving pottage, bread, and apricots untasted. Sleeplessness abraded every sense, her nerves hot itchy threads stitching her flesh. The room felt stuffy, suffocating. Flinging aside the covers, she rose from her bed and pulled on a robe of scarlet brocade over her shift, then shoved her bare feet into gold-embroidered slippers. She crossed to the garden windows and opened one wide, breathing in the cool morning air. Contrary to her mood, the day was serene. Fleecy white clouds gamboled like lambs in an azure field, and sunlight sparked a gaudy glitter of dew on the leaves and the crimson blooms of the roses spilling over the trellis.

"Positively beatific," she muttered, feeling the chew and puff of the words on teeth and lips.

Crossing her arms, she surveyed the walled garden below. Elaborate gravel pathways looped between flower beds, fish ponds, and fountains, arbors, aviaries, and blooming bowers. Espaliered fruit trees wove crisscrossed patterns along the high stone walls. Perfection—but tension raked her usual swell of possessive pride. Behind her on the mantle, her latest prize, a clock of enameled gold and crystal, chimed the hour with metallic precision. Vivian's gaze skimmed over the top of the wall to the enclosed field beyond. Trimmed grass and trampled earth, it was empty still, though as the clock finished striking, Smoke Warren, the captain of her guards, led the men into the field. Her gaze sought out Fletcher immediately, but Viv forced herself to survey them all.

Following her orders, Smoke brought a different group of guards for training every morning. First he scrutinized sword work, then set them fighting with staves or hand to hand. At least the quarrel between Fletcher and Garrin had been useful. Though the guards did little but flex their muscles and rattle their swords when they showed Garnet the gate, it reminded them trouble could come knocking anytime, and from unexpected quarters. Wealth was a deceptive buffer and some men went slack with easy house duty. Trouble waited outside, always ready to knock heads in the streets of London and Southwark. The smartest knew when to dodge it, when to face it down, and when to pound it to rubble. Smoke quickly culled those too stupid or vicious to be of use. The reliable ones guarded the townhouse. If they had a gift for subterfuge, they worked the street games, too. With Garnet disgraced, they needed a new trickster, and Fletcher looked to be a gaming man. It would be a shame to use no more than his muscle, when he might have a brain as well.

If I keep him.

Yesterday, desire had urged yes. Today, anger urged the same. Yesterday, caution spoke a quiet warning. Today, fear whispered incessantly, plucking at her vitals with clammy claws. She wanted to defy it, to defy Nicholas because of it. The anger was a ready weapon, but double-edged. She could chance her life on a bet with less trepidation than arguing with Nicholas. They both had raging tempers, but rarely loosed them on each other.

Jabbing his sword in the air, Smoke called out an order and the men lined up. He tapped them off into pairs for training, singling out Fletcher for his own partner. Vivian hadn't needed to order it. Unless he'd recruited them himself, Smoke always tested the new men. The captain's swordplay was proficient, rigorous and precise, but not fast enough to rank with the absolute best. Where he was truly expert was in spotting strength and weakness in technique. Smoke put his pride in his ability to train. He knew his own worth and demanded respect, and her generous rewards earned gratitude, not greed. Only Izzy was more valuable, more trusted.

Smoke called out another order and the clang of metal vanquished the birdsong of the garden as the men began with sword and buckler. Viv leaned forward, watching intently as Smoke and Fletcher circled, beginning the match with a few tentative thrusts and parries. Smoke increased the tempo to a steady barrage of strokes. Fletcher kept pace but did not push, defending and countering. Viv surmised he was holding back, wondering if he should trounce the captain on the first day. She wondered if he could. So did Smoke, apparently, for he increased his attack again, pressing hard and fast. Fletcher gave some ground, then rallied and battled with equal ferocity.

Rafe Fletcher was magnificent with a sword—even better than she'd hoped. A fencing master must have some skill to earn his keep, but nobles might hire a man of handsome looks and gaudy technique to ornament their courts. Such a popinjay might be adept while prancing up and down the gallery, but have no stomach for the savagery of street brawl or battle. But such a man would not have stolen back his money, then dared enemy turf to claim his job.

"I wish you were just a popinjay. I'd pluck a pretty feather, then shoo you away," Viv murmured as she watched Fletcher. But he was something far prouder and fiercer, a great gyrfalcon.

Dismissing a man with such talent, such spirit, would be folly. Action vitalized the power of his frame, infusing it with deadly grace as he parried Smoke's move and attacked, his sword flashing in the sunlight. Even from this distance Vivian could see how beautiful he was, with his thick, dark hair and brows, his bold features. She watched, savoring a purr of delight as he lunged, thighs taut, sword extended. Desire leapt and crackled, sparks flying like sap exploding in flame, swarming through her blood.

Trouble. He is nothing but trouble.

Anger and frustration collided with desire, a combustion that drove her away from the window. The rushes hissed underfoot as she paced, tapping fist into palm in a staccato rhythm. Energy sizzled along her nerves. She wanted to leap and yank down the tapestries, hurl the tray and plates, smash the clock to a thousand pieces.

The riotous explosion would release her tension, but it would not solve her dilemma.

Dismiss Fletcher, she told herself. *Caution is not cowardice.*

Heavy with coin, Garnet's purse sat on the cupboard. She owed Fletcher nothing, but she would give him the purse he'd stolen. She would pen a letter of recommendation so he could get a job elsewhere, without mentioning the wretched Babington and his cohorts. There were petty nobles who visited the Swift's gambling dens who would take perverse pleasure in taking on such a man.

Harmony with Nicholas is worth more than anything.
Well—almost anything.

Viv gave a short, bitter laugh.

I will not bed Rosy Piper. I will not bear his child.

Last night, she refused Nick what he truly wanted. Why not toss away Fletcher, an appeasing sop? Because Nicholas thought Fletcher was the reason she refused. And Nick would press her all the harder once he was gone.

A rap sounded at the adjoining door and Nick called out her name. She heard a laugh that could only be Ambrose Piper's.

"Satan's serpents!" Inhaling sharply, Viv flexed her fingers, wishing for cat claws. She curled her hands into tight fists, then released them with another exhaled curse. Thankful she had not savaged the tapestries and smashed the clock, she called out lightly, "Come in."

Nick entered, with Rosy following close behind.

Sparks of anger leapt up to burn her throat. Vivian drew another breath, cooling them before she spoke her greeting. Rosy had been here before, but Nick had never brought him so casually, as if it should be expected. Viv held herself erect, waiting for Nick to approach.

Elegant in charcoal velvet slashed with silver, her brother walked toward her, a tiny smile curving his lips. A topaz eardrop dangled from one lobe, and his yellow plume tickled her as he leaned down to kiss her cheek. She returned the salute then stepped away, watching as Rosy wandered the room, pausing to fondle the clock, a tapestry, with slender fingers. Only half-dressed, he tossed his doublet down on the bed, then reached out to filch an apricot from the silver bowl on her tray. Ambling to the dresser where her jewelry was laid out, he fingered the exquisite ruby dragonfly necklace that had been Nick's birthday gift to her last week, then poked amid the scattered rings and trinkets. Lifting a triple strand of black pearls clasped with diamonds, he draped them over his chest and posed in front of the mirror.

Taffeta fool. Street slang for actor, but it fit Rosy as snugly as his hose.

But Nicholas smiled, charmed by his impudence.

Vivian's belly felt like a furnace, flames of anger beating against flesh. She fought the rage that threatened to erupt. Losing her temper would only force Nicholas further away. She would give Rosy no advantage.

How dare Nick bring him here now? Viv could not believe her brother would strike at her so blindly, nor could she believe him oblivious. She faced him directly. Behind his amusement, she saw an edge of defiance, a flicker of anger. But shining over it all was the luminous glow of hope, something between entreaty and buoyant expectation. Nick was in love, and to the lover the beloved was irresistible. Rosy was not a gauntlet flung at her feet, he was a temptation offered up, delectable as marchepane, rare as iced cream. Nick hoped that last night's refusal had risen from shock, that this morning she would see Rosy with new eyes and find him toothsome.

Viv's eyes were well accustomed to the sight. Ambrose Piper was pretty as a girl, even in men's garb. Yesterday's lavender gown had been abandoned for round hose of leaf green velvet and silk netherstocks that showed the shapely mold of thigh and calf. His fine linen shirt was edged with pointed fingernails of lace. The tumble of false curls was gone, but his own long hair skimmed his shoulders, gleaming with hues of apricot and gold. The blurred softness of his lips insinuated he had just been kissed. No doubt he had, but his mouth looked that way always, flushed and tender. She wondered again that Nick had no taste for women, when he preferred such exquisiteness in men.

Rosy flopped on her bed, the pearls now looped around his neck. His insolence was galling. She wanted to jerk away the necklace, tug the bedcovers and send him sprawling, drag him from the room. She wanted to take everything he'd handled and erase his touch with her own. Flares of rage jabbed at her, urging motion, but she stood still. Suddenly the hot anger chilled, congealed, an icy ball of horror hollowing her belly. Last night, Nicholas told her Rosy knew nothing of his hopes, and would not know unless she agreed. Had he lied to her? Her gaze sought his.

Nick looked distressed, and flashed her an apologetic glance. Vivian saw embarrassment, but no guilt. Relief rushed through her. Nicholas had told her the truth. But even the doubt was appalling.

She looked back at Rosy. Lounging among the pillows, he wore his air of faint dishevelment like a perfume, seductive and intimate. However apparent to her nostrils, the scent was meant to entice only Nicholas— and to taunt her. The actor sensed there was a breach between her and Nick and was driving a wedge to widen it. Rosy might not know the reason—but he would mock her the same way if he did.

"You will have to buy him some pearls, Nicholas. Cream or pink, perhaps," she said, studying Rosy critically. "The black looks sickly against his skin."

Pricked, Rosy slung the pearls aside.

"Cream," Nicholas said. "A double rope."

In her mind, Viv took great pleasure in throttling Rosy with them.

Rosy smiled at her, eyes gleaming with hostility and triumph. In the beginning, Viv had been charmed by Rosy's outrageousness, and laughed at his malicious humor. But the more he enthralled Nicholas, the more she disliked and distrusted him. Slowly, he had become an enemy. But did he vie for possession of Nick's love, or only to usurp Viv's power and flatter his own vanity? Rosy was a clever actor, after all. For Nicholas' sake, she hoped it was for love.

Smoke called out an order. Defiantly, Viv turned her back on her brother and his lover, and returned to the open window. Gazing down, she saw Fletcher in a powerful lunge, his thighs taut with exertion, sweat plastering his shirt to his chest. Her energy leapt into the image, lunging to match him. Her thighs quivered with tension that stretched through shoulder and arm to the tip of the sword. The point speared Rosy's heart. *"Touché,"* she whispered.

She made her choice, from anger and desire mingled. She would not have Nick dangling Rosy before her constantly, like some cloying sweetmeat, hoping she would snap him up. Fletcher would be useful, one way or another.

"I told you he'd be graceful with a sword," she said to both Nick and Rosy, watching as the men began anew with rapier and dagger. "He's a born fighter."

Nicholas came to the window and stood beside her, gazing at the action on the field. He had many masks of boredom. Now his half-hooded eyes and weary tone disguised extreme annoyance. "So . . . you are keeping him?"

"As a guard—and perhaps more." Vivian curled the words on her tongue, licking them with anticipation. She would not yield, not with Rosy sprawled on her bed.

Nick tilted his head, studying Rafe as she had studied Rosy in the pearls. "I do see what appeals. But he is rather . . . ?"

"Blatant," Rosy said behind them.

"Just so," Nick remarked. "Like Rosy, I prefer finesse."

Watching Fletcher's eloquent swordplay, the quick jabs of the knife, Viv thought he had finesse aplenty.

Power was still the dominant impression he gave, but it was graced now with speed. Not only his strength, but his vitality and fire aroused her—a fierce animation of mind and body, of heart and sex. Watching Rafe Fletcher with a sword, she saw his fire unleashed.

If such blatant beauty were refined to a smaller frame, she did not doubt Nicholas would find him irresistible. Nick never chose obvious power in his lovers. She had never known Nick to admire a man stronger than himself, or to choose one for a lover. Not since Mortmain. The Earl had been the first—but he had not been chosen, only submitted to. Since then Nick's lovers were never weaklings, but sensuous features and supple grace were their lure. Viv wondered if greater physical prowess meant so much, when Nick's heart was enslaved. But in that, Ambrose Piper was the first.

Rosy sighed, a sound exquisitely wistful and perfectly audible. Too much time was being spent with their eyes fixed elsewhere, Viv thought as she and Nick turned away from the window. The center of attention once more, Rosy gripped a carved post and pulled himself to his feet. Stretching lazily, he swayed back and forth, displaying his supple body. Viv had endured enough languid posturing. If Nick let the sweetmeat dangle much longer, she would shred it.

Deliberately, she moved to her great chair of walnut carved with lions' heads and clawed feet. Her throne, Nick dubbed it. "There's trouble at the docks." She waited a moment. It was Rosy's cue to leave, but he went on idly swinging back and forth. Nick made no gesture or sound to prompt him. All right, a test of nerves. The information was no secret. "Scratch Jones was found dead in an alley, buried under a heap of garbage."

"Was he? I'm only amazed it took this long for someone to slit his throat," Nick said. Viv regarded him quizzically, wondering how he knew Scratch was killed. Izzy had only told her after midnight. He smiled and added, "Or did they bash his brains out?"

"A red smile from ear to ear," she acknowledged. "Down by the docks."

"Wharf rats often drown in their own blood," Rosy commented. "Who will even miss such a creature?"

There was a moment's silence. It was a tiny, petty victory, bitter as it was satisfying. Nick would not urge Rosy to leave, but he should not have spoken aloud. The limit had been reached, and it was Rosy who had crossed the line, not her.

When the moment stretched, Rosy said, "Rehearsal starts soon. Come to the Comet after, Nicholas? We can have supper."

"Yes, of course," Nick said quickly.

Rosy slung his doublet over his shoulder and sauntered out the door.

Nick sighed. He went to the bed and sat down, resting his hand lightly where Rosy had lain. Rising from her chair, Viv settled beside him, reclaiming the territory Rosy had transgressed. A cloud of jasmine hovered in the air, cloying sweet. She ached with anger and sadness. Nick curled up, laying his head in her lap, and she felt a blossoming tenderness. She pulled off his cap with its golden plume and stroked her fingers through his hair, feeling its texture. It was thinner now, receding at the brow. Nick would be thirty-two this month. She was just thirty. They had survived. They had achieved success against the odds, and dominion was within their grasp. Jake Rivett was a powerful enemy, but no one served him from anything but fear. He could be toppled.

When Nicholas spoke, it was not about Rivett or the trouble at the docks. "I was waiting for you to dismiss Garnet, before I asked you about Rosy. I did not expect you to toss Garnet with one hand and take up Fletcher with the other."

She drew a long breath, but never stopped gliding her fingers through his hair. "Fletcher is not the problem. You could have asked a month ago, or a month from now. It will not change what I feel."

Nick would have no son of his body. So Viv had planned never to marry, never to put any man ahead of Nick. Like Queen Elizabeth, her unmarried status had been a ploy to dangle for alliances, then deftly disengage. Viv had kept their hold in Southwark firm for one decade, as Queen Elizabeth had kept England for many, but now there was no heir of her body. And that was bitter, Viv knew. But a child was possible. A child for her and Nicholas to raise.

"I've seen the hunger in your eyes when you look at babes," Nicholas said softly. A hand sought her free one, fingers squeezing hers gently.

Vivian closed her eyes, feeling the deep tug inside her belly. There were nights when longing filled her womb with a hollow ache. She would curl and hold the ache instead of what she desired. A child—a whole world encompassed in your arms.

"You want an heir, too, a son to inherit our kingdom," Nick coaxed.

"I've wanted a child." Vivian paused. She took pride in her survival, her achievement. Truth be told, most lords were no more honest or honorable than most criminals, and got their wealth in much the same fashion. She and Nick were richer now than they had been in their youth. But when she pictured a child, she pictured the green cradle of Hawkfields, not the raucous clamor of the Clink.

"Just one child."

"And I want my freedom. I want my life." Guilt was a better weapon than the knotted coils of her conflict, or distaste for Nick's favorite sweetmeat. She did not shrink from using it. "Mother died in childbirth. I still remember her screams, don't you?"

"Of course," he whispered. "But surely it is worth the risk?"

Her life at hazard so he might have Rosy's child? She had put no other before him, or he before her—until now. The love they shared had been the pure steady flame in the midst of danger. They laughed and danced in the chaos, then came and cupped their hands around the warm glow, protecting it, sustaining it. Now Nicholas had withdrawn his hand, and the winds snuffed the flame. Viv held Nick gently, but she was alone now in the dark.

"I miscarried once. That was bad enough." Smoke's child—Viv had been young and careless. The miscarriage had ended the affair, if not the friendship. Viv remembered the crippling pain, the fear, the bloody sheets. The images spun sickly with memories of her mother's ashen corpse. But even that horror had never drowned the yearning.

"I did not think Garnet would be supplanted so quickly. I thought . . ." Nick hesitated, then said, "Why repeat your mistake?"

"Was Smoke a mistake?" She challenged him. "Fletcher is good with a sword. He's daring and clever. We can use a man with his talent."

"We have no use for trouble." Nick tugged his hand from hers. Her brother might be in love with Rosy, but he felt her attraction to Fletcher as a threat. Jealousy was not only for lovers. "He was a fencing master. Pay him to show you his fancy tricks, then send him on his way."

When you send Rosy on his way, she thought bitterly, though that was foolish. As foolish as plucking up Garnet when Nick had first become smitten with Rosy. Rafe Fletcher might well be as much trouble as Garrin, growing restless, mean, deceitful, when he could not control the woman he bedded. "If Fletcher likes trouble too much, he goes."

"I wish you'd just bed him and get rid of him," Nick said, both more direct and more sullen.

"You've made him the cause of my refusal, because you will not hear no." Tired of the battle, she went on coldly, "Hear it now. I do not love Rosy. I will not risk my life to bear his child. Not even for you. *No.*"

Nick rose from the bed. He paced, desultory and distant, pretending her refusal did not matter.

Viv rose as well. She lit a pastille in a silver perfume pan, her scent of musk and ambergris burning away Rosy's cloud of jasmine. She was glad he had not chosen roses, and spoiled their fragrance for her.

"There's trouble at the docks?" Nick asked.

"Izzy said Scratch Jones was peddling some information about Edward Chettle."

"Chettle's not been our most daring smuggler, but he's been our most reliable," Nick said. "The guns he procured were extraordinary."

"But he's been too broody," Viv said. "I told Izzy to buy the information—but now he says Scratch Jones was found red-throated."

Nick smiled a little. "As I said, it's hardly a surprise when a chattering wharf rat dies."

"It may be no more than a drunken quarrel, or an independent thief with too quick a knife hand." She moved restlessly, squared her shoulders. "But I don't like it. Too many sour notes. Izzy will go on sniffing for information, but I want to talk to Chettle."

Nicholas shrugged. "I'll be at the docks this afternoon."

She did not like how unconcerned Nick seemed, but surrendered the task. "There's wine due from France, and wool to smuggle out. That's excuse enough to see him."

"Or more guns?" Nick said. "A richer profit."

"We are still in disagreement on that," she said, her temper flaring.

"About much lately, it seems." His fingers toyed with starched lace of his cuffs.

"Then let us deal where we agree."

They moved quickly over the rest of their business, assessing the trouble spots. It looked like Maggot Crutcher was skimming the cream, and the tavern keeper at The Dancing Fox drinking up too much profit. They probed for where Smelly Jakes might be trying to dig new holes in their turf, and plotted where they might dig some in his. Rivett was a powerful enemy, but she and Nick might yet rule all of London's underworld. If they didn't hang first.

Another fear cut through her, cold and sharp. What had Nick told Rosy? Love's desire to reveal all could have them both dangling from a rope.

Nick was ready to leave. He stood before her mirror, adjusting the angle of cap and plume. His eyes met hers in the glass. "What is it?"

"Have you told Rosy who we were?" *Have you betrayed us to him?*

He held her gaze silently for a long minute. His face was closed, his eyes gave her nothing. At last he said, "Not yet."

It was no protection—only a warning of disaster. For so long they had been heart and home to each other, guarding that refuge jealously. Infatuation was no stranger, but passion had never breached the sanctuary of their bond. Until now.

What promise would he give her? "Tell me if you do."

Nick refused to answer for a minute. At last he nodded curtly, then turned and left. She gave a little jerk as the click of the door pricked like a knife point between her shoulder blades.

Raging silently, Vivian gave him time to go down the stairs, out the door. Then she stalked to the mantle, seized the clock, and hurled it against the wall. It shattered in a crazed rain of metal and glass, sending bright explosions along her nerves.

The satisfaction was intense but brief. Viv roamed the room, caught in black whirlwinds of apprehension, anger, misery, and scheming. She and Nick had escaped. They had survived. In sixteen years only Izzy had learned their secret. No one else had been trusted with their past, not even Smoke. Now Nick wanted to pour his heart out to Ambrose Piper. She shivered violently at the thought.

Everything had changed, perhaps beyond redemption. She must take some action. Izzy would follow Ambrose Piper for her. There would be the Devil to pay if Nick found out, and it was likely a futile risk. She doubted Rosy had another lover. When he was not rehearsing at the Comet, he was with Nicholas. Was there anything else that could disillusion Nick enough to abandon him? Would even that be enough—or too late?

Walking to the open window, Viv leaned out into the sun and closed her eyes. She willed its warmth to take away the chill that gripped her. The racket of clashing staves and clubs echoed the cacophony in her mind. Then Smoke barked out an order, and silence fell. Viv opened her eyes and looked across at the field.

Exhausted, Rafe Fletcher leaned against the back wall of the field, shirt damp with sweat. She could almost see the rise and fall of his chest, taste the salt on his skin. Imagining the pale blue of his eyes, like water lit with flame, she willed him to lift his head and meet her gaze. His head turned toward her.

Abruptly, Vivian drew back from the window. Already she wanted Fletcher too much. His spirit sounded a clarion call, but what did she know of him except that he was brash and beautiful? Yes, there would be heat there—and satisfaction of a different order than smashing the clock. But such carnal diversion wouldn't solve her dilemma. Pushing the thought of Rafe Fletcher from her mind, Viv resumed her prowling.

She had felt no true fear of exposure in over a decade. She and Nicholas had melted into the mold they'd shaped. Their disguise had long since become their reality. In the Clink, the Swifts lived brazenly, successful entrepreneurs winked at by sheriff and beaks. Thieving twelvepence could put the rope round your neck, but what law there was here valued their presence in a heavier weight of coin. That protection would vanish in an instant if their past was revealed. Nicholas and Vivian Swift could buy safety. Denis and Anne Rive could not.

Sixteen years had passed—but the Earl of Mortmain's killers would be hunted down and hanged.

5

*A*h," the Earl of Mortmain said, bowing low. "The tender fledgling sheds her drab down for pretty feathers."

Anne gave him her brightest smile and descended the staircase. The new gown he praised was white satin embroidered with blossoms of eglantine. Its low wide bodice framed her newly budding breasts. She was fourteen and a woman now. Mortmain offered her his arm and led her into dinner, while Denis trailed behind. She did not like the Earl, but his flattery gave her hope that he might return some of her lost freedoms.

While her father lived, she'd shared the same tutors as her brother—an education of rich red meat to nourish mind and body. Anne rode well and was skilled in archery, even fencing. Now, Mortmain had ordered Denis' teachers not to instruct her, and they were too frightened of him to disobey. The groom who'd let her ride astride had been dismissed. Anne was supposed to content herself with pious tracts and embroidery. In secret, Denis still taught her all he learned. Even in the past they were close, though he'd snubbed her sometimes for being a girl and two years younger. But since their father's death, he'd become her protector—and she his. They shared strengths, and shored each other's weaknesses.

Denis had warned her Mortmain would not relent, but Anne set herself to entertain and impress him. Her father had praised her wit, and she could not believe an intelligent man would value stupidity. The Earl laughed at her jokes, and paid her gallant attention. Denis said almost nothing, shoving about bits of food with his fork, his dark eyes flicking back and forth between them. He looked so pale, she worried he was ill. He had not been so morose since their father died, three years ago

Valor had earned Sir Vivian Rive his title of knight-banneret. Shrewdness and luck won him success in shipping, and his fortune built the rich manor of Hawkfields on his estate near Canterbury. Charm won him dark-eyed, laughing, clever Margaret Nichols. Despite the difference in their faiths, she Catholic, he Protestant, they eloped. The marriage was a happy one, and she gave him two healthy children before dying with the third. Their father had not remarried, but had been a loving and indulgent father till the hunting accident which took his life.

Hawkfields and their wardship were a plum, small but juicy-sweet. Many had reached out their hands to the Crown, hoping to have it dropped into their grasp. Though some of the hopeful were kin closer in blood and affection, Denis and Anne were given over to the protection of Henry Haughton, the Earl of Mortmain, a distant relation to their mother. But Mortmain's hands had been reaching for a far greater prize. The Haughtons had remained Catholic long after the other branches of the family converted, even at the cost of advancement.

The Earl had been petitioning the Queen for a rich barony of mining lands in the north. Instead he received their wardship, and for him the plum was small and sour.

In the beginning, Lord Mortmain brought his family with him for a week in the Kent countryside. He had a wife and a son Anne's age, both with yellow hair as smoothly contrived as their manners and eyes the golden brown of expensive brandywine. But his wife preferred the glamour of life at Court, and the son snubbed them as unworthy companions. More often than not the Earl came alone.

Tonight at dinner, Lord Mortmain was smiling and gracious. He gave Anne's request no refusal, nor any promise, either. It was late when Mortmain summoned her to his chambers. She and Denis were playing chess in her room. Abandoning her play, Anne rose, white satin swishing about her ankles.

"Don't go," Denis said, rising.

"He may have changed his mind." Hope still lingered.

"He's only toying with you, like a little mouse." He poked her. "Squeak, squeak, squeak."

"I'll not squeak." She frowned at him, feeling foolish already. "I have to talk to him. If I don't, he'll certainly refuse."

"I can teach you." He grabbed her hand, but she pulled it away.

"Some things, yes, but I cannot have all your time." Lately Denis had been so restless. "And you'll be sent to college soon."

"If he lets me go," Denis said bitterly.

Anne started for the door, but Denis stopped her again. "Stay here. It's late. I'll say you're abed and beg your case myself."

"Beg? And disprove my ability to argue by letting you speak for me?"

"You're a fool," Denis snapped, startling her. "Go on then, but he'll give you nothing unless you beg, and nothing then either."

And so she went. The Earl stood by a sideboard laid with wine and fruit, casually paring an apple, the green peel snaking down to the floor. He waved a hand lazily, and gave orders to dismiss all the servants for the night. When they were alone, he laid aside the knife and bit into the apple, munching it as he studied her. He washed it down with swallow of wine from his goblet, smiled unpleasantly. "So, Mistress Anne, you think you're clever as a man?"

Obviously *yes* would not get her what she wanted. Fuming, she tried for modesty. "I should like to study all I can, Your Grace, and let the limit of my wit be the limit of my learning."

"I set the limits at Hawkfields. You've overstepped them."

She prickled. "You raise both horses and hounds, my lord. If a bitch or a mare was stupid, you would think it a fault, not a virtue."

"If they were disobedient, Mistress Anne, I would have them put down."

The words, his smile, chilled her. As Denis had warned her, he had no intention of yielding. The meeting was to chastise her.

"There's only one thing a woman need know. And I think it's best you learn young," he gibed. "In this skill, there's no one better than I to teach you."

Realization stunned Anne as Mortmain sauntered toward her. She was abruptly aware of how massive he was, a foot taller and more than double her weight. When she bolted for the door he grabbed her, lifting her into his arms. She thrust her hand between their mouths as he tried to kiss her, clawing at his lips as she kicked at his thighs, knee aiming for his groin. Cursing, he grabbed her legs more tightly.

Denis burst through the door. In an instant the fear and agitation on his face transformed into fury. He snarled at Mortmain. "I won't endure this."

The Earl let Anne drop in a heap. Springing up, she ran to Denis, who pulled her behind him, hissing at her to leave. She shook her head, facing their enemy. Mortmain looked annoyed, then amused. "Quite a pretty pair," he said. "Though you've lost much of your bloom, Denis. I care not whether I bed boyflesh or girlflesh. But I do like a silken cheek."

Denis eyes glittered. "Leave her alone or I tell what you've done."

"What? Amused myself—and you on occasion?" Mortmain smiled. Deliberately, he drew a handkerchief of fine lace from a concealed pocket in his codpiece, the gesture affected and deliberately lewd. He dabbed at the corners of his mouth. "Tell what you please. The word of an earl will squelch the puling whelps of a paltry knight-banneret. I could kill you both and the world would be honor-bound to believe it was nothing but an accident."

Most likely it was true. Anne believed the Queen was wiser than that, but how would she win an audience with the Queen?

A virgin, inexperienced though not ignorant of sex, Anne understood now that Mortmain was forcing Denis. It explained the change in him, sometimes sullen, sometimes servile, when the Earl visited. Explained the strange blend of enticement and punishment Mortmain used to control him.

"In future, if either of you refuses to do what I tell you, I'll punish the other for your disobedience." Mortmain tucked the handkerchief slowly into his codpiece, fingers playing over the stuffed pillar. "Now, Mistress Anne, come back here and kneel in front of me."

Denis lunged at him, but the Earl knocked him aside, a bear cuffing a dog. Rage flaring through her, Anne leapt on Mortmain, but he pulled her off, slapped her to the floor. Her brain reeled. Denis flung himself again, a pit bull ready to go to its death. The Earl's next blow stunned him, knocked him backward onto the bed. Denis gave a groggy moan as the Earl flipped him over, dragging down Denis' breeches and hose to expose his buttocks. Fury swelled in Anne as Denis struggled to escape the pawing hands.

Mortmain leered over his shoulder at her. "A lesson, since your brother knows how. Then we'll see how much you've learned. You did beg to share his tutors."

Pinning Denis to the bed with one hand, Mortmain jerked open his codpiece to free his swollen weapon. Almost blind with rage, Anne snatched the paring knife from the sideboard and leapt onto Mortmain's back. Grabbing his hair, she pulled his head back and plunged the knife into his neck, dragging it across his throat. With a gurgling scream, Mortmain pulled away, his blood spurting over Denis and the bed. Anne jumped to the side as Mortmain tumbled backward onto the floor. Blood spouted from his throat as he thrashed, the hot gore drenching Anne's gown and spattering her face. Horror chilled the hot rush of triumph and twisted her guts. She sank to her knees and vomited in the rushes. Denis stumbled off the bed, pulling his clothes together. He knelt beside the spasming body.

"Give me the knife," he hissed at her.

Anne stared at him, looked down at the knife still clutched in her hand. Denis pried it from her fingers. Mortmain stared up with glazed eyes, his body twitching. Denis took the knife in two hands and drove it into his heart. The Earl jerked, then lay still.

Denis looked into her eyes. "Now we both killed him."

For a minute they said nothing, as the impact of what they'd done encompassed them. Denis stared at the corpse with loathing and revulsion, then turned back to her. "I thought you'd be safe from him," he said. "I thought he liked only boys."

"I'm glad he's dead," Anne whispered.

"They'll hang us for murder. We have to run."

Anne nodded, pushing herself to her feet. "We have till dawn."

"We need money to survive." Denis reached out and pulled three jeweled rings from the Earl's thick fingers, untied his purse, and cut the gemmed buttons off the gory doublet with the knife. He handed her the bloody jewelry.

Anne gripped it tightly, fighting her churning stomach. "Can you get a horse?"

"I'll tell Tom I'm off to tup some wench in the village. He'll grumble, but he won't be suspicious."

They could barely think, but they made what plans they could. Sneaking back to their rooms, they stripped off their bloody silks and hid them in a chest. After washing in pitcher and basin, Anne dressed in her plainest gown, a brown velvet riding habit. If anyone spotted them at first, she wanted to be seen in a gown, to be a girl till they reached London. She packed a bundle of Denis' clothes for both of them while he went to the stable. Her jewelry box yielded a gold chain, a choker of pearls, a few rings to be added to Mortmain's gems. They went into the pack along with needles and thread and a few apples grabbed from a bowl. Afraid some of the servants might be about downstairs, Anne climbed down the tree outside her window.

Each second pierced like a needle, thousands of sharp jabs as she waited. Finally Denis appeared on their mount. He pulled her up behind him, and they rode as fast as they dared in the darkness, taking the shortest route to the Thames. At the river, they unsaddled the horse and slapped its rump, sending it toward Dover. They threw the tack in the Thames, stole a rowboat and headed for London. Near dawn they climbed into an overhanging willow from the boat and set it adrift. They hid in the branches all that day. Even if word of the Earl's death had not reached the local constables, they could not afford to be seen. Vagrants who had no license for begging were subject to arrest. Only the wealthy could move from town to town without a pass. That night they stole apples from an orchard, and another boat to take them further down the Thames.

If they'd been older, they might have fled to France. As it was, London seemed their best chance, a city big enough for them to disappear in, to become someone else. They had a few pounds from Mortmain's purse and jewelry they were not sure they dared to sell. Knowing it meant survival, Anne hid their hoard, sewing the coins into the seams of breeches, doublets, and capes. She could pass for a boy still. When they reached the walls of London after three nights of travel, she threw her dress into the Thames and donned Denis' oldest, smallest clothes.

In the morning, they entered the gates of the city as brothers.

❧

The noise, the smells, the swarms of people were intimidating, but they felt anonymous, safe for the moment. They ate bread and cheese and shared a tankard of ale at a tavern near the gate, then began to explore the streets, uncertain what to do next. The crowd grew steadily, pressing them forward, and they went with the flux of movement, back through the gate and along the north road. Then the man walking beside them grinned, twisted an imaginary rope around his neck, and lolled his tongue. There was a hanging in Tyburn. For a minute they stood in the middle of the road, too stunned to flee, while the crowd swarmed around them. Denis' gaze sought hers, and held, filled with fear and a terrible curiosity. She felt the same horror and perverse fascination. With an act half will, half surrender, they moved on with the mob. They had to know what was at risk, make themselves know what it would mean to be caught. They needed to make their own deaths real.

The gallows had stood in Tyburn for over a decade and were kept busy enough to entertain the crowds. Three men, two women, and a girl scarcely ten were hung that day. The image burned in Anne's mind with grotesque clarity. Even more than killing Mortmain, this was her coming of age. There would be no protection, no trust in her life, except what she and Denis gave each other. The faces around them showed fear, horror, hilarity, lust. She saw a pickpocket lift a purse from an oblivious woman and scuttle through the crowd. A fine gentleman had a coach with a view, and two prostitutes to help him enjoy the show. The sight made her queasy. For a moment Anne felt like Lord Mortmain still held them in his power, like a great fist closing about them and squeezing tight. Fighting off her panic, she vowed to escape his power, his retribution.

She'd never lacked bravery. Even as a child she was far more daring than Denis. Her father, her tutors, all despaired of her reckless exploits. A little pain was a small price to pay for the intoxicating triumph of success. If it was the quick sweep of the headsman's sword, she believed she would not falter. But the sword was for nobility. The idea of being hung, the humiliation of having to jerk and dance on the rope as she died, filled her with horror. Still, she thought, she would stand up and make a fine speech, and persuade the crowd to admire her. The thought of death chilled her less than the thought of long imprisonment. Being cooped up in the dark for months could devour all her courage.

When the woman and the little girl were hanged, a youth about Denis' age climbed onto the platform and flung his arms about the child's feet. He bore down hard, and her neck broke quickly. The youth started to climb down from the platform, but the woman hanging beside the little girl was strangling slowly, flopping on the rope. So he knelt and acted as hanger-on for her, too, though Anne didn't know if it helped her die much faster. Denis was sickly white as whey, but he watched it all, to the end. Walking back when it was all over, she saw the boy from the gallows wandering through the crowd. He looked across at her, death still couched in his eyes.

Continuing the charade of brothers, she and Denis took a room at a London inn. The street seemed shabby but not too dangerous. Playing poor, they carefully counted out the price of a week's stay from both their pockets, dividing the remaining silver pennies as if they were near all they had. The next day, Denis talked the owner into letting him serve ale in the tavern, but there was only work for one. Anne was good with horses, and got work in a stable, but it was hard to hide she was a girl in such rough company. They laughed at the new boy for being too modest to piss against the wall. Anne knew it would not be long before they found her out.

And she and Denis wanted to work together if they could. The jewels would keep them for a year, or two, if they could sell them without drawing suspicion. Denis chose the smallest gold ring and sold the jewel to a pawnbroker. He gave Denis only a pittance in return, then asked if he had more to sell. Denis said no, but the next day their room at the inn was sacked, their clothes cut to pieces, what money and jewels not on them stolen. The landlord tossed them out for bringing trouble and refused Denis his salary. Crossing over London Bridge to the Clink, they found a room in a more dilapidated inn. They had the clothes on their backs, a leaking roof for a week, enough pennies left for bread once a day. Desperation gripped them. They wanted to survive, but they remembered good food, warm beds, clean clothes. They did not want to become scuttling bugs existing on garbage. Anne saw girls, boys, younger than herself selling themselves in the streets. But she saw no point in refusing to submit to an earl, then giving herself over to the violation of drunken strangers.

"I'd rather be a thief than a whore," she said to Denis.

They'd stolen to get to London, been robbed themselves. Watching the streets, they had been quick-eyed enough to see cutpurses at work. In St. Paul's yard, Denis bought a pamphlet that warned the country gentry of the games of nicks and foists, and how best to avoid being the coney caught in the games they played. They read about hooking, but stealing money was safer than stealing goods, where they'd need a middle man like the pawnbroker. Anne's hands were quickest, and they decided she would cut the purses, and Denis would take the pass. She practiced with Denis till he could not feel her cut the purse strings.

They studied all the streets and alleyways near where they lived, learning escape routes and hiding places between their inn and the three alehouses they picked as their first targets. The taverns they chose were not so wealthy they were likely to be run off, nor so disreputable they felt at risk just waiting nearby. They spent three days' ration of pennies on food for supper the night before, to fight off the growing weakness from their meals of crusts. Settling on the alehouse with the quickest escape routes, Anne loitered in a nearby doorway while Denis waited in the nearest alley. Men went in and out of the tavern, and finally one sufficiently drunk stumbled their way. Anne tripped him, let him topple across her, cursing him for a clumsy lout and pummeling him with one hand while she cut his purse strings with the other. She wriggled free of him, the prize tucked into her breeches, and moved quickly into the alley to pass the purse to Denis.

Running on, Anne made her way back through the planned maze to their room. Swarming with fear and excitement, she paced the tiny space until Denis met her there a few minutes later. He'd passed the still oblivious

drunk tottering down the street. Laughing till the tears
ran, they spilled the silver pennies on the bed and
counted out their loot. Not a fat purse, but enough to
keep the roof over their heads another week. Enough to
buy a fine pie for supper and push away the specter of
starvation. They did it once again, at another tavern, and
came away with a fatter purse and a belly full of confidence.

But the next man who stumbled into Anne's path was
more clumsy than drunk. Feeling her go for his purse, he
grabbed her knife arm, dragging her along as he yelled
for a watchman. Filled with terror and fury, she bit his
hand. He yelped and let go. She ran fast, tasting his
blood in her mouth. The coney and the watchman ran in
pursuit—gaining on her every second.

Just ahead, Anne saw a young man beckon at the
mouth of an alley, then vanish down it. She didn't break
stride as she dashed around the corner to see him standing in an open doorway. He gave a quick jerk of his head,
and she hesitated only a second. The unknown was less
threatening than the men close on her heels. She dashed
through the doorway. The youth shut it behind her, then
quickly moved them through an open trapdoor hidden
under the rushes, poking a stick through the slats to
cover it up again. A tallow candle burned in a passageway
behind them, and the youth led her there and closed the
door to block off the light. Anne still had her knife and
kept it at the ready as she tried to catch her breath and
fight off the oppression of the enclosing walls. It was a
tunnel, not a grave, and she had no time to waste on
childish fears.

She faced her rescuer, wondering if he hoped to rob her in turn. "I didn't get his purse," she warned him, forcing her voice lower.

The flickering light and shadow of the underground passage showed her a pair of bright brown eyes. "Too bad," their owner said. "Still, ye've got promise, girl."

Anne gasped, looking to see if some telltale rip in her clothes had revealed her.

He smiled at her shock. "Oh, no one else'll notice, not unless they look close and careful."

"I do my best not to get noticed."

He nodded. "Like I said, ye've got promise. But I think ye've need of some help if ye don't want yer neck stretched."

"What help are you selling?"

"I'm trading, dearling. I'll teach ye how ter file a sharp hornbill ter cut a purse quicker and neater. I'll teach ye places like this, where ye can run when the beaks are closing on ye. I'll teach ye every kind of cozenage—curbing, cogging, charming, and crossbiting—what ye will."

"And just what do you want in trade?" Her bristling tone warned that she was not for tumbling. But she had to warn herself to be wary. The youth made her want to smile.

He leaned forward eagerly. "I heard ye the other day, talking ter the other one, yer brother?" When she nodded, warier than ever, he added, "Ye talk fine. In this business the better ye talk, better ye walk, the closer ye can get to a gold-stuffed gander. That's the trade, dearling. Ye teach me fine manners, I teach ye fine craft."

"And just who are you?"

"I'm Izzy Cockayne," he said. "And ye?"

They'd used different names at every inn. Anne decided it was time for a change. But they might have to stick with these, and she did not have them ready. Izzy caught the hesitation, and winked. "First lesson. Better be swift."

"Swift then," she said, and they'd exchanged the smile of conspirators. After a second, she decided, "Vivian Swift."

She was proud of her father, and she wanted to keep some small part of him alive.

"Viv," Izzy said at once.

She liked that, and she liked how easy he was. She'd known him five minutes, but it might have been all her life. Curious, she looked at him closely. Did Izzy Cockayne's face seem familiar only because it was so ordinary? "I've seen you before," she said.

"At the hanging three weeks past. Ye were the only ones there looked as sick as I felt." The sudden weariness in his eyes aged him decades. He gave a nod toward the door. "I keep a sharp eye on me turf, but I noticed ye special because of that day."

Viv stared at him, recognizing the misery in his eyes as much as anything. "You were on the scaffold at the hanging."

He leaned back against the wall, as if he couldn't bear the weight of the memory. "It was me sister on the rope."

"I'm sorry," she whispered.

"I'd like ter see that ye don't 'ave ter play hanger-on for yer brother, or he fer ye." He met her gaze, and his voice was wistful as he added, "Ye look like ye love each other."

Viv nodded. She tried to speak but the words caught in her throat. Her eyes stung and she blinked back tears. The last thing she'd expected to find in London was kindness.

"I should go back to my brother. He'll be worried," she said. "Come with me."

Izzy showed her the way through the tunnel, which branched in three directions. He led her out across the street through the cellar window of another abandoned building. On the street, he bought a pippin pie, then Viv took him back to the cramped garret to meet Denis. As she feared, he was in a frenzy of worry, and was instantly suspicious of the stranger with her.

"This is Izzy Cockayne," she said. "He helped me escape. I've told him our name is Swift."

"Vivian and I 'ave a bargain, waitin' on yer yea or nay, ter be sure," Izzy smiled, ignoring Denis' tension.

Her brother looked from one to the other, then said cautiously, "It's good to see you safe, Vivian."

Izzy looked at him expectantly. Viv held her breath.

"I'm Nicholas," he said finally, choosing a play on their mother's maiden name.

"Master Nick," Izzy said, giving him a wink.

"And just what is our bargain?"

So Izzy told him.

They trusted their new friend—but only so far. She and Nicholas took his help, but they hid who they were. That reward was too much temptation to put before a thief. Sitting in their garret, sharing the pippin pie, Izzy just nodded when she told him a half-invented story of losing their mother and being abused by their stepfather.

"Ye'll do better if yer 'ave a family 'ere," Izzy said.

"No doubt," Nick said dryly. "Where might we find one?"

"Right 'ere," Izzy said, tapping his nose. "I'll 'dopt you. I be short on family just now. I just be telling Old Warts ye're kin from the country and I be training you."

"Who?" Nick asked, not believing his ears.

Izzy clucked his tongue in disapproval. "Ye be in sore need of some trainin', lad. Old Warts is King o' the Clink, and has been for twenty years. E's upright man to every beggar, apple squire to every bawd, piss prophet, prigger of prancers, master verser, lock charmer, and knight of the post. Old Warts gets a piece of every pie cut in Southwark, and gets it delivered to his doorstep."

"Prigger of prancers," Viv said, remembering her pamphlet. "Horse thief."

"Apple squire," said Nick. "Pimp."

"E's a man to be reckoned with," Izzy laughed, then gave Viv a wink. "Lucky ye and yer brother are swift. Could be summin else'd nabbed you and made you pay up. Don't ye worry. Old Warts'll may lay a bit of stick about if ye come up short of silver—the spongy, bloat-belllied, suck-leech—but he be a better master than most."

"I don't want a master," Nick said tightly.

"Then ye 'ave to become one yerself," Izzy answered, "when yer pizzle's long enough to out-piss him. Meanwhile, let me teach you the tricks, and his stick'll float over you like a feather."

Izzy paused, then took a bite of apples and crumbling

crust. "I paid the pieman, and there's still enough t'go around. Don't ye get too greedy, and we'll do just fine."

They nodded that they understood.

"Viv, ye go on playin' ye'r a boy. Ye'r fast on your feet, no reason to flap skirts around them yet. But if any of our lot hooks it, laugh and shrug like they should've known. We'll make a game of it, long as we can."

"I'll do it," she said. The law would be hunting brother and sister, not brothers. And already she loved the freedom of the breeches.

Izzy told Old Warts that they were country cousins gone destitute, their father a parson, penniless but educated. Izzy promised to train them, and assured Old Warts he'd get a goodly profit. Izzy was known and liked, so no one thought to question his word. His mother was so crazed with drink, she'd finally been locked away in Bedlam. Izzy played mother to his littlest sister, who was too young to doubt him. The other siblings were gone. His older brother drowned at sea, one sister was dead of smallpox, another of the French pox, one hanged. Izzy didn't like to be alone and made them family. He taught them all he knew, and learned what they could teach him. Slowly they wove their way into the underworld.

It was a year later when Izzy took them up to an abandoned garret. He brought out a pippin pie and set it down on a clean rag.

"Before we share this, I've a secret to tell you."

"A secret?" Nick asked. Viv tilted her head expectantly.

"It's your secret," Izzy said. "I know who you are— who you were. I want you to know I won't be telling."

"And who are we?" Nick rasped.

"You were a family named Rive. You killed a earl—sort of like poaching the Queen's deer, that. Turning you in would earn me a fortune—if they didn't decide to hang me, too." Izzy clicked his tongue and wagged his head. "So few people you can trust."

Viv could feel the scratch of the hangman's rope about her neck. The scent of the pie blurred into the smell of the apple Mortmain had peeled and eaten. Panic clawed at her belly. She thought of killing Izzy, and knew he could see it in her eyes. She and Nick both had their daggers, and Nick had a sword.

Izzy was afraid, but he'd expected their reaction. He gulped, then lifted his jerkin and pant legs, slid off his boots, showing them he'd come unarmed. He trusted her not to slit his throat on the spot, so she trusted him enough to listen. Izzy seemed defenseless, but he was a cozener, using his easy babble and meek posture to disarm everyone. Maybe this was only a slick bit of coney catching. Izzy might need the confirmation that he'd guessed right, so as not to spoil his chance for the reward. No point in betraying a friend if it didn't earn your fortune by it.

"Not that I'd not like heaps of money," Izzy said, as if he'd read every question in her mind. "I thought about it, but I could feel how the money would burn. I'd spend it all trying to get rid of it, and be no better off when it was gone. Worse."

"If you discovered us, others can," Nick said.

"Ah . . . but I'm the only one knows you're adopted. The rest thinks you're family. If they were gonna hook you, 'twas when you first popped up. No one's come asking these six months."

If Izzy was going to sell them, he'd had his chance.

"I suppose I'm a fool," Izzy said. "I felt so clever catchin' you fer meself, y'see. I want to be the best. I thought you could make me the best."

"And you were short on family," Viv said.

Izzy nodded. "I couldn't give you to be hung. Not after seeing you that day at Tyburn."

Nick sheathed his dagger and sank down in the corner. Viv knelt beside him, felt the cold sweat on his brow and hands. He squeezed her fingers tightly, swallowed hard.

"There be limits," Izzy went on. "If they catch me and twist up with thumbscrews, say. I'm not fond of agony. I avoid it whenever possible. So if they do catch me, you might want to be running—swift as you can." Izzy smiled at Viv, his conspirator's smile. "Either that or rescue me."

"I'd try," she answered, making it a promise.

He smiled at her. "Thought you would if you could. But I'm not expecting the impossible."

"Why not? We've managed it so far."

6

"Poison?" Silver asked.

"Yes—poison," Topaz whispered. The flame of the candle reflected in his eyes, a hectic light. "It must be odorless, colorless, and it must kill by touch."

Silver smiled. "You have someone the Queen trusts to come so close? Or do you intend to sacrifice yourself?"

"I have someone," Topaz said curtly. "If you cannot procure a poison that will kill in such a fashion, then bring me some lethal distillation that can be added to the Queen's food. But that method will be far riskier for my confederate and for success."

"If the Queen dies suddenly, poison will be suspected," Silver said.

"Of course, but it will not matter. The bastard's minions will have far greater worries. There is no heir of her body to claim the throne. With the succession in upheaval, the Catholic monarchs will unite to place Mary Queen of Scots on the throne in her place," Topaz said. "Secrecy will insure my confederate's safety, nothing more. I do not dare procure such a thing myself."

"I know such a man—one who has already proved both his skill and his silence." Near the tower there was an apothecary named Crabbe, a crooked little man with an appetite for gold. "Tell me exactly how you plan to do it, and he can contrive a poison to fit your plan."

Topaz hesitated, then finally spoke. "Her perfume. My ally will add the poison to her favorite bottle and with luck be nowhere near when Elizabeth succumbs. They must first discover the method, then who tampered with the scent. Before they succeed, Mary will take the throne, and England will be Catholic once again."

"Yes, I can bring you such a potion, if your man can administer it." Silver said *man*, and he supposed it was possible. But most likely it would be one of the ladies-in-waiting. Elizabeth was known to meddle in her ladies' pleasures, chastising any flirtation not directed at herself, and refusing her favorites' requests to marry. He could imagine great hatred festering beneath those pretty, jeweled bosoms.

Topaz hesitated. "This apothecary? He is of the true faith?"

Yes. Silver smiled, remembering Crabbe's greedy eyes. "He believes in money."

"If he is not Catholic, kill him once he has delivered the poison," Topaz demanded.

"The man is valuable, for obvious reasons."

"He is a threat—"

"What threat? He does not know how we plan to use the poison. If we succeed, he will not dare speak—unless he dares to claim a greater reward. Afterward, every apothecary who's traded in such goods will fear or hope the brew was his." Silver gave him a twist of a smile, but Topaz saw little humor in it.

"Make sure he has no suspicion, or he may develop a conscience as well."

Silver doubted that, though terror of the rope might send his Crabbe scuttling. "I will see he does not suspect beforehand."

Topaz withdrew a pouch heavy with coin and handed it over. As his hand closed about it, Silver felt a tingling in his nerves. This was not the satisfaction of greed, but something subtler—the cold, sweet shiver of infinite possibility. Topaz' scheme could succeed. If so, those smoke wreath fantasies Silver had spun could prove as substantial as the purse of gold weighting his palm. One deed, one death, could transform his life. There was great risk, of course. He must trust Topaz and his unknown confederate not to bungle the poisoning. Mary must be rescued. He would see to it that Topaz' men would have the finest guns for their attack, and the Easton cannon as well.

But if the plan failed, Silver could surely escape in time. He had false identities established in more than one city.

The rewards were immense—a pardon, perhaps a knighthood. Why not, if his connivance put the Queen of Scots on the throne?

It did not matter to him which bitch ruled England.

7

*S*words clashed and scraped. Streaks of dirt melted into sweat. It was training only—but training for life or death. In the midst of the fray, Rafe glimpsed Nick Swift and Rosy Piper watching the practice from the door of the stables. Parrying a blow, Rafe fixed his gaze on the adversary before him, but the faint sound of laughter slid between the harsh clang of weapons. Rafe struck with renewed fervor, driving his faltering opponent back. Metal snarled as Rafe's blade caught the other man's, knocking it from his grasp, then twisting back to pin him against the garden wall, point to his heart. The guard signaled his surrender, and Rafe lowered his sword. The man nodded briefly, resentment and respect mingled. The respect was important, and Rafe did not gloat over the victory, only stood aside for the guard to reclaim his weapon. These men were all criminals, and any one of them might have helped kill Gabriel. But it was Swift who commanded them, Swift who drew Rafe's suspicion and incipient hate like a magnet.

Smoke Warren signaled a halt as Swift moved onto the field. Rosy, in feminine dress today, lingered by the stables. Surveying the assembled men briefly, Nick nodded without acknowledging anyone in particular. But Rafe knew Viv's brother had marked his presence, and sensed hostility beneath the feigned indifference. Swift wore the topaz ring again today, the great yellow stone winking malevolently in the sun. Nursing his suspicion and anger, Rafe listened to the dark whisper that urged the intimate revenge of bedding his enemy's sister.

Too intimate.

With a shiver he closed his mind to that whisper and concentrated on the man. Although Swift judiciously posed himself to convey command and assurance, the eternal restless current coursing through his nerves betrayed itself in the small, ceaseless movements of his fingers. Rafe wondered if he was ever still, even in sleep.

Moving forward across the courtyard, Nick gestured to Smoke, and the two men entered the captain's small office beside the guards' quarters. They had had such a conference two of the three days Rafe had been here. The first was quite brief, though yesterday Smoke been summoned to the house for over an hour. Once Viv had accompanied Nick, but not today, it seemed. Well trained, the guards moved to waiting tasks, and Rafe knew he must follow suit. Wanting to observe Swift's expression when he emerged, Rafe chose a bench where he could watch the door and set himself to cleaning his sword. He glanced idly about the yard, assessing the guards, targeting one to strike up a conversation with today. No one thought his curiosity about the Swifts' network unnatural. Ostensibly Rafe was one of them, but he had earned no one's trust, either. He was careful not to pry if they showed any reluctance to disclose details about their work. Better to glean the prize bits that fell unnoticed.

After a few minutes, Izzy Cockayne wandered over and sat beside him. Izzy practiced every morning with the rest of them. His attacks with a sword were pitiful, his acrobatic retreats amazing. He leapt and dodged and tumbled, rolling up to land nasty counter-blows. He was also remarkably good with a stave, at least at keeping his opponent at bay. Now he carried a torn shirt and mending kit in his hands. Rafe watched the thief's nimble fingers enviously, knowing he would have had to jab the thread at the needle a few times. Izzy pierced it with one quick stroke and gave a little cluck of satisfaction.

Izzy began to stitch, talking meanwhile of some whore he was fond of, wishing he did not like her so much, since he did not like the wine at the tavern where she kept a room. Izzy's lazy warmth turned even such apparent trivia into intimacy. But Rafe was sure appearances deceived and the conversation was anything but trivial. Izzy wanted to find out about the women Rafe had bedded. He was gathering information for Smoke, Nick Swift, or Vivian herself.

Rafe resented the probing, though he believed Izzy did it with good will, to ease Rafe's way and to forestall trouble. With the others guards, Rafe had volunteered what he wanted them to know, answered the obvious questions readily, and told a tale or two to make them laugh. Most men would rather talk about themselves, and it was easy enough to twist the conversation when the other men asked about his past. But Izzy had been using the same ploy on him. It put Rafe's nerves on edge.

"What would you do?" Izzy asked.

"Simple enough to take her elsewhere," Rafe said briefly, working on the hilt of his sword.

"Simpler still to stay where she is," Izzy rejoined. He heaved a great sigh. "I'm like to die of love."

As Cockayne drew breath, Rafe said scornfully, "Die of love for a whore? Of the pox, more likely still."

"Bishop and beggar can fear that end," Izzy said with a shrug. "We all risk the pox for the passion."

Rafe guessed Izzy would next ask him to describe the lustiest wench he'd ever had, or some such thing. He had experience enough to make it sound like more. Living in London, he'd gone on some wild adventures with Gabriel, and even in Exeter he had never been chaste. He'd already told Izzy the tale of his virgin tumble with the brewer's daughter, and the night with the French courtesan who had shown him all the sweet portals of sin. Perhaps this time he could recount the escapade with two bawdy barmaids. Those adventures were easy to make light of, but he was sick of the game.

What more did the thief need? Then Rafe sat up, the answer obvious. He turned to face Izzy. "I've never forced or mistreated a woman, if that's what you're wanting to know."

After he spoke, Rafe wondered if he should have tried to make himself unappealing by inventing some sordid tale filled with crudity or cruelty. But there was no certainty that he would be left alone rather than dismissed, and he'd only alienate Cockayne.

Beside him, Izzy knotted the thread and bit it off. Meeting Rafe's gaze, he nodded to the closed door. "Treat her well, and you'll have no quarrel with Nick Swift, Smoke, or me. Treat her ill and they'll chop you into mince—if she's left any pieces of you big enough."

"What about you?"

"I'll watch—then feed the mince to the dogs."

Rafe tilted his sword toward the house. "It's a foregone conclusion, then, that she can take whatever piece she wants?"

"Are you saying that you don't want her?"

Glancing up at Vivian's window, Rafe thought he saw movement behind the curtains, but it was impossible to tell from this angle. Probably he imagined it. Viv had no need to hide—she was brazen about watching them.

When he did not answer, Izzy prodded with an elbow. "Rafe?"

Finally he said, "A man likes to choose."

"Everyone likes to choose." Izzy smiled a little. "Seems to me the choice is mutual."

"I presume the choice was mutual with Garnet—at first," Rafe said sharply. He'd been lucky there. Garnet's ill temper had cost him most of his friends, and no one felt Rafe need be snubbed or punished for his sake.

"He mistook a bit of sport for passion."

"He felt more than was permitted?"

Izzy shrugged. "He felt more than there was answer for. It would be the same with a tavern wench."

"And even a wench might have friends powerful enough to toss him from the tavern?"

"From the city, if they were big enough." Izzy grinned. "If it vexes you so, say no, and there's an end to it."

It was a chance. A *no* delivered through Izzy Cockayne would have been far easier than a *no* to Vivian herself. Rafe did not want to seek a relationship so dangerous, so intimate, and reeking of sin. But he had so little time, only a month before his family was brought to trial. He could not bring himself to close off the possibility, or to invite it. Reluctance was the most he dared convey, and his silence had conveyed that well enough already.

And *no* was a lie. Rafe wanted her.

He returned to polishing his sword, an absurd task since the blade gleamed in the sunlight. There were other chores he could attend to, but he did not want to surrender his view, equally absurd since there was little the door was likely to reveal.

Izzy watched Rafe for a moment, then clapped a hand lightly on his shoulder before taking himself and his mended shirt away. Rafe watched him go. Izzy was affable and generous, and Rafe knew he was not begrudged his supposed good fortune, only thought a bit of a fool to hesitate. Rafe had caught envious and resentful glances from some of the men, but there was no lack of respect for Viv. They seemed to take pride in her exploits. Rafe had heard more rueful comments about her temper than her lustiness. And there was some mutter about Nick's moodiness. Listening to what was unvoiced, Rafe decided that Nick Swift was not hated, but neither was he loved. Viv was loved. Viv was their Queen. Unlike her brother, she spoke to the guards by name, joking with them and asking after the families of those that had them. She moved among them bright and gleaming as a flame, casting light and warmth—when her temper did not burn.

Restless and dissatisfied, Rafe left his useless bench and singled out one of the guards who worked in the armory, trolling for information as he asked advice on what gun he should buy when he got his wages. At last the door of the captain's office opened and Nick emerged. His expression was aloof as usual, so Rafe's watch had gained him nothing. Mounted sidesaddle, Rosy rode out of the stables on his white gelding, followed by a groom leading Nick's bay. Swift mounted, and Rafe watched the two men ride off. Smoke Warren returned and set Rafe to working with four of the men whose blocking technique was faulty.

Late in the afternoon, the captain summoned Rafe to his office. Smoke sat back in his chair, sharp blue eyes studying him closely. Rafe coolly returned the scrutiny. Smoke had already questioned him closely about his past. In this short time, Rafe doubted the man could have searched out any of the weak spots in his tapestry of half truths and lies, but he could have found the men Burne had arranged to verify his false history.

The captain was of medium height, lean and sinewy. His ekename probably came from his prematurely gray hair, pale as smoke. An old rope scar marked his neck, and the hanging had given his voice a harsh roughness. The tale went that Viv had rescued Smoke by bribing the hangman to cut him down before he died. Although Smoke was a criminal, Rafe felt a grudging respect for the man. Rigorous and intelligent, there was no doubt that he merited his position as captain and could skillfully command both men and weapons. Today, Smoke had ordered them to work with sword and buckler, yesterday with sword and dagger. Tomorrow there would be cloak work.

From the guards, Rafe learned that Smoke, like Garnet, had been Viv's lover. The few times Rafe had seen them together, he'd sensed nothing but respect between them. Apparently, the affair was long over, and neither passion nor unease lingered. Rafe didn't doubt he'd be watched like a hawk, but from protectiveness, not jealousy.

"Your morning training continues here as usual, but you have new duties in the house," Smoke said at last. He gave a brief nod toward the guardhouse. "Clean yourself up. A servant is waiting with your new livery."

It was not a subject for debate. Rafe cursed silently, but he felt the tug of desire pulling against his reluctance. He'd thought this the best position—working close by the weapons. The captain was tight as a mussel, however. He would not be charmed. He would not be careless. But Vivian Swift might be both.

"Yes, sir," Rafe answered in his most respectful tone.

"It is an excellent opportunity." There was no innuendo in Smoke's voice and his face was unreadable as he added, "See you do not abuse it."

❧

Rafe sluiced off sweat and dirt in the washroom and toweled himself dry. When he entered the guards' quarters, the waiting servant spread out the new garments on Rafe's bunk with finicky care. Scarlet and black, silk and velvety mockado, the fancy livery was meant for display. The fabrics were extravagant, richer than the best garments of a gun merchant's grandson. The Swifts loved to flaunt their stolen wealth.

Rafe picked up the shirt, fluid silk pouring scarlet over his hands. He remembered Gabriel dying in his arms, his blood red in the flickering candlelight. Rafe would have happily shredded the garment to ribbons, but instead he slid it over his head. The silk flowed over him, cool and caressing against his skin. Rankled by the seductive luxury, he pulled on netherstocks, drawers, and breeches, then shoved his feet into the leather shoes. Over the shirt went the doublet and sleeves of soft-napped mockado. At least he had a sensible collar, rather than a starched plate of lace ruff. Rafe tugged bits of scarlet silk through the slashes along chest and arm. Dissatisfied with his cursory arrangement, the servant stepped forward, deftly tweaking pleats and puffing silk. Finally, he crowned Rafe with a plumed cap and pronounced him satisfactory.

Dressed in his new finery, Rafe followed the servant back to the house, through the servants' quarters and into the main hallway, as richly furnished as a nobleman's home. For that matter, it was probably furnished with objects stolen from any number of great houses, like the elaborate clock that sat on a table by the entrance. His young guide presented him to the butler, who examined Rafe with critical scrutiny, puffed his slashes some more, then handed him the small, heavy, and obviously precious clock. Crystal, onyx, and gold, it displayed its intricate workings within a case flanked by an intricate sculpture of a man spying on a naked goddess, Acteon and Diana, he presumed, since it was crowned by hounds hunting down a stag, Acteon transformed and punished. Admonishing him to carry the treasure with the utmost care, the man indicated the room at the end of the landing above, Vivian's room.

Advanced to errand boy, Rafe thought with annoyance as he climbed the staircase with its ornately carved balustrades, then walked along a corridor paneled in polished oak. He couldn't help wondering what other duties might await him. The guard outside opened the door to the Swifts' apartments, admitting him into an ornate parlor where a lone waiting woman in black silk sat embroidering. Smoke's sister, he'd been told, and she had the same stern visage, the same keen, measuring glance. Viv was well guarded. To the right, an adjoining door led to where he knew Nick Swift's rooms to be. Silently, the waiting woman nodded him to the door on the left.

Opening it, Rafe entered a sumptuous bedchamber of deep amber walls bedecked with tapestries. The floor was thickly strewn with rushes, herbs, and rose petals, Turkey carpets draped the tables, and the coffered ceiling was brushed with scarlet and gilt. The bed was vast, its tall posts thickly carved with grape vines and hung with lavish draperies, their autumnal hues lined with scarlet silk. Pouring through the windows, sunshine filled the chamber with a pale golden haze. Silhouetted against the frame of light, a small, slender man stood looking out at the garden, a jaunty cape slung over his shoulder. Rafe halted, recognizing the impertinent profile even as the figure turned to face him with a bright smile.

Not a man. Vivian. Tightening his grip on the clock, Rafe stared in disbelief at the outrageous display. Under the short flared cape, she wore a doublet of scarlet brocade and black trunk hose brightly slashed with satin. Encased in parti-colored hose, the muscles of her thighs were taut and supple, the swell of her calves shapely. Glossy black shoes displayed the trim curve of her ankles. Rafe tried to smooth his censure into bland indifference, but it was too late. The welcoming smile vanished and the bright light in her eyes went cold and dark. The clock ticked inanely in the silence. She nodded to the fireplace mantle and Rafe placed the fabulous gold-worked thing upon it. He hadn't intruded on a naked goddess, but the mythic sculpture atop the clock was newly sinister. Vivian Swift had hounds aplenty to tear him apart. Inhaling deeply, he turned to face her.

"You disapprove?" She gestured to her exposed legs with one hand. The other curled about her sword hilt.

Surely he was not the first man she had shocked? Would she dismiss him for showing his surprise? Rafe temporized. "I have heard great ladies sometimes dress so, when they hunt." In his mind, he heard his grandfather railing at the gentlewomen who donned such unseemly and impious garb. Then Rafe had secretly thought it daring, exciting, for a woman to so defy convention. Now his own dismay unsettled him. He'd thought himself more worldly.

"I am always hunting." Smiling dangerously, Viv stepped to face him. "And I always catch my quarry."

Rafe stood utterly still. "I'm sure you're a most skillful huntress."

Her eyes scanned him from head to foot, then lifted to meet his own, glinting with challenge. Laying one hand on his chest, she rubbed slowly against the nap of his mockado doublet. "Soft as fur."

Her touch was both caress and threat. Rafe's heartbeat quickened beneath her hand, but he held her gaze steadily.

"Yes. You do look splendid in my livery." Her fingertip skimmed the collar, her nail grazing lightly along his throat. Then she stepped back. Her voice was low, but every word was hard and distinct. "Now—take it off."

Rafe drew a sharp breath. Lust and mutiny clashed in his nerves, stringing every lineament taut. He didn't move. She read the tension in his body and laughed softly, mocking him, knowing that her aggression disconcerted him. He glared defiance.

"Take off your clothes." Her voice was low, as menacing as it was enticing. Her eyes calculated his opposition. Only a flicker of laughter in their depths leavened her brazen tyranny.

Rafe wondered if his resistance made him more compelling. Was it that few resisted, or she preferred those that did? He did not think she wanted subservience, but neither did he know how much mastery she would accept.

Her voice softened to a seductive whisper. "Take them off . . . I want to see all of you."

A jolt of arousal shot through him. He'd thought that she might be summoning him to her bed, but he had never imagined such a confrontation. He had known proud women, but he never seen any but a whore so bold. But it was he who was the whore, selling himself to her. Rafe dropped his gaze, queasy shame tainting his lust.

Except that his honor lay in vengeance for Gabriel and safety for his family. It could bear a bit of tarnish.

For two days he had done his best to ignore her, hoping reason would prevail over carnal urges. Now this provocation. Desire uncoiled from his loins, thin scarlet flames heating his blood. Nick Swift's topaz burned in Rafe's mind, glowing with baleful yellow fire. Lust and anger twined together in his heart, scorching hot.

Defiantly, Rafe started to undress. Eyes gleaming with triumph, Viv watched as he removed the doublet and scarlet shirt and flung them aside, kicked off his shoes, and finally tugged off breeches, codpiece, and hose and stood naked. Feeling his bravado stripped with his clothes, Rafe ran his hands through his hair, disconcerted and aroused by the boldness of her gaze.

"Don't move." Her voice was quiet, but there was no doubt it was a command.

Rafe eyed her askance, but forced himself to stand so, his legs braced and his hands still tangled in his hair. With no way to cover himself, he felt doubly exposed. He was already half hard from her teasing. She began walking around him again, the velvet nap of her cape brushing him occasionally. Catching his gaze in brief glances, her eyes mocked and teased and praised him.

"Mmmmuum." Viv made one of her small throaty sounds as she looked at him. "Beautiful. Very, very beautiful." Her gaze leveled at his groin as she spoke. "And very . . . impressive."

Her lips parted, the tip of her tongue stealing out to moisten them. Rafe could imagine its delicate wetness gliding over his skin. He flushed as his cock rose higher, jutting out from his body. At least her command for stillness was not meant for that part of him. He tensed as Viv smiled at him and reached out—gasped as her fingertips grazed the skin above his hip.

"Where did you get this scar?" Her voice was soft, her touch curious and possessive.

He swallowed. "A childhood scrape, trying to save a cat from a stoning."

She lifted her hand to his shoulder. "This?"

"From a beating my grandfather gave me, when I ran away from home."

She moved round him, tracing the sword slash on the back of his thigh. "This?"

He could not tell her it was the result of a sneak attack during the war. The fencing master had not served in the Netherlands. "A cowardly acquaintance of Babington's, who was annoyed I was the better swordsman."

"And this?" One fingertip followed the old path of a knife across his shoulder.

He remembered the fight—he and Gabriel against six drunken students bent on raping a sobbing flower girl. "A tavern brawl."

Viv continued her slow circling. Brief at first, her touches began to linger, to caress, fingertips skimming lightly over his back . . . his ribs . . . his chest. Cool as a breeze, the delicate touches trailed fire in their wake.

"Don't move," she whispered again. Almost inaudible, still the words were a challenge.

Rafe stood, rigid and quivering with tension. She knew well enough her fondling was exquisite torture. Everywhere she looked, his nerves ignited, everywhere she touched, his skin burned. He wondered if she were a witch weaving some spell, her fingers stitching threads of fire through his flesh, binding it to her own. Still she circled, stroking him till he was wrapped in a flaming web. Her fingernails followed the line of his collarbone, sculpted the hollow of his throat, then trailed over the ridge of bone to the other shoulder. He shivered at the touch, sharp currents of ice cutting through the fire. A subtle ache began in his raised arms. Her hand flattened to caress the planes of his chest. Sliding down, her fingertips brushed a small circle around the nub of one nipple, till it tightened under her touch. They lowered fractionally, tracing the line of the knife scar down to his rib cage, then angling up to his other nipple. Her fingertips claimed the nub, pinching it to an aching hardness that echoed in his sex.

Viv made a soft noise of sympathy. Rafe closed his eyes, then opened them, gasping as she twisted his nipple again and whispered, "Don't move."

Descending the midline of his body, one fingertip dipped into his navel. Her hand hovered torturously close to the top of his straining cock, so that he drew a sharp hissing breath of frustration when it swerved, gliding over the edge of his hipbone, her fingertips riffling the edges of the hair at his groin. Moving down, her palm molded to his thigh, stroking the hard swell of muscle. Viv moved behind him. Her fingers teased the sensitive skin behind his knee, then slid up the back of his leg to curve over the mound of one buttock. That hand massaged in slow circles while the other ran up his spine, unfurling skeins of fire as it rose. Rafe's hands curled into fists, tight in his hair, and Viv's touch slid up his arm to caress them, too. Her lower hand tightened on his hip, another unvoiced command for stillness as the teasing fingers descended his back, her fingernails raking lightly over his vertebrae. He shivered again.

"Don't move." Soft and coaxing, her voice belied the command. Exhaled, her warm breath flowed down his back. "Ohhhhh . . . so much to feel."

Involuntarily he gasped, arched, as her fingertips trailed provocatively over the cleft of his buttocks. He blushed hotly as one fingertip slipped between his cheeks, teasing a tight circle over tender flesh, then cursed silently as it slid away. Her hand slid lower, over the bottom curve, pressing between his legs until her fingertips lightly brushed his balls from behind. He gave a choked cry as fire branched, blazing through every limb. His cock throbbed ominously.

"No. Not yet," she whispered even as her other hand slid around him, caressing the straining column, stroking up the shaft, squeezing over the head.

Breaking away from her grasp, he whirled around. The need to burn his body into hers flared unbearably, and he seized her, lifting her against him. Her eyes flashed, desire mingling with a spark of anger. He did not care, was glad of it, and pulled her into a fierce kiss. The spark blazed, and they coiled together, fire licking fire. A moment's fusion, then Viv struggled and he felt the sinewy strength of her as a shock. He held her more tightly, but she bit his lip, then jerked her head away. She slid her forearm between them, pressing hard at his throat.

"Stop," she ordered, her eyes darkening with warning. "Put me down."

He released her, but slowly, pressing her close as he eased her down. The heat of her body burned through the textured brocade, tormenting him as he lowered her to the floor. She jerked away even as he released her, and they both stepped back. They watched each other for a moment, panting, glaring, catching their breath. Under the anger, desire seethed in the blackness of her eyes. Viv wanted to control him, but however much she played and taunted, Rafe knew she burned as hot as he did. Complete submission would bore her, just as surely as continued aggression would have unleashed her wrath.

"Reckless," she whispered.

"Yes," he answered her. "Very."

For a moment, her gleaming eyes still dared him, then she tilted her chin up, crossed her arms. "You can get dressed now."

Rafe drew a harsh breath, trying to will his flaming arousal to subside. She had taken full measure of revenge for his disapproval. Well, today she needed to prove her mastery—perhaps next time she would need to be mastered. He felt a rush of anticipation which did nothing to appease his still aching cock, but the draught was a tonic for his spirits. Meeting her mocking gaze, he gave a low laugh. She raised her eyebrows, but her lips curled in a smile. One by one, he gathered his scattered garments, aware of each posture as he did. Another game, but he enjoyed it as much as his fuming body would allow. Viv settled in a chair by the window, slinging her booted feet up on a table, head propped on her hands. Facing her, Rafe dressed again, slowly, while she watched every move.

"Enough room in that codpiece?" she asked solicitously.

"Barely."

When he was done, he gave her the barest suggestion of a bow.

Viv rose and walked over to him, reaching up to tilt his cap at a more rakish angle. "Better."

Rafe smiled and flipped the edge of her cape over her shoulder, displaying the silken lining with a gallant's flare. Viv set a cap over her brow, a golden hawk pinning on its plumes. His glance surveyed her male attire. "It suits you," he said, half praise and half insult.

They regarded each other for a moment, opponents and conspirators in the unfinished game. She laughed, at him and at herself. The sound of it mingled with his dissipating tension. Rafe felt sweetly giddy and laughed with her, not knowing how she could make his veins feel streamed with fire one minute, dancing motes of sunshine the next.

"What now?" he asked.

She laughed. "I think—a tankard of ale to cool you off."

8

*S*unset dyed the sky like a cloth dipped in deepening shades of scarlet. Rafe wondered if Vivian Swift had commanded the hue to herald their walk. As the sun lowered, leaves in the orchards took on a glossy darkness and garden flowers began to fold up their petals. He followed her through the lush suburbs surrounding her townhouse; Viv greeted everyone she met as she sauntered through her kingdom. A breeze riffled the jaunty froth of plumes on her cap as she nodded to the passersby, the golden hawk on its brim glinting red-gold in the sanguine light. With her hair coiled under the hat and her velvet cape draped over a shoulder, many simply mistook her for a man. Some of the more observant were shocked. Others looked indulgent, no doubt because they'd seen her dressed so before. Still fascinated and perturbed by her brazen garb, Rafe's gaze returned again and again to the sculptured curves of calf and thigh displayed by the form-hugging hose. Viv caught him looking and laughed, her small white teeth flashing. So he smiled in answer and shrugged.

Townhouses, trees, and gardens gave way to the raw, teeming streets of the Clink. Viv led him directly to the Lightning Bolt. Crowded and boisterous, the interior buzzed with activity. She called out greetings all around, and

Rafe nodded to Izzy and some of the guards. Nick and Rosy had the largest table to themselves. Viv headed straight for it, swinging her legs over the bench. Following close behind, Rafe glanced about at the crowd, catching surreptitious glances and a bold wink or two. It was disquieting knowing that everyone here suspected he'd bedded her. Or rather, they suspected that Viv had bedded him. *Not quite,* he thought. He wondered if he'd garner any information of worth tonight. It was only four days since he'd staged his own robbery here. Viv's men had not fully accepted him yet, but most greetings were more friendly than envious or mistrustful—with notable exceptions.

Resplendent in maroon velvet, Nick ignored him pointedly. Despite his expression of indifference, he radiated hostility. Rafe feigned nonchalance with equal enthusiasm. Nick draped an arm about Rosy. Rouged and powdered, the actor was gowned in tiers of peach satin embroidered with pink rosebuds, pearls, and ribbons. Lace frilled the sheer cuffs and circled the double ruff. Rafe was used to men dressed so for performance, but off stage the counterfeit unsettled him, much as Vivian's masculine garb first had. But now when he tried to imagine Viv in Rosy's layered and lacy gown, it shocked him to realize that he preferred her as she was, quick and vibrant as a flame in her doublet and breeches.

Smiling up at him, Viv patted the plank beside her. Rafe took the seat, feeling the warm pressure of her leg and answering it with his own. The heat radiated through his thigh and pooled in his groin. The attraction was far too distracting, but he could not deny it.

They'd just settled comfortably onto their seats when Rosy gave Rafe a candied smile and commanded lazily, "Bring me some wine, Fletcher—the red."

Before he could protest, Nick Swift said, "Two goblets."

"And two for us as well," Viv said, nodding Rafe to the bar. Rafe knew she wouldn't undermine her brother's authority, even though this game of fetch and carry was only sport for Rosy's amusement. But she made it her will, and made Rafe a beneficiary of it.

The tavern keeper, a square and ruddy fellow dubbed Brick, filled the order instantly and gave him a friendly grin. Rafe returned a rueful one, and he carried back the goblets on a tray, serving Viv and Nick first. Entertaining himself briefly with the image of red wine dripping from Rosy Piper's glossy hair and splotching his lacy ruff, Rafe set the actor's drink down with exaggerated care. As if reading his thought, Rosy quickly closed his hand about the base of the goblet. The barmaid swooped through the crowd and took the tray from him. Rafe settled back onto the bench, smiling at the quick wink Viv gave him.

Wine in hand, Rosy studied him for a moment, then drawled, "Tell us, Fletcher, you are newly baptized? Dipped in the waters of power?"

The question dripped lewdness. Rafe did no more than tilt his head in question.

"Isn't that what you do with them, Nick? Baptize them into the order of rogues?" Rosy queried, twisting his question to new intent.

"Ah, yes, the beggars do that—give a good dousing with a pint of booze." Nick glanced over at Rafe, his expression one of cool indifference, but Rafe's skin prickled as if stung with poison needles. It was in Nick's bad moods that he most resembled his sister. "Stalled to the rogue, they call it. It's the claim of the upright man over his inferiors. The king of the beggars is the upright man to every beggar in the Clink—but he does homage to us."

"Fletcher should do you homage as well," Rosy wheedled.

"I am no beggar," Rafe said.

Nick smiled derisively. "Just because you're a thief, doesn't mean you're not a beggar."

Viv gave Rafe a quick smile, her eyes warning him not to take such roughing seriously. If she or Izzy had found some reason to play out this game, Rafe knew he would be laughing. It was he and Nick Swift who rasped like crossed blades.

"Rogue I will answer to." Rafe tried for more lightness.

"He's new to the brotherhood of thieves," Rosy insisted. "There should be a baptism."

Nick climbed from bench to the tabletop. With one hand he raised the goblet aloft, with the other he gestured for Rafe to stand beneath him. Knowing Viv would order him to obey, Rafe did not look to her for confirmation. Instead he stood directly, then looked her in the eye, making it clear that only for her would he submit to this nonsense. The crowd had caught on now, and bellowed approval.

"Take off your hat," Nick ordered.

It was only one garment, but the command had unpleasant reverberations. Viv's gaze flickered, and Rafe did not hide his irritation. He drew a quick breath and pulled off the cap.

"Good," Nick murmured, as if he knew how much it rankled. Holding the goblet high over Rafe's head, he proclaimed to the room, "I, Nick Swift, do stall thee, Rafe Fletcher, to the rogue."

Swift poured slowly. Rafe stood still as the wine cascaded over his head and soaked his shoulders. Rivulets ran down his face and into his collar. When the stream stopped, he lifted his hands to comb back his dripping hair.

"Don't move," Nick said.

Rafe felt a jolt of anger. He met Viv's eyes for a quick flash, then lowered his hands and stared at his boots.

"Rosy, give me your wine as well."

Piper laughed gleefully, and handed up the other goblet. Rafe could envision the cup poised above his head.

"You are too big a beggar for just one cup, Fletcher." Nick's voice was smug.

"Or too big a rogue," Viv said, picking up Rafe's cue.

Rafe sputtered as the second full goblet was upended over his hair and clothes. A goodly quantity made its way down his back. The target of choice would be his crotch, Rafe thought, if Nicholas could angle the goblet more acutely.

"Don't move," Nick commanded.

Rafe fought down the urge to punch him.

"Now Fletcher's wine," Nick said to Rosy. The third goblet went up. From the corner of his eye, Rafe saw Vivian sit back, holding her own cup close. Fuming, Rafe waited as the third dousing dumped over him, leaving his shoulders and back drenched to the skin. Wet strands of hair plastered his face and neck. Sticky streams flowed over his fingers. He reeked with the sour honey smell.

"Done," Nick said.

Rosy gave a little sigh of satisfaction.

Taking a breath, Rafe shook himself vigorously. His wet hair flashed back and forth, flinging spatters of wine indiscriminately over Rosy, Nick, Viv, and the other watchers. Vivian laughed, Nick and Rosy muttered, the crowd cheered. Rafe sat down and mopped face, hair, and clothes with the towel the barmaid brought him. Now that it was over, it was silly, nothing more.

Seeing his bit of entertainment complete, Rosy stood, flicking red droplets from his lacy ruff. He gave Nick a beguiling glance. "Take me back to the Comet? I need to change before we discuss the opening of the play."

Nick nodded agreement, and rose from the bench, making their farewells.

When they had gone, Viv looked Rafe over and smiled ruefully. "I expected this livery to last a little longer."

He plucked his collar, his doublet, and laughed. "Still dripping wet."

"There's another set in the making, and you can give those out to be cleaned." Under the cover of the table, he felt her touch his thigh—first with her hand, then with the heavy weight of a bag of coins. Rafe covered her hand, stilling it. She smiled up at him. "Buy what you please—with this."

The gesture mingled extravagant generosity and manipulation. Rafe hated feeling bought. He lowered his gaze, tempted to flow with his feelings and refuse. But he sensed she needed gratitude, not rejection. He lifted his eyes to meet hers, promising loyalty. "You know you don't have to give me so much."

"I want to."

"Thank you," he murmured, then gave a little shrug. "I suppose I could use a new pair of boots."

Viv laughed. The money she'd just given him would buy boots and spurs, horse and saddle. "Something spectacular," she coaxed. "Blue velvet? I would love to see you in a blue velvet doublet."

Memory provoked him to whisper, "And out of it?"

"Ohhhhhh . . . even more." Her fingertips brushed the back of his hand. Lightning crackled between them, suddenly too intense for a game. They both leaned back, sipping their wine.

From out of nowhere it seemed, a dark-haired boy popped up beside Izzy. "Did yer spot me?" he asked.

"Not a hair," Izzy answered with a grin.

The boy whispered something in Izzy Cockayne's ear, then gave a nod to the door. Izzy thanked him, pressed a penny into his hand, and the boy melted into the crowd. The thief slid over to the seat beside Viv and gave her a nudge. "Smelly Jakes is on his way. That oozing pox-pustule's strolling through the Clink like he owned it."

Catching Viv's gaze, Rafe leaned forward, including himself. "What do you think he wants?"

"Usually he calls for a meeting if it's something specific. Maybe this is just a foray to make his presence known. We do the same," she said to Rafe. But to Izzy she added, "Jake's slipped behind a pillar for too long, now this. It makes me wonder what he's plotting."

"Shall I go after Nick?" Izzy asked, but Viv only shook her head.

They hadn't long to wait. Viv's attention kept straying to the door, and five minutes later she tensed, squaring her shoulders and lifting her head. Outwardly formal, her posture emanated a wary calculation. "The jackal himself, come trotting round."

Rafe turned, expecting someone lean, but the man who stood in the tavern doorway was short, not heavy, but squarely built and square-faced, with high cheekbones and thin, hard features. Jacob Rivett reeked of arrogance, haughty as the proudest duke. Gemmed brooches circled the tall crown of his hat, and two inches of fine lace embellished his starched white ruff. Standing motionless, he gleamed like a silver chessman in doublet and trunk hose of silver damask slashed with yellow satin. A chain of jeweled plaques draped his shoulders, set with bulbous pearls, moonstones, citrines, and lumps of pale amber. Studding its center, a huge topaz glittered like a malevolent eye.

The noise in the Lightning Bolt stopped, then rose to a mutter as Jacob Rivett walked toward them, shadowed by four guards in fancy breastplates. As he approached, his gaze fixed on Viv, the hair on the back of Rafe's neck prickled. Deliberately, Rafe moved from the bench to stand behind Viv, drawing Rivett's attention. Cold, opaque eyes met his, pewter gray and soulless. They did not flicker once as they assessed him. For some men greed and power were a drunkenness, a consuming blaze. Rafe saw no wildness or heat in Rivett's gaze. It was iced with sin. A man with those eyes could seize the world and hold it frozen within his grasp.

Rivett stopped at their table, acknowledging Vivian with a small bow. He glanced dismissively at Rafe's wine-sodden garments, nostrils flaring in a sniff of disdain.

"Recruiting from the scullery, Vivian?" Rivett asked, still looking at Rafe.

Rafe said nothing, only held his gaze like a drawn sword across Rivett's, claiming his own place in the game—knight, not pawn. He was aware of Rivett's guards moving closer. Rafe ignored them and held fast against Rivett's unblinking gaze. He did not look away until Vivian murmured his name. Then Rafe showed his loyalty, looking to her instead. For a second their glances held, her dark eyes flickering with sparks of amusement and warning, gratitude and annoyance, before she turned her attention back to Rivett.

"You must be lost."

"I'm never lost, Vivian. It's you who tend to wander into dangerous territory." Rivett spoke well, though his voice was oddly flat, and his thin, cold smile seemed something learned by rote, an imitation of the life animating other faces. Despite the glistening silks, there was a strange stillness about him. He was like some clockwork contrivance, the flat silver carapace filled with oiled metal gizzards—tight springs and inaudibly clicking cogs and wheels.

"Why are you here, Jacob?" Viv asked.

"Business, of course. I have legitimate ventures bordering

Southwark." He paused, then added, "And I plan to acquire more."

"Keep piling such acquisitions one atop the other, and you'll find the weight has toppled you into the Thames."

"You underestimate my strength."

"You equate it with your greed," she said coldly. "Boundless. But there are boundaries here."

"Boundaries shift," Rivett said. "Wisdom dictates we combine our forces."

"Wisdom counsels. Greed dictates," Viv countered. "The Clink is ours, and the rest of Southwark stands against you. You couldn't take it before and you won't now."

"I don't know that I need to take it. I can simply wait for it to fall." His brocades and satins hissing like snakes, Rivett rose to leave. Then he paused, drawing on his yellow gloves. "One last thing, Vivian. If you want to keep your territory, don't throw your refuse onto mine. After I've cleaned up, the boundaries may have been wiped away."

Vivian regarded him narrowly. "And just what refuse have you tripped over?"

"A bloated thing named Chettle. One of your creatures, I believe—a customs officer?"

Rafe felt more than saw Vivian tense. She answered tersely. "I know him."

"You bound and weighted him well enough, but the body tangled in some fishing nets," Rivett continued. "Be more careful next time."

Rafe stood very still, keeping his face a mask. Any problem at the docks was of interest to him.

Jacob Rivett waited, toying with the heavy chain circling his shoulders. His thumb caressed the giant topaz in the center. The stone gleamed with an evil yellow light.

Vivian studied him coldly. "For all I know, the handiwork is yours. Carrion steams like bloody droppings in your wake, Smelly Jakes."

"You've never known enough, and never will." Rivett bristled at the hated nickname. "What I know is that the beaks are pecking me with questions about a corpse that belongs to you. If I swat them, they may fly through the air and land here."

"Ummmmm," Viv gave a little hum, contemplating the thought. "Then we can play a game of bat-the-beak, and send them squawking back and forth across the Thames."

"Aren't they squawking enough already? This is the second corpse you've left in their path. Control your turf, Vivian, or I'll control it for you." Rivett turned abruptly and stalked from the tavern.

After Rivett left, Viv stayed long enough to cool tempers and lighten the atmosphere in the tavern. Rafe watched as she strolled about the room, making sure the ale kept flowing, laughing and joking with her people. She murmured something to Izzy then moved on among the men. As the next round of ale passed by, Izzy grabbed a tankard, climbed atop a table, and began to sing. Soon the crowd joined in the raucous chorus of "The Bedbug's Lament." When the tavern grew noisy with laughter, Viv signaled Rafe and they left through the back door.

Behind the inn, Viv exploded. Energy blazed around her like lightning as she kicked over a pile of empty ale kegs.

Curses sizzled in the air as she demolished whatever was breakable or crushable, then flung the debris down the alley. Panting with the release of anger, Viv turned and stalked back toward the townhouse as Rafe strode apace. Jake Rivett was capable of striking in the heart of the Swifts' territory, and Rafe kept alert for attackers as they walked under the dim lanterns. But curiosity buzzed like a wasp. When her pace eased, Rafe asked, "Who is this Chettle?"

"You heard Rivett. He was a customs official."

"He smuggled for you? Cheated you?" Rafe tried, not risking to ask if she had killed him.

"Everyone cheats," she snapped. He gave her a wounded look and she temporized, "Almost everyone. Good business is figuring who'll cheat you and how much."

He tried from the other angle. "You think Rivett is involved?"

She did not answer for a moment, then said, "I don't know what he knows, or thinks he knows. I don't know what he wants."

Her answers were too ambiguous. She was disturbed, but was it because she had not known about Chettle's death, or because the body had been discovered? "What reason would Rivett have to kill him?"

"None I know of." Viv gave a short laugh. "Smelly Jakes has killed men for coughing."

Rafe realized he wanted Gabriel's killer to be Rivett. Even more than he wanted him to be Nick Swift.

"Vivian—" he began.

"Enough!" Her eyes flashed dangerously. "I have to think."

He walked in silence for a moment, and she gave him another glance, contrite. Stopping, she pulled his face down to her, his mouth against hers. He held still for a moment, then wrapped his arms around her and pulled Viv close, pouring all his frustrations into the kiss. There was no pretense. The fencing master would feel as he did—angered that she would shut him out, trapped in the coils of desire that bound them. Willing and unwilling.

Her response was fierce, lips, tongue, teeth dueling with his. But at last she pushed him away. "I have to go back," she said, and led him down the street to the townhouse.

She brought him inside, but as soon as they stepped through the door, Nick Swift came out onto the second-floor landing. In a precise voice, he said, "I'm told Smelly Jakes is stinking up the Clink."

Vivian looked up at him. "Yes. He complained that they've found Chettle's body in his territory."

"A pity." Nick did not look in the least surprised. He surveyed Rafe imperiously for a moment, then said to Vivian, "The two of us should talk." He folded his arms and stood above them, waiting.

Viv turned back to him. She gave a little shrug, and there was no sharpness in her voice as she said, "Go back to the guards' quarters, Rafe."

There was no way he would be included in the upstairs talk. Instead, he asked quickly, "When will I see you?"

"Tomorrow, after training. It's time you learned more of our territory—I'll give you a tour." She gave him a last flash of a smile, then turned and ran up the stairs.

Seething with frustration, he watched her go up to
Nick. There was also a guard at the upstairs corridor.
Rafe made his way out the servants' entrance, then hurried out onto the training field. He glared across the garden wall at the great house. An alluring light gleamed
through the draperies, but the windows were all closed
fast. Rafe was willing to chance the patrols, but there was
no tree close by, and the rose trellis was too flimsy to support his weight. Disgruntled, he returned to the guard
house, hoping to do better there. Rafe stripped off his
wine-drenched livery, laughing along with the jests of the
other guards. Taking advantage of their good humor, he
wandered about as the men readied for bed, dropping
questions between jokes, but getting few useful answers.

When the candles were extinguished, he lay on his bunk
and stared at the ceiling. Frustration knotted his nerves.
He'd begun to gather intelligence for Nigel Burne, but there
was still too much he didn't know. Everyone he'd asked had
some gut-curdling tale about Jake Rivett. But Rafe had
learned no more of Chettle than he already knew, that he
smuggled wine and wool for the Swifts.

And guns?

❧

Viv walked along the landing toward Nick. He held his
stiff posture, his glare, till they were face to face—then
his lips quivered at the edges. He nodded after the
departing Rafe. "The wet dog slinks back to the kennel."

Exasperated, Viv thumped his chest with her fist.

"Very large dog." Laughing, Nick mimed an animal shaking water from its fur. "Very, very wet."

She thumped him again, twice.

"Fiend! Not so hard." He caught her fist in his hands.

"You've had too much to drink."

"Not too much. I still make absolutely perfect sense," Nick enunciated carefully. At her frown he looked sheepish and defiant. He'd removed the doublet Rafe had spattered with wine droplets, but his breath was heavy with it. Rosy was a bad influence, though she did not say that now, wanting to avoid a quarrel. Nick's hair was awry. She smoothed it back from his forehead.

He pulled away. "Your new pet hates me already."

She faced him down. "Well, you've put him well on the road to it."

"I don't trust him."

"Smoke will check out Fletcher's story," Viv said, fighting her annoyance. Here the present was more important than the past. Information was always useful, what could be had. Rafe's story was not uncommon. Many a man came to them with crimes to his credit, a price on his head—some bragged of it, some hid it for fear.

"You're bringing him too close too fast."

"Me?" she asked, coaxing his humor. "You're the one who anointed him, Nick."

He flashed her a look that said he wanted Rafe boots-up in a vat of wine, but the darkness quickly twisted into a smug smile. "I'm sorry."

"No, you're not." She gave up and laughed.

"No—I'm not." Nick straightened, resuming his controlled posture. He licked a fingertip, touched it to her nose, and pronounced, "I, Nick Swift, do stall thee to the brotherhood of wet dogs."

Vivian rubbed her wet nose, and he dissolved into a drunken giggle. She gave up and laughed with him.

"Come, I have something for you." Nick grabbed her hand and tugged her toward the door. She followed him through the salon and into his own room, hung with indigo velvet, burgundy brocade, and cloth of silver. He went to the chest by the bed, took out a folded cloth, and unwrapped it. "Look what was brought in tonight."

Nick extended his arms, displaying a marvelous sword belt, gilded leather set with rubies and clasped with a fierce panther with diamond eyes. Viv gasped with delight. She unbuckled her old belt, transferred the weapons to the new, and fastened it on. The belt sat easily about her hips, beautifully crafted for use as well as show. "Magnificent!"

She drew her sword and executed a series of parries and thrusts to dispatch an imaginary opponent, then slid the blade into back into its sheath.

"Smelly Jakes?" Nick toed the invisible corpse, and sniffed. "Definitely not."

"Not Chettle either."

"About the guns—"

"Oh, leave them where they are for now," she said, as casually as she could. When Nick was inebriated, she preferred him silly to morose or belligerent. She wanted no fight about the snaphances tonight, or anything else for that matter. Nothing useful would be achieved anyway. She put aside the last of her own urgency. "Business will wait till morning."

Viv did not want to talk about Rosy, either, but it would make Nick happy. The Comet was a safe enough topic. She sat cross-legged on the bed, as they'd done since childhood, and patted the mattress beside her. "Tell me about Piper's play."

Nick swept an arm across his face, as if hiding behind the folds of a cape. He stalked across the rushes to the edge of the bed, and intoned, "Harken—I bring you a dark tale of betrayal and revenge."

"Called?" She should remember. Rosy had gone on and on about his debut as the hero.

Nick flopped onto the bed beside her, feet dangling off the edge. "Hamlet—by Thomas Kyd."

9

*C*urbing his frustration, Rafe waited in the courtyard for Vivian. As the sun approached its zenith, she finally appeared. One hand wrapping her sword hilt, one fisted on her hip, she studied him for a moment, a faint challenging smile curving her lips. He smiled in answer, prepared for the mannish garb she wore again today. Gold-brocaded scarlet, her doublet and trunk hose blazed in the sunlight, and a jeweled sword belt wrapped her hips, gems winking. High boots of fine black leather shaped to her calves and thighs. Satisfied with his response, Viv gestured for him to follow, then strutted through the gatehouse and down the road.

Bodyguard to the Queen of the Clink, Rafe assumed the arrogant mien that befitted his position and kept pace beside her. He averted his gaze from the supple curves of her legs and watched for trouble around them. Trouble within was another matter. Alternately perturbed and intrigued, he was always acutely aware of Vivian. Her brazen garment shone bright as the sun, the rays of her energy brighter still. They penetrated him with a quivering heat, sparking random facets of anger and laughter, guilt and desire. He had never known anyone whose presence was so palpable. Every mocking glance, every movement, every word pulsed and scintillated within him.

Exasperated with his own response, Rafe forced his attention back to their current expedition. "Where are we going?"

"Here and there," Viv said. "First we'll gather golden eggs from some Winchester geese."

A brothel then. Whores had gained the ekename Winchester geese when that bishop controlled the property of the most lucrative business this side of the Thames. Rafe nodded casually, suppressing the fierce jolt of disappointment. He had hoped Viv would lead them to the docks, where he might learn something about her smuggling operations and the death of the customs official, Chettle. Well, he would see what other information might be had today.

They strolled through the leafy suburbs. The sky stretched overhead like a vast celestial field, blue furrows heaped to either side with hazy mounds of soft white cloud. A rippling breeze carried the lush scents of late summer flowers and ripening fruit. The neighborhood was more lavish than any in Exeter, but the sweet scent of peaches stirred memories of his grandparents' orchard and a wave of homesickness swept over him. Nostalgia ebbed, and underneath lay the raw worry for his grandfather and cousin. Had they reached London yet? Did their prison cell show a glimpse of the fine blue sky?

Vivian Swift led him to a half-timbered house near the alley where he'd attacked Garnet. No cheap stew, the brothel had a fine walled garden without and comfortable furnishings in view through the windows. The doorman had enough muscle to handle a troublesome client, but he had a pleasant smile for Viv as he gestured them through. Rafe nodded to him, settling back into his role.

Inside, no customers were apparent yet today, though several whores were lounging about the parlor. They were a pretty flock, dressed in glossy satins. Framed by starched lace collars, their bared breasts were powdered white, the nipples rouged like ripe berries. They all greeted Viv, and there were a number of glances cast his way. Some looks the whores gave him were hostile, displaying a dislike for his sex they wouldn't dare reveal to a customer. Some looks were cool and assessing, as they wondered what weight to give the new piece in the game. Others regarded him with lewd curiosity. Rafe judged they had little interest in the strategy of the board—they simply wanted to play with the pawn. He assumed a cool façade himself, learning their faces and names, keeping his gaze above their shoulders.

The bawd appeared, a dainty little old woman, brightly painted and beribboned, who Viv introduced as Saucy Nan. The bawd quickly shooed her flock upstairs, and had a servant bring a dinner when Viv admitted hunger. Hunger pangs attacked when he caught scent of the food, and Rafe gladly accepted the invitation to join them at the table. They ate chicken pie, cheese, and pears washed down with rich ale as the bawd portioned out the week's earnings.

As she stacked the piles of gold and silver, Saucy Nan regaled them with tales of the week's business. Rafe saw Viv watch the accounting with a hawk's eye, but still laugh lustily at the old woman's outrageous tales. With her wrinkled poppet's face and wig of red curls, the bawd had a way about her, describing her patrons' vices like the scrapes of naughty toddlers. She tattled on the lawyer with an obscene taste for gold, who must suck coins as he swived the wenches, and the two barons who liked to be saddled and raced by the whores, with deftly placed crops to urge them to the finish. Lord knew he'd heard crude talk from men, but Rafe laughed then blushed at the plenitude of lewd detail. Saucy Nan reached over and pinched his cheek, and gave Viv a wink. "Oh, a juicy prize, indeed, a man who can still blush!"

Viv didn't answer, but the look she gave Rafe was so hot he flushed more brightly, arousal overriding his annoyance. He leaned back against the wall, crossing his arms over his chest and staring at her defiantly. She held his gaze, her eyes alight, lips smiling, tongue tip playing lightly along the edge of her teeth. His loins throbbed so fiercely, he wondered if she would drag him upstairs before they ignited the bawd's parlor. Then Viv gave a throaty laugh and turned her attention back to Saucy Nan and the money. Rafe mentally assembled matchlocks till his need subsided.

The bawd finished counting and filled the purse Viv handed her. She gave Rafe another speculative glance before asking, "So Mistress Swift, will this one be taking Garrin's place—picking up the money?"

Viv ignored the innuendo and shook her head to the question. "It will be someone you know well, Red Harry or Dick Sunder. Maybe Prancer Potter."

"Ah, that Prancer is a charmer. And Harry has always been a good-natured fellow."

"So they are. You will see one or the other." Viv had not asked the old bawd's opinion directly, but Rafe realized that Saucy Nan had just lopped Dick Sunder from the list. This was a prime route, with a little dalliance at the last stop if the collector chose.

Viv stood and gave a nod toward the hall. "We'll be off now, Nan. The short cut—by your leave."

"You have it, lady. There's no handsome rogue between my sheets this morning." Saucy Nan gave her a wink. "I'll lock up after you."

Though Viv had made it clear that it was too soon to be trusting Rafe on his own with collecting, she tossed him the fat purse to guard. Rafe tied it to his belt as Viv left the parlor. He followed her, expecting they would head out the door. Instead she led him the other way, down the corridor and into a bedroom which was small but lavish, with gaudy tapestries thickly embroidered with roses, and more white plaster roses blooming on the ceiling. Viv nodded to Rafe and he stepped inside. She pushed aside a close stool padded with pink satin and pulled up a trapdoor, revealing steps leading down into a tunnel.

"Go down," she ordered curtly. "There's a torch at the bottom, matches and tinderbox beside."

Rafe descended into the gloom. When he'd found and lit the torch, Viv came down the wooden steps. Saucy Nan appeared above them to close up the entrance. Viv turned to Rafe, her mobile face smooth and expressionless as a mask. Her hand felt unexpectedly cold as she took the torch from his hand and forged on into the narrow tunnel. Packed earth walls were shored with wood and planks laid on the ground against seepage. She walked quickly, the torch casting manic shadows on the wall. Rafe silently counted steps as they walked. A hundred paces from the brothel, the tunnel ended at a wall. A small sliding panel showed the wine cellar of a tavern, and Vivian tripped the lock that let them out of the tunnel into the empty room. Rafe saw that she drew a breath of relief as they stepped into the relative spaciousness of the cellar. She disliked the close confines of the tunnel, he thought, but forced herself to confront her weakness.

They climbed stone stairs to the kitchen, where she introduced Rafe to the keeper of the Buzzing Hornet, a jolly fellow named Culpepper, and collected another purse. They made their way out the back door and into the street.

"We do a lot of business at the Buzzing Hornet," she said when they left. "More than at the Lightning Bolt, where our own gather."

Rafe nodded, for Izzy had told him the same. "You didn't ask the Hornet's keeper what new collector he preferred."

"Saucy Nan has earned a few privileges over the years," Viv said. "Besides, I know what those men are like in their cups, but not between the sheets—and I know Culpepper favors Red Harry. A good bawd like Nan can tell you a lot about men, the worst and the best of them."

Continuing the tour, Viv showed him a half dozen other hideyholes and tunnels. Some were guarded by bawds, innkeepers, or gamblers, others were simple escape routes. "Toward the river all our escape hatches are above ground— doors between walls, connecting attics," Viv said.

"Do all the thieves know these places?" Rafe asked.

"Most such tunnels and closets are common knowledge." She smiled a little, pressed a finger to her lips in a mock hush. "We keep a few secrets, of course."

He didn't doubt it. One or two secret tunnels known only to the Swifts' followers. One or two more known only to the Swifts themselves.

"I keep my people safe from the beaks. Few of us are caught—unless it's with a clumsy hand down a pocket," she said. "Izzy will show you other places next week. Bit by bit you'll learn them all. The Clink first, then all of Southwark, then the common ground in London."

Next, she led him to an old house in a shabby section near the docks, tapping a rapid signal at the door. A small dark man let them in, goggle-eyed and thin-lipped. He nodded respectfully to Viv, doffing his cap with the metal hook that served for one hand. "Good day to you, Mistress Swift," the doorkeeper said, giving Rafe quick scrutiny.

"Good day, Frog. How's the Tadpole?" Viv asked.

"Lad's a streak, quick as I ever was." Frog's thin lips stretched in a wide smile. He twirled his cap on the hook. "Quicker. He's helping out with the other little wrigglers."

"We'll have a look," Viv said.

"Last on the left," Frog told her, resetting his cap.

Viv ambled down the hallway and Rafe followed, listening to muffled noise and laughter behind closed doors. They opened the door that Frog had indicated and slipped inside, Viv nodding to him to stand against the wall and watch. Within, four clothed dummies hung suspended from the ceiling, silly expressions painted on their stuffed heads and their garments stitched about with little brass bells. Motley batches of children were clustered about each dummy. Many young faces glanced at them curiously, until Izzy Cockayne, schoolmaster, tapped his cane against the wall.

"I'll teach you to look the other way—after you've learned the art of a quick nip," he said.

Dutifully, they turned back to their suspended victims. Taking turns, each child tried to cut the purse tied to belt or girdle without setting the bells jangling. Izzy moved among them, cajoling, coaxing, and scolding. He used the cane to startle them with a sudden crack of noise, but Rafe never saw him strike a child. He proved a gentler schoolmaster than any Rafe had ever had.

Rafe recognized one boy as the messenger who'd brought warning of Rivett's visit to the Lightning Bolt. With his floppy dark hair, wide eyes, and narrow lips, he was presumably Frog's Tadpole. His adroit fingers cut purse strings without a sound and tucked the prize smoothly under his jacket. He gave a cocky little bow and the other children cooed envy and appreciation. Vivian applauded and tossed him a shilling from her own purse. Then she handed out silver pennies all around, laughing at the hubbub. Izzy rolled his eyes and set about arranging the dummies so that the coins were in their pockets rather than their purses.

Leading Rafe into the hallway, Viv showed him other classrooms, introduced him to Izzy's assistants. In one room, the children's size was put to use. A false house front was set up, and they squirmed through a narrow open window into a dark room, then crept round to unlock the door and let in a man to finish the burglary. In another section, they crawled through a dark maze filled with teetering objects, bringing out different treasures. "Izzy dubbed this craft wriggling." Viv smiled. "After that, we took to calling the children wrigglers."

From there she gave him a brief tour of the dormitory laid out with pallets, the kitchen, the cellar with its tunnel. "Only for emergencies. The children don't know it's here, or they'd be sneaking down to try it out."

He nodded, not trusting himself to press for information. His mind was buzzing with questions, but anger was simmering close beneath the curiosity and amusement the place evoked. They treated the children well, but he could not let himself be charmed by their playful wickedness. It was sinful to lure innocents to such a life—and such a death. His tension eased when she led him out to the backyard, and from there and through a gate to another house. The guards at the door of this school were more formidable, the rooms filled with as motley a crew of knaves as he'd ever seen in one place, from raggedy beggars to a gentleman or two in bedraggled lace. The children had touched him, but these men were here by choice. Some were only pathetic, others obviously dangerous. He wandered about with Viv, watching as they practiced card tricks or tested their trick dice.

"None of these are wild rogues born," Viv said. "Like you, they've all come late to the law."

Calling such sinful crafts *laws* amazed Rafe, but he just gave a knowing nod. At least when his training was done, no one would ever be able to cheat him at cards or pass off weighted bones or bristle dice. "Useful skills," he said dryly.

"There's none better than Izzy to teach you lock charming. But the wise men here are the best with cheating law and crossbiting cozenage." Viv smiled at him. "Marking cards is craft, but much of coney-catching is quick thinking. You've already proved you've a gift for conniving. There's no one here who'd have dared what you did."

He mixed a modest shrug with an insolent smile. "Maybe they'll live longer."

"And die poorer?" she asked.

"Short or long, it's a poor life I want to avoid."

She laughed at that. "Stay with me and you'll live rich enough."

"I'm feeling rich already," he said softly, letting her know he knew the worth of other wealth than money. She looked at him speculatively, wary yet pleased by their rapport.

As they left the house, Rafe saw a little girl running toward the children's school. Seeing Vivian she veered off, rushing toward them instead, then tripped and sprawled in the street by the gate. She began to sob wildly. Rafe leapt down the last steps, ran to the street where she lay, and gathered her in his arms. She looked about eight, with hair like amber honey, and blue eyes, huge and round in her tear-streaked face. As soon as he scooped her up, she stiffened, and when he kissed her cheek and told her not to cry, she wept hysterically, pushing him away and squirming to escape. Dismayed, he tried to hold her gently but firmly so she would not fall.

"Don't fear," he said. "I'll not hurt you."

"Give her to me." Vivian's voice was almost casual, but her eyes brooked no argument. She reached out her arms and Rafe handed the little girl over. The child gripped Viv tightly, arms about her neck and legs wrapped about her waist.

"Hush, Mary. I've got you now." Viv's voice was gentle, and gently scolding as the frightened child went on crying. Viv bounced the girl for a minute, then began again in the same scolding, cajoling tone. "Mary, Mary Blue, you must tell me what happened."

"The beaks nabbed Dickon," she cried, and burst into a fresh flood of tears.

"Have they?" Viv asked. "Well then, we must save him, mustn't we?"

"But they've nabbed 'im," Mary sobbed. "They'll lock 'im up. They'll hang 'im like Mama."

Rafe's heart gave a twist and he stepped closer, but Viv shot him a warning glance and he stopped where he was.

Viv set the little girl down on the step and took her hands. "Be brave and you can save him." More tears, but Viv waited them out. "Deep breath," she said, and the little girl sucked in air and released it in a whoosh. "You were out on the bridge?"

"Foistin', we were. We saw a fat old cove what looked slow."

"So Dickon got caught with his hand down a pocket?"

Mary nodded. "The fat cove grabbed 'im. 'E shook 'im, 'n slapped 'im about."

The memory frightened her, and she began to cry again. Viv gave her a minute to stop herself, and this time she did. "That's my brave Mary," Viv said, brushing her knuckles softly over the tears. "Now tell me, Mary, after Dickon was nabbed, which way did the sergeants go? This way or across the bridge?"

"This way."

"And did you hide so they wouldn't catch you, Mary Blue?"

"No, they didn't see me. I ran here, Mistress Viv."

"Brave, and clever too, Mary," Viv praised. "Let's take you to Izzy."

They went back in the door, and Frog went for Izzy. When the thief appeared, Viv handed Mary over to him, and she locked herself around him as she had around Viv. Izzy stroked Mary and cooed at her while Viv told them what had happened, with honors due to the little girl's quick action. Then Izzy carried Mary off to be put to bed with a posset.

As soon as they were gone, Viv gave her orders crisply. "Frog, you go find Prancer Potter, he'll be doing the rounds on the west end. He and his guards are to detour to the Southwark Counter, and ply Sergeant Tripp with silver."

Frog nodded. "If we're lucky we can stage a little escape right off. But I'll wager the coney's close by, wanting his revenge."

"Dickon's likely to get thrown into the hole till they know he's mine," Viv said. "The money will get him good food and a clean bed to sleep on tonight. It's likely it will be tomorrow before we can arrange an escape."

"It'll be costlier still if they move him over to Newgate," Frog said, and hurried off.

Bribe arranged, Viv beckoned to Rafe and set out toward the bridge.

"Are these are the children of the people who work for you?" The questions Rafe had pushed aside came up to the surface. He thought of the doorkeeper's stump and wondered that the man would set his son on the same path. And little Mary Blue said her mother had been hanged.

"Many of them. Some are foundlings. Izzy is always finding homeless strays," Viv answered. "If they're too little, he takes them to the orphanage at Christ's Church, though it breaks his heart."

At least the orphanage would find them honest work, Rafe thought. Though he and his family gave generous charity to such homes, the children he had seen there often looked half-starved and wretched. But that path, however hard, would not lead them to the hangman's noose.

"If they come to us this young, and we treat them well at all, there is a chance for loyalty we can get no other way." Viv smiled. "And we create the most skillful thieves in England."

Rafe thought of her shower of silver pennies, like royalty tossing largesse. Queen of the Clink, Viv commanded both obedience and adoration from her subjects. He asked, "And what if they've no skill for it? Or no stomach?"

"Izzy finds work for them in the taverns, the stables, as servants, with the merchants, whatever it looks they can do best."

"After they've trained as thieves? What merchant will have them?" Surely Mary would be better with such work.

"Izzy knows which ones can be trusted, children and merchants both," she said. "If nothing else, they can beg."

"Or whore?" he asked coldly, remembering her brothels with apprehension. Judgments coiled uneasily in his head. A thief was worse than a whore, yet training a child to whore was far more evil.

"Not children," she said sharply. "Nowhere that I control."

At least there were some sins that Vivian shunned. She seemed to know all the wicked arts, but Rafe had heard no talk of her whoring. But if she had, he could imagine her boasting of her prowess. "Did you ever . . . ?"

She whirled on him, her eyes glinting black sparks. For a second Rafe thought she'd dismiss him on the spot. He swallowed hard and met the hard bright anger in her gaze.

"No, Fletcher. I've never whored," she said finally. "Though I worked for some of the bawds for a time, like Saucy Nan, keeping accounts when Old Warts ruled the Clink."

Rafe lowered his head and hoped he looked suitably abashed. "I meant no insult," he said softly. "I want to know everything about you."

She gave a little snort of exasperation, but the cold light in her eyes warmed. "I forget you're newly come from the honest world."

"Where my honest patron ran off with my salary and my savings." He played with the irony, smiling a little.

"Exactly. And where he tupped any serving wench he wanted, then tossed her out in the street if she grew a belly." Coldness gleamed again in her eyes. "Did he tup any as young as Mary?"

"No!" he said, as outraged as if she had accused him. Perhaps she was accusing all men. Perhaps paying him back an insult.

"Well, little Mary had a trundle in the attic of a fine house, and was learning the fine arts of dusting and polishing, with some nightly chores besides for a fine gentleman who liked his women to stand no higher than his manhood could stretch."

Rafe shuddered, blinking back a hot prickle of tears. Such things were common enough, but they sickened him always. In an instant the cold anger vanished from her eyes, their darkness warm and glowing. She reached out, stroking his cheek lightly. "You have a tender heart."

"Thieving is a better fate than such lewd polishing," he said.

"Mary finds it so."

"That's why she screamed so when I held her," he said quietly.

"She was upset, but yes, Izzy's still the only man she lets touch her without flinching. He makes a good mother, does Izzy. Much clucking and soft feathers."

"What of the fine gentleman? Where does he live?" Rafe thought the fine gentleman's manhood would make finer dog meat. There was no tenderness in his heart when he thought of such a man. The first hot flash of anger turned cold and calculating.

"Live? Why sir, I promise you he does not." Her words were mocking, but her eyes were merciless. "He has taken up residence in the stews of hell."

It shocked him, yet he felt a hypocrite, for the same thought had been in his heart.

The sun was setting as Viv led him from the school, casting light like a pirate's treasure of glittering golden crowns and silver farthings on the water of the Thames. She pointed out the boundaries of their territory in London, a small but invaluable piece of docking she had inherited from one of Jacob Rivett's rivals. It was the area where Gabriel had gone to meet Scratch. "Shall I get us a wherry?" Rafe asked, hoping she'd take him across.

Viv shook her head and kept walking. "Southwark first, then London."

He followed along beside her, forcing lightness to counter his own frustration. "I'm surprised you don't want it all."

"Of course I want it all." She flashed her eyes in exaggerated exasperation. "But I'm not so greed-addled I'll drop my prize to snap at what's still beyond my reach. For almost a decade, the Southwark alliance has held firm against Jake Rivett. That's our first priority. We've got one juicy piece of London, but we're not strong enough to take the whole pie yet. We wouldn't gain anything and we'd likely lose our teeth."

Nearing London Bridge, Rafe saw ravens take flight from the heads rotting atop the spikes of the Tower Gate. He fought through a sickly wash of fear. There must be proof of his family's innocence. One way or another he would find it.

Seeing the direction of his gaze, Viv set her jaw and squared her shoulders pugnaciously. "You've seen that I keep my people safe. There's few of us that have been caught. Fewer still that died on the gallows. And there's none that's had his head or quarters on the ramparts."

The fear was for his family, not himself. Rafe pushed it deep, letting the alloy of anger and desire rise to the surface—a dangerous but potent alchemy. He lowered his voice to intimacy. "I know what I've chosen. And it wasn't safety."

Her eyes kindled, but her smile was tinged with irony. "Stay with me then, and I'll keep you well steeped in danger."

"How can I leave, when you promise such a surfeit of riches and danger?"

"I don't want you to leave." She tilted her chin defiantly, but the small catch in her voice made her words more admission than banter. It was a tiny crack, yet through it he glimpsed loneliness and vulnerability.

Rafe told himself it was only a flare of victory he felt, but the warmth that suffused him blossomed not only in his groin but in his heart. However watchful his mind, sometimes he could not separate his emotions from those of the brazen fencing master. But the fencing master did not have family accused of treason—Rafe Fletcher did. Whatever he feigned or truly felt must serve his purpose. "Not till I have your leave to leave you, lady," he said, returning her banter.

Flares were being lit as they walked through Southwark. With the image of the ravens swooping across his mind, Rafe pressed his advantage. He sauntered beside Vivian, smiling warmly but peppering her with questions, exploiting what she'd revealed so far. How many brothels did they own? How many gambling dens? How lucrative were their legitimate businesses? Did they make more from robbery or burglary? Who was the richest, most famous coney they'd netted? Who brokered their stolen goods? How many customs officials worked for them? Viv expected his boldness, but she ignored more questions than she answered. Most frustrating, Rafe could learn nothing from her about their smuggling operations. It was their most profitable and dangerous venture, and he was still on the periphery of the organization. It seemed Vivian had already decided how much he was to know. The more rebuffs she gave him, the more suspicious his prying.

When he persisted in a query she had adroitly dodged, the warm laughter in her eyes flashed to hot anger. Her mood shifts were cat-quick as her movements, and he had to stay attuned to each one. But he seemed to know their rhythm instinctively, as if they danced. Nonetheless, her temper was dangerously volatile, and he might not escape an explosion if he probed about business. Rafe wanted her to believe he belonged in her world, that he was an asset, not a threat. Showing too much curiosity, too much ambition would be dangerous—showing too little, unbelievable.

Quelling his frustration, he shifted to talk of the people, wooing tales from which he could perhaps glean some precious bit. What was Saucy Nan's history? When did Frog lose his hand? How did she meet Izzy? Warmth quickly returned to Viv's eyes, and Rafe enjoyed the snap and roll of her voice as she finished off the tale of Saucy Nan and the gilded codpiece. Rafe wondered if he'd circled round enough to raise another question about Jacob Rivett.

Before he could frame one, Viv took his arm and pulled him into the closest tavern, the Dancing Fox. Only a week ago, he'd trailed Garrin Garnet from this spot. Inside, Viv settled at a table and called out for ale. Obviously flustered, the red-nosed tavern keeper hurried over with two tankards of his finest. Viv took a long draught. Then she leaned forward, her eyes gleaming with curiosity, warmth, and calculation. It was her turn to question him. Silently, he prayed she would not ask some question to which he could not quickly find or invent an answer.

"So, Rafe Fletcher, you say the Devil owns you?" Viv asked.

Rafe remembered he'd said that when Nick and Viv first questioned him. He gave a shrug and leaned back against the wall. "So my grandfather said—often enough there seemed no point in arguing."

"You decided to prove him right?" she asked.

"Obviously."

She leaned her chin on her hand, and tilted her brows interrogatively.

He began a story that closely resembled his own. "My mother ran off with a fencing master, against her parents' wishes. A love match. When they died of the plague, my grandfather took me home with him. After a vagabond life, a Puritan household was little better than a prison."

"A Puritan? Did he preach?"

"Yes." Hoping to submerge his memories of the wicked theatre life in a sea of piety, his grandfather had deluged him with sermons, inundated him with commandments. "Incessantly."

"And whipped you when you disobeyed?" Her eyes flicked briefly the shoulder that bore the scar of the worst beating.

Rafe remembered the skimming touch of her fingers on his naked skin, then thrust the thought away. He gave her a bitter smile. "Sometimes I thought every breath I drew was disobedient. His preaching was harder to bear than his whip hand. I ran away—often. Each time, he caught me and beat me harder. But pain only made me fight harder, too."

"Anger is better than grief."

"Yes." Anger hurt less. Rafe leaned back, guilt twisting as strangely as he twisted his own past. It was only the first year that had been so wretched. One night he found his grandfather weeping, and understood he also mourned, a pain that could be shared with his own. Once he made an effort to please, his grandfather had been as generous with love and approval as he'd been with punishment. If he had not, Rafe would not have endured it. The fencing master hadn't. Here the story crossed the far edge of the truth. "One day I ran fast enough to escape—or perhaps he simply decided I was too old to chase."

"And did you run straight to the Devil?"

The rest was easy enough to invent. "I tarried at a whorehouse or two. I'm sure the Devil was watching from the corner. Then I found an old friend of my father's and apprenticed myself to him. Marisco taught me what he knew of the sword, till I was good enough to work on my own."

"Marisco?"

It was one of the few lies she could trace. The great swordsman had bought all his swords from Easton Arms, and had indeed given Rafe lessons. Burne had Marisco's promise to tell the tale as they wished.

"Are you so very good?"

"You've seen me in practice. You know my worth."

"I know your worth is considerable—in practice. But it is not fully tested in action."

"Then we must take action." He smiled.

Viv leaned forward, mock serious as she queried. "Surely you must admit to some flaw?"

"Many—but not in technique, I hope."

"Or in spirit."

"None, save excess."

"Ohhhh . . . you are the best, then?" she provoked.

Rafe Fletcher, fencing master, was arrogant, but not a fool. "No. You will not fault my courage. I have strength, endurance, and excellent speed for my size—but others are quicker, more deft."

She smiled at him. "A very few others, I trust, Master Fletcher."

"Scarcely a handful, Mistress Swift. You can wager on my winning." He leaned forward, letting the air of intimacy enfold them, more important than the words. "If you want to know my flaw, I am not a good teacher. I earned my skill and have little patience with those who expect to acquire expertise like a new ruff."

"And no patience at all for those who will not pay for the ruff."

"None." He smiled again, then gave a nod toward the door. "Here's Red Harry."

Keeping track of the customers, Rafe recognized the man's fiery beard as soon as he entered the tavern. Red Harry was a tough, burly man, capable but a bit lazy. He must be on his own collection route, which meant more guards waited outside while he collected from the tavern keeper. Viv let him handle business, then signaled him to come over. She had Rafe pass over the money they'd collected so far. Harry took it, then hovered anxiously.

"What?" Viv asked.

"I'm just back from the Blackjack," Harry answered. "Maggot Crutcher sang me songs of poverty. I had four men, not enough to force the issue."

Viv frowned. "That would depend on how forceful they were."

Harry cleared his throat. "Maggot had a tavern full."

"Counting the gamblers and the whores?" Viv said, disgusted. "Maggot has no intention of fighting us. Especially not when he can keep what he wants with whining."

The man looked sheepish. "I'll go back, but I'd like a show of arms, if only to make an impression."

"Finish your collections and head back to the barracks. I already know how to make an impression on Maggot."

"Mistress Swift." Harry touched his cap and left the tavern.

Finishing off her ale, Viv gave Rafe a measuring glance. "You are singularly impressive."

"Together we are doubly so."

She stood. "So—are you ready to move off the practice field?"

The glitter in her eyes meant danger, but Rafe didn't care. Her heightened energy reached out to stir him. He rose from the bench. "I'm ready for anything."

With a quick movement, Viv drew her dagger, tossed it high, and caught the hilt snug in her hand. "I'm very good with this," she said. "In case you think my weapons are naught but gauds."

"I believe you."

"Good." Sheathing the dagger, Viv gave him a roguish smile. "Then follow me."

10

*T*he Fringes were the worst of Southwark, a grimy warren southeast of the bridge, dangerous by day, and even more so by night. With Rafe keeping guard at her side, Vivian led the way through the first clump of dockside taverns, then into the dark, mucky streets of the warehouse district.

"Just who is this Maggot Crutcher?" Rafe asked

"A worm who lives in the dark," she answered. "Crutcher is one alliance Nick and I formed to keep Jake Rivett out of Southwark. Maggot held this patch even when Old Warts was alive. He is smart enough to rule the Fringes, but he can't keep his wriggling fingers out of richer pies. Sometimes he gets a whiff of trouble and takes to playing poor, thinking we'll be too distracted to collect from him. We never are, but the fart-brained fool never learns."

"What trouble?" he asked.

She gave him a quick glance. "Nothing of import. There's always trouble at the docks, if you want to find it."

Rafe looked disgruntled, but knew enough not to press her. Viv liked his persistence, but only to a point. He'd learn only what she wanted, and only when she wanted him to. Besides, the situation at the docks was as nebulous as it was disturbing, and talking to Rafe about it would accomplish nothing. Nicholas was right that a scheming wharf rat like Scratch Jones might have had his throat slit for amusement. But Jones had had information for sale about Edward Chettle, and Chettle had disappeared as well. Viv doubted the disappearance was coincidence.

A lame beggar gave them a startled look, then hurried down an alleyway, his limp healed. "One of Maggot's sentinels," Viv said.

"Then he'll be expecting us."

"Of course."

The Blackjack was tucked into a small, boisterous section between the warehouses and the river. Lit by greasy tallow light, the alehouses and stews were swarming with customers. The reek of urine from the alleys added its sharp odor to the decomposing garbage and the stench of the midden. The miasma of desperation and predation was as noisome as the piles of waste. Maggot's tavern offered cheap beer and cheap whores, but gambling was its main attraction. As Viv led Rafe to the door, she flashed him a warning glance. He answered with a nod and dropped back a step, guarding her back.

"Good. You watch the others. I want my attention on Maggot." She flung her cape over one shoulder, set her hand on her sword hilt and sauntered inside.

Filthy rushes covered the floor, and the air was rank with smoke, sweat, and sour beer. Men clustered about the card tables and dice games. Those bored with gambling tugged the women to the rooms upstairs, or made do with a dark corner. Maggot Crutcher sat at the far end of the room, his ugsome bulk enthroned on the one massive chair behind a long table. Three whores draped about him, fresher and prettier than could be had elsewhere in the Fringes.

Crutcher caught sight of her as soon as she entered. Viv gave him a warning smile, striding across the room toward the table, aware of Rafe keeping pace behind her. Maggot looked far too comfortable, so Viv didn't stop when she reached the table. She stepped up, planting one boot on the seat of the bench and the other beside his plate. Resting one hand on her knee, she stared down at Maggot and savored her vantage point.

Crutcher's pasty skin had earned his nickname. He looked like an great, unleavened lump of dough, though there was still power in him, a bulk of muscle beneath the flab. Wisps of yellowish hair hung about a puffy face. His thick tongue lapped nervously at the slack mouth, but the gray eyes that watched Viv from within the fleshy pouches were shrewd. Leaning away, Crutcher looked over her shoulder to Rafe and back to her again. Only two of them, but it said what she wanted. She wasn't afraid of him.

"Vivian," Maggot said, with false surprise. He had a deep, oozing voice. The whores pressed closer to him, eyeing her with a mix of envy and contempt. He gave them each a squeeze on the buttocks and chuckled, then nodded behind her. "And someone new?"

"Rafe Fletcher," Viv said tersely. "My bodyguard."

"Rafe." Maggot pursed his lips and nodded judiciously, checking Rafe's muscle and guessing at his skill with the sword. "I'm Maggot Crutcher."

Echoing her attitude, Rafe looked Crutcher over contemptuously. "Maggot," he said. "That's unique."

Affronted, Maggot frowned at Rafe, then returned his gaze to her. Viv wasted no time. "You're late again, Maggot."

"Again?" Maggot strummed his lower lip with a bent knuckle, turning up the wet pink underside. Behind him, the whores frowned at her and pouted sympathetic irritation. "It can't be that often, Vivian."

"It can. It is. We're tired of it."

"Ah yes, we. Just where is your brother these days? He seems weary of business."

Viv felt a surge of anger at Nick for so obviously neglecting business, and at Maggot for thinking he could toy with her. She had slowly squeezed respect out of men like Maggot by being cleverer and more ruthless than any of them. She would hold onto it, even without Nick's help, but she knew it would be more difficult, the tests more frequent, if his presence wasn't felt throughout Southwark. Crutcher needed a lesson.

"The money, Maggot," she said, icing her voice. "Plus twenty percent to urge you to swiftness in the future."

Maggot flinched, then he began his negotiations in earnest. "I can't piss silver, Vivian. The last two weeks have been slow as slugs. The coneys would rather speculate on the length of Babington's guts than toss bones."

"I'm sure you're turning the speculations into odds, Maggot." Viv nodded to the players in the tavern. "Business looks the same as usual."

"I've building costs to pay on the tavern closer to the docks. But when it's done, there'll be more profit all round, for you and Nick as well as me."

"I'll anticipate an abundance of riches. For now I just want what you owe—plus twenty percent." Being a more generous overlord than Rivett was to her advantage, as long as men like Crutcher didn't see it as weakness or fear. Maggot was going to pay for his weasely evasion.

"Just give me another week, Vivian, and we'll take up the payments from there. If I have to pay you back so much, I'll be forced to borrow from Jake Rivett."

Viv leaned forward, studying Maggot narrowly. "What will you do when Jake wants his silver and you don't have it?"

Maggot shrugged, like dough rising. Like buns to his bloated loaf, the whores imitated his gesture.

Viv knew Jake had been sniffing around Maggot less than a month ago, and that nothing had come of it. But she did not tell Maggot she knew. "A week late and you'd be paying him in pieces—pieces of your turf or pieces of flesh."

Maggot shrugged again. "Jacob is a reasonable man."

"Reasonable." One by one, Viv tasted the syllables. "No, I don't think so, Maggot. He just kills before he loses his temper, instead of after. Defy me again and you'll find me just as reasonable as Rivett."

Maggot pursed his lips and wrapped his pudgy fingers tightly together, as if to hold onto the gold. "Ummph," he said, a deep hollow grumble from his gut.

Viv set her hand on her sword hilt and leaned forward, her gaze locked on Maggot's. "I know you won't let Smelly Jakes into the Fringes, Maggot, and for good reason. You'd never get him out again, not without our help. And I'd much rather rip a few pieces out of you myself, than to fight off Rivett after he sets his fangs in Southwark."

Crutcher opened his lips for yet another argument.

"I want our money. I want it now." Viv rapped her hand on the table, a staccato beat. "Now, Maggot—or I'll lose my temper."

Maggot regarded her morosely. She knew he was not ready to defy her. Crutcher was greedy, but he was lazy, too. And he was not stupid. If Maggot killed her, Nick would find him if he had to burn down the Fringes. Maggot shrugged off the whores clinging to him and gestured to one of his guards. The man came over and Maggot whispered in his ear. Viv flashed Rafe a glance. There was a quick spark as his eyes met hers, then he returned to his watch, tracking the smallest movement of Crutcher's men. The guard plodded over to the barman and repeated the messages. The barman produced a purse from under the counter, and counted out a smaller one. The guard returned and Crutcher nodded for him to hand the money to Viv.

"It's all there," he said sullenly.

"I'm sure it is, Maggot." She gave him a smile. "At this point, anything less would be a grave offense."

Viv stood and tied both purses beneath her cape. She turned her back on Maggot and walked out of the Blackjack, acutely aware of Rafe moving smoothly in her wake. Outside, they began to retrace their steps, moving from the bright flare-lit street of shops, taverns, and brothels into the murky shadows of the warehouse district. Rafe's eyes flashed as he glanced about, and the moonlight etched the clean strength of his profile, the firm sensuous curves of his lips, with silver. She appreciated both his beauty and his alertness, feeling totally attuned to the taut readiness of his body as they traveled swiftly through the deserted streets. Viv expected no trouble, but this was still Crutcher's territory.

"It doesn't seem like Crutcher had much to gain," Rafe said, keeping his voice low.

She gave a snort of disgust. "Maggot thought all he had to do is puff and wheeze and blow Jake's name like smoke to sting my eyes. Then he'd get our money and our protection, too."

"I think you convinced him otherwise."

There was a sound behind them, distant but recognizable, the careless splat of a boot in a puddle. Falling silent, they both began to turn toward the noise. Catching his movement, Viv let Rafe check behind them, keeping her own eyes on the mouth of the alley ahead. Already wary, she felt a fiercer energy flooding her nerves, like a stream of fire edged with ice. Her vision sharpened, shapes within shadows emerging with new clarity.

Rafe touched her arm lightly, his voice low as he said, "We're being followed."

"Yes. I can't believe Maggot is this stupid," Viv hissed, gripping the hilt of her sword. "He likes profit, not trouble."

"Maybe they're on their own. Some men only want enough silver to escape London."

Moonlight gleamed at the top of the alley, revealing the silhouettes of several men. Alarm, anger, and anticipation seethed, a volatile mix in Viv's gut. "Ahead of us too. Those aren't independents. Not so many."

Rafe reached for his sword and knife, but Viv stayed his hands, scanning the buildings for a vantage point. The high, flat fronts of the warehouses offered no way to climb quickly. Diagonally across the street, an overhang jutted above the door of an abandoned two-story house. It was higher than either of them could leap, but it was their best chance.

She gave Rafe a quick nudge, then ran for the building. The attackers rushed the alley as soon as she made her move. Reaching the building, Viv braced herself against the wall, bending her knee to make a step of her leg. Rafe hesitated, but he was the one with the strength to pull her up.

"Up!" she said, urging him.

Using the ladder she created, Rafe climbed onto her knee, then onto her shoulder, and boosted himself up to the overhang. Lying flat, he reached down for her. Viv crouched, then leapt up, grasping his wrists as he gripped hers. He pulled her up beside him, out of reach of the men who appeared below. The overhang creaked precariously as they repeated the maneuver to clamber onto the dormered roof, and from there up and over the crest.

They leaned against the roof, panting lightly. So close to her own, Rafe's face looked as it might on a pillow, washed with moonlight and sweat, his lips parted, his eyes gleaming. They were attuned, danger thrilling a wild music in their blood. Impulsively Viv kissed him, feeling the lush firmness of his lips against her own, the moistness of his tongue as she dipped into his mouth. Excitement intensified, licks of wet fire, and when she drew back they were both panting harder than before.

Rafe met her gaze. "Aren't you afraid?"

"Oh yes," she said, feeling the fear like a coal of black ice that fed the unfolding blaze of her excitement. She laughed aloud. "Aren't you?"

His answering breath of laughter mingled exasperation and euphoria. "Not enough."

They heard a scrabbling noise as two of the men from the street rolled up a barrel and began their climb onto the overhang. They were outnumbered. There would be no quarter. Viv drew her dagger, waiting till one man got a hand purchase on the edge of the roof and pulled himself up. Grasping his hair, she slashed her dagger across his throat. Blood splashed over her as he gave a gargling cry. She let him fall. The body tumbled backward, knocking the other man off the edge of the roof and collapsing the overhang. A cacophony of curses, groans, and shouted directions rose up from the street.

"That lowers the odds," she said with grim pleasure.

"Let me know when they're in our favor."

Watching over the roof, they saw the attackers separate, half of each band running back toward the alley to try and cut off their escape. Rafe pointed west, the easiest pathway over the steep rooftops. Weighing their options,

Viv tapped Rafe's arm, then pointed back down the way they had come. They'd ambush the attackers left below.

Quietly, Viv eased into the shadowed angle of the dormer, Rafe following her lead down to the roofline. Beneath her and to the side, she saw four men scattered about the corpse and the groaning man on the ground, arguing their best tactics. Viv drew her sword. Rafe grasped her dagger arm and silently lowered her over the edge of the building, lessening the gap of her fall. He released her and she dropped directly behind one of the men. Startled, he turned at the soft thud of her landing. He lunged, but Viv blocked his sword arm with a downward drive of her own. Closing on him, she shoved her dagger under his ribs and into his heart.

Rafe leapt down to join her, rolling to break his fall. As he started to rise, the man who'd tumbled from the roof got to his knees and seized Rafe's cloak, jerking him back into the muck. Moonlight glinted off the blade of his dagger. Viv sprang forward and slashed the knife from his hand with her sword. Rafe kicked up, his foot meeting the man's jaw with a crack of bone. The attacker grunted with pain and collapsed. Rafe surged to his feet, sword in hand.

There were three men left. Two had circled around, moving at Viv from behind. As she turned to meet them, the third slipped between her and Rafe, cutting him off from her. Viv heard the man urge him, "Help us kill her and we'll give you a cut of the money."

"I'll cut you instead." Rafe attacked ruthlessly, meeting the man in a harsh clash of blades. Viv concentrated on the first man confronting her. He was short and stocky, his face bristling with a thick growth of black beard. He drove forward, his blade engaging hers with a jarring clang. Viv felt the blunt force of his muscle, but he was overconfident of his skill. She had far greater expertise, greater speed. Deflecting the thrust of his blade, she trapped his sword with twist of her blade and sent it flying. The man leapt back, running to retrieve his lost sword. Her other opponent moved in swiftly to fill the gap, sword glittering as he thrust, parried, then thrust again. Sharp pain flashed along her ribs as she deflected a jab to her belly. Blood seeped from the shallow wound, wet fire flowing over her side. This man was an a accomplished bladesman, a deadly threat. Her only advantage was quickness, and she danced and retreated, trying to keep him at bay. For a moment there was nothing but the metallic flash and scrape of their swords.

A piercing scream rose in the air—too high for Rafe's, Viv thought, but she did not dare look back and reassure herself. The cry was followed by the hard thump of a body falling to the ground. The next instant, Rafe moved up beside her. Relief rushed through her, and renewed excitement. With this man for her partner, fighting for her life became a savage, joyful dance.

Viv eased back, relinquishing her adversary to Rafe and whirling to pursue the man who had chased after his weapon. She was surprised Blackbeard hadn't renewed his attack after he'd retrieved his sword, but he skittered nervously, afraid to press his advantage, even with Rafe still occupied behind her. She snatched the offensive and attacked. The man sprinted for the bottom of the alley, then stopped and turned. He'd found some courage. Two of the other men had circled back and rejoined him. The moonlight showed them all clearly: the black-bearded one who'd fled, a bigger man with slabs of muscle and a smooth, bald dome—and Garrin Garnet.

Viv gave a low hiss of anger, though she should have known he'd try for revenge. Eager for blood, Garnet moved into the lead, followed by the black-bearded one and the muscular bald man. Then, as Garrin approached her, the bald man grabbed the man in front of him and gave his head a hard twist, snapping his neck. Garrin whirled and stared in disbelief as the bald man let the corpse fall.

"Garnet's the one you want," he said to Vivian. "Consider him a present—from Maggot."

"Late as usual," Viv said to the bald man. "And more payment than present."

"You've carved a good percentage already," the man nodded to the bodies around them.

"Maggot is the one richer for it."

The bald man gave a snort of laughter.

Garrin looked back and forth between them, his eyes glittering with panic. Behind her, the rasp of swords ceased, replaced by an explosive curse and retreating footfall. The man dueling with Rafe must have taken to his heels. If he ran into his compatriots, Viv doubted they'd try to rejoin his captured leader. Trapped between her and the bald man, Garrin gave an enraged cry and rushed her. He was quick, but anger made him careless. She snarled her sword blade on his, sliding down to press hilt against hilt. In the same step, she drove her knee between his legs.

Dropping his sword, Garrin sank to the ground with a cry. Viv hooked her sword point into the grip of his sword and rolled it toward Rafe, who picked it up. Garrin still clutched his dagger, and she pricked his hand with her sword point till he dropped that as well. She kicked the knife away, set her foot on Garrin's shoulder, and toppled him sideways. He lay in the muck, curled up around the pain in his groin. Sheathing her sword, Viv knelt over him, pinning him beneath her with her knee on his chest and the heel of her sword hand hard on his forehead. She angled the blade of her knife across the artery in his throat. He went still beneath her.

"Good luck, Garnet." The bald man gave a harsh laugh, then retreated down the alley. Rafe stood to one side, watching in silence.

"So," Viv said to Garrin. "Maggot didn't put you up to this. Did Rivett?"

"No," he snarled.

She let the knife blade etch across his skin, drawing blood.

"No," he repeated, and then, too eagerly, "Yes. Rivett sent me."

"You're lying," she said, cutting deeper.

"Rivett wants you dead," Garrin gasped.

"True enough. But you want to make trouble." Viv increased the pressure. She could smell his blood, and his fear. "I know the sound of a lie in your mouth, Garrin. Tell me the truth and you'll live."

Garnet was silent, except for the harsh drag of his breathing.

"My word on it," Viv pledged.

Finally, sullen-voiced, he answered. "It was my idea. Maggot seemed soft, careless. I thought if you were dead, and I'd grabbed control of the Fringes, Maggot's men would back me against Nick. I'd cut a deal with Rivett if I had to—take Maggot's piece and give him the rest. A piece is better than crumbs."

"Rivett wouldn't give you a piece, or even toss you some crumbs. He'd make you a feast for worms instead."

"Devil's bitch," Garnet swore, rubbing his aching crotch.

"Well, you have one chance left in hell—to escape." Disgusted, Viv stepped back from Garnet. He rose, one hand pressed to his bleeding throat, the other clenched into a fist. Rafe moved in closer, his extended sword guarding her from any surprise maneuvers.

"Got you in a roiling frenzy, has she?" Garrin glared at him, anger and jealousy rising as his fear subsided. "You pizzle punk, think she'll treat you any better than she did me?"

"I know I'll treat her better," Rafe answered him.

"You're wasting precious time, Garrin." Viv crossed her arms and regarded him coldly. "Tomorrow you'll be worth more dead than alive in London. Be on the road when the sun rises, with whatever you can steal by then to fill your pockets."

With a low curse, Garrin turned and ran into the night.

Rafe stepped up beside her. "You let him go."

Viv heard approval in his voice, and surprise.

"I keep my word." She gave him a twist of a smile. "Except perhaps to Jacob Rivett."

"Not worth giving if not worth keeping," Rafe said.

"True enough."

He began to clean his blades, his expression suddenly grim in the moonlight.

"You killed to protect me," she said. "Was it the first time?"

"No," he answered, but she could see it disturbed him still.

"You've proved yourself," she told him. "You are one of us now. A bond of blood."

"Thieving wasn't enough?"

"You were audacious—but you only took back what Garrin stole from you. That was for yourself, not for us."

"Perhaps you should baptize me this time," he said. The humor was edged—Nick's dousing must still rankle.

"A shower of gold," she said lightly.

He turned and looked at her, his gaze intense. "Gold has a pretty glitter, to be sure. But there are things I value more."

Her heartbeat quickened. Even standing still, they ran together through the darkness, each sensing the other as if linked by invisible threads.

Abruptly, Rafe turned away and sheathed his sword. "Will you put a price on Garnet?"

"Oh yes, that I will do," she answered, tending to her weapons in turn. She felt strangely disoriented by the shift, the tight connection suddenly lax.

"He still wants revenge," he warned.

"Yes—but not more than he wants his life." If she had wounded no more than Garrin's pride, it probably was not worth it to spare him. But he had been infatuated with her once, or with her power. "I promised him nothing. He threw away what I did offer. If he wants to throw away his life to have another chance at mine, so be it. But Garrin, like Maggot, wants what he thinks will be easy."

"Where do you think he will go?"

"Garnet? Who knows. Like most of us, he can't go home again."

They began moving, wary while they journeyed through the maze of warehouses toward the docks. Vivian admired Rafe's vigilance. He kept watch for any new attack, but his mind continued to play out the moves on the board. "So, Maggot knew Garnet's game, and set his own man as sentinel?"

"Maggot knows the scent of greed. Probably he told that black-bearded Judas goat to help Garrin incite any troublemakers," she answered. "Maggot wasn't willing to challenge us himself, but he'd let Garrin snatch the chance to kill me."

"None of the men Garnet recruited will dare go back. So Maggot's rid of them as well."

Viv nodded. "If Garrin had succeeded in killing me, Maggot would have done him in turn, and tossed the corpse to Nick for appeasement. Then he'd try to play Nick and Jacob against each other. It was clever enough. He's only stupid because he doesn't see he can't win alone against Rivett."

Ahead of them, the streets looked livelier, with more flares burning to light their way. Rafe paused beside a doorway, reaching out to stay her. Moonlight slanted over his face, his eyes gleaming silver blue, watching her intently. Silence enveloped them. After a moment, Rafe asked hesitantly. "Did you love him—Garnet?"

The invisible strings drew taut again, tugging at her heart. Viv drew a deep breath and answered him honestly. "No. I never loved him. I thought for a time that he loved me. If he did, he loved his pride more. He thought a tumble in my bed would set him on the throne of Southwark."

Rafe's gaze held hers steadily, and he smiled, taking her warning without rancor. During the attack, wildfire had burned between them, uniting them in its blaze. But Garrin's final betrayal had dampened the flame. Viv did not know if she wanted to ignite it again. She laid her hand on Rafe's chest, feeling the rhythmic pulse of his heart. He had unexpected depths. Under his brashness lay tenderness. Under fiery impulse lay cool calculation. And under the calculation, she suspected a deeper, hotter fire. She wondered if anyone had ever reached it.

"And you, fencing master—have you ever been in love?"

His heartbeat surged. The heavy pulse seemed to beat in her blood.

"No, I've never been in love."

Rafe drew her toward the darkened doorway. Viv held back for a second, and his hand gave a small tug, urging her. He gazed down at her. Shadowed now, his eyes looked huge and black. Cupping her face, he kissed her, not roughly as he had this morning, but softly. His lips barely touched hers before they withdrew, then brushed again, again, their touch warm and soft as his breath. Then his mouth pressed more firmly, lush and hot, and his moist tongue tip flicked at the seam of her lips. Desire erupted, flaring out from her core. A fierce heat burned between her legs, the flames licking down her thighs, up through her belly. Her nipples drew tight. His arms tightened around her, lifting her against him.

For a moment, the danger of where they were vanished, fading along with the sharp pain of the wound, the smells of blood and street muck that covered them. The walk home to a wide bed and clean sheets was too long. Viv wanted him here and now. The hard heat of his body pressed against her. She felt the solid muscle of chest and thigh, the sudden, insolent thrust of his cock. Abruptly he tensed, then drew away. His eyes looked wary, but there was a breathless edge to his voice as he whispered, "This is not safe."

"You knew that when you started," Viv said, still not caring. She wrapped her arms around his neck. "You don't like things that are safe."

"I like to be alive to enjoy them."

She kissed him quick and hard, biting the cushiony flesh of his lower lip. Rafe moaned, and she felt the hardness of his sex surge against her again. Viv thrust against him, feeling the pulse of life in him, energy pounding out in waves. She wanted to ride that energy, drown in the waves. He pressed closer, his arms tightening, then drew back with a harsh gasp of laughter. Licking his lip, he added, "Alive—and in one piece."

Viv took a deep breath. What she wanted and what she could allow were different. She must beware her own desire, as well as the danger of these streets. A moment ago, she would have mounted him, heedless of everything but the wild ride to completion. She had never wanted anyone with such sudden, blind fervor. Letting the ferocity of the moment ebb a little more, she said, "Do you think you can live till we get home?"

"If it doesn't take too long." His voice was deep, roughened with desire, and she could feel its reverberation in the marrow of her bones.

11

Viv found it a long walk from the Fringes to the heart of the Clink. They said little as they moved through the flare-lit streets, but caution and anticipation played back and forth between them in glances. At last, they passed through the guard house gates and entered the courtyard. Smoke was waiting there, with a dozen men ready to scour the Fringes. Viv dismissed them, then motioned Rafe to follow her back to Smoke's office. Perching on his desk, she gave him a colorful account of the night's adventure, inviting Rafe's comments.

Rafe shrugged. "Maggot's smarter than I thought at first, but not as smart as he thinks he is."

Viv made sure her rendition was filled with praise for Rafe's prowess and loyalty. "Fletcher never failed me. He stood fast at every turn."

Smoke glanced over at Rafe, cautious and contained as ever, but his expression warmed. Viv knew Rafe had passed a crucial barrier by protecting her.

"I promised Garnet I'd set a price on his head by morning. I always keep my word."

"Ten pounds?" Smoke asked. A year's wage for a poor man.

"Five should insult him—and still frighten him off," she said. "I want him out of London."

"I'll see to it. You'll want Maggot closely watched."

"Yes. Keep him on a tight rein." Bidding Smoke good-night, Viv left the office. Rafe followed close behind her, like a great shadow, dark and warm.

She turned at the fountain, gazing up at him. The vividness of their skirmish still radiated from him, his dark hair straying over his forehead, his eyes glowing like sapphires from the Indies. She wanted him so much she ached with it. But beneath the heat of their adventure was a stone-cold warning. Her last lover had just tried to kill her. Garrin's betrayal reminded her all too well how dangerous it was to trust anyone beyond her small, proven circle. The praise she'd given him he'd earned. There was no doubting his courage—but would his loyalty stand the test of time? Would the taste of power make him greedy?

Rafe's gaze held hers, the flare of his desire matching hers, but beneath that she saw another longing, and it was kindred to hers, too. His eyes said he wanted more than the just recognition of his brains and talent. What he craved was her trust. Tenderness welled up in her that he yearned for the very thing she wanted to give him. She reached up and stroked his cheek. He drew a soft breath, as if his skin burned where she had touched him.

"Come with me," she murmured.

She led him inside, her desire shivering through her limbs like the air that brushes bare skin anticipating a touch. Making her way by the light of the beeswax tapers that gleamed richly on wood, bronze, and silver, she listened to the sounds of his steps behind her. Awareness of him filled her, a possessive pleasure edged with aching tenderness. Many men had looked at her with desire, and with many kinds of need. How did Rafe Fletcher reach into her heart and stir unnamed longings of her own so sharply? She took him up the great staircase to the balcony, and opened the door to her withdrawing room. She passed through, turning his hand and she led him into her bedchamber with its carved bed and scarlet hangings. They had privacy. Joan would not attend her unless summoned, but a faint spicy scent told Viv her lady-in-waiting had anticipated her comfort. She smiled to herself as she guided Rafe into her bathing chamber.

A fire burned in the small fireplace, reflected in the steaming water that filled the wooden tub. The flickering illuminated painted sylvan scenes of cavorting nymphs and centaurs. Dangling grape clusters ornamented the ceiling. Everything seemed suffused with life, glowing with the desire that burned between this fascinating near-stranger and her. She watched Rafe's response to the scented soaps, perfumes, and fine oils arrayed on the chest beside the tub, the abundance of soft cloths and towels. From his expression she suspected he had never seen such sybaritic luxury, perhaps did not entirely approve. She hoped he found it intriguingly wicked. For a moment they stood looking at one another, feeling the heat of anticipation simmer and rise between them.

"Take off my clothes." She said it softly, making it an invitation, not an order.

Kneeling in front of her, Rafe tugged off her boots. She lifted her head, wordlessly challenging him, offering him the fastenings of the breeches he had found so improper. To her delight, he caressed them. Whatever else he thought of them, they had an erotic effect. With a soft brush of his fingers he guided them over the curve of her hips, drawing them down her legs and over her feet, then tossed them into a corner. He stroked her calves and thighs through the tight hose, his touches praising the pliable agility of her body, making her all the more aware of the profound strength of his. She watched his hands with fascination. They were huge as the rest of him, with the same long, elegant bones to give them grace. She felt their power controlled behind his gentle caresses. His thumbs stroked the crease of leg and hip. Her sex pulsed hot, only the thin fabric between it and him. She caught her breath.

But he did not careess her there yet. Instead he unfastened the points of her hose and stripped them from her, leaving her bare from the waist down, her femininity exposed beneath the masculine doublet. She was acutely aware of his gaze on the hollows of her hips, the taut skin of her belly gleaming pale gold in the firelight, the black triangle of hair that did not entirely hide her sex. His fingers curled as if they wanted to shape themselves to the flushed lips barely visible beneath the curling thatch. She felt the answering heat of her own moisture.

He lifted his gaze to hers, and she saw how much he wanted to touch her, but instead, he blew softly on the tender lips, teasing them with nothing more than his breath. She answered with a small yearning sound. He drew back, looking up at her with laughter in his eyes, teasing her as mercilessly as she had him.

"Not yet," he whispered.

Impatient irritation flashed through her, like lightning that flickered then vanished. Acknowledgment overwhelmed it, and she laughed softly at his deliberate provocation.

He rose and unfastened the front of her doublet. When she lifted her arms for him to remove the sleeves, a ragged edge of pain caught her. She tensed involuntarily. He glanced at her as if uncertain, then with caressing hands he released her breasts from the tight garment. The quiver of his desire was palpable to her as he brushed her nipples through the thin linen. He slowly removed the doublet, but abruptly went still. His pupils flared with shock, darkening his eyes. "Your shirt is covered with blood."

She glanced down. So it was. The darkness had spread into the white cloth, alarming in the candlelight. She shrugged, hiding that this cost her some discomfort. Her anger at receiving the wound was returning, and she did not want it spoiling their mood. She could bear the pain easily enough. "Only a scratch."

Gently, he lifted the bloody garment over her head and tossed it with the others in the corner. Taking one of the cloths, he dipped it in the water and gently washed away the blood on her side, revealing the long, shallow cut left by the sword.

"You see," she insisted defiantly. "Nothing."

He touched the skin on either side lightly with his fingertips. "Not deadly, but not nothing."

Wine waited on a small table. Rafe poured some over

another cloth and cleaned the wound; it stung so that she had to grit her teeth. He cleansed the cut as thoroughly and carefully as a physician, moving the cloth so gently and solicitously that at last she pushed him away, laughing.

"Enough." She pointed to the tub. When he hesitated she commanded, "In."

Rafe shook his head, but it was not a refusal. She saw exasperation in his face, and frustrated desire. Quickly he stripped, revealing solid muscle and taut sinew, density balanced with the grace of harmonious angles, the tender textures of lean hips and lightly scattered chest hair. The firelight licked the tender rim of his navel, the knotted core sunk deep. Below it the hair grew in wild patterns, like darker flames spreading upward from his manhood. He climbed into the tub, and she watched his face relax as he leaned back. His nostrils flared as he inhaled deeply of its scent, and the water glowed transparent gold over his skin. He closed his eyes as if he wished he could dissolve and be carried off in the rising steam.

"You possess subtle and insidious weapons," he murmured. "I am vanquished with oil and water."

Not if she had aught to do with it. Viv murmured, "Are you? Touch oil with fire and it will burn in water."

She climbed into the great tub, feeling the hot fragrant bath rise, making her legs feel silky, then her torso. Its lapping heat eased the wound. She sighed and quickly sank in up to her neck, the water almost sloshing over the rim. Laughing she sat up before it could spill and grabbed a cloth. The firelight poured over him as she cleansed his body. She washed away the dust and sweat, thick lather oozing through her fingers, making them slippery on his skin. As she leaned over him he laved water over her breasts, then caught one nipple in his lips and sucked with a fierceness that made her gasp. She loved the supple sweep of his tongue against its hard point, and the way his lips pressed the soft swell of her breast. At last, languor and impatience mingling, she handed him the perfumed soap. He turned it over and over, working up a creamy foam to caress her buttocks and flanks. Viv dipped her hands deeper into the water to toy with his manhood, the thick rod that swelled to her caresses, and the soft vulnerability sheltering beneath. He moaned, his legs parting, increasing his exposure to whatever she chose to do.

Though she herself was inflicting the sweet torture, it was more than she could endure. She stood, water cascading. Laughing at her volatile change, he clambered from the tub. She tossed him a towel and backed away. He followed, wiping away the worst of the wetness, then flinging the towel aside. His arousal stood stiff and demanding, and her mouth watered as she imagined it between her lips, imagined coaxing its liquid spice. Feeling contrary, she darted around the tub, away from him.

"Stand still," he commanded her.

She arched her eyebrows at him, but decided to please him, and did as he told her. Rafe tore thin linen into strips, binding it over the sword cut and around her ribs. Impatient with such concerns, she was hard put to not to squirm.

"It makes you look like an Amazon from the ancient myths," he murmured, tucking in the ends of the linen.

"Are you satisfied now?" she asked.

He pressed closer, the thrust of his sex grazing her belly. "Not quite."

With a low laugh, Viv curled her fingers about it, and then backed away, leading him by the hard handle of flesh. Flushed and laughing, too, he followed through the door and into the bedchamber. She did not release him until they stood by the bed. She pushed aside the hangings, flung back the embroidered covers and lay down. Her black hair spread in serpentine coils on the pillow, its fragrant dampness a sensual pleasure to her, and one she saw he appreciated. His body glowed pale against the scarlet silk of the hangings. Shadows outlined his musculature, and the light of the tapers licked the upcurved shaft that jutted from the tangle of dark hair.

He moved toward her, but Viv held him back with a gesture, smiling provocatively. "Look at me," she whispered.

Sliding back among the pillows, she opened her legs, giving him full view of the tender, parted lips and the still more tender flesh within. She opened herself like the petals of a rose, showing him the swollen bud that throbbed like fire made flesh.

"Don't you want to taste me?" she whispered.

"Yes." His voice was hoarse. The tip of his tongue flashed over his lips, leaving them glistening.

A web of need vibrated between them. Viv sucked in her breath, trembling as he knelt between her legs, the bud at her center pulsating fiercely. He moaned and his cock jolted fiercely, rearing back to tap his belly. She inhaled his scent—clean soap, amber oil from the bath, warm skin, all mingled with the dark musk of his sex. He bent and licked her fingers where she held herself open to him. Then, leaning closer still, Rafe touched the bud with his tongue. He pressed gently, but her flesh throbbed against the touch like a beating heart. He flicked her with his tongue tip, stroke after stroke igniting sparks that leaped along her nerves. He moaned as if her pleasure and need shot through own his body. Pressing his tongue flat against her, he licked in slow, widening strokes. He reached beneath her, and she lifted for him, letting him gather the round of her buttocks in a firm grip that shaped itself to them. Pressing his face against her, he sucked at the hot liquor of her sex, pulling her closer still to him, devouring her with lips and tongue and teeth.

She squirmed, turning beneath him, tugging at his hips. His moan as he realized she wanted to do the same to him sent a hot tremor through her. He moved as her hands bade him, kneeling over her, all his strength commanded by her touch. She wrapped her fingers around his rigid shaft with greedy adulation and took the head between her lips, sucking with thirsty delight at the springy tenderness crowning it. The pulse of his desire raged so fast and hard she felt it against her tongue, felt it in the shivering, sobbing breath he drew as her tongue rubbed wet and hot against the living power of his flesh.

She stroked the curves of his buttocks, grasping and

kneading the lush muscle, then slid her fingertips inward, savoring the heat within the deep cleft. He moaned a protest that was a plea, muscles contracting as she stroked one finger between his cheeks. She teased the tender hidden opening as his tongue caressed the portal of her body. She pressed into him, his tongue invading her, sending shocks through her one after another. His sex throbbed wildly, and he tried to tug away, but she pulled him closer, pressing her finger further into the secret tightness of him, feeling the silken vulnerability of that inner skin. He gave a cry, pulsing hotly into her mouth as his tongue thrust deep into her. Explosions burst in her body, her brain, racing through her in shock waves of blinding light. She drank greedily, filling herself with his bittersweet seed. Rafe groaned against her, each dazzling pulsation, each rush of brightness, a new oblivion as they drowned together in a sea of opalescent white flame.

❧

Afterward Rafe lay beside her, dazed and throbbing. The drowsy torpor of aftermath flowed thick as poppy syrup in his veins, drugging his limbs and mind. Rafe had scarcely thought of who he was, why he was here, since she led him into the bedchamber. All that time, had he been the rogue fencing master, or only himself? He did not know which. But one careless word now and he would be dead. He struggled to grasp the emotions lost under the lazing waters of satiation. Nothing was clear. Anger was a dim ember, sunk almost too deep, beyond his grasp. Without it he felt defenseless. Apprehension moved slowly forward, a cold slither twisting with wariness. The bright remnants of triumph were edged with bitter shame at using her, at being used. But the sweet shame of pleasure blurred the effect, and unwanted tenderness invaded everything he felt.

He desired her too much. Admired her too much—her fierce passion, her courage, her sense of honor even in the midst of the corruption in which she lived.

Rafe watched as Viv leaned over, still entranced with touching him. Her fingertips traced a circle on his nipple, then drew a line up his throat, his chin, rubbing lightly in the small cleft. She kissed him, her teeth delicately seizing upon his lower lip and sucking till it felt swollen. "You have the most luscious mouth I've ever seen," she said, smiling at him lazily, lips nuzzling where she'd sucked and bitten. "Like a plum begging to be bitten. And your eyes . . . so blue." Her fingertips teased the tips of his lashes, so that he blinked. Smiling, she traced the arch of his cheekbones and brows, then stroked her finger through the thick mass of his hair. "It's seldom a man so pretty still looks like a man."

Her talk made him uncomfortable, but Viv only smiled when he blushed. She seemed as fiercely possessive as if he were some jeweled object. Rafe knew he should compliment her, too, yet sincere words seemed forced following her lavish praises. She was handsome enough to warrant praise. Women he had once deemed beautiful now seemed pallid and dull beside her. The fervor that animated both her face and body fascinated him more than her features. But her eyes were extraordinary. He gazed into their blackness, a universe at once cold and hot, starred with flame.

"Making love with you is like embracing fire," he said. "Brightness burning into darkness."

"We burn in the same blaze."

A breeze stirred the hangings, framing the bed in rippling scarlet. *Hellfire.* Rafe closed his eyes, staring through the red haze on the inner darkness of his eyelids. But it was not the flaming pit he saw. He saw Gabe, drenched in blood and dying. He saw his family in the black pit of prison, saw their heads on pikes above the Tower Gate. Feeling sick, Rafe rolled over, burying his face in the pillow.

"What . . . what?" She leaned over him, her voice quick and breathless with concern.

He shook his head, unable to think of anything, truth or lie, that was not too dangerous. Finally he said, "I don't want to want you. Not so much."

"But you do," she murmured, almost purring with satisfaction.

"Yes." The truth would serve his purpose better than a lie.

"You are too proud." She sounded pleased with that as well.

"Yes," he replied, glad she had chosen her own answers.

The night's adventures spun through his mind. Rafe

had killed in war, from a distance and during battles far bloodier than tonight's encounter. It was a paradox that he loved the raw savagery of a fight, no matter how desperate, but loathed killing. Vivian shared his excitement, but not his regret. Rafe wanted to draw far away, to think of her as purely evil. Instead, he saw a feral beauty inseparable from its ruthlessness. Viv pranced light-footed through her territory, or leapt with unsheathed claws to defend it—the Queen of Cats. For Viv it *was* a battle, part of an ongoing war to hold her territory against betrayal and invasion. He could not deny that the shared adventure had fused a bond between them. And in the midst he had been her protector, her knight, her comrade.

In truth it was nothing more than a tawdry skirmish between criminals. And he was her enemy.

Viv began to stroke him, her hands massaging the muscles of his neck and shoulders. Moving down his back, her fingers skimmed with soft touches of the pads, the sharper accents of her nails raking lightly down his torso. His body drank the energy flowing from her fingers. Rafe tensed, relaxed, tensed again as fire began to build, his body rising to her conjuring touch.

And because there was no escape except the flames, he pulled her close, needing to obliterate his own need of her. She did not protest his fierceness—until he tried to enter her, then she twisted like an eel, slithering down his body. Rafe cried out in protest, then in searing pleasure as her mouth fastened tightly on his straining flesh. He had wit enough to recognize her wisdom and pulled her thighs over his face. She moaned around him, urging him feverishly, as he lost himself in the wet fire of her.

❧

Rafe woke to the sound of a door opening. He sat up and his sudden movement woke Viv. "It's only Joan. I know her step," she murmured.

He glimpsed the woman's movements through a crack in the bed curtains, then Viv pulled him back under the sheets. Rafe burrowed there with her, feeling the shape, the warmth, of her body curled against his, savoring the dark cozy intimacy, yet disturbed by its ease. He listened to the soft rustling movements as her lady-in-waiting attended to the bath and came out again. When the bed-chamber door closed, he lifted back the covers and opened the bed curtains to let the sunlight fall across them. Viv stretched, sleek as a cat, then smiled at him.

Reaching out, Rafe stroked her face lightly, brushing the slope of her cheek. Remembering her fingertips tracing more intimate scars on his own body, Rafe followed the curving line of the scar. Oddly, Rafe did not think it marred her attractiveness, as it might a woman prettier but less fiercely animated. He had wanted to ask before, and now dared venture, "How came you by this?"

She tensed, as if the tip of a whip had flicked over her nerves, then exhaled. Her eyes met his. "Jacob Rivett."

"He cut you?" Outrage flared from his gut, heating his whole body.

"Oh yes. Before we had power, Smelly Jakes thought to pimp me. The scaly, split-tongued viper tried to lure me from Old Warts with rich promises. When I refused, he thought more forceful persuasion might bend me to his will. He caught me alone one night. I was young, but I knew how to fight. It took a knife to dissuade him." Anger and amusement glittered in her gaze. "His own scar cuts closer to the quick. He gave me this in answer— but it was worth it."

His blood chilled, but his own thoughts about the man who'd harmed little Mary had been no different. Rafe asked her levelly, "Did you unman him?"

"I should have," she said. "I may yet."

Rafe wondered what she would do to him, if she found out who he really was. "How old were you then?"

"Fifteen. I'd been wearing breeches more often than skirts, and Rivett thought he'd appeal to my vanity." She gave a little snort.

"How did you . . . begin all this?"

"A tale much like any other. Our parents were dead. We were destitute. Izzy's crazy mother was a distant cousin. She was beyond care for us, but Izzy took us in and taught us what we needed to know to survive." She gave a little shrug, glancing away. Rafe wondered what pain, or what secret, she was hiding. Facing him directly, Viv went on, "We started late, but we had an instinct for the game, the same as you. My hands were quick—and my wits. Nick hadn't my deftness at thieving, but he had a gift of seeming totally aloof that was useful for coney catching—as if he were too disdainful to cozen anyone."

"It seems a long way from nipping and foisting to this magnificence."

"Old Warts was the King of the Clink, then. He treated us well enough, but Nick and I never liked anyone giving us orders, so we set ourselves to be the ones to give them— beginning with organizing the wrigglers. Izzy never wanted the responsibility of control, though he's always been a good manipulator, a good diplomat. The three of us worked together." Toying with Rafe's hair, Viv told him how they began to climb the rickety ladder that would give them more money, more control. The climb that would give them dominion over the Clink.

From what he'd seen, Rafe believed Vivian loved the power quest even more than Nick. She delighted more in it, certainly. "And Rivett was your enemy from the first?"

"In an instant," she said, her eyes narrowing. "Bart Rivett, his father, held sway over half of London's criminals— though Smelly Jakes was already more hated than his father. When Bart died, we all thought Smelly Jakes behind it."

Rafe pictured Rivett's soulless eyes and thought it possible. Such deeds were done for kingdoms, both lawful and unlawful.

"Old Warts was cunning and wise, but growing lazy with age. We never betrayed him, but we gathered more and more of the strands of his power. When apoplexy struck him down, we tended him, and ran things in secret for a bit, while we tried to gather strength. Then Old Warts died, and there was a frenzy to grasp at his territory. Maggot, One Eye Wallace, and the others were all trying to grab what Nick and I had staked out.

"Jake was voracious, and he thought it was his chance, but he attacked too soon. His invasion did what our warnings had not. After he failed, we made the alliance. That was ten years ago—five to consolidate the alliance, five more to claim all the Clink as our own. Rivett had encroached into Paris Gardens, but we have a foothold in London now, too. His chief rival died last year, and hated Rivett enough to give us a foothold in the London docks."

Where Gabriel died, Rafe thought, wariness prickling. *And Chettle.*

"In London and in the Clink, they fear Rivett, but they hate him, too. We cultivate their hate and battle their fear with greed. We take a smaller percentage of the action of the gambling, brothels, and robberies in the territory we've claimed, or give them better in return. But we strike hard if they're fools enough to take our generosity for weakness, like Maggot."

We meant Viv and Nick, but she might have been a queen, speaking only of herself. "Rivett won't think you weak, not after you've cut a piece of him."

"It was a small piece. Far too small." Her lips pursed in a mischievous pout, and her eyes sparkled. She captured his hand in hers, curling his fingers down—all but his forefinger, which stood solitary and erect as she traced her tongue up its length. Despite the cold warnings buzzing, Rafe felt a hot throb in his groin. Then, closing her lips over his finger, she sucked softly, her mouth hot and slick, her tongue tip lapping at the pad. Her teeth took hold of the base, etching into the flesh, deliberately aggravating both his arousal and his apprehension. He moaned, hardness nudging her thigh.

But she was deliberately teasing, for she gave his finger a last lick, and drew away from him. "You'll be late for practice."

"In a worthy cause," he answered, reaching after her. He caught her and started to pull her back. Viv squirmed fiercely and he let her go free. He wanted no animosity to mar the morning. He saw the heat and the hesitancy in her eyes. She wanted him, but she did not want their affair to be a disruption. She was right that he best not shirk the practice. Perhaps there was more to gain leaving her wanting him, as he was wanting her. Rising from the bed, Rafe saw his training leathers laid out on a chest, and he pulled them on quickly. She watched all the while, which was of little help to his aching cock. When he was dressed, he leaned over and kissed her amid the pillows. She nipped his lower lip lightly, one hand rubbing his chest.

"I'll see you this afternoon," he murmured. In case that was too presumptuous, he added, "When I come on duty." Perhaps today he'd convince her to reveal at least the outer workings of their smuggling operation.

"I've plans with Nick," she said, shaking her head.

A flash of jealousy flickered, white hot. He drew back, angry with himself for feeling too much—angry with her because she had more distance than he did.

"I still want to see you in blue velvet," she murmured, pulling him back for another kiss. "After training, take the purse I gave you and buy yourself new clothes. Tomorrow you'll escort me to the fair."

A bit of bribery, Rafe supposed, to sooth any ruffled feathers. Well, she'd given him the excuse he needed to see Burne. He felt a flare of triumph, a flare of shame. He wanted to warn her against desiring him, trusting him. Instead he deepened the kiss, silencing them both with the thrust of his tongue. Her arms circled him, pulling him back down on the bed. She kissed him fiercely, sucking on his tongue as if to draw his soul. Then with a supple twist, she turned and pushed him out of bed. "Go—or we'll be here all day."

12

"Yes?" The tailor eyed Rafe's shabby fustian dubiously. "Were you recommended to us, sir?"

"This will recommend me," Rafe said, counting out a hefty deposit from the weight of gold and silver in his purse. It was too early to try to make contact with Burne, so he'd chosen this handsome shop near St. Paul's for his other errand.

"It will be a pleasure to serve you, sir," the man said, his tone now smooth and unctuous. He handed the money to his assistant, then led Rafe to the back of the shop. Conversing glibly about the latest styles, the tailor measured him, then gestured to his array of fabrics. "Black and white are favored at court. And what, sir, I ask you, could be more elegant? Embellished with a touch of gold braid perhaps?"

"No. Blue velvet."

"Most complimentary, sir." The owner unfurled bolt after bolt, darkest indigo and palest milk-and-water, gaudy peacock and popinjay, cornflower, violet, and sapphire. Rafe chose the sapphire for doublet and trunks, with slashes of sky blue silk for contrast. Twinges of guilt plagued him, for he could hear his grandfather's voice condemning such prodigal luxury. To counter it, he conjured his father filling the room with color as he displayed the opulent costumes for the latest play. Like his father, he must wear the right costume for the role. The rebellious fencing master had a taste for roguery and riches. The fencing master, he decided, also disliked ruffs. He pointed to a collar of cobweb lawn, narrowly rimmed with lace.

The owner pursed his lips. "Subtle," he said dolefully.

Rafe ordered a fine linen shirt and two pairs of blue hose.

"Your cape!" The merchant unwound another bolt, cut velvet this time, scrolls of midnight blue. "Short, of course. Double dagged collar? And for the lining—crimson satin!"

Rafe ran his hand over the textured velvet, the nap lush and faintly ticklish under his palm. He imagined Vivian's small, strong hand caressing it. Then he remembered the heat of her palm moving over his chest, her hair a black curtain around them, glossy as any silk in the tailor's shop. Arousal speared through him as he remembered the deft twist of her fingers on his nipples, the sweet, sharp edge of her teeth. Flushing, he nodded agreement to the cape, confirmed the deposit, and left the shop.

Rafe walked quickly, blindly, fleeing the erotic images that plagued him. Viv's dark eyes laughed at him, daring him to escape if he could.

With a soft curse, he turned and walked back toward St. Paul's.

Lightning had taken its steeple, but the great cathedral stood as it had for centuries, stone walls towering hundreds of feet above the square, dominating the entire landscape of London. Beneath the vaulted arches of the vast interior, crowds gathered for reasons both pious and profane. Much commerce had moved to the gleaming new quarters of the Royal Exchange, but still the walls echoed with the hubbub of intrigue and trade, as courtiers and countrymen paraded the central isle.

It was difficult, but Rafe found a group in prayer and joined them, whispering a plea for his family's wellbeing. But there was more that he could do here to help them, so he rose and made his way into the churchyard. Outside, crowds roamed a morass of stalls filled with the latest books, pamphlets, ballads, and plays, and gathered in clumps to debate. The situation was still combustible, Protestant fervor the spark to set off riots. Screened by a bookseller's stall, Rafe listened as one small dissenting group, Catholics, no doubt, conversed in low voices. The Queen of Scots denied Queen Elizabeth had the right to try another sovereign prince, but her protest would carry no weight without the military support of the Catholic nations. Would any dare? Would Elizabeth, after choosing imprisonment rather than death for Mary these seventeen years, at last order the ax to fall?

At sunset Rafe made his way to the tavern Burne had named. Though he had leave to be gone, Rafe double- and triple-checked the streets to make sure no one had been sent to trail him. He passed by the inn and rounded back to it. The interior of the Tilted Jug seemed pleasant enough, plain and respectable. Rafe had met none of the other intelligencers working for Burne, but he recognized one man. He was an occasional customer at the Lightning Bolt, and he had been at Maggot's last night as well—trailing Garnet, no doubt. Rafe gave no sign of it, simply rented the private room as he had been instructed, ordered a tankard of ale and a beef pasty, and went upstairs to wait. He expected a delay of an hour or two while messengers came and went, but ten minutes later there was a light rapping at the door, and the same man he'd seen below entered.

"Master Fletcher, I am Christopher Marlowe." The young man smiled pleasantly. Wide at the temples, small at the chin, his smooth, soft face was rimmed with a narrow beard. Large, dark brown eyes gazed from under high curving brows that gave him a questioning look. "Sir Nigel told me to bring you to Whitehall."

So, Marlowe had been awaiting his arrival. Rafe's heartbeat quickened with excitement, though he wondered if a trip to one of the Queen's royal residences was wise. The agent carried a light cape with a hood, which he handed to Rafe. He put it on, raising the hood, and together they took the back exit from the inn. Marlowe led him first through a maze of alleys, checking behind them as Rafe had.

"I saw no one following when I came," Rafe said.

Marlowe nodded. "We're as like to find trouble here as leave it behind." Soon they left the alleys for a broader and safer street leading toward the Thames.

"Do you know the reason for this meeting?" Rafe asked.

"Not I," Marlowe said, with a quick smile. "Though I know who you are, and the general purpose of things. With Babington jailed, Burne has me sniffing out information about Jake Rivett."

As they walked to the river, Rafe learned that Marlowe was twenty-two, six years younger than himself, sometimes a student at Cambridge, and an aspiring playwright. The waters of the Thames gleamed ruddy bronze in the waning sunset. Choosing a wherry, they set off down the river, the great houses sliding by as they passed seamlessly from London to Winchester, the rosy light slowly absorbing the purple hues of dusk. With the boatman close by, Marlowe stayed to safe topics, talking of the latest plays, and his interest in the Comet, the new theatre just opened in Southwark.

"Do not be surprised if you see me wandering about there as well," he said. "On business."

"I have already," Rafe said.

Marlowe laughed. "You have an eye, sir."

"What can you tell me of Burne?" Rafe asked.

"What, indeed? That our mentor is the eldest son of the baron, Lord Enstone? That the family is moderately rich, and Sir Nigel has married richer? But that much anyone at court could tell you. I can tell you that his true marriage is the Queen's service. There his love, his faith, and his ambition are one. In the past he operated more secretly, on missions such as you or I might undertake, but that is changing. He is not so known or feared as Walsingham, but his connection is recognized at court and few are comfortable in his presence."

"Has he dealt with you honestly?" An unsubtle question, but Rafe had no time to plan some clever strategy to woo the information.

Marlowe hesitated, then replied, "He has had no reason not to."

Hesitation and ambiguity were both deliberate, Rafe thought, and so as true an answer as Marlowe dared give.

At last the boatman rowed the wherry into the dock at the rambling palace of Whitehall, the stone walls glimmering in the torchlight. Marlowe gave a password to the guards before they passed into the jumble of townhouses, gardens, tiltyards, tennis courts, and cockpits cobbled together with long galleries and elaborate gateways. The motley collection of buildings were deceptively plain without, richly embellished within. Still hooded, Rafe followed his guide through a maze of hallways, their walls hung with paintings or vast tapestries of hunting scenes, their ceilings carved and picked out in gilt. Marlowe led him through a lavish waiting room off one of the galleries, and from there through a concealed closet, up a stairway into a small antechamber.

Signaled by some device, Burne appeared a moment after their entry. He gave a quick nod for Marlowe to exit as he had come. When the younger man had gone, Burne regarded Rafe critically. Rafe slid back the hood and returned his gaze. Burne seemed even more remote and frosty than usual, but showing the impatience he felt would give Rafe no advantage.

"Sir Francis wants to see you," Burne said abruptly.

Rafe drew a deep breath, excitement tinged with

apprehension. So, Walsingham wanted to make his own assessment of the new intelligencer. Over the past decade, the Queen's secretary of state had woven an intricate net of spies throughout England and across the continent. Walsingham hovered in the shadows, listening acutely to even the faintest vibrations that quivered along its strands.

Burne led Rafe through an oak door into the next chamber, a study intricately paneled and shelved with books, its floor covered in neatly plaited mats. Walsingham sat at a massive desk, looking up as they entered. Burne stepped to the side, standing between them both. "My lord, I present Master Raphael Fletcher."

"My lord." Rafe bowed in acknowledgment, assuming his most deferential manner.

Walsingham scrutinized him wordlessly, his gaze as critical as Burne's had been. Refusing to be disconcerted, Rafe took the time to study the man before him. The spymaster's visage was stern and saturnine, dominated by a strong nose. A gray cast dulled his swarthy complexion, as if he had been ill. Grizzled brown hair thinned back from his forehead, but his beard and mustache grew full and shapely. Intent, cautious brown eyes were deep-set beneath heavy lids and dark brows. He possessed an unnerving stillness, a blink of the eyes his only movement. His intelligence was obvious, as was his ruthlessness.

When at last he spoke, Walsingham's deep voice had a faint rasp. "Our offices do not speak well of you in the Netherlands, Master Fletcher. Your reputation names you trouble maker, rabble rouser."

Subduing his alarm, Rafe kept his gaze steady. Either they had sent queries when his family was first arrested, or the Earl of Leicester had maligned Rafe when he claimed credit for the discovery of the sabotage. But if Walsingham intended to fit his neck for a noose, it was more likely Rafe would be answering these questions in jail. "Is that my captain's opinion of me?"

Burne's mouth twitched slightly, though Walsingham's expression remained impervious. "No. Your captain said you were headstrong, but otherwise praised your courage, moral and physical. You are fortunate that Sir John holds your own views on the war."

"Are they so different from the Crown's?" Rafe asked evenly. "In the Netherlands, Protestant and Catholic unite to fight against the oppression of Spain. Are they not our natural ally, my lord, both practically and morally?"

"The war in the Netherlands is of great import. As is any struggle in which we can weaken the grip of the papists," Walsingham said. "You claim to be patriot, but some say you fought harder against the crown than against the enemy."

"Those who fight with words and paper might say so," Rafe responded. "But my sword, my heart, have always been for England."

"So you say. Words again."

"Words and deeds, my lord." Rafe felt the old rebellious anger rise, but he held Walsingham's gaze and spoke firmly. "Like many other soldiers, I volunteered to fight for freedom, not to starve so that our commanders could fatten their bellies with our food and their purses with our wages. Such corruption decimates our effectiveness."

"You consider yourself fit to judge such matters?"

"Starving bellies make their own judgments, my lord, and they are difficult to silence. They rumble their complaints most loudly."

"In truth, Master Fletcher, you never starved." Walsingham smiled grimly. "And I doubt if most bellies are as articulate as your voice."

"In truth, my lord, I saw our soldiers starving while their commanders feasted. They sent their men to die, then lied about their deaths to collect a handful of Judas silver." At best such men were thieves, at worst traitors. But Rafe could hear Gabriel's voice in his mind, cautioning him. These arguments led straight to denouncing Leicester, the Queen's eternal favorite. Despite his outrage, Rafe heeded the warning. "There is a great deal of trouble in the Netherlands, my lord. But I did not make it, only pointed it out. You must sift through a dross of rumor and lies to find precious grains of truth. I do not think you are a man to kill the messenger because the truth is not to your liking."

"That depends on whether I wish the news to be heard," Walsingham replied bluntly. "You have the courage to speak, Master Fletcher. Whether you have sense enough to hold your tongue remains to be seen."

Rafe chose silence as the most prudent response. After a moment, Walsingham nodded and settled back into his chair. "Apparently, your attempt to infiltrate the Swifts has been successful."

So he had passed the test, at least the first one. Rafe relaxed slightly, though he remained wary. "Yes, they've hired me as a bodyguard."

Burne moved closer to Walsingham. When the spymaster did not look at him, Rafe knew they had agreed to question him together. Burne's gaze swept Rafe from head to toe, his pale green eyes like ice over pond water. "There are rumors that you have found your way to Vivian Swift's bed."

The guards must be gossiping, enough that a man like Marlowe might pick up the tale at the Lightning Bolt.

"Yes," he admitted, disliking that they knew, though his skin prickled with heat at the memory.

"Good," Walsingham said. "Such access is invaluable."

"If it continues." Feeling pushed between Vivian's sheets, Rafe wanted first to pull away—then to shelter within, and draw the curtains against their prying gaze.

"You have a handsome countenance," Burne commented, as if this were a defect of character. "Surely you can make further use of it."

"I want to find Sir Gabriel's killer, and clear my family of these false charges," Rafe reaffirmed. "You can be sure that I will use any means within my power to do that."

"Do what you can to encourage her interest," Walsingham ordered.

"Such a creature must love flattery," Burne added with a shrug.

Rafe felt nothing prurient in Walsingham's interest or in Burne's. But their very coldness was a kind of obscenity, their smug scorn an insult. He felt even more the whore than he had with Vivian, whose fire ignited his own. He could not deny his desire, as much as he deplored its rashness. "Vivian Swift rules her domain like a queen bestowing favors. If I have no daring, she will forget my presence. If I am too presumptuous, I will be dismissed from her court."

"Or tossed into the Thames?" Burne muttered.

A common enough way to dispose of corpses, but Rafe wondered if the choice was significant. "Like Chettle?"

Both men stilled, regarding him more closely. A palpable hit.

Walsingham spoke first. "What do you know of Edward Chettle?"

"That he was a customs official, found floating in the Thames. He is the reason I've made contact with you, though I did not know if his death had any significance. Last night Jacob Rivett came to the Lightning Bolt. He complained of the police finding Chettle's body afloat in his territory, though his visit seemed more an attempt to taunt and threaten Vivian Swift." Rafe suppressed a smile as he remembered how Viv tossed back both taunts and threats.

"What else of Chettle?" Burne asked.

"Mistress Swift admitted they were involved in smuggling, but nothing else. She would not say if she killed him, or if she thought Rivett did."

"She would not say," Burne echoed, his voice edged with sarcasm. "What do you think? Did the Swifts kill him?"

Rafe felt his felt his own ambivalence rise again. "Her reaction was guarded. The news surprised her—but it may only have been that Chettle's body was not supposed to be discovered. When I questioned her, her response was evasive, then angry, though the anger seemed more at Rivett than me. If you want only my guess, it is that she is innocent. But Nick Swift showed no surprise when he learned of Chettle's death."

"That is suspicious," Walsingham remarked.

"Yes, my lord, and there is something else. I've seen both Nicholas Swift and Jacob Rivett wearing yellow jewels that could earn the codename Topaz. Swift wears such gems often, but not every day, and not the same stone. I've only seen Rivett once." Rafe paused, then added, "I've not discounted Nick Swift, but of the two, Jacob Rivett seems the more likely suspect."

"And why is that?" Walsingham asked.

Rafe frowned. "I have no facts. Only instinct. Perhaps all is as it seemed, and Rivett only used his annoyance at Chettle's death to goad the Swifts. But he is arrogant enough to play at such a game if he himself was the killer."

"They are all criminals," Walsingham remarked. "By nature ruthless and arrogant."

"To plot treason requires someone of great heat or great coldness. The Swifts have a hot fervor, but only to rule their own domain. Jacob Rivett possesses a calculating coldness. His pride would fatten upon such an evil secret."

"More evidence links the Swifts," Burne argued. "The territory is theirs, and the connection with Chettle."

"The territory is disputed, and Chettle may have rowed both sides of the Thames," Rafe countered.

Reflective, Walsingham stroked the edge of his beard. "If you believe Jacob Rivett is the more likely traitor, then you should find a way to switch your allegiance as soon as possible."

"Presuming I could accomplish that, no one will trust me if I change sides without motive." The strength of his resistance surprised Rafe, even as he argued. "I have earned some small measure of confidence from the Swifts. For now I may learn far more about him from them than Rivett or his men would confide in me."

"You can find a motive. This flirtation with Vivian Swift can easily be manipulated into a quarrel," Burne retorted. "Perhaps with the woman, perhaps with her brother."

"A quarrel may ruin my rapport with the Swifts, yet bring me no closer to Rivett," he argued.

"Many men would chafe at serving under a woman's command." Walsingham's tone was carefully neutral, since they all served the Queen. "If Rivett believes you unhappy, perhaps he will make some attempt to recruit you, if only to aggravate his rivals."

"Since I've been there such a short time, my value to him would lie in keeping me with the Swifts," Rafe pointed out.

"True," Burne said. "If he is as calculating as you say, he would find a spy so close to the heart of his rivals' organization of far greater value than the dubious gratification of appropriating a new favorite. But the necessity of exchanging information would dictate that you have contact with him. A foot in each camp."

"Perhaps. At double the risk."

Burne surveyed him disdainfully. "I thought your purpose was to save your family's lives, not protect your own."

"You know I am no coward." Rafe glowered at him.

"I know you hesitate."

It was perverse to feel such a peculiar loyalty to Vivian, but Rafe did. Spying on her for the Crown was one thing, for Jake Rivett quite another. Then he realized he had only to tell Vivian if Rivett approached him. He spread his hands, magnanimous. "You are right. That situation would double our chances."

Burne looked faintly surprised at his acquiescence, brows drawing together in a small frown. Rafe realized his dislike of the man had heated Burne's resistance. Rafe would have to be more cautious or defeat his own purpose.

"It is agreed then," Burne said brusquely.

"Agreed." Rafe smiled casually and was amused to see Burne's frown deepen. If Burne's arguments were also aggravated by dislike, it would be a way to manipulate them.

Burne looked him up and down. "Make Rivett aware of you—subtly if you can."

"Subtlety has many masks, sir." Rafe's smile broadened as Burne's frown deepened yet again. Burne definitely underestimated him. He gave another shrug. "This is naught but conjecture. Rivett has yet to approach me. If he does, I will seize the chance."

"See that you do," Burne ordered, asserting control.

Walsingham watched them both, his expression inscrutable. Rafe faced the spymaster. "I have told you what I know of Edward Chettle. Will you tell me what you know?"

Another pause. An invisible nod that Rafe could sense but not see passed between Walsingham and Burne. Taking the cue, Burne spoke. "Chettle was a papist, and dangerous. Our investigation uncovered a violent history. His family was involved in one of the Northern rebellions when the Queen came to power. His father and brother were hanged for treason when Chettle was still a child. We think now that he nursed his faith and his hatred of the Crown in secret for two decades."

"Revenge," Rafe said quietly. He felt Gabriel's weight in his arms, felt his blood sticky on his hands. For an instant he saw Gabriel's room as if he hovered above it, then London, England, the world, a map soaked in blood. Burne's voice drew him back to Walsingham's wood-paneled office.

"Chettle was not only helping to smuggle goods from France into England," Burne said. "He also transported Jesuit priests. We found evidence that Chettle was involved in a secret cell, one far more clandestine than the one which plotted the Babington conspiracy."

"What evidence?" Rafe asked.

"We captured a conspirator," Walsingham replied. "A Jesuit."

"Captured?" Something in the spymaster's flat tone alerted him. "He escaped?"

"The priest is dead," Burne said succinctly. "He revealed nothing more than Chettle's name."

Dead by torture then. Silently, Rafe cursed both the men before him.

"I had just uncovered Chettle's smuggling connection to the Swifts when Sir Gabriel brought me the pistol." Burne frowned. "I was most keen to hear what Scratch Jones had to say."

Burne sounded more disappointed in this loss than in Gabriel's death. Rafe's dislike grew to pure loathing. "My family's guns would be of great use to such a conspirator. Chettle had every reason both to sabotage the guns meant for the war and to steal the others for himself."

"Or to buy them," Walsingham said.

"You do not believe that," Rafe challenged. They wanted a collar about his neck, a leash to tug on. Fear for his family was only a way to manipulate him. "The sabotage occurred in London, under Chettle's direction. My grandfather and cousin were never involved."

Walsingham only looked at him. Like a bell sounded for the third time, the hollow silence echoed within Rafe, filling him with a new foreboding. He remembered Burne's critical appraisal when he arrived, Walsingham's first wordless scrutiny. Perhaps the spymaster was not just twitching the leash. Perhaps there was some other damning evidence he was concealing, or some guilty knowledge he hoped to surprise.

"I believe you believe in their innocence," Walsingham said at last. "And you have the chance to prove it."

"Whatever evidence you have against them is falsified," Rafe asserted, "and I will bring you proof."

Walsingham leaned forward, commanding Rafe's gaze with his own. "Do you know what Sir Gabriel said of you?"

Rafe felt disconcerted, though surely Gabriel had spoken well of him. "He must have told you how fiercely I'd fight to clear my family's name."

"Sir Gabriel argued most vehemently that you be given official sanction to investigate." Walsingham nodded toward Burne.

Because he knew I'd investigate with or without your sanction. And you know it, too.

Burne spoke again, a faint smile hovering at the edge of his lips. "He claimed you were astute. Loyal. Resolute."

Gabriel would probably have told Rafe he was stubborn and headstrong, but his heart warmed at his friend's praise, despite Burne's sarcastic tone. "Your tongue twists virtues into vices, sir."

"He said you were one of the most honest men he knew." Burne gave him another tiny smile. "And one of the best liars."

"If Gabriel said so, both were to recommend me as an agent in your service," Rafe returned. Their quick wits had rescued them from several scrapes.

"The latter you have demonstrated full well, by winning your place with the Swifts," Walsingham said.

"You have my honesty, my lord."

"Keep it so. The accusation is treason, Master Fletcher. Your first loyalty must be to your Queen, not to your family. Bring me proof of their innocence if you can, proof of their guilt if you find it." Walsingham's eyes were implacable. "Play me false in any way, and you will be imprisoned with them—executed with them."

"Yes, my lord." Rafe's voice was level, but his heart beat furiously. Had he been played skillfully or truly warned? Either way his task was the same. He must disprove his family's connection to the sabotage. In such a vengeful climate, even the taint of the association might hang them.

Walsingham returned his gaze to the papers on his desk. "You are dismissed. Sir Nigel will show you to the dock."

Rafe hesitated, but to question Walsingham now would count against him in ways he could not calculate. Drawing up the hood of his cape, he followed Sir Nigel out the door.

As they emerged into the hallway, a movement at the far side of the room caught Rafe's eyes. He glimpsed a flash of yellow satin skirts as a young woman vanished into a doorway. There were guards, but otherwise the hall was empty. Burne walked swiftly ahead, and Rafe strode beside him, determined to get his answer from the chief intelligencer. "Sir Nigel, have my cousin and grandfather arrived in London? Can they be detained privately?"

"No," Burne said brusquely. "They will be held in the Fleet when they do. If they have been falsely implicated, I do not want to warn whoever is truly responsible that we are searching for another culprit. They will be installed comfortably, do not fear."

Of course he feared, but Rafe nodded. Burne quickened his pace, walking swiftly to outstrip more questions.
Rafe glowered at his retreating back. Walsingham and
Burne considered his family no more than useful pawns
in the religious war they waged for England's sake—and
pawns in their private game of politics at court. But more
than one game was in progress. The chequered field of
Southwark was Rafe's board, and there the moves were
his own to make.

13

Rafe moved swiftly to catch the evasive Burne. Midway along the elaborate corridor, a door opened between them. Dressed in mourning, a woman stepped out and turned toward Rafe. The pale, determined face beneath the black veil belonged to Claire Darren, Gabriel's younger sister.

"Rafe! Rafe Fletcher!" She moved to him swiftly, her hands outstretched toward him. Rafe reached out in answer and clasped them in his own. She gave him a fleeting smile. He would have embraced her had it not been so public a place. As it was they only met the pain in each other's gaze.

"Claire," he murmured, his voice catching on a rush of affection and grief. He had no siblings, and Gabriel's sister had seemed like his own. Like Gabriel, she was slender and graceful. She had the same slanting cheekbones, but her face was more oval, her coloring darker. Under the drift of black veil, her long hair was deep chestnut. In the sun it glowed auburn, he remembered, the same shade his own mother's had been. Smudges of sleeplessness lay beneath her hazel eyes.

"You know," she said. The husky voice that had once toyed with ironies was hoarse now with grief.

"Yes," he answered, and then low and quick, because

Burne was returning, "I will come see you when I can. But it is best if you have not seen me here, Claire."

Turning, she saw Burne and understood at once. "Of course, you are here to help your family," she murmured. She gave his hands a gentle squeeze then released them.

"I am here because of them, and because of Gabriel."

Her gaze intensified. "I am glad."

Claire knew what Gabriel had done as well as Rafe, and kept him apprised of court gossip. Rafe wondered if she had any piece of the puzzle he did not hold as well. "Had he spoken to you recently?"

"I had not seen him for over a week. I know nothing, but I will help you any way I can." Her eyes blazed behind the veil, anger burning through the grief.

"I will let you know if you can, Lady Claire," he said formally, for Burne had joined them. Rafe knew Claire was trustworthy, but he expected Burne to rebuke him.

Instead, when Burne spoke it was not to Rafe, and his voice was soft and solicitous. "Lady Claire."

"Sir Nigel," she said, offering him a solemn smile.

"I hope you fare better today," he said.

"Little better," she said. "But I thank you for your kindness, Sir Nigel."

Kindness? Burne?

"Sir Gabriel's death was a great loss to us," Burne said.

Remembering the intelligencer's chill composure over Gabriel's body, Rafe felt a surge of mistrust and anger. But the emotion Burne showed to Claire did not seem false. Gazing at her, his eyes were tender. On another it might be no more than compassion, but Rafe thought

Burne must be in love with her. He did not think Gabriel would approve. *Nor do I,* he thought.

"Is your wife well?" Claire asked him.

Some of the warmth went out of Burne's eyes, but he answered with appropriate civility. "Lady Burne is well. You also are kind to ask."

No, cruel, Rafe thought, though he did not think Claire intended it so. She did not see Burne's warmth as uncommon, only what someone who had honestly cared for her brother might have shown. He was glad Burne was married. Obviously it would not change his interest in Claire, but he hoped it would prevent her forming any for him.

"You've suffered much this past year," Rafe said gently. First the terrible boating accident on the Thames, which had injured her and killed her betrothed. Now Gabriel's death.

He saw Claire's hands curl into fists, but she only shook her head. She did not wish to speak of it anymore.

"I did not expect to find you at Court," Burne said.

"The Queen gave me leave to go, but I thought it might be easier to stay." She made a small gesture. "I am on a quest for Her Majesty. Three of us were sent to look for a token she misplaced, a handkerchief. It is not so important in itself. She welcomes the distraction from things of greater import."

"We will leave you to your errand then," Burne said to her, then he nodded to Rafe. "Fletcher."

"I have but one more question for Rafe," she said, glancing from Burne to him and back again. "Only a moment, Sir Nigel."

Kindness put to the test, Burne stiffened slightly but then gave her another bow. "A moment," he said with a warning glance to Rafe, then withdrew beyond hearing.

"It is only that I thought of you as I looked through Gabriel's belongings," Claire admitted quietly. "I wanted you to have some memento."

"I have the ring he gave me still. It is all I need."

She nodded. "I wanted the dragon brooch you gave him for myself, if you would not mind. But I could not find it among his things. . . ."

Guilt tangled with Rafe's grief. Gabriel had worn it pinned to his cap the night he died, but had returned bare-headed. He remembered Gabriel's pale hair spilling across his arm, face white as chalk, death in his eyes. "It is lost—or stolen." His voice was grim. "If I find it, it will be yours."

His words showed Claire that he knew far more than she did about her brother's death. She pressed his arm, a quick hard clasp. "We must talk, about Gabriel and about your family, when there is time."

"We will," he promised.

A door slammed, and a flurry of movement erupted on the gallery above. A sharp voice rang out. "God's garters! Cannot my simplest commands be carried out?"

Rafe drew a deep breath as the Queen appeared at the top of the staircase. She paused, glaring down at them. Instantly, Rafe swept back his hood and knelt, aware of Claire sinking into a curtsey beside him. Queen Elizabeth descended, four maids of honor and a handful of courtiers trailing behind her. Her movement was graceful and vigorous, though she was displayed within her garments like a painted idol within a baldaquin. Lifted by a crown of gemmed flowers, a veil of gold net framed tight curls of red hair. She wore a gown of white satin embroidered in flowers of black and gold. Full over-sleeves of cloth-of-gold trailed from shoulder to floor.

"Is this what kept you from my errand, Lady Claire?" The Queen's voice was tight with censure.

"Yes. Forgive me, Your Majesty." Claire offered no clarification. Rafe knew it was because she was unsure what it was safe to say about him.

The Queen's gleaming skirts stopped two feet away. A dew of pearls and diamonds glistened among the embroidered flowers. A fan of carved ivory and white feathers dangled from a cord at her waist. More diamonds flashed from the satin rosettes of her slippers.

"You may stand," Queen Elizabeth said to him.

Rafe rose and her gaze scanned him from head to toe, an appraisal less blatant than Vivian's, but quite as thorough. Distance had taken decades from her face. Close up, he saw the red curls were a wig. A myriad of fine wrinkles showed beneath the mask of white power, and behind the rouged lips her teeth were blackened from decay. Gazing out from the mask, the glittering eyes were ageless.

"Such a pretty fellow—and so large."

"Your Majesty," he murmured, for there seemed no appropriate response.

"Have you a name, pretty fellow?"

Rafe hesitated fractionally, though he knew he must answer. Behind him there was a faint scrape, a sword scabbard grating against the floor. *Burne.* The Queen glanced over at the sound, and when she looked back at Rafe there were shrewd new questions in her eyes. He answered as best he could, without words.

"Never mind, pretty fellow. I will give you a name." She tapped him with her fan on either shoulder. "I dub you my Centaur. Even those of small vision can imagine the larger horse parts."

Tittering ran through the maids and courtiers, but they would not remember he had not given his name to her, only that she had chosen a ribald one for him.

The Queen turned to Claire, smiling more kindly now. "You have leave to say farewell, Lady Claire. Rejoin us presently." She turned and swept up the stairs again, her attendants following in a bejeweled gaggle.

Rafe breathed a sigh of relief. There would be no incriminating questions. Whatever the Queen wished to know she would discover in private, from Walsingham and Burne, and from Claire.

Burne rose from where he knelt, his expression thoroughly peevish. He walked over to them, and Rafe knew his moment with Gabriel's sister was long past. As they spoke their farewells, a door in the far corner opened. The young woman Rafe had glimpsed earlier emerged and came quickly along the gallery, her yellow satin skirts glowing brightly. She walked with her head bent, straight flaxen hair spilling down from her cap, and a lace handkerchief clenched in her hand. She looked up as she approached, and Rafe saw she was lovely, though a sullen anger creased the wide, high forehead and thinned her soft lips. A month ago her charms would have dazzled him, but now her prized fairness seemed pallid compared Viv's flaming darkness, her softness bland contrasted with Viv's supple strength. Seeing them, the young woman quickly straightened, tilted her chin up, and smoothed her agitated expression into blank indifference.

"Lady Barbara, you have achieved the quest," Claire said.

The young woman answered the small pleasantry with a curt, "So I have." She swept past them, then turned back and studied him for a moment before moving up the stairs. The pale hair was distinctive, her fair brows and lashes almost invisible around eyes of deep blue. Rafe was sure he had never met her, but he felt discomfited nonetheless.

"I should return to Her Majesty," Claire said, drawing his attention back. She bade them both farewell, then followed Lady Barbara back to the Queen's apartments.

When Claire was out of sight, Burne turned and stalked toward the doors. Rafe followed him outside and down the steps to the dock. Gesturing for a wherry, Burne instructed Rafe to take a succession of boats back to Southwark, as if he had not the sense to do it himself, and waited for Rafe to settle into the boat, as if he might sneak back to the palace if Burne did not see him underway. The boatman dipped the oars and the wherry slid out into the Thames.

A lantern glowed on the prow to light their way along the river. Streaks of gold rippled on flowing darkness as Rafe stared into the water. For a moment, Gabriel gazed

back at him, black cap slanted above his forehead, its rakish golden plume pinned with the dragon brooch.

Rafe had been seventeen and scarce a week at the Inns of
Court when he met Gabriel. London was new—fascinating, exhilarating, intimidating, appalling. Rich and poor,
students from Oxford, Cambridge, and less prestigious
universities came to finish their education at the Inns of
Court. Many were young aristocrats who merely
skimmed over the surface, permitted by privilege to grad-
uate in four years, while merchants' and yeomen's sons
had to study the full seven. Rafe smarted at the injustice,
but seeing the leisure, the dazzling finery of the noble-
men's sons, he confessed the sharp nip of envy. Rafe's
good wool doublet looked unfashionably severe, his plain
flat collar even more so—but his rapier was among the
finest in London. Not gauded with gems, still it was rich,
the sheath inlaid with ebony, ivory, and mother of pearl,
the hilt damascened, the perfectly balanced blade embellished with fine engraving.

His possession of it offended a young lord, Oliver
Haughton, Earl of Mortmain, strolling with his friends.
He was the richest of the fair-haired trio known as the
Midas Men—and not simply for their golden locks. All
three possessed vast wealth, vaster vanity, and a title be-
ginning with the letter *M*. Obviously, neither Millefleurs,
Marshland, nor Mortmain knew of Rafe's connection to
Easton Arms, much less that he had supervised the mak-
ing of the blade himself. Certain a challenge would yield

him the weapon, the Earl goaded Rafe to prove his worth to handle such a prize. Smirking, the young noble wagered a gold brooch set with a fat ruby, worth double the sword's price. His bejeweled friends were adding inducements to the pile, trying to intimidate Rafe with the weight of their disdain and wealth.

"A test, then. If you will, my lord." Smiling, Rafe stripped off his hat and doublet, watching as the other followed suit. Proud of his own skill and prickling with animosity, Rafe did not make the mistake of presuming Mortmain's arrogance proof of incompetence. The Earl was taller though more slender than Rafe, and he could afford fine training.

A slight movement behind the circle drew Rafe's gaze, and he looked over to meet an assessing gaze from pure blue eyes. The stranger measured the Earl with the same precision, then sauntered over to stand beside Rafe. His rich clothes proclaimed a noble heritage, and Mortmain's coterie glared at the newcomer for daring to favor such an obvious inferior. Smiling, the young man unfastened his pearl earring, tossing it onto the grass, followed by his embroidered gloves, and a gold ring set with lapis lazuli, matching the other's bets.

"Sir Gabriel Darren," he said with a slight bow to all, and then with a quirking smile for Rafe alone, "Gabe."

"Raphael Fletcher—Rafe." Unsheathing his blade, he raised it in salute. Then, plucking his knife from its scabbard, Rafe turned to face his opponent. Mortmain flung off his cap and drew sword and dagger, his indolent demeanor sharpening as he moved into stance.

"First blood?" Gabriel asked.

The young noble twitched his blade. "By all means, let us be brief." His friends sniggered as if this were the greatest wit.

"No," Rafe said coldly. "Three strikes. We must entertain this gentleman's friends."

Lord Mortmain tossed back his yellow hair. Although the Earl abounded with such decorative gestures, Rafe sensed its artifice was a distraction. When a sudden lunge followed, he quickly parried, and struck in turn. The point of his rapier pricked the other man's shoulder, eliciting a hiss of outrage. A trickle of blood stained the fine linen.

They engaged their blades again, steel rasping against steel. Still warranting Rafe's strike no more than luck, nonetheless his opponent was cautious, not wanting another nick of humiliation. Rafe gave ground briefly, parrying and retreating, coaxing his opponent's vanity as he took measure of his expertise. Mortmain was good, but not excellent. His tutor had permitted him to think otherwise, probably because the Earl preferred having his pride coddled to having his proficiency increased. Confident once more, Mortmain attacked with a flurry of fancy tricks. Rafe countered every one and deftly sent the point to the other shoulder, drawing forth a twin rivulet of blood.

"Twice," Sir Gabriel announced.

Ignoring the gasp of Mortmain's friends, Rafe attacked. He lunged forward again, and again, his aggressive thrusts driving his opponent back, ending with Mortmain's back pressed to a tree and Rafe's blade pressed to his breastbone.

"Thrice," Gabriel enunciated with delicious satisfaction.

"Drop your sword, my lord," Rafe told him. There was a moment's hesitation, and then the sword fell from the Earl's hand.

"You should not have won. You are nobody," Lord Mortmain hissed, livid as if he'd caught Rafe cheating.

"I am the man who bested you, my lord," Rafe answered. "And so one better than nobody."

If he had not just lost the duel, the Earl might have challenged him again for his insolence. As it was, he snatched his discarded doublet and stalked off, his friends following in petulant silence.

Rafe turned to Gabriel. They regarded each other in silence, savoring the victory. "An old enemy?" Rafe asked.

"A new one. Freshly minted," Gabe answered, and glancing after Lord Mortmain's retreating back, added with a shrug, "Ha'penny."

Laughing, Rafe scooped up the winnings and held the pile out to Gabriel Darren. "We must share this. What will you have?"

Gabriel shook his head, smiling as he gathered up his own things. "Your skill, your prize."

"I laid but one wager, and you should have some profit for your risk."

"I saw no risk." Gabe smiled.

The ruby brooch was the richest trophy. Rafe plucked it out. "Take this—a memento."

"An exchange of tokens rather," Gabriel suggested. He took the ring he'd wagered, deep blue lapis, and offered

it, tilting his chin to indicate the enameled brooch in
Rafe's hat, lying with his doublet. The enameled dragon,
small but ferocious, held in its claws a lump of amber.
Within the amber a tiny insect lay embedded like a tiny
homunculus. It was an ornament of roughly equal value
to the lapis ring. To Rafe the brooch was worth a great
deal, for it had belonged to his father. But the affinity
Rafe shared with this man seemed of great value as well.
Certain of the rightness of the gesture, Rafe knelt and
unfastened it from the felt. Standing, he made the trade,
sliding the ring on his finger to seal the pledge of friendship as Gabe pinned the brooch to his own hat.

To celebrate, Gabriel took him to the theatre. Rafe
had not been since his parents died, and never to one
housed in a building as marvelous as Burbage's new
building, the Theatre—the first of its kind. Filled with
shame and delight, tender nostalgia and vivid excitement, he watched as the play unfolded. This was the
other, the secret reason he had lusted to come to London,
the same reason his grandparents had feared. A decade of
their devout, uncompromising pressure had reshaped
him, but not demolished this core. Sitting in a box with
Gabriel, Rafe ate apples and drank clary, the rich wine
sweet with honey and spiced with ginger and pepper. But
he needed no wine to give sight and sound vibrance, to
give taste brighter flavor. He was intoxicated with happiness, with freedom.

Rebellion, long smothered by gratitude, rose against
the constraints of his future, and for a time Rafe wondered if he might not carve a life for himself in London.

Then, in the midst of the city's bounty and brutality, he would feel a sweeping homesickness for the wilder landscape of Exeter and the enveloping affection of his family, simple and wholesome as bread. His grandfather sensed his conflict and chose to blame Gabriel, but his anger only alienated Rafe more. Then his grandmother had fallen gravely ill, so Rafe had gone home, first to tend to her, then to comfort his grandfather after she died. Shared grief mended raveled affection, and need bound him close to his family, closer still when his aunt and uncle were slain by highwaymen and his cousin came to live with them. After their time of mourning was past, his grandfather had urged Rafe work on the development of the snaphances. Even though Peter was heir to the business, Rafe had both the talent and fascination for it, a place within it. And his grandfather needed them both.

But the longer Rafe stayed, the smaller and tighter that world had pressed, and infrequent trips to London glowed with promise of a richer life. Peter gained in skill and maturity, so Rafe felt his cousin's help alone might suffice. Then the war in the Netherlands escalated. Rafe thought he would have joined the fight for freedom even had he lived in London, but the war let him escape Exeter with his grandfather's blessing.

He had never had to face the choice of returning or not.

With a soft bump the wherry landed at the Southwark embankment. Rafe paid the boatman his sixpence fare and tuppence tip, then headed into the Liberty of the Clink. It had been his grandfather's greatest fear that he would become an actor. Rafe wondered if spying were so very different, playing a role in the theatre of life.

The Swifts' townhouse came into view, flares burning at the gate and candles at the windows. Rafe felt a sudden hot buzz of excitement swarming through his blood, as if he readied for a duel. Today he had met with the Queen of England. Tomorrow he would go adventuring with the Queen of the Clink.

14

S ilver?" The urgent whisper followed the raps.

He opened the door, irritation edged with a twinge of fear. "What is so important that you summon me in the middle of the night?"

"There is a new piece moving across the chessboard. I do not like it." Topaz paced the room. He had come in a hurry, Silver decided, not bothering with his commoner's disguise. Beneath the cape, Topaz wore saffron velvet, a lace ruff, perfumed gloves.

"Who is the piece and what is its value?"

Topaz turned to face him. Light from the candle shimmered fitfully in the glossy yellow hair. Under the peaked brows, golden brown eyes reflected the flame in yellow facets. Silver had always thought the codename suited the man. "Two days ago, George Easton's grandson was observed at court. Whether he is a wandering pawn or a charging knight remains to be discovered."

"Why wasn't he arrested with the others?"

"I don't know why not," Topaz snapped. "Defective or sabotaged, the ruin of those guns should have ruined the family. I do know Fletcher was walking free and in peculiar company. He spoke with Lady Claire Darren, though that is to be expected—"

Silver broke in impatiently. "Expected? What connection has he with the Darrens?"

"Gabriel Darren was his closest friend at the Inns of Court. A decade ago they were inseparable." His voice coiled with scorn. "An earl's son cavorting with merchant's get."

"Indeed, what could they have in common?" Silver gave Topaz a mocking smile. Faith had brought the Earl of Mortmain far lower than friendship, down to the gutter.

"Aside from a taste for wenches, extraordinary skill with weapons," Topaz answered literally.

"If he was Darren's friend, an offer of sympathy is not remarkable."

"He was accompanied by Sir Nigel Burne, a man too often closeted with Walsingham. That is worth remarking."

Silver liked this news even less.

Reaching into his purse, Topaz withdrew an object, opening his palm to display the small brooch—a dragon clasping a round of amber. "You remember this?"

Silver looked down on the jewel. A paltry thing. He nudged it with a finger ringed with a huge topaz surrounded by diamonds and pearls. It amused him to wear such gems lately, and irritated his confederate. "Yes, I remember. You found the brooch but lost Darren."

"The wound was mortal. He could not have lived long," Topaz contended.

"Not long enough to reveal what he learned, or you would be in the Tower."

"Demonstrably, I am not," Topaz rounded.

Silver picked up the thread. "What of the brooch?"

"I first saw it a decade ago, pinned to Fletcher's hat."

"Fletcher?" Silver tensed, though his voice stayed even.

"Raphael Fletcher," Topaz said. "George Easton's grandson."

Silver nodded, concealing his shock. He was alarmed that Fletcher had invaded his world. But the information was a more valuable jewel than the dragon brooch, and he would pay in kind. "The piece proves to be a knight. He has invaded the Clink."

"What?"

Silver told him what he knew.

"A dangerous piece," Topaz said. "And far too close. Kill him."

"If he knew about the snaphances, Walsingham's kennel would be unleashed already."

Topaz considered. "If he wants to clear his family, he may dislike what he learns."

"We want time to put all the elements of the plan in place." Time for Silver to decide if he should dispense with Topaz as well as Rafe Fletcher. He wondered what other surprises Topaz might disclose. "You know Fletcher? You bear some sort of grudge?"

"I told Agate to find a supply of Easton Arms—they are the best. Repaying Fletcher's past impertinence is sauce to the meat."

"For the moment Fletcher may serve us better alive than dead." Silver held out his hand. "Give me the brooch."

"Why?" Topaz closed his hand over the brooch.

"It is a tiny weapon, but perhaps I can devise some use for it," Silver said. Topaz handed the trophy over reluctantly. Silver slipped the brooch into his purse.

"When will you bring the poison?" Topaz' voice quickened with impatience.

"Soon."

"The apothecary should be dispensed with as well," Topaz stated.

"My domain, Topaz, my judgment."

"I will not trust my fate to a heretic."

Silver did not want to trust his to a fanatic. "You make no use of Protestants? I am to believe a Catholic will be let close enough to the Queen to administer the poison?"

A secret Catholic perhaps? But no, he had hit the mark, for Topaz glared at him. "I have but one Protestant ally."

"And why should I trust your one Protestant ally with my life, Topaz?" Silver countered.

Topaz hesitated, but decided to confide in him. "Because she has a secret lover who is soon to be executed."

"Anthony Babington?" Silver asked.

"No. Babington was his friend, and came begging help at his door. Out of pity he gave the fugitive bread and water, nothing more—but it was enough to earn him the sentence of traitor. Though he had no part in that conspiracy, he will suffer the same fate as the others. They are to be hanged but taken down alive. Their bowels will be drawn out and burned before their eyes, their privy parts cut off, and their bodies quartered."

Silver might attend death sports, but he had no plan to provide such entertainment himself. For once he might forego the amusement. "Unless Elizabeth dies first, and the Queen of Scots grants their pardon?"

"Exactly. Do not fear. She is resolute," Topaz told him.

"So you say. I can only take your word for it, as you must mine."

"Such an ally we can trust. But the apothecary is no ally. And Fletcher is an enemy."

"Fletcher will be dispensed with. In time."

Suddenly, Topaz laughed. "You must test the poison. What better victims could you choose?"

Silver smiled in answer. "I have already considered that very question."

15

*S*hading her eyes, Vivian glanced up at the motley-hued pennants snapping in the breeze. Blue sky arched overhead. The sun shone bright as a king's ransom, and white clouds swarmed like roving bands of thieves. A perfect day for the fair, with the breeze blowing the fresh scent of the fields through the pungent odors emanating from the booths and pens around them, and the rooftops of London crisply outlined to the south. Rafe stood close beside her, surveying the colorful chaos. Filled with zesty anticipation, she smiled at him, then lifted the hem of her vermillion damask and led the way among the booths, tents, and animal pens clustered around the ancient church. She halted at a crossways, surveying the multitude of possibilities. Nick's birthday was close at hand. He'd asked for scent, and Viv was determined to add another gift or two.

"You've never been to St. Bartholomew's before?" she asked as Rafe looked about them curiously. It was a national holiday, and the greatest fair in England—different from all the others, for here the merchants were Londoners, the visitors from far and wide.

"Once or twice—with old friends," he answered.

An old friend or an old lover? Viv wondered, hearing the slight catch in his voice. The twinge of jealousy was small but sharp as a cat's claw. She waited for Rafe to say more, but his gaze moved restlessly over the crowd. When he spoke it was a question. "Is Rivett likely to be at the fair?"

"Probably," Viv answered curtly, closing off in turn. This morning was not for business. Too many things were vexing her: Nicholas and his obsession with Rosy; the continuing mystery of Chettle's death; Rivett and his insatiable appetite for power. She laid a hand on Rafe's arm, a light touch to soothe the sting of her words. She wanted to lose herself in the adventure of the fair, submerge herself in its scents, its sounds, its tastes. She wanted to savor the pleasure of her handsome lover beside her, the heat of his body, warm as sunshine. She wanted to delight in the quickening of her heartbeat when his gaze sought hers. Later she would consider her problems with a clear mind.

"Probably? Then I shall probably keep a keen eye," Rafe said.

His tone was tart, but his vigilance was commendable, so she smiled and added, "The fair is neutral ground. There are nips and foists from both London and Southwark here. There will be independents about, too, hoping to filch their fortune."

"So much danger all around?" Rafe stepped closer. His voiced deepened, low and intimate now, sending a humming reverberation through her blood. "I had best guard you very closely."

"Little danger," Viv murmured, caressing his chest lightly, the velvety mockado of his livery teasing her fingertips. Only the rankest beginner would dare try to steal from her. And a rank beginner would find his fingers cut before her purse. "More's the pity. I like being in danger with you."

His eyes flashed in answer, and for an instant she was back in the alley off the Fringes, arms about his neck, sharing a ferocious kiss. She moved closer, feeling the heat of his body radiating against her—heat too intense for what was possible now. Viv drew a deep breath. "Who will guard me from you?"

"That is the one thing I cannot do," he answered.

"And who will guard you from me?" she teased, her blood still thrumming wildly, sweetly.

"I fear there is no safety for me, either," he said softly. His eyes darkened, desire smoked with a pain and yearning that moved her.

Viv felt the fair fading to a blur, the urge to kiss him, to ravish him, rising. She drew another long breath, backed away slowly. "What shall we do?" she bantered.

The gleam in his eyes told her what he wanted. She shook her head. "Later," she said, though her eyes told him she wanted him now. She gestured around them. "What else?"

Rafe heaved a theatrical sigh, then looked about them. He pointed out an open air theatre at the far end of the aisle. Viv shook her head. She was far too restless to stand for a long play just now. She nodded to the freak show that promised such multitudinous wonders as a two-headed sheep, a homunculus in a bottle, a mermaid, a camel, and a pineapple.

"I've never seen a pineapple," he said, mock serious, as if mermaids were commonplace.

Down another aisle, the throng parted to show a group of children and adults gathered about a painted and curtained booth. "There's a motion!" Viv exclaimed. She darted down the aisle. She squeezed through to a good vantage point, and he stepped up close behind her. Together they laughed aloud as two hand puppets pounded each other with gleeful abandon. Rafe pressed closer as they watched the show, the solid muscle of his body sweet against her back. She rubbed against him slowly, a teasing dance of hips and thighs, hoping her movement stirred him. When the performance finished, he looked flushed and Viv felt giddy with laughter and desire.

"Babies! Buy my babies!" A woman's voice boomed through the crowd. "Fresh baked gingerbread babies, still warm!"

Viv discovered she was starving. Clasping Rafe's hand, she pulled him across the aisle to the source of the voice. "This is Maud," she said, introducing him to the buxom woman who glowed as toasty gold as one of her gingerbread dolls. "She bakes the best Bartholomew's babies at the fair."

"That I do, Mistress Vivian," Maud replied proudly. "The sweetest, spiciest, crustiest best in all England."

"Give us two—those two." Viv pointed unerringly to the largest.

"As if I didn't know, my lady." Maud handed over the two gingerbread dolls.

"Beware!" Bible clutched to his chest, the preacher seemed to appear from nowhere. The young man looked no better than a Tom O' Bedlam. His countenance was almost childish, with its small, soft mouth and huge brown eyes. But masses of long brown hair and beard hung in greasy snarls about his dirt-streaked face, and the whites of his eyes were bloodshot, his gaze wild. Patched clothes flapped loosely about his limbs.

"Be off with you, brimstone-breath!" Maud shooed him with her hand.

Ignoring her, the preacher addressed Viv and Rafe. "Beware. Those are the Devil's wares you buy."

"What do you want?" Rafe growled from behind her. Vivian felt a ripple of pleasure as Rafe move protectively closer. The preacher presented no threat she could not handle herself, but she gave Rafe a little nudge with her shoulder, savoring his presence.

"Want? What do I want?" The preacher's clarion cry sank to a whisper. "I want to bring you the Master's word, if you will hear it. Warnings and omens." The man might be mad, but Vivian sensed he was enjoying himself immensely. She found him almost as funny as the puppet show. She broke off the foot of the gingerbread doll and bit into it, wondering what he would do next.

The preacher turned from Rafe to her, eyes gleaming. "Take care, sinner. Every bite is a taste of hell."

"A taste of hell, you say?" Hovering between amusement and irritation, Vivian carefully examined the nibbled foot, then regarded the intruder mockingly. "I see no signs of scorching." The preacher's eyes grew wide as she ate it up. "Honey, nutmeg, and ginger I can taste, but not a hint of sulfur. I'd call them a taste of heaven."

"Blasphemy," the preacher breathed, caressing the word like a lover. "The fires of hell will rise and consume you."

"Not for such a sweet consummation, surely?" Breaking off the other foot, she popped it into Rafe's mouth. He swallowed the treat, gave her a quick glance, then returned his gaze to the preacher. He seemed far more concerned than she did, one hand tense on his sword hilt, the other holding his crumbling gingerbread doll. Viv smiled. "You should try one, preacher. It's sure to sweeten your disposition."

"I'll not poison my soul with such sinful excess."

Maud was livid. "You spindle-shanked, sorrow-farting, mammering piss-prophet—I'll have you up before the Pie-Power Court for driving off my business!"

Viv thought the silly preacher would likely love to hold sway before the fair's official court.

"Far more foul than fair," the preacher proclaimed.

"I fear 'tis you fouling our nostrils," Viv sniffed.

"You do not fear enough!" The preacher turned on Vivian, seething with his own passions. "Confess your sins, harlot, or be buried in the foul stench of hell."

Humor flipped to anger, and Viv braced herself. One step closer and her knee would give the preacher a taste of hell on earth. Then Rafe surged past her, grabbing fistfuls of the man's jacket, dragging him up onto his toes.

"Submit to your Master," the preacher exclaimed, "and to me his messenger."

"I submit to no one," Rafe snarled, pushing him back through the crowd. The throng closed around them, the disturbance too minor to interest more than a few. Few were taller than Rafe, and Viv could follow the back of his head as he dispensed with the bothersome preacher. A moment later he returned, brushing dust and gingerbread from his hands, anger still simmering in his eyes. Glancing at them, he muttered, "The preacher proved not so eager for martyrdom after all."

Vivian regarded Rafe with interest. He had been protective of her, certainly, and perhaps still felt he must prove his usefulness. She'd needed no help dispensing with such a buzzing gadfly. Rafe had told her his grandfather had punished him with preaching as well as whip strokes. Perhaps that was why the gadfly had incensed him so.

"Well, sir, you've trounced that lily-livered lunatic." Maud glowed with pleasure. "He'll find a nice cozy hole to hide in."

"We'll see no more of him," Rafe said, smiling a bit. "I've given him a boot hard enough to send him back to his Master."

Maud generously bestowed a second gingerbread baby on each of them, then strolled off through the crowds. "Babies! Buy my gingerbread babies! Heavenly sweet babies!"

Vivian laughed. They ate some of the gingerbread, and tucked the rest into their purses. Viv looked around, then pointed over a row. "I see something to take the stench of the preacher away," she said. Rafe followed her

to a booth well-stocked with glass vials of scent, poman-
ders, and potpourri. Subtly obsequious, the perfumer
hurried to attend her. Vivian conferred with the merchant, aware of Rafe beside her, scanning the crowd restlessly. The incident with the preacher had honed his
edge.

"This is a great favorite at court," the merchant suggested, offering a glass vial.

She inhaled and wrinkled her nose. "Too cloying."

Viv sniffed at others, daubing one or two on her hand
for Rafe's approval or rejection. She set aside a scent of
civet and spicy stock gilliflowers for Nick's gift, and a mix
of marjoram, lemon, and mint for Izzy. Finally Viv found
one she thought would suit Rafe. "What is the blend?"

"A bold yet subtle mingling, my lady." The perfumer
spoke in hushed tones. "Rare woods from the East.
Ambergris for warmth—and rich musk to deepen the
tone."

She offered it to Rafe. "What do you think?"

"I think I have a headache from sniffing so many
scents," Rafe responded.

"Then I shall have to choose for you."

"Do, for I shall only wear it for you."

"No gentleman goes without scent," she scolded him,
though the pure male fragrance of his skin was exhilarating.

"Puritan gentlemen do."

"You are no Puritan." She took his hand. An invisible
spark leapt between them at the touch, and his hand
tightened on hers.

"Apparently not," he said, his voice low and rough.

Smiling, her nerves tingling, Vivian daubed the scent on the back of his hand and breathed the warm, lush aroma. "Perfect."

Vivian gestured to her choices, and waited while the booth keeper wrapped the three vials. Rafe moved closer, pitching his voice low as he asked, "What of Chettle? Any news?"

Vivian fought a surge of annoyance. The fair had helped her escape such concerns, exactly as she wished. Now Rafe set her thoughts swarming like hornets. The mystery surrounding Chettle and his death was deepening rather than clearing. As a matter of course, she had investigated the customs official when they started business. Then his life had seemed ordinary in the extreme, pinched and solitary. No family. No compelling vices. Now that he had disappeared, the vacuum around him seemed ominous.

"Nothing much," she said tersely, angry at how little they actually knew. Rafe nodded, but his face closed off. Well, she had shut him out again. "Too little information. That is the problem."

"Do you think—" he began.

She pressed her fingers to his lips, feeling the full curve of his lower lip, the warmth of his breath. "No business now. We're at the fair."

Rafe nodded again, and she could feel him subduing his impatience. He was curious, and ambitious, eager to climb in the organization. Still, he was expecting too much too soon. Only last night, Nick had warned her against revealing too much to him. But if she would not yield in the greater thing, she could give way in the smaller. No doubt Rafe was tired of buying fripperies. "What would you like to do?"

His gaze told her he wanted to talk, to learn, but he considered for a moment, then said, "Find a fencing match if there is one—or wrestling. Perhaps I will take a match myself."

"The preacher was too weak to pummel properly?"

He gave a little snort of laughter. "Yes. I find I have an urge to manhandle someone."

"I should like to watch you wrestle," Viv murmured. She imagined him stripped, his skin flushed with exertion, sweat trickling over the broad planes of his chest. She could almost taste a salty droplet on her tongue. The image aroused a delicious pulse between her thighs.

He gave her a quick glance, a slight flush patching his cheeks, as if he could read her thoughts. From the first day she had felt the link between them, as if they were stitched with invisible threads of flame.

"Would you?" he asked, the question filled with a thousand intimate touches.

"Yes," she said again. "I would."

They began to amble toward the green, making their way past the thicket of booths and toward the pens of the horse-coursers. Brightly colored ribbons braided the manes of the steeds for sale. The fair was known for fine horseflesh—and not so fine, tricked up to fool. Viv prided herself on knowing the difference. "Let's come back after we've watched the wrestling," she suggested.

"I've a mind to buy a new mount for Nick's birthday, if I can find a worthy one."

"When is that?"

"Two days from now." She had a magnificent chess set for him already, and the new scent, but she wanted something more.

They strolled beside the roped pens, commenting on the horses they passed. Vivian paused to look at a promising chestnut, but even as she speculated on its merits, the horse-courser came and removed the red ribbon from its mane. Perhaps she had made the prospective buyer nervous and helped close the sale.

When Viv turned around, she saw Rafe standing across the aisle outside another pen, stroking the muzzle of one of the ugliest horses she had ever seen, a massive brute of mottled gray. Dapples were highly valued, but this animal would not fetch a high price. Rafe offered it a bit of gingerbread on his palm, and the beast lipped it eagerly. Glancing back, Rafe shrugged at her questioning look, then slipped under the rope and began to canvass the horses within, moving from the gray gelding to a sorrel, then on to a handsome bay. He gave the animal a cursory examination, then beckoned to the horse-courser and began to haggle.

Surprise streaked through Vivian. Rafe had said nothing of wanting to buy a horse. She did not know this courser, and did not like the look of him, stout, pink, and greasy as a ham. Following Rafe under the rope, she paused to examine the pretty little sorrel. The mare pranced when Viv patted its rump and she suspected the horse had been beaten to make it step lightly and run swiftly at the tap of a whip. It was a common practice, but her anger flared anyway. Beating such beautiful animals infuriated her. Walking over to Rafe, Viv slid her arm through his. He followed with obvious reluctance as she drew him away from the courser. "Don't buy from this man. If you must have a steed, let me take you to a courser who's trustworthy."

She nodded toward the other pens, but Rafe shook his head. "Have a look at the bay. I think you'll find it's sound."

Vivian frowned, disliking that he did not heed her. Garnet had been like that sometimes, deliberately ignoring good advice because it came from a woman. "It's likely besieged with glanders, and had a nose full of mustard and garlic juice to clean out the filth."

"I see no evidence of that. It's a young animal, sound limbs and teeth. Spirited."

"Whipped to liveliness like the sorrel," she countered. Catching wind of their argument, the courser eyed her nervously. Viv frowned at him to keep his distance.

"I know the tricks," Rafe said impatiently. "It is not the first time I've been to a horse fair. Look for yourself."

Prickled, Vivian stalked away from him and began to examine the bay, taking far more care than Rafe had done. At first it shied at her touch, but when she fed it some gingerbread, it quieted and let her stroke it. Skittish then, but still a handsome mount. She wondered where the courser had stolen it.

Still annoyed that Rafe had chosen to ignore her advice, Viv eavesdropped on his haggling. Prices bounced back and forth for a time, till Rafe and the horse-courser came to a standstill, each refusing to budge. The amount the man asked was high, but not unreasonable. The courser was unlikely to sell it for less, so early in the fair. Perhaps Rafe's purse was too light? Viv did not know how much he had spent on new garments. She had enough to purchase any animal at the fair. Despite her annoyance, she was willing to buy him one—

Suspicion chilled her. Was all his bargaining a sham to wheedle more money for the bay? Rafe did not seem so greedy, but he was clever enough to manipulate her that way. Clever enough to try anyway, if he was getting a taste for easy living. Instead of offering, she said nothing, simply folded her arms and waited. But Rafe made no effort to woo money from her purse. Unbelievably, he returned to the dappled gelding she'd seen him stroking earlier, and began bargaining for it. Was this a different ploy? She decided to test him. The price of the better horse would be cheap if she found Fletcher thought to cozen her. Then he would pay dearly.

She approached the two men, taking Rafe's arm and leading him back a few steps. She kept her voice low, so the courser would not hear. "The dapple is an hideous creature. Let me buy you the bay."

"Buy the bay for Nicholas," Rafe answered her sharply. "I like the gray."

Not a trick, then. An odd stubborn look had settled onto his features. Rafe fully intended to buy the monster. What Vivian could not fathom was why. However mixed his past reactions, they were easy enough to comprehend.

Fletcher was new to the rogues' world. She understood the defiance and bravado with which he'd faced her in the courtyard. She understood the anger he'd shown when she commanded him to strip, his defiance mingled with lust and the hint of innocence that clung to him like the scent of fresh grass. Now his response made no sense, unless he simply rebelled against her authority, as Garrin Garnet had.

"Why?" she queried, irritation sharpening her voice. "I doubt there's an uglier horse at the fair."

"There are more ways to measure worth than looks," Rafe replied with equal sharpness. He went back to the gray, toying with the yellow ribbon in its mane.

Was his pride ruffled? Did he feel too much her plaything, dressed in fancy livery and daubed with perfume? She had refused to answer his questions earlier. Now she doubted his integrity when he was in earnest. Feeling a twinge of guilt, Viv softened her tone a fraction. "What worth does this creature possess?"

"It's a powerful animal, sweet-tempered and intelligent."

"Having a taste for gingerbread does not make the beast sweet. It has yet to bite you, but that may be a sign of its stupidity." She regarded the gray critically. "Massive—you should ride a strong mount—but we can find another of equal power. Its head is disproportionate to its size."

His mulish look increased. "Have you never taken a sudden fancy to an animal?" He flushed a little at his careless phrasing. Turning, he scratched the big dapple between the ears. It nickered and rubbed his nose against his thigh.

"Oh ye . . . if he's handsome and spirited," Viv smiled, hoping to tease him.

"Are you sure it's spirit you want?"

"If it's coupled with intelligence," she shot back. "I thought you valued that as well."

He drew a sharp breath. "So I do. Power is dangerous without it."

"Perhaps a sweet temper is most valuable of all then." He laughed at that, a small victory. Viv pursued her main objective. "We are agreed—anyone can have such a fancy. But the gray was not your first choice . . . it was the bay you bargained for."

"Subterfuge?" Now he was the one smiling, teasing, cajoling. "A deliberate ploy?"

Viv bristled with suspicion, but of what she didn't know. She could not believe he had only distracted the horse-courser to get a better price on the gray. The man would be eager to sell it. "I want to see you mounted on a handsome beast. I will buy the bay."

The smile disappeared. "For yourself, if you will. For your brother. Not for me."

They glared at each other. Viv now doubted there was a reason for Rafe's obstinacy. He was rebelling because it was his nature, no more. Sensing the loss of a sale, the horse-courser suddenly offered a lower price for the dapple. Swiftly, Rafe turned and agreed. A hot burst of anger flared through Vivian.

"It is my money buying it." The instant she snapped the words, Viv knew they were a mistake, and a petty one. She did not like to be thwarted, but the money had been a gift.

"Yours?" Rafe's eyes went cold. He tugged loose the purse from his belt. His voice was low, a growling whisper pitched only to her ears. "A dozen others owned it before Maggot stole it from them. It went to him, to you, to me—and now back to you again."

"No." She shook her head, angry that she had spoken foolishly, angry at his cutting scorn. "Keep it. Buy what you please."

She thought for a moment he would fling the purse at her feet, but finally he tossed it once in the air, then closed it tight in his fist. His eyes, his voice, were adamant. "This horse pleases me. So I will buy him."

He turned and counted out the money for the dapple. Still fuming, Vivian bought the bay for Nick. She wanted to return home, and the new mounts were the quickest way. Aware of the discord, the courser sold saddles and bridles with little haggling. Mounting the bay, Viv gave a sharp tilt of her chin, gesturing Rafe to follow her back to Southwark.

❧

"Keep the horses saddled," Viv said to the groom, as they dismounted.

Rafe regarded her warily.

"I thought we might take our new mounts a ride in the country," she told him with feigned casualness. She intended to test their paces on the open roads. Rafe would admit yet he'd been a fool to buy the gray.

"If you wish," he said. He gestured to his fancy livery and she nodded that he could change.

"Wait in the upstairs hallway when you are done." She watched his retreating back as he headed for the guards' quarters. She looked down at her own heavy skirts, and decided they were too awkward.

"Resaddle the bay," she told the groom. "I'll ride astride."

Upstairs in her chamber, Viv summoned Joan to help her out of the damask and into a shirt of scarlet silk and riding breeches and doublet of embroidered leather. Joan's quiet presence was calming. By the time she was dressed, Viv's anger had simmered down, and she felt foolish once again. The bed looked tempting, the afternoon sun bathing the coverlet in warmth and light. Why not summon Rafe? It would be as easy to work off this snarl of energy amid the pillows as in a breakneck ride through the countryside. Vivian's pulse quickened at the thought.

"You're free to leave, Joan. Take the day to visit the fair," Viv said.

Joan's smile warmed her severe features. "It's a good day for it, to be sure."

"Buy a present for Smoke—and a shawl for yourself." Viv pressed some silver into her hand. As Joan closed the bedroom door, Viv added, "Send Fletcher in if he's waiting."

Listening, Viv heard the hallway door close as well, then open again a minute later. Smiling, she turned to welcome Rafe. Stepping into the bedroom, he paused, his gaze quickly scanning her attire. His unease was far more fleeting than the first time, but it was enough to make her temper flare. He saw it in her face, for he looked contrite. Too late. She gave him a goading smile and sauntered back the fireplace, leaning against it. The new clock ticked a warning.

"Are we going riding?" he asked.

"I thought I might do my riding here," Viv answered.

"Here?" His voice was guarded, though he knew perfectly well what she meant.

She lifted her brows in question. Rafe's glance dropped for a second, and she knew he was deciding whether or not to comply. All her anger returned in a rush. When she spoke her voice was low, more menacing than seductive. "Take off your clothes."

"No." Rafe stood unmoving, mutiny tautening every lineament.

Viv felt his resistance, like the hard pressure of steel against her will. He closed his eyes, shutting her out, summoning challenge or capitulation. On the mantle each tick of the clock crackled in the silence. The atmosphere bristled with static, boding a black storm.

"Take them off." It was a whisper, but every word was hard and distinct. Vivian knew she was pushing him too far, but she could not stop. All that mattered was that he yield.

"No." Rafe opened his eyes and their gazes locked. Fury pulsed between them, repelling one instant, magnetizing the next.

"Now," she hissed.

"No. Find yourself another mount." He was adamant again, as he'd been at the fair. He would not submit. "My sword arm is for hire. The rest of me is not."

"Who are you to tell me no?" She was in a seething rage—at him and at herself.

"No one," Rafe answered. "No one you will miss."

He turned his back on her and walked out the door.

Viv stared after him, hardly able to believe he'd gone, even as she knew she had pushed him to it. She waited, the clock ticking in relentless mockery as she willed him to return. But he had already defied her will.

"Fool," she whispered furiously, not knowing if she raged at him or at herself. "Fool. Fool!"

His pride would not bend to her. And she would not bend to him. She could not hold power if her knights thought they could rule the Queen of the Clink. She eyed the clock, loathing the rational chiding of its measured ticks. A breeze rippled over her, and she shivered despite its warmth. The bed hangings swayed, as if asking to be ripped from their posts. Her hands curled and uncurled on hot pulses of anger. Wreaking havoc was tempting, but surrendering to the impulse seemed to acknowledge defeat.

Pay him off and have done with it!

Vivian stalked from the room.

16

*H*ardly able to separate instinct from rage, Rafe moved swiftly along the corridor, down the stairs, through the townhouse, and out the back door to the guards' quarters. The room was empty. Quickly he stripped off the hated silken livery and tossed it onto the bed. He pulled on his own leather training gear, stuffed his belongings into his pack. No one came to stop him. Why should they? *Why should she?* Slinging the pack over his shoulder, Rafe stalked to the doorway, then paused, waiting, his heart thudding like an angry fist. He had defied her because he must. Part of him had hoped defiance would draw her where submission would not. But he'd been wrong. She did not need his strength to match her own. She did not need him at all. There were a hundred handsome rogues who would be happy to take his place.

He had enjoyed bedding her too much, letting his emotions twine with the lust he should have controlled, or manipulated to serve his purpose. Perversely, Viv had seemed more friend than enemy, till her need to dominate him had seared away the camaraderie that linked them. But this show of pride might cost his family their lives. For their sake he should have played out the game. If he had yielded to her demand he could have hated her, despised her. And he knew, bone deep, that she would despise him, too. If he had gone to her bed then, he would never have been more than her whore. When she dismissed him, it would not be back to the ranks of her guards, but back to the streets, with a whore's payment to weight his purse.

Swearing under his breath, Rafe made his way to the stable. Both Atlas and Nimble were there, saddled and waiting. The dapple turned to greet him but his cousin's nervous bay, far more elegant but not half as bright, ignored him as usual. He stroked Atlas' flank affectionately. Most likely the horses had been stolen after his grandfather and cousin were arrested. Perhaps they had even been confiscated and sold to the horse-courser. Theft, either way. Rafe would have bought them both if he could, but he would not risk Atlas being sold to someone too stupid to appreciate him. The gray was far more horse than he looked, faster than his massive bones suggested, and smarter than any horse Rafe had ever known.

The gelding turned and nuzzled his hip, snuffling for treats in his purse. Atlas was ugly, but his ugliness had endeared him to Rafe. His first owner had beaten him half to death, permanently disfiguring his head. Tears suddenly prickled his eyes as Rafe remembered how his grandfather had stayed up with him, nursing the battered, skeletal colt back from the edge of starvation. His grandfather's tenderness showed itself in protecting the weak. Rafe knew he'd been foolish to cross Vivian, but abandoning the dapple would have been like abandoning his family.

It had been a shock to see the horses at the fair—a second stunning blow following Marlowe's bizarre appearance as the preacher. Rafe had been uncertain if Marlowe brought news of Rafe's family, important intelligence, or was only there to show Rafe that Burne was keeping watch on his watchers. He played out the charade, but all Marlowe had told him was that Burne wanted to meet three days hence at the Tilted Jug. He thought for a moment that Marlowe might whisper more, but after a hesitation the intelligencer had only shrugged. Marlowe had scowled, then winked when Rafe's last, frustrated shove had landed the counterfeit preacher on his buttocks.

Rafe led Atlas outside. Viv had responded after all, for Smoke Warren met him in the courtyard. The captain said nothing, only handed over a purse of gold. Rafe tossed it in his hand, feeling the hefty weight of the coins. Smoke's somber gaze did not waver when Rafe threw it back. "Keep it. The price is too high."

"Perhaps you overvalue your worth," Smoke said, though his voice was so neutral it was more suggestion than insult.

"Perhaps so. But I will put no price on what she wants of me." Rafe drew a breath, stroking Atlas' neck. "I have no more than I brought with me, except for the horse. I guarded her well when Garnet attacked. The gray is worth that."

"I have no quarrel with that," Smoke answered. He gave the horse a frown, not understanding its worth any more than Vivian had, but Rafe saw there would be no quarrel, no effort to stop him. Instinct had always served

Rafe as well as reason, but this risk had recoiled against him. He mounted and rode out the guard house gate, moving through the rich residential streets of Southwark and out to the great road. The hammering fist of his heart slowed, hardening to a lead weight in his chest. He headed west, seeking the quiet of the countryside to clear his mind. For half an hour, he rode quickly, steadily, past the outlying inns and into the green rolling hills splashed with oak trees. He tried to think of nothing but the wind moving over his body, the August sun hot on his back, the steady rhythm of Atlas' big hooves on the road.

The heat of her hand moving between his thighs . . . intimate . . . knowing . . .

Cursing, Rafe drew rein. That was over. He had thrown it away, and with it his best chance to save his family and discover Gabriel's killer.

He forced himself to consider his next move. His grandfather and cousin were still in danger, and he must do something to save them. Walsingham and Burne had agreed with him that Rivett was their likeliest target. Rafe must return to London and try to maneuver his way into Rivett's organization. Would Viv send someone to skewer his liver if he dared go to work for her enemy? He had believed her threat against Garnet. If Rafe dared her wrath, would Rivett hire him, if only to antagonize Viv? Rafe did not care about the danger. Neither did he want to waste his time in profligate stupidity. Rafe would be distrusted as a possible spy for the Swifts. He could not imagine inveigling any secrets from Rivett—he still suspected he could gather more intelligence about Smelly

Jakes from Vivian. No information would be divulged by Rivett. Rafe would be watched too closely to discover it on his own, and killed the first moment he looked suspicious.

He thought of Rivett's dark eyes, cold as metal—and then of Viv's warm brown ones, alight with laughter and desire.

Too late. There was a strange hollow in his gut knowing he would not see her in the morning, would not bed her again. Rafe drew a harsh breath. What was stopping him from returning and begging Vivian's forgiveness? Pardon, not punishment, might await him if he went to her, and surely his pride was worth the risk? If she threw him out again, he could still try to trap Rivett. But the hollowness inside him only grew deeper, blacker. He had begun to win her confidence, but Rafe could not imagine Vivian confiding her secrets to someone no better than a slave.

He must formulate a scheme, manipulate Rivett into hiring him.

But it was Vivian's face burning in his mind's eye as he turned Atlas around and faced toward London.

The lead weight of his heart surged to life, pumping hot blood through his veins. On the crest of the nearest hill, within sight but not hearing, he saw a lone rider. He stared at the distant figure, unable to see anything but the silhouette. When he did not move, the rider galloped down the hill and along the road. He could see now what his heart had told him—it was Viv. She surged past him, then swerved around, reining her horse before him. Rafe met the fierce confrontation of her gaze. He could see the remnants of her fury—at him for leaving, and at herself for following—but she had followed nonetheless.

"You turned." Her triumph was new, glittering bright over the anger. "You were coming back to me."

"Was I?" he replied, not knowing if what she said was truth or lie, but refusing to give her any advantage. He would not return docile and repentant. Yet even to his own ears his defiance sounded like a confession.

"Liar." She laughed harshly. "You were returning."

"You wanted me gone. I left."

"No. I wanted you. And you want me."

"You want to own me," he challenged. "No one owns me. No one."

For a moment Viv only stared at him, seething with anger and desire. With a quick movement, she swerved her horse off the road, riding not back to London, but toward the hills. He nudged his mount to follow. Had she come to summon him back, or only to have him one more time? For the moment, Rafe did not care. She had come after him. Victory pulsed through him, a hot, bright rush from heart and loins. They rode swiftly through an open field thickly stalked with sunflowers, their great dark eyes fringed with gold. Hills swelled around them, and she led him around slopes crested with oak and yew till they came to a shaded grove by a narrow tributary of the Thames. It was cooler here, the breeze flowing over the water breathing moisture into the air. Berry bushes crowded the banks on one side, a stand of old willows graced the other, trailing their long withes into the river.

Viv dismounted beneath the trees, and Rafe did the same. She was still dressed in her leather breeches and man's shirt. The snug leather gleamed in the sun where it stretched tight over the firm muscles of her legs. Warring impulses did brief battle, and censure lost to the surge of eroticism. The image of her galloping through Southwark in doublet and breeches excited him with its daring. Before, he had known her wanton fervor, the giddy delight of her playfulness, the rasping abrasion of her dominance. Now, he felt her rebellion, her defiance, as kin to his own spirit.

Vivian faced him. Desire burned in her eyes, but she squared her shoulders defiantly. "You followed me here."

He was aware of her bristling pride. His own victory was sufficient now. "Yes."

"I don't own this land." She gestured around her, though her gaze held his own.

He did not understand at first, but then he realized she acknowledged herself outside her domain, and Rafe outside her rule.

"Here and now I own no more than you do, a horse, a weapon, the clothes on my back," she said. "Here we are only a man and a woman."

Past and future burned away in the black fire of her eyes. He did not know what would come after this. He did not care. *One more time,* Rafe thought, and for the length of that time nothing else would matter—not her coercion and manipulation, or his own lies. There would be nothing but the truth of their flesh. His breath quickened, his aroused sex shoving rock-hard against his breeches.

"And as for the clothes on my back—" Viv tossed her cap aside and stripped off the closely fitted doublet and breeches. Wanton, she pulled off the shirt and flung it to lie in a blaze of scarlet under the shadows of the trees. She freed the ends of her braided hair and raked her fingers through it, the loosened strands flying about her face, black, gleaming, serpentine. The rich musk of her perfume wove an exotic note into the scents of earth and grass and water. Her dark nipples stood erect as her breasts moved softly against the firmer musculature of her torso and arms, and the dark triangle between her thighs pointed to the hidden secrets of her sex. His body throbbed as he thought of the tight grip of her legs, the hot clasp of that secret flesh.

"You want me," she repeated, her voice rough as a cat's purr, soft as a hiss.

"Yes." He had never wanted anyone so much. He was rigid, aching with need.

She stood naked as a forest nymph—but her elemental wildness was beyond that of any gentle sprite. It belonged to some fierce pagan spirit. Fury and laughter mingled in her eyes, and her disheveled hair glinted with flashes of blue and silver light. She shimmered with the fierce beauty of a feral creature alive in every atom of its being, exquisite in its deadliness. The risk of the game he played in London seemed nothing compared to the danger of confronting her unfettered being. He thought of the maenads who would tear a man apart in their frenzy. He knew Vivian was capable of killing him, but the stab of fear sharpened his arousal to an excruciating pitch.

Desire seized him, a madness, a shivering fever sweeping through his veins. Already panting, gasping for breath, he tore at his clothes, stripping them off and flinging them aside, wild for the touch of her skin against his. Ridding himself of everything, he stood naked before her. Power and vulnerability merged into one.

"You want me," he challenged in turn.

"Yes." Her gaze met his, then traveled down, fastening on his sex.

Rafe moaned as if she touched him. He thought she would lie down, open her legs for him, but she was more unbridled, more ferocious. She ran to him, sprang, so that his arms were suddenly full of her. Strong and slender, her arms circled his neck, her legs wrapped tight around his waist. He clasped her to him as her lips devoured his, her tongue invading his mouth with slippery heat. The softness of her breasts crushed against his chest as his hands cupped the taut rounds of her buttocks. She pressed her hips closer, rubbing sex against sex. Then she was lifting herself as he lifted her, intent on the same goal. Rafe gasped as he felt the hot wetness of her furrow sliding up along his shaft. He had never been within her before, and he drew a sharp breath as she paused atop him, the lush portal of her body nudging, promising. The breath he held fled in a long groan as she opened to consume him, her tightness embracing his length with drenching fire, the clasp of her sex as ruthless as every aspect of her being.

For an endless moment she held him fast, then she moved, rising up and plunging down. Rafe cried out wildly, trying to brace himself to hold her—but the sensation staggered him. The only balance he could find was to move with her as she thrust onto him again and again. Long silky grasses, rough brush and branches lashed them as he bore her about the grove. Viv twined tightly about him, driving herself onto him as he lunged into her, carrying her. Slick with sweat, she pressed close, skin rubbing skin in a delirious friction. Her rapid cries blurred with his harsher gasps as she buried her face in his neck, her tongue licking at the pulse. Her teeth found his earlobe and bit, the small sharp pain spurring the crazed rush of pleasure that besieged him.

Fire leapt from his core, streaking up to match each consuming thrust of her flesh. He grasped her fiercely, wrapped in her, around her. He moaned, beyond words, and she had only one, whispered over and over between quickening breaths. "Yes." Gasping, hissing, snarling, "Yes!" And again, crying out, "Yes. Yes!" Her cry rose, a wild keening twining with his. Her body clutched his tighter still, her arms and legs gripping savagely, her nails, her teeth, sinking into his flesh. Her sex clasped his in searing ripples until he screamed and came in an explosion of fire. Locked in orgasm, he held her tightly, jolting with the ecstasy that rent his body, tearing him limb from limb and hurling the burning remnants into oblivion.

He floated, spinning, dispersed in bits and pieces, motes, atoms of his fire one with hers, burning in the quivering darkness of eternity.

When the sustaining intensity of the climax faded, Rafe sank to his knees, still holding Viv, still trembling as she was. She clung close for a moment, then let him lower her back to the grass, both of them earthbound again, breathing in gasps. Rafe shivered as he felt himself slip from the wet heat of her body. Rolling to lie beside her, he gave a low moan of awe, satiation, and regret. The warm breeze flowed over them, cooler than their hot, sweat-drenched bodies.

She raised herself over him, her body glistening with their mingled sweat. He gazed up at her, still stunned beyond words. Her face blazed with triumph. "It was the best you've ever had, wasn't it?"

Rafe stared up at her, beyond anything but honesty and answered, "Yes." He had known passion—but not this absolute obliteration.

"You love me."

"Yes," he said again. Shame, anger, longing swirled together, suddenly lanced by a cold spear of fear. He should not feel so much. Would not. He was dazed with lust, no more. "No."

"Liar," she said, her dark gaze intent on his.

He would not answer her. It was too dangerous to speak now.

"I want you to love me," she whispered fiercely.

"Do you love me?" he challenged.

Vivian drew a slow breath, then slid over him, skin against skin. The lissome movement made him shiver. She was seductive as Eve, wise and wicked as the serpent. "I adore you," she murmured.

She wanted him to love her, but she did not love him. Or would not say so. Would not risk such a yielding.

Anger rose to the fore, and he pulled away from her. "Nothing has changed. You still want to rule me."

Her eyes went black when he thwarted her, a darkness that could devour him. Then a small flame flickered in their depths. Silent laughter. "Maybe I want you so much because I can't rule you."

"That won't stop you from trying."

"Or you from resisting." Her lips curved, the small taunting smile mocking herself as well as him. "Are you afraid of losing?"

"No." A lie to add to all the other lies. Already too much had changed because of her.

"Then savor the struggle, my rebel." Viv laughed openly now. Her gleaming eyes invited him to join in the mockery.

As always, some part of him wanted to join with her in that laughter, that freedom. Still angry, he fought his response, his lips quivering.

"I adore you," she whispered again, her tongue tip flicking delicately at the corners of his smile. She drew back, gazing into his eyes. "So you need only adore me. That will be enough."

"Will it?" he asked. "Will anything ever be enough for you?"

"I have yet to find my limits. Do not set any on me." She rose and gathered the scarlet shirt and breeches. "You are coming back with me." It was not quite an order, but neither was it a question.

"To be what?" He would not surrender what advantage he'd gained. He reached up, grabbing hold of the trailing clothes, refusing to let her dress while he was naked.

She looked down at him, her gaze wary again. "To be what we are, for as long as we are."

"And then?"

"That can only be answered then," she said.

"I deserve better than to be your—your pet," he said bitterly. He released his hold on her garments, but she made no move to put them on. She stood, regally dressed in the inky spill of her hair and a transparent glitter of arrogance.

"Garnet is banished from London. Smoke Warren is my loyal captain, rich and well content," Viv said. "I punish betrayal and reward loyalty. Whatever you deserve from my hands, you shall have."

Already she spoke like a queen to a knight, not a woman to her lover. "I will escort you back to Southwark," Rafe said, promising nothing more. He reached for his breeches, but she stepped on them.

"Leave again, and I will let you go."

He gazed up at her defiantly. "Order me to bed for rancor rather than desire, and I will leave again and not stop till I am well gone."

He waited for her anger to explode. Instead she knelt beside him on the grass, her eyes gleaming. Her lips quirked in a small smile and she reached out, fingers toying with the strands of hair that tumbled onto his forehead. She leaned forward, her lips brushing softly back and forth across his own until they tingled. She dizzied him, one moment proud and imperious as a cat, the next as playful, as sensuous. Nails sheathed, her knuckles rubbed his cheek in a soft cat's paw caress.

"Come back with me?" Now her tone was coaxing, almost wheedling, so blatantly manipulative he had to smile. But he must win more of a concession.

Rafe subdued his voice, murmuring, "After we raided the Fringes, I felt a bond between us. But when I tried to deepen it you ignored me, refused my questions."

He felt guilty pressing his advantage, but his first loyalty must be to his family. Whatever he felt for her must be used in their cause.

She regarded him steadily, speculation and tenderness mingled in her gaze. "I do not know yet if I can fully trust you."

"You know I will risk my life for you." Giving her an ironic smile, he added, "And within reason, my dignity. I have endured both tests of wine and tests of blood."

"And stood fast in both," she smiled in answer. "You have capability and courage. Your discretion remains to be proved."

He must not injure her pride, only assert his own. Meeting her gaze, he said, "I do not expect reward beyond what I've earned, but give me the means to prove my worth."

"How?"

"Let me serve you with my mind as well as my sword arm, or my cock."

"And your heart?" she asked.

"Entirely," he whispered.

Her nod was infinitesimal, but he knew it was his victory. He lowered his eyes, took a deep breath, then gazed up at her again, showing not exultation but gratitude.

Vivian's expression shifted, neither anger nor delight now, but a muted sadness and longing. She reached out, her fingers caressing the lax curve of his manhood. "I was careless today. I cannot let that happen again."

Her meaning struck him suddenly. He had not thought of the consequences of a child, only of his burning need to be inside the seething excitement of her being. His alarm must have shown on his face, for she said, "In future, we must not be so foolish."

"There are other portals to our pleasure," Rafe said softly.

She nodded, but did not look at him. One hand curved over her belly, then fell open, empty, on her thigh. Watching her like this, her bowed head veiled by the dark curtain of her hair, her body stippled with the shadowy tapestry of the leaves, he was touched by her sadness. For all her ferocity, there was this hidden vulnerability that stirred him.

Suddenly, an image came to him of Viv in prison, swollen with child, begging her belly to defeat the hangman. The thought filled him with horror. Even if she were free, he would give no child of his to such a life as she led. For her sake and his own, he prayed there would be no babe to complicate his revenge. Prayed there would be no revenge against the Swifts. Instinct still said that Rivett had committed the sabotage. But whatever he told Burne could easily be used against the Swifts—though bribery had kept them safe so far. If Nick was guilty of treason, Rafe didn't know yet how to destroy him and not Vivian, only that he would spare her as much as he could.

"Rafe?" Viv whispered, lifting her face to his. Her lips curved into smile, but the strange sadness lingered and made him feel guilty again. "When you left, I told myself not to follow. I should not indulge such a trouble-maker—but I came after you."

For you and no one else. Unspoken, the words hung in the hair between them.

It was an offering. Her sudden generous gifts came from the wealth of her heart as well as from the ill-gotten loot piled in her coffers.

"I would come back for no one else."

She reached out, weaving her fingers through his. Her dark eyes were alight as she whispered, "Together we are fire."

"You cannot abandon that—any more than I can." Rafe knew they were words that she needed to hear. But as her fingers tightened again in his own again, he felt the fire she spoke of flickering in his loins. He'd wanted to believe her passion as wicked as the world she lived in, yet it seemed elemental, pure.

It was dangerous to want so much. More dangerous to care so much.

"You are coming back with me?" Her gaze was level, and this time it was a question, although the answer was certain.

"Yes."

Pressing their clasped hands between her breasts, Viv leaned closer, brushing her lips against his with delicate seduction. Her tongue tip stroked a line of wet heat along their parted edges, then licked, lush and velvety, full across his lips. The simple touch sent a rush through his body. Rafe knew himself lustful, but he had never known the full blaze of his desire. Her flame found some spark deep within him and ignited it, consuming all other fires. He gasped aloud as the flowing muscle of her tongue filled his mouth, exploring with lascivious insistence. Arousal surged. Disturbed by her power over him, Rafe broke away from the kiss, rose, leapt into the river. Water rushed around him, dousing the furious heat in his loins. Surfacing, he scattered water from his hair and swept it back from his face.

"So, does that cool you?" Arms akimbo and legs braced, Viv stood on the bank above him. Her nipples puckered into hard points. Like a tiny fist, her pugnacious navel popped from the encircling rim of flesh. The black bush at her loins curled riotously, and beneath it he could see the tender curves and clefts of labia and buttocks. She smiled as his gaze lingered there, and her own sought what was hidden below the flowing surface of the river. She ran her tongue tip lightly across the edge of her teeth. Rafe surged to life in an instant, his cock rising hot in the cool water. He shook his head, exasperated and aroused. Laughing, she tossed aside the clothes and dove cleanly into the river, rising a few yards away with her hair a spill of black rivulets over her shoulders. She dove again, a pale shape in the moss green water that vanished behind him then emerged, wriggling slippery as an eel between his legs. Her body skimmed his as she rose to the surface, then turned to float on her back. He parted her legs and slid between them, licking the droplets from her thighs. She drifted, surrendered to him on the rippling surface of the water as he tilted her hips, bringing her sex to his mouth, his tongue caressing the rose flushed skin of the parted lips.

"Yes . . . your mouth," she whispered. "I want your beautiful mouth. And your tongue. Deep inside me."

Then he was lost in her, drinking from her body as the cool water lapped them both.

17

$\mathcal{A}$fterglow surrounded Rafe in a sensuous haze. He watched Viv rise up naked from the tumble of bed linens, lace spreading like pale sea foam over her calves. Sunlight gleamed scarlet through drawn silk curtains, then danced bright gold as she pulled them open. Her hair fell like a black wave down her back, and he remembered it yesterday clinging wet as seaweed. Beneath its dark cascade, the sinuous curve of her spine pointed to the deeper cleft of her buttocks, and between her parted thighs he glimpsed the tender lips and soft thatch of her sex. She turned her head, smiling at him over her shoulder. If he weren't so freshly spent, he'd rise again at the sight of her heedless wantonness. He reached out and pulled her back laughing among the pillows, and kissed her till she squirmed and gasped, then kissed her to quietness. He held her close, feeling the quivering life of her, skin to his skin. The giddy serenity faded slowly, pleasure shadowed as purpose moved forward.

Raising himself up, Rafe teased her lips with a fingertip. "Take me to the docks today? I'd like to know more of that side of things."

Viv caught the fingertip with a bite, then smiled at him. "If you like, though it seems best to use the skills you have already. You could work with Smoke training the men. And I want to develop our armory."

"Yes, I could be helpful there," he said smoothly. He had focused on the smuggling at the docks because Gabriel had died there, but he had yet to see their armory. It was a chance to trace the link backward from the weapons themselves— or prove there was no link to the Swifts. He gathered breath to ask about Rivett, but she spoke first.

"Tomorrow is Nick's birthday, I'll be tending to the preparations for the feast today. It will be a day or two before I show you."

He'd planned to beg tomorrow free, for it was the date Marlowe had whispered to him at the fair. She would want him by her for the festivities. He must go today. "Perhaps my velvet doublet is finished," he said. "Unless you would prefer me to wear your livery tomorrow?"

"The new doublet, if it is ready," Viv said, giving him leave to go. She stroked the skin over his ribs with teasing fingertips. "I like you best in such naked satin as this. But blue velvet, too, will be a pleasure to touch. And to strip from you."

❦

There were gaudy gallants aplenty strolling the neighborhood about St. Paul's, but Rafe felt as conspicuous as a peacock in his new plumage. For the third time, he checked behind him, making sure no one followed him to the Tilted Jug. Once inside, he had only a brief glimpse of the agent keeping watch. Going straight to the innkeeper, Rafe took his room upstairs and waited impatiently for an hour before

Burne appeared, alone and equally impatient. Burne's pale green eyes swept quickly over the new finery, but he made no comment about it.

"You bring news, Fletcher?"

Rafe shook his head. "No. Slipping away tomorrow will be impossible."

"Coming here is a risk. It should not be taken unnecessarily." Burne frowned. "To say nothing of the inconvenience."

"The choice was this day or several hence," Rafe retorted. "And hence the chancier prospect. After that jape with Marlowe at the fair, I presumed it was you who had news of import."

Burne ignored his request for enlightenment. "So, nothing has changed?"

"I did not say that." Rafe had already decided to tell Burne as little as possible. "The Swifts trust me more. Soon I'll be given a tour of the docks and a chance to assess the armory. When next we meet I expect to have intelligence for you— enough to know whether to focus on the Swifts or Rivett."

"While you dawdle, events race swiftly by," Burne snapped. "Babington and the other traitors will be tried and executed within a month. Your grandfather and cousin cannot expect to live long after them."

Rafe's guts twisted into a knot. Because of Babington's treason, panic ruled the council. Guilty and innocent would be struck down with the same blind frenzy. "They too must be tried."

"And so they shall be. Their names are on the docket ten days hence."

"They have arrived then?" Rafe suspected that was why Burne had summoned him.

"A week ago," Burne replied.

"You lied to me." Rafe surged forward, but Burne held up a hand. Rafe controlled the urge to manhandle him, but only because Burne had power over his family. "It was necessary to question them. Your intervention would have served no purpose."

"Except to give them hope."

Burne gave him an acid smile, suggesting hope was an undesirable commodity unless parceled out by the Crown, like ha'penny alms to beggars. "They have been interrogated, not tortured. But if you uncover no refuting evidence, I doubt they will be spared. Treason is the most serious charge."

"This is madness," Rafe protested. "My grandfather is a man of impeccable integrity."

"Your grandfather is a Puritan of extreme faith. Such men can be as dangerous as recusant Catholics."

"But hardly likely to conspire with them. No Protestant wants Mary of Scotland on the English throne," Rafe retorted. He doubted his grandfather's beliefs were more radical than Burne's.

Burne shrugged. "True, though I doubt such reasoning will prevail in an atmosphere of panic. They are linked to Chettle through the guns. Greed has tempted many to treason."

"We argue in circles," Rafe said. "My grandfather would not succumb to greed."

"We argue pointlessly," Burne said sharply. "Your opinion is not proof."

Rafe held his tongue. Burne was right. With nothing to stand against the hard reality of the sabotaged weapons, Rafe feared his family's trial and execution would be as swift as the one given Babington and his cohorts. Little more than a week till their trial, perhaps no more than a month till their execution. "Take me to them," he demanded.

"That is why I summoned you here, Master Fletcher. And it is my consent that will permit you to see them." Burne's voice was chill. He handed Rafe a plain hooded cloak. "Conceal your face. We must ride through the streets of London."

Rafe followed Burne down the stairs, slinging the cape about his shoulders and drawing up the hood. In the warm August weather, it was another sort of conspicuousness, but better than his face associated with Burne's. He led Rafe out the back door of the Tilted Jug, where his groom awaited with two horses.

"We go to the Fleet?"

"Yes," Burne answered tersely. Mounting, he guided them through a maze of alleyways to Ludgate Hill.

More than one prison housed lesser political prisoners and religious recusants. The confines of the Tower housed those of nobler birth, but the Fleet claimed those named by the Queen's decree. They guided their horses up the hill toward the western wall of the city, following Farringdon Street to the massive gate of the prison itself. As they dismounted, cries rose up from the begging grate, where the wretched denizens of the Hole crowded to plead food and coins from passersby. Burne gave a curt nod toward the gate, but Rafe was appalled by the misery of the prisoners, men and women pressed together in the same foul dungeon. He gathered all the small coins from his purse and scattered them among the hands outstretched through the bars. Such prisoners' very survival depended on paltry charity.

Burne ignored the commotion. Turning his back on Rafe, he stalked across the courtyard. Hurrying after, Rafe followed him inside the building and over to the desk where the records were kept. "Easton," Burne said to the warden.

"Master's Side," the man replied, summoning a guard to lead them through the maze of corridors. A decade past, Rafe and Gabriel had spent two nights in a prison after the tavern brawl. They'd had enough coin to pay the jailer's garnish. The bribe bought them a room on the Master's Side. It had cost a shilling for every door that took them away from the hell of the Hole. Six shillings bought them a small cell draped with a fine lacing of cobwebs, comforted with dirty sheets and dirtier straw, the whole dimly lit with a single candle stump. On the Knight's Ward, such a room would be shared by a dozen. Beneath that, the black Hole was a wretchedness beyond belief, crammed with diseased and starving prisoners waiting for trial. To be poor and in prison was to be buried before you were dead.

"Let me talk to them alone," Rafe said to Burne, when the guard stopped before a heavy door at the end of hallway.

Burne eyed him narrowly. At last he nodded. "You have half an hour. Use it well."

The guard unlocked the door to the cell and Rafe moved through, pushing back his hood. It looked as dismal as the cell he'd once shared with Gabriel, a bit cleaner perhaps. George Easton sat on a stool beneath the barred window, crosshatched by the pale sun falling through the bars, his hands clasped before him. His head was bowed and he did not lift it. Rafe's cousin Peter leaned against one wall. "Rafe!" he exclaimed, his eyes lightening. He stepped forward then paused, glancing at their grandfather, who still had not moved.

"Grandfather," Rafe said quietly, a chill fingering his spine.

This time his grandfather looked up. He rose unsteadily to his feet, one hand grasping at the rough stone for support. Rafe's breath caught. The shock was brutal, like ice crackling suddenly to plunge him into freezing water. He drew a harsh breath. His grandfather had always been a powerful man, tall, broad, his posture erect, righteousness steeling every sinew, keen brown eyes hawk-swift to spot any transgression. Now his frame was wasted, his face gaunt, his eyes rheumy. He drew himself up, seeking the dignity of proud bearing, but his head seemed too heavy, listing unsteadily on his neck. His grandfather looked like an old, wounded lion, his white hair loose and tumbled like a mane. Rafe's heart twisted, and he moved to his grandfather, enfolding him in his arms. There had always been a great heart under the sternness, and his grandfather returned the clasp with his own, at once fierce and frail.

"You too, Raphael?" he asked, his voice cracking.

Rafe felt a surge of fury at Burne, who obviously had told his grandfather nothing.

"No, I have not been arrested, grandfather. I am here to help you."

"They refuse to believe me." The scorn of an old lion besieged by whelps.

"Here you are surrounded by enmity and indifference. But when you return to Exeter, people will know you were falsely accused."

"What can be done?" his cousin asked.

"I can discover who is guilty."

His grandfather lifted his hands. Rafe saw scabby sores where chains had rubbed the skin raw. "They unlocked the shackles, but I feel their weight still. Iron is heavy, but shame is heavier."

"You have no need to feel shame, Grandfather," Peter broke in furiously. "You have done nothing."

His grandfather shook his head, swaying as if buffeted from within. "'For the mouth of the wicked and the mouth of the deceitful are opened against me. They have spoken against me with lying tongues.'"

"'Let mine adversaries be clothed with shame, and let them cover themselves with their own confusion, as with a mantle,'" Rafe quoted in turn, hoping the words of the psalm would have greater effect than his own.

But his grandfather only shook his head again, that strange blind motion. He staggered, but Rafe was there to catch him. Peter rushed forward to help and the eased the older man down onto the bed. He pushed them away and knelt beside the bed, locking his hands together, his lips moving silently.

"Let him pray," Peter said. "It calms him."

George Easton had stoically endured every grief that decimated their family. Rafe had never known him to become so lost, floundering in a murky pit of misery and confusion. Expecting granite, he found crumbling sandstone.

"How long has he been like this, Peter?"

"He is better today, a little." Only three years younger than himself, Peter had the russet hair and light brown eyes of the Eastons, though a rounder face and finer bones. Freckles spattered his nose and cheeks, and at twenty-five he still looked like a gawky youth. As he spoke, distress hardened to anger. "The sergeant who escorted us from Exeter was leisurely in his progress to London, with a strumpet to visit in every town. He lingered for three days in Winchester, and we lingered likewise in jail. Our keeper judged us guilty on hearing the charges. Here they want bribes for every breath you draw, but he had no care for such garnish. He stripped us naked, chained us, and threw us in a stifling hole. He tossed us offal to eat, and used our prison as his privy."

Rafe shuddered. His grandfather would have preferred pain to such degradation. "But he has always been strong."

"At first anger sustained him. Then he took ill in that horrible place, and riding in the grip of sickness served him little better. It is luck only he did not die on the way to London. The fever passed two days ago, but it sapped both strength and spirit." Peter Easton darted a quick look at his grandfather then chewed nervously at his lower lip. "I fear it's addled his wits."

"He recognized me when I entered."

"Sometimes he seems as always."

"And you, Peter?"

"Alive still, with my guts still looped in my belly." His eyes flashed, accusing Rafe. "No thanks to you."

Rafe felt a queasy guilt spreading though him. "The guns had been sabotaged. Of course I reported them. You cannot imagine they would have gone unnoticed. Good Englishmen died because of the tampering."

"Men died. . . ." his grandfather whispered. He lifted his head, awareness returning to his gaze. "You acted rightly, Raphael."

Rafe felt a surge of relief that his grandfather had been attending to their conversation. Then the distracted gaze sharpened, and his grandfather rose and approached Rafe, pushing open the dull cloak that covered the tailor's finery. "What wickedness is this? Velvet and satin and lace. You have lapsed into sinful ways, indulging in vanity and vice. It is that wastrel Darren, leading you astray once more."

"No," Rafe said, stricken. "Not Gabriel."

"Where is your pretty lordling now that you have need of him?" his cousin scoffed. "Such gentlemen are conveniently not at home when common traitors come begging help?"

"Wallowing in the corruptions of the flesh," his grandfather accused.

"It is the corruption of the grave which consumes his flesh." Rafe flung the words at them, anger overriding pity. "Gabriel Darren is dead—from trying to discover who has falsely accused you."

"Dead?" They stared at him in disbelief. Then fear washed over his cousin's visage, and shame over his grandfather's.

"Yes," Rafe said bitterly.

"And Chettle?" Peter asked. "We were told he was dead."

"Yes. He, too, was murdered."

"Whatever was done was done by our London agent, Chettle," Peter declared. "He would have had your answers, but his mouth is stopped."

"I am trying to discover who killed him, in hopes that the crimes are linked," Rafe told them. "When the truth is known, you will both be freed."

But prison had already corroded their health and their spirits. Though Peter had always been more dutiful, his easy smiles were stifled and the bitter attacks were unlike his amiable nature. But Peter was young and resilient. Rafe feared prison would destroy his grandfather before he was even brought to trial. This wavering was frightening. His grandfather's mind had always been keen. His judgments were stern, his punishments swift, but he had patience and tenderness. Rafe remembered him teaching his grandchildren the workings of pistols and the nesting habits of birds with the same devoted attention to detail. He told Bible stories with a drama that Rafe's father would have relished, with grand gestures and a voice that boomed or whispered to send chills up the children's spines.

Rafe sat down with them, going over the method of shipping their weapons to London. His grandfather could not follow the line of the questions for more than a moment or two. Peter slipped back into sullenness, brooding on his fears, countering questions with stinging accusations. They paused as the jailer brought in their supper, thin beef broth with a bone, a tough capon, dry bread, and sour wine. His grandfather said grace, and insisted Rafe share a bite of each dish. Rafe took a bite and no more. He should have thought to buy food. Ripe red apples, something bright and alive.

"We pay richly for such dainties," Peter said, pointing his spoon at the scummy broth. "They will bleed us of every farthing, then punish us for our poverty."

"The trial will be soon," Rafe warned them.

His grandfather was oblivious to the danger, but his cousin turned pale. "Have you found anything at all?"

"Only more mystery, but I believe it is linked."

Rafe talked to them as they ate, hoping to lure some forgotten bit of information to the surface, but he learned little more than he had before. His grandfather remembered Chettle, but had not gone to London in three years. He had closely tended the transport of the guns from Exeter, but his responsibility in that would only be twisted against him in court. Peter handled matters in London, and claimed to have met Chettle only twice and that nothing extraordinary had occurred. Rafe made note of the dockmen his cousin mentioned, and planned to investigate their connection, however slender. "Has there been trouble with any other shipments?"

"No reports of sabotage have reached Exeter," his grandfather said. "We received full payment for the guns."

"Thefts?"

"What are you hunting for?" Peter muttered. "You'll not be wearing hemp for a ruff."

"There are those who wish to fit me with one," Rafe replied, though the words cut him.

Peter dropped his gaze, sopping up the last of the greasy broth with the bread crust and cramming it in his mouth. Rafe waited, but Peter refused to lift his eyes. Suspicion, swamped by guilt, rose suddenly to the surface.

The jailer came in. He cleared away the dirty plates and warned Rafe that his time was all but gone, then left them alone again. Filled with qualms, Rafe rose to go. Embracing his grandfather, he murmured, "'Judge me O Lord, for I have walked in mine integrity.' That is you, Grandfather. Hold fast to your faith."

"I will trust in the Lord for my deliverance. Surely he has chosen you for his angel, Raphael, and placed a holy sword in your hand."

Again, his grandfather knelt by the bed and prayed. Rafe clasped Peter by the arm and drew him toward the door. Feeling resistance, he tightened the grip of his fingers. Pitching his voice low, he asked, "What aren't you telling me?"

"Nothing." Peter's eyes evaded his.

A dreadful fear seized Rafe, that his cousin was truly implicated. "You are lying and it will come out. Better I know."

"Better you know? You've already proved you would hang us to save your own hide."

"Stop it!" Rafe commanded. "I have done nothing but point out destruction I had no part in, and knew was not Grandfather's fault."

Peter hung his head, biting into his lower lip. Rafe's fingers tightened, digging into his cousin's arm. "Did you sabotage the guns?"

True horror blanked Peter's features. "No!" he gasped. Suddenly, he clutched Rafe in a hard embrace and whispered, "I would never commit treason. I swear to you, Raphael."

Then what was he hiding? Before Rafe could question him further, the jailer opened the door and gestured him out. Peter pulled away, retreating to the back of the cell. His eyes wide and pleading, he looked fifteen instead of twenty-five. Rafe told the jailer to wait, but Burne loomed in the doorway. He could not confront his cousin with Burne watching. Frustrated, Rafe drew up his hood and returned to the corridor. They walked in silence, following the guard back through the maze of corridors and outside. Rafe used the quiet to calm his agitation.

Alone in the courtyard, Burne asked, "What have you learned?"

Rafe shook his head. "Nothing I did not know. Neither of them is involved in the sabotage."

"You are useless to us and to yourself if you can do no better than that," Burne said. "Your cousin did not tell you of his debts?"

"Debts? Easton arms is—*was* thriving."

Burne surveyed him coldly. "Gambling debts."

"Gambling?" Rafe repeated, shocked. But that explained Peter's ambivalent responses.

"Your cousin has been embezzling money from the company to pay for gambling debts he accrued on his trips to London. We think he sold the guns and arranged the sabotage with Chettle to cover those debts."

Fear sent icy tendrils through Rafe, chilling his blood. "Perhaps he has been reckless, but he is not seditious. He was horrified at the thought."

"He is at best a hypocrite, at worst a traitor," Burne said. "Do not play us false, Fletcher. You will save neither yourself nor your family."

"None of us is guilty of treason," Rafe snarled at him.

"At least one of you is a liar." Burne gave him one of his chill smiles, then said, "There is something else you should know."

Rafe waited, suspicious of his smile.

"The Earl of Leicester is returning to England soon. He found you overzealous in the Netherlands, snooping after the business of your betters. Even if you do not hang with the others, do not be surprised to see your family's business placed in the hands of some associate of his. The Queen may find you a handsome centaur, but the Earl was long her Master of Horse. I doubt she will lift a finger to stay his whip hand. It may fall heavily on you."

"'The privileges of a few do not make common law.'"

"One of the privileged few may strip you of your livelihood, Fletcher," Burne observed. "Will you quote St. Jerome then?"

"If I prove my family innocent, Leicester can do nothing. If they are condemned, I will care little what he does. I can make my way in the world."

"As a fencing master, an actor?" Burne scoffed.

"Actor, mercenary, spy—what you will." Rafe did not want to see Easton Arms handed to some minion of Leicester's, but saving the business was nothing compared to saving his family's lives.

"Take care, Fletcher, or you will find yourself a corpse."

*B*eware," Viv said, advancing her knight to threaten Nick's queen.

Sunlight slanted through the windows of the great chamber and across the board of onyx and ivory, gleaming on the array of jeweled and enameled chess pieces. Diamond-crowned royalty commanded castles of pearl, ruby-robed bishops, and knights charging with golden lances at the ready. Reining her tension, Viv watched as Nick studied the lay of board. Rafe sat beside her on the bench, watching the play as intently as she. He looked magnificent in his new blue velvet. At last Nick's hand lifted, hovering over a black pawn carved in the likeness of an archer. He tapped with a fingertip, hesitated, then chose his bishop instead, sliding it across the board to topple a pawn and pin her knight.

"You've softened your center." Nick gave her a smug smile. He fondled the white pawn, half in pleasure of its capture, half in pleasure of possession of the set. "You take too many risks."

Viv leaned forward, steepling her hands about her mouth to suppress the quiver of a smile, pleased that her gift delighted Nicholas, and pleased that her gambit had led him where she wished.

She felt a gentle pressure against her knee, and glanced

over to Rafe. His expression was carefully guarded, but his eyes held a knowing gleam. Viv suspected he had divined her strategy. She would have to play him, and see what sort of opponent he was. That thought stirred memories of other games they played, sweet carnal games. Only two days had passed since their tryst by the stream and the glow enveloped her, giddy-sweet as wine in her veins. As if he saw the images dancing within her mind, Rafe's gaze intensified in answer. He inhaled a slow breath, his lips parting. Teasing, Viv blew him a kiss, then forced her attention back to the board.

"Too many risks?" Viv asked Nick. "What of your unwary knight?" Her deflecting jab captured Nick's piece and set her queen into a commanding place, hedging his king on one side.

Rosy shifted restlessly, skirts of silk taffeta rustling noisily. He wore pale pink, setting off the long strand of creamy pearls that adorned his throat. Nick was not only receiving presents today, he was also giving them, at least to Rosy. Coiling the shimmering rope about his fingers, Rosy smiled at Vivian triumphantly, cheeks flushed bright beneath the powder, his eyes flashing. Vivian smiled back at him, happy enough not to care about such petty rivalry. She had not even complained when he borrowed the opal and pearl earrings from her jewels this morning, though he'd best not plan to keep them.

Rosy pressed closer to Nick, stroking the chartreuse satin of the doublet that had been his own birthday gift to his lover. Nick gave him a perfunctory smile, then returned to his study of the board. Rosy sighed audibly.

Tilting his head, he swallowed the last of his wine, then set the Venetian goblet down by the chessboard. The sun pierced the crimson glass, casting a shadow like a pool of blood on the squares. Rosy clinked his fingernail against the rim, then offered Rafe a honeyed smile. "Fill the cups would you, Fletcher?"

The wine game again. Viv flashed a irritated glance at Rosy. The actor sensed enough of the growing intimacy between her and Rafe that his command had been couched as a request, but if Rafe hesitated Nick would endorse Rosy's order with one of his own. Nick did not look up from the board, but Viv could feel the new current of tension.

"Do you want more wine as well?" Rafe rose and turned to her. At the stream he had referred to Nick's dousing. The wine itself was nothing—but the intent to humiliate him rankled. Viv could hear the slight edge in Rafe's voice, but he had initiated the next move, taking control from Rosy and giving it to her.

"Please—more red," Viv said, extending her goblet and smiling into his eyes.

Rafe smiled in answer, his hand brushing hers before he took the goblet and sauntered over to the sideboard. Viv watched his movements as he filled her goblet from the decanter then returned it to her. Once he served her, he took the other two goblets and wandered back to fill them.

"Are you coming to see the new play, Vivian?" Rosy asked, drawing her attention. He leaned close to Nick, sucking on a strand of the pearls. Really, he was tedious, unhappy unless he was making someone else unhappy.

"Of course." Viv could hear the soft plashing of liquid, then Rafe's approaching footsteps.

"Your wine." Rafe leaned over to set the glass goblets carefully beside Nick and Rosy.

"Fruit." Rosy murmured the request with his most beguiling smile, nodding back toward the sideboard where a silver bowl held late peaches and early apples. Rafe went back, gathered the bowl of fruit and two silver dishes filled with marchepane and nuts and placed them beside Rosy. Vivian gave a tiny snort of amusement, smiling as Rafe slid back into place beside her. She inhaled the clean scent of his skin mingled with the spicy cologne she had bought at the fair.

Nick moved a pawn to hem her queen's threat.

Viv studied the board. Rafe sat quietly, trying not to distract her. Rosy offered Nick a drink from his goblet and sipped from Nick's, licking the dribble of wine with a pink tongue tip. He poked a finger at the marchepane, then tugged the bowl of fruit closer. Choosing a glossy red apple, he drew a jewel-encrusted knife from the sheath dangling from his girdle and cut the fruit in two. Nibbling on one half, he stabbed the other half with the point and presented it to Nick, who pulled it free and munched the crisp white flesh while Viv weighed her next move. Rosy sheathed his dagger with a faint metallic scrape.

With insolent assurance, Viv thrust her pawn forward, a deceptive attack.

"Your last knight falls," Nick countered, moving his queen to seize the exposed piece, threatening her castle.

It was the move Viv had hoped Nick would make, but made far too quickly. Had Nick recognized her ploy? Had she sacrificed her knight in vain? She studied the board intently. Rafe was a warm, solid presence beside her and she fought the urge to press her thigh along his. Rosy fiddled with his pearls, took little nips of apple, little sips of wine. He offered his cup again to Nick, and they exchanged swallows. Nick offered him a bite of apple. Rosy shook his head. He took a piece of marchepane instead, sucking at the treat. The minutes ticked past, but Viv could uncover no weakness in her strategy.

"I shall keep my king a while longer," Viv said, feigning irritation as she moved her king forward, sheltering the piece behind two slightly advanced pawns and leaving her castle exposed. She felt Rafe tense slightly and then relax. He comprehended her strategy. Nick set aside his cup and leaned forward, frowning. Would he spot her gambit or take the bait? If he went for her deepest defenses, she would checkmate in two moves.

Rosy put down his goblet and rubbed his cheek against Nick's shoulder. His voice was plaintive as he said, "I've got a headache, Nick. Take me home."

For once Nick looked annoyed. "Why don't you lie down? If you don't feel better after the game is over, I'll walk with you back to the Comet."

A small smile twitched the corners of Viv's lips. Rosy no doubt made things difficult if his complaints were dismissed, whether real or counterfeit. Was it too much to hope that Piper's charms were wearing thin? That would be worth far more than victory in one chess match.

"What?" Nicholas asked her.

"What . . . what?" Viv asked in answer. Nick always humored Rosy in such distractions, but it was unlike him to use the ploy himself.

"I thought you said something." Nick pressed a hand to one ear, frowning.

"I said I want to go," Rosy reiterated. "I feel cold."

"Not yet. I want to win," Nick popped the last bite of apple into his mouth and licked his fingers.

"Then you had best leave now," Vivian laughed.

"Don't be so certain." Nick sent his queen on a diagonal attack, toppling her far corner castle.

Triumph swelled through Vivian, a brightness that filled her veins. Nick had been far too greedy. Viv angled her bishop into position and sighed with utter satisfaction. "Oooooooh . . . but I am certain."

Whatever Nick did, her next move would send her bishop racing to place Nick's king in check. If the king tried to escape in the other direction, he would fly to the lethal embrace of her waiting queen—a perfect crisscross mate.

Nick pondered the board, started to moved his king, and frowned. He rubbed his head, looking perplexed, combed his fingers through his hair. Rafe pressed his thigh to hers and a delicious surge of desire drummed in concert with the pulsation of victory. She smiled into his eyes, sharing the moment of triumph.

"I feel hot," Rosy announced.

"First cold, now hot?" Rafe commented, not bothering to hide his skepticism. His gaze never left Viv's, his eyes filled with praise for her skill.

"Yes. I'm hot and thirsty." Rosy said petulantly. He picked up the goblets and moved behind her to the sideboard, setting them down with an ostentatious *clink*.

Nick stared at the board, head in his hands, palms pressed to his ears. Viv waited for him to concede the game. But when he lifted his head, his eyes looked unfocused, as if he were listening to something. "Do you hear a ringing?"

"A ringing?" she asked.

"I hear it," Rosy said behind her, "I hear—"

Glass shattered and Viv whirled to look around. The decanter lay in pieces on the floor. Red wine splattered Rosy's pink skirts and flowed through the wreckage. He took a step forward, lifting his hand to his brow and swaying unsteadily. The gesture seemed worthy of some staged swoon, but Viv wondered if he were feigning his headache. He looked pale and bilious. Suddenly Rosy collapsed onto his knees, leaned over, and vomited onto the fine carpet. The foul mess stank of wine. "I'm sick," he gasped. "I told you. I told you."

Nick knocked over the bench as he rose. He took one step and faltered, gripping the table to keep from falling and staring at each of them in turn.

"Nicholas?" Vivian asked, alarm clanging in her heart.

"I feel strange," he said slowly. "Dizzy. My ears are ringing."

Rosy let out a keening wail. He lifted his hand to point at the goblet, then jabbed his finger at Rafe. "Fletcher has poisoned us."

"Yes!" Nick's gasp echoed with horrified comprehension. "Oh, God."

Viv looked at Rafe, who stared back at her. Emotions swept quickly across his face—stunned disbelief gave way to horror, but fear followed close in its wake. Then he set his jaw and shook his head. His voice was firm. "No. No—I didn't."

"He's poisoned me, Vivian," Nick whispered. His face was pale, paler than Rosy's. "He brought the wine. Your goblet first, then mine."

"You're ill, Nicholas," Viv said, though the suddenness of the attack filled her with fear. "Rafe, send the guards for a doctor."

"No!" Nick snarled as Rafe moved toward the door. "Stay where you are."

Rafe halted, looking back for confirmation of her order. Rosy picked up dishes from the sideboard and began hurling them. "You've murdered us!" he screamed at Rafe. The assault of porcelain and silver ended abruptly as Rosy sank to the floor, moaning, his arms wrapped around his stomach.

In the wake of the noise, two hallway guards burst through the door, swords drawn. They paused inside the threshold, shocked, looking back and forth from her to Nicholas for their orders. "You . . . guard the door," Nick gasped, pointing to the first man. His breathing was rapid and sweat poured down his face. "And you . . . bring Smoke Warren."

"You need a doctor," Rafe said to Nick. "It may be sweating sickness."

Vivian's heartbeat quickened in hope, then dread. She was praying for plague rather than poison. "Have Smoke send for the doctor," Viv ordered the departing guard.

Drawing his sword, Nick advanced on Rafe. His gaze swarmed with loathing and hatred. He struggled to speak. "I need . . . nothing . . . but your death."

Rafe lifted his hands, weaponless. His gaze held Nick's, and he made no attempt to deny the animosity between them. "I have not poisoned you. If I wanted to kill you, I would not choose so conspicuous a way."

"You want to take my place . . . beside Vivian. Rule the underworld." Nick's voice was slow and slurred. He advanced but he was sweating, his movements unsteady. "But if I die . . . I will take you with me."

Rafe cast Vivian a desperate glance then moved backward, refusing to draw his weapons. "I swear I have not poisoned you."

Viv moved between him and Rafe. "Nicholas—"

"Stand aside." His eyes accused her.

"No."

Nick shoved her, a fierce push that sent her stumbling backward. He started toward Rafe, then sank to his knees, retching. Vivian caught her balance, then rushed to kneel at his side.

Smoke came through the doorway, four guards with him. He moved to her swiftly. "I've sent for the doctor. Nicholas is planetstruck?"

"Yes," Viv agreed. "A sudden sickness. But he thinks—"

"We are poisoned!" Rosy cried out. "Fletcher has poisoned us both!"

Smoke's eyes questioned Viv. She shook her head, but suspicion clouded every emotion like black ink. Smoke saw her doubt and looked up at Rafe, his own assessment far colder. Nick whispered Smoke's name, then picked up the fallen sword and handed it to him. Smoke took hold of the hilt. He gave Viv a brief uncertain glance, then moved within thrusting distance of Rafe, point extended.

"Remove your weapons," Smoke ordered Rafe. Still watching her, Rafe unbuckled his sword and knife, handed them over.

Viv pointed to the sideboard. "There are their goblets, unbroken. Test the wine on some rat."

"Test it on Fletcher," Nick demanded, raising his head. "The larger cup was mine. Have him drink that." Nick bared his teeth, an agonized rictus that showed the skull beneath the flesh. Viv's heart caught. Seeing that smile, she believed Nick was going to die.

"Yes," Rosy hissed. "Have him taste his own poison."

Silence filled the room. Rafe stared at the cups, apprehension plain on his face. Viv felt the black suspicion spreading through her. Rafe's disbelief had seemed so genuine. But if the wine was safe, Rafe could drink it without harm as she had.

"Drink it or die now," Nick commanded.

"Rosy could have poisoned the wine," Rafe said cautiously.

"Me! How? With the touch of my lips?" Rosy laughed hysterically, a wild sound that turned into retching.

The black murk of suspicion flowed toward Rosy, and Viv had to fight against its pull. However much she detested Rosy, he had no motive to harm Nicholas and he was wretchedly sick.

"You hate me, Fletcher." Nick's eyes glittered. He spoke each word on a harsh breath. "Rosy loves me. We shared both cups. He put nothing in them."

Viv walked to Smoke, pressing down the blade of the sword. Her heart drummed fiercely inside her chest as she went to the sideboard and took the larger cup, Nick's cup. Light filtered through the crimson glass, staining her hands. The goblet was a quarter full. She carried it to Rafe, held it out. "Drink the wine."

Rafe covered her hands with his. They were cold, proof of his fear. But his gaze held hers, protesting his innocence. Taking the goblet from her, he lifted it to his lips and drained the wine in three swallows. He handed the empty cup back wordlessly, but his breathing had quickened.

"I hope there is enough left to kill you," Rosy said.

Viv placed the goblet back on the sideboard. Then she went and knelt beside Nick, holding his hand as they waited to see if there was poison in the cup. No one spoke, but sound swarmed around her. Nick's breathing rasped, Rosy rocked and moaned, and her own heart continued its feverish drumming, pounding against the wall of her chest. Suddenly Rafe doubled over, stomach throwing up what he had drunk. Vivian felt her own guts clench and twist. Rafe leaned forward for a minute, then raised his head, his face blanched and sweating. His gaze met hers. Even darkened with fear, his eyes still vowed his innocence.

Nick gripped her shoulder, demanding she look at him. He pulled himself up a little, his breath rapid gasps. "I want to see him dead."

Viv looked at him, seeing the terror there, the vengeance, the need. "If the poison does not kill him, I must question him."

Nick's eyes accused her. "He's killed me. Your lover . . . has killed me."

"No." Viv shook her head.

She could still not believe it. Rafe had resented Nick's presence, as Nick had resented his. Such resentment could turn to hatred, if he believed Nick blocked his way. Ambition did not even need hatred to commit murder. Rafe did not seem to lust for power—but others had fallen to its lure. Did Rafe think with her brother gone she would raise him up instead?

Was the poisoned wine perverse repayment for the public dousing? A mortal wound returned for such a tiny prick?

Nick convulsed. She and Smoke gripped him as his body arched and twisted in their grasp. Vivian bit her lip, her own guts knotting as she struggled to hold him. Finally the spasm faded and Nick gazed up at her, gasping for breath. "Kill him. Promise me."

"I promise I will kill whoever has killed you." Viv kept her gaze on Nick, refusing to look at Rafe, though she could feel him standing a few feet away.

"Even Fletcher."

"Yes. I give you my word." Pain cut her heart like a knife, twisting, cutting deeper with each shift of emotion. "Lock Fletcher in the cellar," she ordered two of the guards.

The men took hold of Rafe's arms, but he jerked them away. "I'll go with you," he said. But then he tottered and they caught him, dragging him through the door. Rosy was sick yet again. He crawled to a corner and curled into a ball, mewling piteously. The room stank of vomit.

Nick sagged back onto the floor. His hand grasped her skirts, tugging. "What?" he whispered. "What did you say?"

"I didn't say anything," she answered. Then, "I love you."

"You look strange," Nick whispered, gazing up at her. "Yellow. Everything looks yellow."

Vivian bit back a panicky laugh. Nick's pallor had increased, his sweat-slicked skin glowed with the faint yellowish-green tinge of his doublet, as if the dye had seeped through his skin and tainted his blood. It was too bizarre to be real.

Nick clasped her hands, his fingers cold and clammy. His breathing, so rapid at first, was growing slower and slower. He shivered violently and Viv felt an echoing shiver run through her. "My blood feels like ice." His words were sluggish, as if he could barely lift his tongue.

Nicholas convulsed again, and again, and again. Viv called out to him, but Nick could not hear. For a time there was only the horror of holding his body as it bucked out of control. All her will was bent on keeping him still. When the last paroxysm faded, Nicholas could not speak, could barely breathe. His body stilled, his flesh icy as a corpse. His face was a frozen mask, though his eyes gazed up at her, burning with suffering. Strangely, the pain wiped years from Nick's face. He looked young and completely helpless in its grip. They had protected each other since the Earl's death. But Viv could not protect him now. Only wait with him. He took a breath, his chest barely moving. She waited for his next breath and it did not come. The pain left his eyes, their stare cold and blank.

"He's dead. Oh God, he's dead!" Rosy crawled toward Nick. His face was filled with fascination and revulsion. He stretched out a trembling hand to touch Nick's cheek, then snatched it away again. "I'm going to die, too."

At that moment Viv hoped so. Rosy could see it in her eyes and began to scream at her. "It's your fault! You brought Fletcher here. You've killed Nick. You've killed me."

Viv could not summon a shred of pity. Her grief, her horror was for Nicholas. Her fear was for Rafe. "The doctor is coming. He will tend you."

"What can a doctor do? Take me home. I don't want to die here," Rosy shrilled. "You hate me. You'd poison me yourself if you could. I hate you! I hate you!"

Viv clenched her fists, trembling. It took every shred of control not to slap Rosy. She forced calm. "You're still alive. You may survive. Let the guards help you upstairs."

"No!" Rosy retched again, dry heaving, for there was nothing left to vomit. When it was over he sobbed helplessly. "Take me home. I want to die at home."

She should keep Rosy here. Nick would want her to tend him, at least with outward kindness. But Viv could not bear his presence while she mourned. She beckoned to a guard and ordered a litter to be brought to the front. "Take Piper back to his rooms. Fetch whatever doctor he wants, and I will send mine later." Quietly she added, "I want guards posted outside, day and night, keeping watch. Let me know who visits. If he recovers, follow him wherever he goes. Don't let him leave London."

Your lover has killed me, Nick's voice accused in her mind. Rafe had reason to murder Nick. Rosy had none.

The guards helped Rosy from the room, leaving her alone with Nick's body. Leaving her alone.

19

The metallic rasp of the key woke Rafe. He sat up as the door swung open, bringing the flicker of torchlight into the darkness of the small dank room in the cellar. Fighting off a swell of queasiness, he rose from the straw, struggling for balance against the manacles clamped around his wrists and ankles. His body was bruised and aching from the last beating, his innards abraded from vomiting, but if he was going to die, it would not be from the noxious wine. Blinking, he focused on the forms backlit against the doorway. Vivian entered the cell first, Smoke following behind her, and Rafe glimpsed more guards waiting outside. He concentrated on Viv's face, though her eyes were only a glimmer till Smoke lit the lantern overhead, casting a dim yellow light on their faces. She met Rafe's gaze, her eyes black with suspicion. The cold appraisal chilled his blood, but beneath it he saw flickers of both pain and uncertainty. She had not stopped caring. He had no doubt she could kill him—but she had not condemned him yet. She gestured for Smoke to close the door, then nodded Rafe to the stool in the center of the room. He sat down on it, looking up at her.

Smoke had already interrogated Rafe, alternating blows with questions—asking what poison he had used, if he had acted alone or been hired. Still trapped in the hideous bouts of vomiting, Rafe could do nothing then but protest his innocence, heave his guts, or sink back into wretched sleep. But the worst was over now. His body was leaden, but his head was clear and wariness sharpened his senses. He even had wit enough to appreciate the irony of his situation, accused of betrayal, but for the wrong sin. He'd felt a fierce antipathy to Nicholas. Destroying him would have been easy, if Rafe had ever been certain the man had contrived his family's ruin and murdered Gabriel. But that surety had never come.

"I did not kill your brother," he said.

Vivian stepped forward, confronting him directly. Rafe knew she wanted to believe him innocent, and knew that she struggled against her own desire to search for justice—and for vengeance. She drew a deep breath and said, "You hated Nick. With him gone, you saw a road to power open to you."

"I cannot blame your suspicion. But I would not claim power at such a cost." How much of who he was would she believe, set against who he had pretended to be? Power would have tempted the fencing master, but he would not have murdered to grasp it. Behind Vivian, Smoke gave a harsh snort of disbelief. "Smoke does not believe me, even though he himself puts love and loyalty before power."

"Nicholas is dead of poison. My willingness to believe you is therefore tainted," Smoke said.

Rafe kept his gaze on Vivian, answering to her. "You doubt my honor. What of my sense? Why kill Nicholas in a way which points suspicion straight at me?"

"You did not know Rosy would drink the wine as well," she answered. "You thought that only Nick would become ill, that the poisoning would be taken for illness. Sweating sickness, you said."

"No," Rafe said flatly. "I can tell you ways now I might have killed him and deflected suspicion. Someone else has done it and deflected it to me. Since I know it was not you, it can only be Ambrose Piper."

"Rosy had no reason to murder Nicholas. You did."

"Rosy had no reason you know of. It is not the same." He leaned forward, challenging her. "You cannot believe Rosy loved him. Rosy loves nothing but himself."

"No, I do not believe Rosy loved Nicholas. I believe Rosy benefited from him—a wealth of adoration and adornment."

"Someone offered him more."

"No one could have matched the adoration," Viv responded. "And Nicholas showered him with jewels, perfumes, gowns. He wanted for nothing."

"Rosy reeks of vanity and malice. He would delight in playing the central role in a drama of deception."

"Not at such a risk," Vivian said.

"Then there was threat as well as reward. Rosy, I think, would be easy to threaten."

Viv shook her head. "Nick would have protected him."

"Perhaps—from someone like Maggot. But from Jacob Rivett? Rosy would see him as the greater threat. If you want someone with motive, Rivett has much to gain."

"This only delays the inevitable." Smoke stepped forward, laying a hand on Viv's arm. "Fletcher offers tempting lies in place of the ugly truth of his betrayal. Let me torture him. We will discover the truth soon enough."

Rafe sat very still. "If I do not confess, it will only prove my strength. If I do, it will prove nothing but my fear."

"I am no fool. When you confess, you will give us particulars," Smoke said.

"But I am innocent." Rafe drew a harsh breath, facing Vivian. "I am in your power. If you do not believe me, you will kill me. You presume my guilt. For ten minutes, presume Rosy is guilty."

"You hope to live long enough to escape," Smoke said, his own wrath simmering close to the surface. "But the longer you delay your confession, the longer you will suffer the torture. And I will see to it the length of your dying will match it moment to moment."

Rafe knew those choices did not belong to Smoke. "Vivian," Rafe implored. "Do not look only where the finger points. Look at who points it."

"Ten minutes," Vivian said. "And then I will leave you with Smoke. Tell me how Rosy poisoned Nick while we all watched."

Hope and despair twisted within Rafe. "I paid Rosy little mind. I watched the game. I watched you. You must help me discover how he did it."

Viv said nothing only looked at him, waiting.

Rafe drew a long breath. "If I poisoned Nick, you know how it happened. I added something to Nick's goblet, hoping the symptoms would be taken for illness. It is simple enough."

"Yes," Vivian agreed. "Such simplicity has virtue."

"The shape is simple, but the fit is too loose." He gathered the tattered scraps of thought that had whirled through his sickness, trying to piece memory and conjecture into a pattern. "We all drank the wine but only Nick is dead. I am alive. Rosy is alive."

"You drank less, that is all," Viv said.

"Perhaps. Or perhaps what we drank was different. Nick became ill quickly, but not so quickly as I did."

"Nick and Rosy sipped little by little. You drank it all at once."

"We don't know how much Rosy drank," Rafe said. "If he knew the cup was poisoned, he might have feigned drinking."

Viv shook her head. "I watched. Rosy drank, he swallowed. He licked the drops from his mouth."

"Perhaps he did no more than wet his lips," Rafe said.

"I doubt he has the courage to sip heedlessly at a lethal brew. He is not so good an actor."

"His sickness seemed genuine," Rafe admitted. He remembered how smug Rosy had been that day, and could not conceive it either. "He has been as sick as I have?"

"Yes. My men say he's been abed for two days, tossing his guts up."

"That might be feigned," Rafe said, but it was impossible to prove.

"He's summoned half the apothecaries in the Clink, to

beg their best physics." He glanced up quickly, and she added, "They will all be questioned."

"What were Nick's symptoms?"

"Dizziness. Vomiting. A ringing in the ears. A yellow tint to all he saw. His breathing was rapid, then a slow agony." Rafe saw a shiver run through Vivian's body, but her voice was even as she went on. "He said his blood felt like ice water, and his body was cold as a corpse even before he died."

Rafe shook his head. "I have had headache, horrific nausea, sweats—but no coldness. No difficulty breathing. Nothing of the ringing in the ears Nick mentioned and Rosy agreed to."

"You did not drink a lethal dose," Viv said.

"Perhaps—"

"This is absurd," Smoke broke in. "You waited until Vivian was distracted, and added the poison to the wine. All eyes were intent upon the game."

"She did not see me put the poison in the wine because I did not do it."

Viv frowned, holding out a hand to quiet Smoke while she thought. "I watched Rafe pour my wine. I was annoyed that Rosy asked him to do it."

"He poured yours first, and added no poison," Smoke argued.

"Rafe went back to the sideboard to fill the other goblets. It was Rosy who distracted me to look away."

"Why should he?" Smoke asked.

"Presume Rosy is guilty," Rafe countered.

"If Rosy is guilty, he planned to throw suspicion on you," Smoke answered, but without conviction.

Viv said, "If Rosy poisoned Nick, then he chose it do it when he could implicate you."

"He would not want you to see what I did with the wine, for it would prove my innocence, not suggest my guilt."

"And I did not pay attention when he went himself, and poured more wine from the decanter." Vivian looked at Rafe. "He could have added something to the wine then."

She was his ally at last. Rafe leaned forward eagerly. "Rosy did not dare only pretend illness. His life depended on deceiving us. He added a weaker concoction of the same poison—or a different one, less lethal. He drank it then, and became sick quickly, as I did. Before that he needed only to mimic Nick's symptoms."

"If it was a different drug, he need not feign illness— nor fear death," Viv said.

"Then how was Nick poisoned?" Smoke asked. His voice was skeptical, but not as harsh as before.

"The marchepane?" Rafe asked, remembering Rosy sucking on the almond sweet.

"Only Rosy ate the marchepane," Viv said. "They shared the apple, so it cannot be that."

Rafe summoned the image. "They did not pass it back and forth. They each ate half."

"A poisoned apple?" Smoke scoffed. "Venom from the serpent's tooth?"

"Wait." Viv held up her had, her face intent. "Nick offered Rosy a bite of his half of the apple. Rosy refused it and ate the marchepane instead."

"Rosy would," Smoke said. "And you cannot easily poison half an apple."

"Rosy took the apple from the bowl and cut it in two. He handed one half to Nick. . . ." Viv paused. "No. He pierced it with the blade and offered it."

Then Rafe knew how it was done. He said to Vivian, softly, "Rosy is an actor. He has an actor's arts—and an actor's tools."

Rafe could see her replaying the sequence in her mind, watched as his own knowledge become certainty in Viv's eyes. "The knife—he injected the poison with the knife."

"Yes." On stage, actors used trick weapons to kill falsely, hiding mock blood within secret channels. Rosy had used his dagger to kill in truth.

There was silence, Viv speechless with rage, Smoke assimilating the knowledge. After a moment, he asked sharply, "But why? Why would Rosy murder Nick?"

"I don't know why," Rafe answered. "I only know he did."

"Rosy will tell us—eventually." Viv's eyes were black, filled with a pure, cold fury. Rafe knew Ambrose Piper was a dead man. She turned to Smoke. "For now, no one but those of us here now, Izzy, and Joan, will know Rafe is alive. I will tell Rosy I have avenged Nicholas. He will be far more careless if he believes himself safe."

"Izzy and I will dump a weighted shroud into the Thames, so there is no gossip to alert him," Smoke said.

"Arrange it," she ordered. "Dismiss the guards at this door and at Piper's."

"Tonight." Smoke nodded and left.

When Viv turned back to him, Rafe saw hatred for Rosy burning in her eyes. But as she looked at him, it cleared. She knelt in front of him—to unlock his chains, but it was a gesture of surrender, too. Emotions swarmed in her eyes—tenderness, guilt, remorse—but her gaze, her voice, were direct. "I've wronged you."

Silently he held out his hands, and she worked the key in the lock. He drew a long breath of relief as the chains clattered to the stone. The energy of the confrontation deserted him abruptly, leaving him hollow and aching. Her fingers curled gently about his chafed wrists. She kissed each palm, then lifted her hands to his to his face, stroking the bruises left by Smoke's battering. Rafe felt far too vulnerable to the simple touch of her hand. He drew away.

"Forgive me?" she pleaded.

"I don't blame you," he said wearily. "I understand revenge."

"You wanted me to believe you."

"You hardly know me," he whispered, turning his face aside.

"Don't I?" she whispered in answer.

"Trust was too much to ask." True enough, but it implied his own forgiveness was as well. His reluctance drew her closer and he let her come. Yet he wished she would heed his warning. But she reached out to touch his cheek, turning him back to her. He looked at her directly. "You've survived as long as you have by not trusting anyone."

"No. I trusted Nick." Grief roughened her voice. She waited a breath, then went on. "I trust Izzy. Smoke and

Joan have been at my side for a decade. I've built my life on the few people that I can trust. Now you are one of them. Closest to my heart."

"Am I?" he asked.

For answer, she leaned forward and kissed him on the mouth. "I love you. I will not ever doubt you again."

Rafe held her close, caught in a swirling vortex of joy and pain, triumph and dread.

20

I love you, Vivian whispered silently, gazing into Rafe's face. He looked so weary. She did not want to beg his forgiveness again.

But he must forgive her. Not only from his mind—from his heart.

But why should he? She had forced herself to cold detachment, so Nicholas might have justice. But her coldness had wrought cruel injustice on Rafe and ravaged the special affinity they shared. He had said her betrayal did not matter, but how could it not? His body bore the marks of it, and so must his spirit. Grief and guilt clouded her joy in his innocence. Nick's loss was a bleeding wound. Half her life had been ripped away, and she still felt blinded by the pain. The thought of losing Rafe as well cut deeper into her wounds.

She must keep him. Her actions now must prove her trust.

"Follow me," Viv said, taking Rafe's hand and leading him from the cell. He returned the pressure of her hand, then pulled gently away. Even such a simple loss hollowed her.

She went to a rough cupboard set into a corner near a stack of ale barrels and pressed the hidden hinges, opening it to reveal a narrow stairway leading up from the cellar. With

Nick gone, only Izzy and Smoke knew all the passageways within and without the townhouse. Now Rafe would know them as well. Lighting a taper, she drew the cupboard shut and guided Rafe up the tight circle of steps to the second floor. The secret panel slid back and they stepped into the withdrawing room between her chamber and Nick's. The paneling fit seamlessly as she closed off the passage.

From there, she led Rafe through her bedroom to the bathing chamber. He followed willingly enough, obviously tired and aching, and stood patiently while she stripped off the soiled, torn velvets and tossed them into a corner. She removed her own gown as well. There had been no time to prepare a tub, but she poured scented water into a basin and cleansed him with a sponge, wringing cool streams over the ugly bruises that Smoke's beating had left on his skin. A beating she had ordered, when he was already in pain. Tears stung her eyes as her hands laved him, soothed him. He had known her cruelty, now he must know her gentleness. She dried him with a linen towel, then chose an herbal oil and rubbed the healing, aromatic balm into his skin. He closed his eyes, swaying with the movement of her hand.

"You look likely to fall asleep where you stand," Viv murmured.

"Tired . . ." He sighed the answer. She coaxed him through the door to her bedroom and peeled back the embroidered coverlet. With a sigh, he lay down on the white linens. "Thirsty," he whispered.

Viv went toward the pitcher and goblets, then paused. "There is only wine."

He gave a harsh gasp of laughter.

She could call for something else to be brought, ale, cider, anything—but that would break their tenuous intimacy. Instead she poured a goblet to the brim with the garnet liquid. Standing by the bedside, she held Rafe's gaze and drank a swallow. Tart, bittersweet, it filled her with memories both dark and joyful. Wine was an ancient sacrament in rituals of life and death. Death must not triumph. She handed the cup to Rafe. He hesitated, then sipped from the rim. When he was done, Viv kissed him, tasting the wine on his mouth. She shivered with pleasure and the echo of fear. His lips yielded, but did not respond.

Setting the drink aside, she moved about the chamber, lighting more candles. Bright, fragile, their soft golden halos were small blessings in the night shadows. They seemed to shine in her heart, in her mind, holding back the consuming dark. She mourned Nick, but grief made Rafe all the more precious. Like the simple purity of the candles, his presence glowed, a beacon in the blackness, kindling an answering light and warmth within her.

Returning to the bed, she sat beside him, simply watching him for a moment, then reached out, her fingertips skimming the bruises on his face. He gazed into her eyes. There was no accusation, no anger, no fear there now, just the strange sadness. Had all his passion for her died? She murmured to him, a soft crooning of remorse and delight, fear and entreaty. Her hand glided down, fingers gently tracing the strong column of his neck, the wide sweep of his shoulders, the hard muscle of his arms.

She wanted him with a consuming, tender ferocity. Her own need appalled her, for she knew he was weary from the illness and abuse. She must seek no more than to comfort him, to lull him to sleep. Her hands moved gently over the arch of his ribs, touch too soft for a massage, too soothing for a caress.

"I love you," she murmured, as much to herself as to him.

The discovery still bemused her. Never had she felt such longing, such hunger, for any man. Lust had always burned swift and hot, like fireworks streaking through the night. Explosions of sensation burst in chaotic splendor, bright and enthralling for the moment, then dissipating quickly in a hazy trail of smoke. However intense, lust was familiar, a greedy delight that sated only the flesh. But what she felt for Rafe did not wane. From the beginning, she had only wanted more of him—his body, his mind, his heart. She had called it infatuation, then adoration. But it could have no other name but love. The unfolding tenderness was bewildering, overwhelming—a desire to give, to receive, as fierce as the desire to take. It was a bud of life blossoming in the darkness of death, and she nurtured it with a joy and fear bordering on desperation.

Rafe lifted one hand, stroking the back of hers as she caressed him, his fingertips skimming as lightly as her own. Unable to resist the beauty of his body, Viv smoothed the broad planes of his chest, tracing the diamond of soft hair at its center. Moving outward, she idly circled the bronze disk of a nipple, the nub rosier, sensitive to her touch. He whispered something inaudible, a protest perhaps, as it peaked beneath her fingertips. But when she started to withdraw her inquisitive fingers, he captured her hand and pressed it back against his chest. She could feel his heartbeat thudding against her palm. He met her gaze, and she saw a blue flame of desire flare in his eyes, sudden and bright.

"You're too tired," she whispered.

"Too tired to argue," he countered softly, then reached up and drew her down into a kiss.

Viv felt the fullness of his lips under her mouth, firm and yielding at once. She licked delicately, tiny flickers, teasing with tongue tip and the moist inner flesh of her lips in delicate, devouring touches. One demanding gesture might crush all her hopes. She felt the exhalation of his breath against her lips as his own parted in answer, his tongue tip questing with soft touches. She lured him within, their tongues dancing in languorous rhythm as the kiss deepened. The shared taste of honeyed wine was sweet and terrifying. She shivered again. In response, his arms encircled her, warm and hard, wrapping her in his embrace. She reveled in his strength and his gentleness, her heart filled with a sense of protection and an urge to protect. She would be his refuge and he hers.

Viv captured his tongue, drinking the winey liquor in a sensuous suckling, intoxicated with his flavor. Tenderness and desire mingled, sweetening the harsh bitterness of grief. Her heart brimmed, overflowed, the aching sweetness pouring into her breasts and belly, flowing into her limbs, down to her hands and feet, even into her fingers and toes. Tears spilled from her eyes, a welling of pain she could hardly bear, but the love flowed after, infusing loneliness with hope. Her blood turned to liquid gold, liquid light. Her bones seemed to glow within her, her skin to sing without. Love spilled from her lips, her fingertips, and seemed to fill Rafe as well, for he moaned to her, drowning with her in shared sorrow and sweetness.

He drew a shuddering breath, and she felt his arousal stretch against her thigh, a slow, insistent pressure. Death had come too close to him as well, but life clamored even through his weariness. She reached between them to caress him, the satin skin drawing taut over his rising shaft. He throbbed in her hand, and an answering throb pulsed within her. Her hand tightened, feeling the heat and hardness of him. He gave another low moan, arching to her. Drawing him over her, she guided him close, rubbing the blunt tip between the tender wet furrow of her lips, licking him with the wetness.

He gasped aloud, drawing back to look at her, his eyes wide. "We shouldn't," he warned. "Not that."

Caution was nothing now. She could not bear not to receive him. There must be no barriers between them, of flesh or spirit.

In answer Viv wrapped her arms and legs around him, pulling his hips forward, sheathing his sex within her own, pleasure so deep, so pure, it cleaved a path to her heart. Rafe's wounded cry echoed hers. He plunged deep to meet her, then held utterly still. They trembled together, sensation radiating from the hot core they shared. Slowly, he began to thrust, a subtle friction that awakened every atom. She moved with him sinuously, heart and soul speaking though her flesh. His hands reached to caress her, stroking her back, her flanks, her buttocks, molding every swell and valley in an erotic mapping. She clung to him, rocking to his rhythm, surging as he surged, limbs entwined, skin and muscle melting. The tempo increased, the long thrusts demanding yet questing. She could feel his manhood swell to fill her, each intimate stroke breaching the barrier of flesh, piercing her, opening her. Loneliness welled, almost impossible to bear except for the love that flowed through the pain. She let it hollow her so that she could take him deeper still. Grief, longing, hunger fused with the overwhelming tenderness. She moaned to him, held fast to him.

"Viv . . ." Rafe sobbed her name, over and over, the sound desperate then joyful. Everywhere they touched they joined, skin melting to soul. They became one flesh, moving together. She was sobbing, too, calling his name in answer. He cried out sharply, his arms tightening around her. She felt his power, but she felt his trembling also, as he lost himself within the greater power they conjured. With a final cry he plunged deep inside her, straining to find the pinnacle of ecstasy. She could feel his seed pumping, his life filling her. She gripped him fiercely as her passion exploded like an infinity of suns, each brighter than the last. Her whole being pulsed around him, one with his rapture, dissolving in the light.

• • •

They held each other close. There was only the hushed silence of the room, the slowly quieting pounding of their hearts. Afterglow spilled from them both like light, merging with the diffuse glow of the candles, warm and golden. Peace permeated and cocooned them. They sighed together as Rafe slipped from her body and lay beside her on the bed. The sense of union dimmed but lingered. She wrapped a leg over his thighs and pressed close to his chest, caressing him with possessive awe.

"I love you—as I have never loved anyone," Viv said softly. "With you anything is possible."

"You ignite fires in me that would have slumbered my whole life." His gaze held hers. Then, more hesitantly, he whispered, "I do love you, Vivian."

Her heart gave a strange twist, hearing the admission and the hesitation.

He sagged back against the pillows, staring at the ceiling. "This is madness."

"Is it?" she asked. "We are where we belong, in bed, in each other's arms . . . in love."

He closed his eyes.

"What?" she asked.

He shook his head and his arms tightened around her. "Nothing. I don't want to think. Only to feel."

What she felt was the barrier rising after their perfect communion. There was a turbulence in the pit of her belly, dark stirrings of anger, of fear, of need, but the shared warmth still shielded her from them. She stroked his cheek, his jaw, her fingertips pressing lightly till he turned to face her. Her voice stayed calm. "You are afraid I will try to own you?" It was what he had said in the past.

He did not deny it.

You are mine. Mine. She felt the greed for him rising as he withdrew and subdued it, breathing deeply. "I am possessive, I admit it." She moved closer still, intent. "But haven't you proved that you won't be owned?"

"Will that stop you from trying?" The corners of his lips curled in an ironic smile.

"Just now I did not own you, or you own me. Tonight we belonged to each other, heart and body given freely."

"Yes," he murmured, but the sadness had returned. Then he drew a breath, visibly steeling himself. "When I began here I thought I could play knight to the Queen of the Clink. Perhaps I can serve you still, Viv. But I can't be ruled by you."

Viv made her decision. "Then rule with me, Rafe."

He stared at her.

She knew he spoke of his own spirit, but she could think of nothing else that would answer him so completely. World and spirit would be one offering. "Nicholas and I shared our empire. Now I will share it with you."

"Will you bring me as close as he was?"

"Closer," she whispered. She knew what she must do. "I almost took your life. I'll give you mine now—my life and my trust. I will tell you who I am."

And so she told him how Anne Rive and her brother had killed the Earl of Mortmain and fled to London. How they'd met Izzy Cockayne, who sheltered them in the underworld. How they'd slowly risen to power. Rafe gripped her more tightly, his hands a hard anchor. His gaze never wavered, mirroring, magnifying, the outrage and pain the years had dimmed. For her, the telling brought memories of Nick, who had been steadfast at her side for so long. Rafe had not known her brother when he was young, full of jests and easy tenderness. Mortmain had broken a part of Nick which never mended—and Rosy had completed his destruction. Pain sank claws in her heart, but Rafe's presence beside her made it bearable. When she was done, there was a new peace, a new freedom. "No one knows this now, except you and Izzy."

"This secret is safe with me," he said. "I give you my word."

"You didn't want to be owned. I am yours now, as much as you are mine. Are you mine?"

"Yes," he said softly. "I'm yours." His arms gathered her protectively, and she drifted in his embrace. The harmony that had seemed suddenly precarious returned, enveloping them. He stroked her hair, spreading it over her shoulders. Comfort, tenderness, acceptance flowed from his caresses. "Our tales weave together," he said quietly.

"How so?" she asked, raising to look at him.

"I never met the old Earl of Mortmain, but I once had a skirmish with the young one. He lost a fortune in small wagers because he would not believe a commoner could wield a sword as skillfully as he."

"Bravo." Vivian smiled, pleased to share an enemy. "From what I know of him, the heir's arrogance is equal to the father's."

He gathered her close, protective still. "Would he recognize you if he saw you?"

"Perhaps. I make sure he does not."

Rafe nodded, his hand sliding under her hair to caress her back. After a time, he said quietly, "Perhaps the Queen would pardon you."

"The Queen?" Viv smiled bitterly. "It's true I used to imagine her listening to my woeful tale, and granting me a pardon. But that time is long past."

"She is a woman. She would understand."

"I do not doubt the woman would understand. But the Queen rides the crest of power, and her nobles are the great wave which bears her high. She cannot afford to forgive me," Viv said. "I could be hung a thousand times over for the life I've lived since the Earl's death, but bribery keeps the hangman at bay. That one act would insure the rope around my neck. Nothing but a miracle would save me."

"Then I shall pray for a miracle," he said, smiling slightly to ease the growing darkness of the mood.

"Why should I want to be saved?" Viv jested in answer. "Here I am Queen in my own right, and a fine gaudy, bawdy kingdom it is."

"Tell me true," he whispered. "Would you not reclaim your birthright if you could?"

"Of course," she said. "But that will never happen."

"Perhaps—"

She laid her fingers over his lips. "I will hold onto what I have. Elizabeth rules her realm. I rule mine. Queen above and Queen below."

$\mathcal{T}$he last flames of sunset were fading above the roofs of Southwark, but Vivian felt an inferno rising in her. All day the fire had mounted, feeding on the fuel of her grief. Now mourning and fury merged into a single element, and only by appeasing one could she begin to heal the other. "Izzy reports that Rosy Piper lay about in his rooms all day in silk and tears, mopping his brow and saying he must be strong enough to perform tonight."

Rafe smiled contemptuously. "No doubt everyone is impressed by his valor."

Vivian snorted. "Especially since tonight is his first performance as leading man." Rafe was cloaked, and they were taking a deserted back route to avoid being seen. Gossip was abroad that Rafe was dead, and she wanted no contrary whisper to reach the Comet. She strode along freely in her doublet, trousers, and boots, pleased Rafe no longer showed any trace of disapproval, that he accepted her for who she was. All of who she was. She glanced at him walking beside her along the narrow lane. Odd how she felt not less safe now that he knew her secret, but more. Even without touching him, she felt the tension and anticipation crackling through his body, too. Eager for anything, both of them. Ready to face it together.

"I approve of these night performances at the Comet," she remarked. "The taverns and stews in our territory will be bustling with business, to say nothing of the opportunities for the pickpockets."

The theatre itself would bring her little. The Comet stood within the border of the neighboring Paris Gardens, officially under the rule of One Eye Wallace. The backing for the theatre was from entrepreneurs in both London and Southwark, and Wallace had his piece. As with Maggot, she had a portion of that. Rivett had tried to acquire a partnership, she knew, to sharpen the wedge he was driving into Southwark, but Wallace kept him out of it. The mere thought of Rivett sent scarlet spiraling before her eyes. She had no proof that Jake had hired Rosy to kill Nick, but all knew that if the power of the Swifts was broken, Rivett would swoop down like a vulture before the crows like Maggot and Wallace could glean many pickings. "He underestimates me," she murmured, teeth clenched. Her power was not broken.

"Considerably," Rafe agreed, knowing who she meant. She liked the way their minds worked together. Even after so short a time, in some ways he understood her better even than Nick had. She and Nick had been of one mind in their deviousness, but Rafe was ingenious in his own way. Nick's moods had swung between lassitude and feckless energy, seldom finding a steady course. Rafe was the firm rudder to her sail.

"I wonder if Rosy did other damage we have not discovered yet?" Rafe mused.

"Not likely, in my organization. No one paid him any

heed but Nick." She gripped the hilt of her sword. "Rosy Piper is nothing. His paymaster would see at once he's good only for cowardly mischief and poisoning."

"And spying."

"He could discover only one secret that really matters."

"Do you think he has?" Rafe asked quietly, accomplice now.

"Nick said not. But no, I do not know for certain." She squared her shoulders, taking on that challenge. Fear of the past was far away tonight, even knowing her enemy might possess her secret. "I need two pieces of information from Rosy Piper. Who he was working for and whether Nick told him of our past. Then all I need is to watch him die." She looked Rafe in the eyes, offering the gift of this revenge, which he must crave nearly as much for his own sufferings. "In agony and terror, if possible. As Nick died."

Rafe nodded, then looked away. Rosy had tried to contrive Rafe's death. She knew he must understand and want this gift, but though he looked back almost at once, nodding acceptance, she did not see the eagerness she expected. She frowned. "You are fully recovered? No lingering ill effects?"

He paused fractionally, increasing her worry. But he answered firmly, "I am equal to this."

She smiled, the blaze mounting again. "We have both journeyed through hell, and come out triumphant together."

"If it was Rivett who paid Rosy, what next?"

"That depends. If it is safe for me to stay in England, I shall deal with him. If I must flee, I will still make him pay. As soon as I can." She felt her back muscles tighten. Though she would not be without resources if she must leave the country, her empire, her home, were here in London. "Either way, whoever is behind Nick's death made a mistake leaving me alive."

They reached the end of the lane where it opened to the street. Ahead were the tall, broad, timbered walls of the Comet Theatre. People had gathered at the end of the street, paying their penny for admittance, milling about in conversation, waiting to join friends. It was a motley crowd, the laborers and other groundlings hoping for a lurid spectacle of play-acted revenge, the merchants and their wives eager to display their wealth, nips and foists eager to relieve them of it. Clusters of young gallants from the Inns of Court disputed the merits of the play before they had seen it performed. All were familiar with the playmaker, Thomas Kyd, whose *Spanish Tragedy* was such a ferocious success. This new work was taken from a French tale of a prince called Hamlet whose uncle murdered his father and usurped his throne. Rumor had it Kyd would repeat some of his most successful gambits from last year's vengeance play in this new one. Perhaps too many, according to snatches she'd heard of the gallants' talk.

As she and Rafe moved through the crowd, young men ignorant of Southwark stared openly at her male attire. Rafe bristled slightly, moving closer. Viv spared him a quick smile of camaraderie, amused at his protectiveness. He was still her knight. Then she focused on the business at hand. She searched for Smoke near the main entrance. He'd been awaiting her arrival and met her glance, nodding slightly. *Excellent.* Rosy was in the theatre as expected. She sighted two of her men by a side door, a few others milling about as if waiting to go in, their alertness concealed. All wore plain clothes rather than the scarlet and black of her livery.

"Instead of some forceful hero, Ambrose Piper?" The scoffing remark was followed by a puff of laughter.

"That choice in the role intrigues me," a softer voice responded.

The words close at hand caught her attention. Vivian turned to see a young man with thinning brown hair, keen eyes and fine, arched brows in conversation with another. Neither was richly dressed, but their beards were neatly trimmed, their hands uncalloused. They carried themselves with more flair than clerks—actors, perhaps.

"Intrigues you?" His friend gave a puff of laughter.

"It opens new possibilities," the first fellow went on. "No man of action, a Hamlet too thoughtful—too tormented by the thousand implications and uncertainties that lie within all actions to strike directly. Is that not what humanity has come to?"

Not me, Vivian thought.

"What, a bumbling philosopher for a hero? They would pelt him with rotten eggs!" His companion laughed again, glancing toward the doorway. His voice was vaguely familiar, and Vivian looked at him more closely.

"No, mark me, I mean it," the first answered. "What uncharted territory might we explore if the action of the simplest play were turned not outward, but inward?"

"Then write your own version, Will. But can we go in before the best cheap seats are taken?"

Playmakers, then. Vivian did not recognize the second man, and she rarely forgot a face, but something about the soft mouth, and the expressive dark eyes under the wide temples was peculiarly familiar.

Putting her hand on Rafe's arm, she whispered, "That fellow, who is he?"

Rafe gave the man a brief glance. "No one I know."

"Look again more carefully, I feel should know him. Perhaps I've seen him at the Lightning Bolt."

"What about that one over there?" Rafe nodded toward a man in a red cap and black stubble. "Isn't that one of Rivett's dregs?"

Vivian snapped around to where he pointed. "It is." Anger flared, parching her like thirst. There was only one way to appease it. "I will enter now. You know what to do."

Rafe's fingers closed on hers for a moment, conveying awareness of her pain, and her need. She watched him go through the crowd. She was so fortunate to have found him it almost frightened her at times. Yet this new vulnerability only Rafe Fletcher had ever awakened made her love him all the more. Vivian made her way to the entrance. She paid three pennies, the price for the best seats, and climbed the stairs to the first gallery. In the gathering twilight, its seats were dark but for torches placed so the spectators could see their footing. The stage was covered by a high canopy of wood, but the groundlings' area surrounding it was roofless. The stage flickered brightly in the light of well-placed torches, the smoke drifting into a deep blue sky where stars glittered like flakes of gold and silver gilt.

Vivian made her way to the seats directly overlooking the side of the stage. Izzy sat there, holding a second seat for her. Vivian settled in it and looked down at the stage, anticipating the unique performance to be enacted for her, Rafe, and Izzy, and only for them.

Izzy nodded at the stage. "The light from those torches is falling on us. The players will see us."

Vivian smiled. "Rosy Piper acted prettily for us before. Let us see how he performs when the play is mine."

"I, for one, want my money's worth. I want to see that fawning, plume-prancing, twist-tongued, venom-spewing measle skewered on a spit and roasted slowly." Izzy's good-natured face was hard. But then he frowned. "Do you believe in ghosts? I keep feeling as if Nick is here, like he can't rest till it's set right."

"If that's so, I will send Piper where Nick can deal with him. And you shall have your wish."

"Yes, but do you think—"

She squeezed Izzy's hand. "No more of that." Heaven and hell were beyond reckoning. She only knew what she could not tolerate here on earth.

The musicians struck up a tune, recorders, hautboys, and drums measuring out a stately tune appropriate for a tragedy. Vivian watched the last of the audience find standing room, the hawkers moving amid the crowd to sell apples and meat pies. The tune finished, and the chorus entered. The crowd quieted to hear him recount the plot in brief, the tragic murder of a king by his own brother, the murderer taking both throne and Queen, the filial prince avenging the wrongs but suffering ruin in the course of doing right.

Apt enough, Vivian thought, waiting with surging, enforced patience.

At last Rosy Piper entered. In mourning black, lugubrious as a puritan, he was very masculine tonight, very much the leading man, the only touch of coy prettiness his shining hair. From this far away she could not tell if he had really spent the day in tears, but she did not doubt he had the skill to weep when he wished. The clarity of his voice gave the lie to grief, and the untroubled grace of his gestures proclaimed his guilt loudly as a shout. With a small, bitter smile Vivian watched him quake and fall to his knees before his father's ghost and vow vengeance on the murderer.

It was a fine scene. As he rose, his gaze swept the best seats to see how his performance was admired. His eyes met hers, and widened. He recovered his line, but as he described his vision to his friends, Hamlet's glance stole to her and Izzy. Izzy kept his face as neutral, as unreadable, as hers. Of course he would have heard gossip of Rafe's death, and must believe himself successful. Piper could pretend courage and duty had brought him to the stage, but seeing Vivian enjoying an evening out mere days after her brother's death had shaken his performance noticeably. She would have given much to know what he made of it.

Yet as the prince outlined his scheme to feign madness and escape suspicion, conviction suddenly returned to his voice. Encountering his uncle and his mother, he whirled with grace into a wild speech and extravagant gestures. As he doffed his cap, taking leave of them, Piper glanced at her again, and let grief flicker over his face, and mournful sympathy.

Vain, mewling, maggot-pie.

Vivian choked down her rage. So he thought she was here to offer her patronage, did he? And lost no time milking it. Poor, dead Nick would have wanted her to be generous to his Rosy, would he? As Rosy exited, Vivian ground her teeth.

A scene unfolded without him, and Vivian held herself in her chair with difficulty, fingers tapping the hilt of her sword. At last he entered again. The king hired a courtesan to wheedle Hamlet's secrets, but the crafty prince would have none of her tricks. Piper was busy wriggling from her amorous arms and did not notice when Izzy slipped quietly away and Rafe took his place beside her. The audience loved the scene's bawdy thrusts and parries. Knowing Vivian's earthy humor, Rosy glanced to see if she was enjoying it.

Hamlet's shock at his father's ghost was put to shame by the disbelieving terror that distorted Rosy Piper's face. Lips working soundlessly like a fish, he stared at Rafe, and then at her. His fellow player waited for his line in growing alarm, then picked up the dropped line, twisting its words to make them the strumpet's and feed him his cue. Rosy responded sluggishly, tearing his gaze from them, if not his thoughts.

Beside her, Rafe was intent on Rosy Piper, his calm face as implacable as an executioner's. As he spoke his next lines, Rosy looked wildly about the theatre. He saw her men were watching all the entrances and realized he was in a trap. When he looked up at her again, Vivian allowed a smile to steal over her face.

Rosy's terror grew, and with it his acting galloped faster, wilder. Hamlet no longer feigned madness but transformed to a hollow, frenzied lunatic in truth. Vivian watched over her prey, flexing her fingers on her sword hilt like a hawk stretching out her talons to take a squeaking rat. "He knows these are his last moments," she murmured to Rafe. "If I were he, I would drag out each one, not spur them on,"

"If nothing else were in my power, I hope I would at least play out a last scene the crowd would remember me by, not earn their catcalls," Rafe answered.

The valor of his answer pleased her, as did its truth. After the fine beginning, the crowd felt cheated by Piper's awkward faltering. From disapproving silence they were moving into sullen buzzing, and now in the back a voice rose, openly heckling him. Vivian watched Piper wince as if under a lash. She narrowed her eyes with fierce satisfaction. If his vanity was more capable of shame than his loyalty, let them wound him there where it hurt him most.

The players exited, and others entered with the king's councilor and queen. Hamlet was not among them, but Vivian was not concerned. If Rosy tried to bolt, her guards would catch him. They knew exactly what to do: silence him before he could raise an alarm, and take him alive to a certain nearby cellar until she arrived. She did not doubt Piper checked the doors, but he had the sense not to try them, for Hamlet called at his mother's door, and the councilor slipped behind the arras to spy on him. Rosy entered, looking strained but no longer panicked. The dread had left his eyes, but so, seemingly, had hope. In the torchlight they looked flat and dull as old coins.

After some disdainful incoherence about the lustfulness of donkeys, monkeys, and ladies, the mad prince dismayed his mother by crowing like a rooster and flapping his arms. The playwright's shabby device was transparent even to the groundlings. Flopping thus, he could not fail to brush the arras and discover the spy. Only Piper's distraction explained his bad judgment in drawing it out so long. Then, understanding, Vivian gripped Rafe's arm. Rosy chose that very moment to careen, arms flailing, into one of the torch stands. It crashed over, hurling the torch into the arras. A line of flame swept up the cloth, and the spy behind them fled, heedless of the play. Rosy ran for the back exit.

Cursing, Vivian vaulted over the rail of the gallery onto the stage. Rafe leapt beside her, but fed by the breeze, the vanguard of the fire licked the posts holding up the wooden stage covering, and the boards of the stage itself began to ignite, sending players and stagehands running from the wooden structure to seek escape among the screaming, shoving groundlings. Those backstage rushed after Piper. The rest leapt from the stage and raced up the isles. Some hero, imagining she was running toward the flames in panic, grabbed her wrist and pulled her back, refusing to heed her command to let go until Rafe gave his arm a sharp twist. The stampede had cleared the stage, but Rosy was gone, and vines of flame twined up the exit.

Vivian saw flames spreading fast among the backstage clutter as she plunged through the fiery ring. As she had known he would be, Rafe was right behind her. They sped beneath rafters catching flame toward the back door. It was closed, but there was no other, and Piper would not hide in what would soon be an inferno. The door yielded, but the blaze mounted with the in-draft. Smoke billowed through the doorway with them. Outside, both guards she had posted lay dead, blood drenching their doublets.

Leaving hell, they entered chaos. The inhabitants of the populous lane had realized their danger, and were struggling under hastily gathered possessions, or trying to drag furniture through the narrow, crooked way, or calling frantically for their children. Rafe grasped her arm and pointed. Without the advantage of his height, Vivian could not see Rosy in the turmoil, but shoved and clawed her way through the frantic bodies in the direction Rafe had showed her. Then through a brief opening in the crowd she spotted tawny hair above black shoulders, Piper darting into a side alley.

Vivian knew the alley well. It twisted for some distance, intersected by other alleys before crossing one which led to a riverside dock. Some were blind ends, but if Rosy knew this warren he might easily escape. But

Rosy was a creature who delighted in strutting down the broad public way, and might easily take a false turning. With Rafe's size and strength they made headway through the confusion, but not fast enough. By the time they reached the alley Piper was out of sight.

The crooked way angled toward the Comet, and no crowd filled it. They pursued unhampered now, peering into each doorway and cranny they passed. The alley bent away from the theatre again, but above the rooftops the sky glared lurid scarlet, and Vivian could hear the shouting. Another score to settle with Rosy Piper. Some of those lanes housed her investments, and people who looked to her for protection.

Rafe reached the first intersection just before she did. Piper ran not far ahead, silent in his soft costume slippers. Their swords rang, and their boots clattered behind. The player wasted no time glancing to see if it was them, but put on desperate speed. He swerved into the rathole of another alley. Exultation filled Vivian. "Dead end," she panted fiercely to Rafe. Piper could go nowhere now.

Beyond the turn, the alley continued only the length of a few buildings before ending with a high wall. They approached quickly, but on guard. Rafe gave her a silent look, then sprang forward, protecting her by exposing himself first. Almost on top of him, Piper leapt from the shadows and thrust. Steel clashed as Rafe's blade hammered his down. Vivian struck while Piper's guard was down, but he had anticipated that, already dodging back. He was fast, maybe even as fast as she was. Vivian's need blazed, filling her with demonic urgency hotter than the scarlet sky. Fueled by it, she drove on, making Rosy leap back again. He struck at her, but she saw the warning in a tiny flicker of his eyes, and parried, gritting her teeth at the heavy blow of metal on metal. Rafe circled lightly behind her, blocking Rosy's only way out of the alley, but waiting until she needed him, letting her fury claim this moment.

She watched Rosy's eyes in the dim scarlet glow. A slight flick presaged the direction of his next move, and she swerved. He shortened it in time, keeping his guard up. Despite his seeming indolence he was strong and well trained, and his quick reactions were formidable, but in the end his athletics were for the stage. He was not aware his own eyes betrayed his strategy. "Scar-face slut," he hissed, trying to goad her. "You'll never rule the Clink on your own."

He was ready for her. Even on fire, she was no fool. She circled, watching his eyes, listening to his breathing for an involuntary change.

"If that pretty brute standing behind you does not take it from you, the next one will."

In a deadly purr she countered, "You will not survive to see it. Even if you escape me, do you imagine your paymaster will let you live?"

Rosy laughed scornfully. Lurid glow on his face, cinders drifting on the breeze that stirred his hair, he looked like a fiend, mawkish and heartless.

So a deal had been struck, and Piper was confident of it. Whoever his master was, he could deliver on promises. Vivian struck at Rosy's heart, but he managed to turn her blade, and pressed his advantage ferociously. "Nick was amusing—for a while," he taunted. "You never were. I wanted to kill you, too." He smiled. "Now I will." He snapped his sword in a small circle, tip pointed at her face—a showy move loved by audiences and calculated to make her cringe away.

Puffed toad. By the time the trick turned itself to a lunge, she had seen in his eyes where he was going. Keeping her own eyes carefully unreadable, Vivian awaited the final instant, then sidestepped, driving her blade below his upraised arm. She felt it catch in soft flesh. Piper cried out and lunged against his own impetus to escape a deep wound, throwing himself off balance. His sword arm flailed. If she had wanted, she could have spitted him then like a coney. Instead she kicked the leg he rocked back on, all the force she had craved to put into her sword transferred to her boot. With a cry he went down.

Standing over him, Vivian set the point of her blade in the soft hollow of his throat. "Drop the sword."

He stilled instantly, opening his hand so his weapon rolled onto the packed dirt of the alley. Vivian kicked it out of reach.

"Who paid you to kill my brother?"

Terror distorted his face, but he summoned up all his acting skill, changing it to a derisive smile. "I tell you that, and you'll no longer have a reason to keep me alive."

Vivian smiled back. "I have none anyway. But would you rather a quick stroke, or a slow slicing to ribbons?"

"Neither. What about a bargain, instead?"

Rage tightened her grip on the hilt. She wanted to peel him like an apple. "There is only one bargain, Rosy. When I look at you, I see my brother in agony."

"You will torture me anyway," he whined.

"Tell me and you will die quickly. I give you my word." She pierced the skin at his throat, blood welling around the point of her sword. "Speak now or suffer."

"Rivett," he gasped.

Viv eased back the point a fraction, "Tell me."

"Soon after Nick began courting me, Jacob Rivett came wooing. At first he wanted only information. Then . . ." Rosy's voice trailed off. He tried again, with little more success, "He promised me—"

"What? What was the price of Nick's life?"

"Ownership of the Comet. Rivett's bought control of it secretly."

"From One Eye Wallace?" Would she have to contend with both Wallace and Maggot trying to tug both ends of the rope?

"No. He was blackmailing two of the investors. He forced them to buy for him when Wallace shut him out."

Viv was glad she had not misjudged Wallace. She would need all her allies to destroy Rivett. She gazed coldly at Rosy. "Rivett said he would give you the Comet."

"You're a businesswoman, Viv. You know what that would mean." His hand went to his heart, as if he imagined that made them secret intimates. "Nick offered me only baubles."

Nick had given Rosy Piper his very soul. Vivian's ears roared with the mounting wave of rage. But she could not let it fall quite yet. Choosing her words carefully, she countered, "You had only to ask. You had only to tell Nick."

"Rivett said he would kill me. Nick couldn't protect me from him." Rosy whimpered piteously.

Viv remembered when he had mewled exactly so as the beleaguered heroine in his last melodrama. She pushed the sword point back through the skin. Now the choking gasp Rosy gave was honest, and the blood that stained his neck was real. "Nick would have killed Rivett for the threat," Vivian hissed at him. "He would have protected you—but he couldn't protect himself from you."

"Please . . ." he croaked.

Viv eased the point back. There was more she needed to know. She kept her voice soft, as if she was only grieving for the past. "Nicholas would have stood by you. He must have told you how we came to London?"

"I know Izzy brought you," Rosy answered, confused. "You were poor relations, but you could speak well. You climbed out of the gutter together."

There was not a flicker that suggested Rosy believed anything else.

"When Jacob Rivett wants your territory, you'll be back in the gutter where you belong." Finding his courage, Rosy mocked her, flourishing one hand to indicate the offal around them. His other hand crept into his doublet.

Rafe shouted a warning at the same instant Vivian drove down two-handed, stabbing Piper through the gullet. Amid the blood she saw for a moment a shadow of the terror she had seen in Nick's face. But before it could register fully, it was over.

Heart pounding, Vivian was aware of Rafe's sword point at Piper's heart. If she had missed, Piper's knife would not have gone home. Rafe would have had him first.

She bent, drawing out the hand still clutching the jeweled knife Rosy had worn the day Nick died. Carefully she pried open the dead fingers. "You were right. It is an actor's bauble." She turned it so he could see the hidden plunger. "A squeeze on this stone ejects the stage blood."

"Or the poison," Rafe answered grimly. "I'll wager he's kept it on him for fear of you."

"He did not fear me enough," she answered, but she was numb. The satisfaction she had imagined had eluded her. She had been forced to dispatch him too fast, and in any case he was not the real murderer, only Jacob Rivett's tool. She had not yet accomplished the justice Nick's death demanded. Wearily she said, "Let us begone, we have plans to make." Amid the drifting cinders and smell of ruin, the only thing that had reality was the proven loyalty of the man standing beside her, his hand on her arm, warm and gentle.

22

*S*ilver held out the metal flask, its plain surface deceptively ordinary.

"The poison?" Topaz reached out eagerly, taking the
sealed flask in his hand.

"There is a glass vial within this, stoppered and sealed
tight with wax."

"It is odorless, colorless?" Eyes fervid in the candlelight, Topaz examined his prize. "Nothing must betray
its presence before the heretic succumbs."

"It is a lethal distillation of monkshood. A single drop
will cause death whether it is placed in food or merely
dropped on the skin. Whoever handles it must understand the danger. Though if they spill it, they won't survive to implicate you."

"You are sure?"

"Absolutely." The crooked Crabbe had been well
rewarded for his expertise.

"You tested it—on the apothecary? Is it painful?"

"Excruciating I'm told." He smiled. "The victim was
Nicholas Swift."

For an instant Topaz looked angry, then he laughed.
"You had it placed in perfume?"

"No, but the manner was similar enough. Fletcher
was made to look the poisoner. He is dead and rotting

on the bottom of the Thames." Perfume would have worked well enough. Any guard or servant with access to Nicholas' room would have been suspect, Fletcher among them. But Rosy would have been suspect as well. The actor had been entranced with his own scheme to throw suspicion on Fletcher. Since it had worked, Silver could hardly quarrel with it. "This is doubly advantageous. Fletcher and whatever he's learned are destroyed, and Walsingham will direct his attention where we have pointed."

"Toward Vivian Swift." Topaz gloated as if she were his personal enemy. Mortmain had always seemed amused by this part of the plan, ever since Agate had pointed Vivian out one night, when her patrol swept by their hiding place.

"We will fell two queens with one blow," Silver said. One way or another, Vivian would soon follow Nick, and his way would be cleared in Southwark. No need to relinquish his illegitimate control of the docks simply because he would soon have a legitimate one. They were but two gloves to fit the full grasp of his hands. When they succeeded, Sir Jacob Rivett would be more powerful than many lords of greater title.

"The apothecary lives?" Topaz asked.

"Yes." He had use still for his crooked Crabbe.

"You know my thoughts—I would give him a sip of his own brew."

Silver had no intention of relinquishing so useful a prize without reason. "If he fears the death of a queen, it is the Queen of the Clink."

"See he has no reason to link them," Topaz said.

Silver ignored him. "Are you ready to receive the guns?"

"Yes. Be ready to move north. Rumor has it that Mary will be taken from Chartley to Fotheringay for trial. I have chosen a location that should serve wherever she is taken. The one place it will not be is the Tower, since the bastard's whore mother lost her head there."

"I've already had my jarkman drawn up the false passports for the men. Tell me where to send the wagons."

Topaz gave him directions to the farmhouse. "The building is secure, the owners loyal to the cause. Once the weapons are in the hands of my men, we will move swiftly. My spies have chosen the best points of attack, both on the road and against Chartley house."

Topaz would have the prize snaphances and the cannon. But would it be enough? "How many men do you have? How skilled are they in the use of these weapons?"

"Enough men, with enough skill."

Rivett nodded, hating to be involved in any plan where he had so little control. But he could do nothing in Staffordshire, and Elizabeth's assassination was the crux of the matter. If that failed, he must be ready to flee. He said, "I will set out tomorrow, after midnight."

"I will arrange another meeting with my confederate. She said the heretic Queen has been expecting a new perfume from France. She will be sure to choose it—and that day she will choose death," Topaz said, closing his first tight about the flask. "And then the Queen of Scots will claim her rightful place on the throne."

"I will pray for success." Rivett crossed himself quickly, then walked to the door.

"Silver?"

Rivett paused, waiting.

"Do you still have the dragon brooch?" Topaz asked. "It would make an amusing token, since it is no longer of any use against Fletcher."

Rivett shrugged. "I will see if it can be retrieved." He went down the stairs, and out into the street. His bodyguards moved out of the alley to his side. One man pointed down the alley. "Fire across the river, sir."

Between the buildings Rivett glimpsed flames bright against the darkness, and the night breeze brought a heavy scent of smoke. Idly, he wondered what was burning in Southwark.

23

*S*prawled beside Vivian in the bed, Rafe reached out one hand to stroke her back, fingertips gliding down her spine. The silk curtains made a soft red cave of their bed, a world apart. Beyond them, a faint whisper of rain sounded at the windows, lulling, peaceful. Nothing could touch them here.

"Mmmummmm . . . ooooooh . . . muumm . . ." Viv murmured her enjoyment, stretching catlike beneath his touch.

He clung to the languorous pleasure a moment longer, but the prickings of conscience resumed their attack.

I must tell her.

If only Rafe could be a little more sure of her, he might chance revealing his true identity and ask for her assistance. He had almost told her a dozen times since she had revealed her own secret. Would joining with him to catch Rivett win her a pardon? Surely helping to uncover treason would excuse Vivian Swift's common crimes. But the death of a peer was another matter. Rafe would reveal what she had told him of Mortmain to no one.

"Mmmmmm . . ." he murmured to her in turn. He kissed her shoulder then bit it gently, licking a taste of salt.

The betrayal he had worked would enrage her. But she had killed to protect her honor, her family. Surely, she would understand what he had done to protect his? Understanding did not mean forgiveness, but promised hope of it. She loved him—or loved the man she believed him to be. But how much of what she believed was false? Only his willingness to live as a criminal. He would not have succumbed as easily as the fencing master, but it was a path he might have been driven down, if it meant his survival, as it had hers.

Viv turned to him, smiling, cupping his face as she gave him a kiss, tender and succulent. He started to pull her closer, but she wriggled free. She shook her head, a little smile curving her lips. "There's no more time—we must plan the attack."

She opened the bed curtains and rose, letting in the dim morning light. The soft patter of rain on glass continued, but Rafe could see shafts of sunlight opening in the distance. He settled back on the bed, watching Viv as she walked naked into her bathing room. His hands tightened in the covers, linen still warm with the scent of her body. He wanted to tell her here, now. It would be an offering of trust to tell her when he was as naked as she was, still warm from their loving. But the same vulnerability could be too painful for her. If she gave way to fury there would be no escape without violence. She might try to kill him. If she summoned her men before he could subdue her, he might not get away. Nick's murder would make her feel his own betrayal more keenly. Telling her where either of them could walk away without harm was the wise choice. But where was the wisdom in loving her?

It must be today. Rafe could not carry on the deception any longer. He must still discover who had sabotaged the guns, but Rivett was the far more likely target. Vivian's quest for vengeance was now at odds with his own. Rivett had hired Rosy. To avenge Nick, Viv would want to kill Rivett as well. Rafe had to have him alive. Rivett had to be questioned about the guns. Rafe must choose a time, ask Vivian directly about Chettle. When she had cleared away the last of his doubts, he would confess, offer her the protection of the Crown to help him take Rivett.

And pray she did not desert him in her fury.

Still naked, Vivian emerged from the bath and sat on a velvet padded stool in front of her dresser. Arrayed before her were pots of paint and powder, carved or lacquered boxes of jewels. "I don't want to summon Joan," she said, glancing at him. "You help me."

"Me?" Giving her a smile, Rafe rose from the bed and moved to stand behind her. "With me to help, you'll be back among the pillows, naked and well disheveled."

"A most excellent plan." Tilting her head back, she smiled, moving ever so slightly to tease the fall of her hair back and forth across his body. Rafe arched back with a low gasp, his cock rising under the caress of her hair. He drew a deep breath, amazed at what her slightest touch could do to him. She straightened and sought his gaze in the glass again. "When I'm with you I want to be abed all day. It will not do."

"No?" He played with the fall of her hair, running the weight of it through his hands and teasing the ends against her back like silken tassels.

"No." She laughed and shook her hair free. "Rivett will have his plans in order. I must organize. Let me dress, then there is something I want to show you."

Knowing she was right, Rafe moved back from the temptation of her golden skin. He went into the bath and doused himself with water to cool his arousal. His whole body still tingled with awareness, as if she were a magnet he would be drawn to whether he would or no.

Reentering her chamber, Rafe found she'd donned a linen shirt and trunkhose. She pulled on the body of her doublet, the gleaming black satin piped with white in a pattern of fish scales. He helped her tie the doublet sleeves, then tugged on his own clothes as she watched, smiling, obviously hoping to stir him with her smile alone. He turned his back, not that it was much safer, for her gaze teased his buttocks like a touch, and every second he expected her hands to come exploring, if only to torment him.

Only when he was completely covered did Viv turn aside and move back to the dresser. Safe for the moment, he watched as she opened her jewelry boxes, taking a pearl earring from one, a ruby ring from another. From the largest she lifted a heavy gold chain set with jet, the plaques snarled with a mass of thinner chains and gems. Impatiently she set to untangling the mass. After coiling the chains back in the box, she held the jewel that had snared them on her palm and examined it thoughtfully. It was a brooch—a dragon of enameled gold grasping a round of amber, a tiny insect trapped within its depths.

Breath left him. The room dissolved into swarming motes of light and dark. For a second her hand, the jewel, were all he could see. Rafe inhaled, and when he spoke his voice was barely above a whisper, though its softness could pass for intimacy. "A curious piece. Where did you get it?"

Viv hesitated, her expression shadowed as she gazed at the brooch. Then she shrugged. "I gather such trophies easily enough."

Rafe's heart twisted. He willed himself to breath evenly. "Do you?"

He had shown too much. She met his eyes in the mirror. "What is it?"

Find a truth to tell. "My father wore a brooch in the likeness of a dragon."

Viv hesitated again, then smiled and pressed the brooch into his hand. "Then you take it. It means nothing to me."

His fingers closed tight round the jewel. His voice was tight, too, as he whispered, "Thank you."

"Do you remember him well?" Vivian asked tentatively.

"Yes."

"You were so young when he died."

"I remember it vividly. . . ." Gabe dying in his arms, the air reeking with blood.

Rafe fought down the turmoil, willed silence over the pain, the rage.

"You know I understand," Viv said softly, inviting his confidence.

When he said nothing more, she faced the mirror and slipped the gold chain over her shoulders—a man's heavy

chain such as she often wore. She had a man's promiscu-
ous lusts, a man's ruthless instincts. How many had she
killed on her rise to power?

He clenched his fist. The pin of the brooch stabbed
his palm.

It means nothing to me. Her words echoed in his mind.
Rafe knew she gathered booty from her men. Perhaps the
explanation was no more sinister than that. Perhaps Gabriel's murderers had not taken the brooch. Perhaps Gabriel
had lost it on that last bloody journey rather than in the
fight. Rafe did not trust himself to question Vivian now.
If she was guilty, it was too dangerous to focus her attention on the jewel. Pain twisted his heart again, knotted it,
but he slipped the brooch in his purse and asked, "What
is your plan for Rivett?"

She paced restlessly, her rising energy palpable. "Now
that Rosy is dead, we must be quick. Rivett will not
know if Piper confessed his involvement, but he must
suspect it. He will be planning both defense and attack.
We must strike first. I've already contacted Maggot, One
Eye Wallace, and Harry Corker. They have all agreed to
commit their men. None of them feels safe after learning
Rivett arranged Nick's death."

"The men admire you, that's an advantage. Rivett is
much hated, but he's much feared, too. Their courage
may falter when you most need them to press forward."

Viv gave him a quick, ferocious smile. "Follow me.
There is something I want to show you."

Going out of the bedroom door, she opened the secret
passageway and took him down to the cellar, then led

him to another room beside the one where he'd been held. She took out a key and fitted it to the lock. "In an hour Smoke will go over the arms with the other men. Not all of them own pistols, but all have had training in their use. But I've newer and better than any they've awaiting them. A small advantage, but one that will fire their spirits."

"Pistols?" Rafe's spine turned to ice, freezing cold branching out along his limbs and cracking open his heart.

"Yes, they were stored across the river. But our holdings Londonside are the first Rivett is like to attack. I had Smoke bring them here yesterday."

The territory near the Tower—where Gabriel had gone the night he died.

The door swung open and Vivian stepped inside and lit the hanging lantern. The room was filled with smugglers' prizes, crates of wine, wool, silk, and furs. She led him to two unmarked wooden boxes placed to one side of the door. "We'd not decided whether to sell these weapons or use them ourselves. It's good we kept them. I want all the advantage I can get against Smelly Jakes."

Rafe felt dizzy as the light flickered uneasily over the small wooden crates. Smiling, Viv gestured for him to have a look. He lifted the open lid, and the expected yet dreaded shock of recognition was like a blow. At his sharp inhalation, Viv murmured, "Beautiful, aren't they."

"Beautiful . . ." His voice was a hoarse whisper. With a surge of hope, he took one of the pistols from the nest of straw, raised it to the circle of lantern light, and ran his fingers over every part. There was no flaw, nothing to indicate that Nicholas and Vivian had been duped by the saboteurs. He took a second and searched it. No sign of tampering. "These guns are perfect."

"The finest snaphances to be had," she said. "Chettle was good for something before he died."

"Easton Arms," he said, stroking the engraving. He took a third snaphance from the crate, examining the firing mechanism. Perfect. "There are no better weapons than these."

Viv moved behind him and embraced him, reaching round to caress his hands as he held the gun. "Take one, if they please you so much."

"Thank you," Rafe closed his eyes, willing his hands not to shake. His fingers tightened hard around the weapon, and his guts knotted tight inside him. He had been a fool for love, believing what he wanted to believe, searching for truths to match those beliefs. He had been thinking of how to save Vivian, a ruthless killer, rather than how to save his grandfather, the soul of honor.

Schooling his voice, he asked, "How did Chettle acquire these?"

"Chettle knew of some gentleman from the provinces with gambling debts to pay and access to such fine stock. His losses proved our gain."

Still he hoped. "You bought these two cases from Chettle?"

"A trade. A night's labor on his own project, the weapons in return," Viv answered. "Smuggling pays more than the gambling dens and brothels. That's where we've made our greatest fortune."

Smuggling. An innocent name for treason.

Did you murder Chettle as you did Gabriel? Rafe had many more questions, but he no longer trusted himself to speak. He examined another weapon at random, but there were no defects. The truth was obvious. There might be an explanation for the guns, or for the brooch, but not for both. The weapons that had been sent to the Netherlands had been sabotaged here in London, by Chettle in league with the Swifts. In return, Nick and Viv had kept these untampered ones for themselves.

He replaced the gun and Viv led him back into the cellar. On the wall across from the secret stairway to her chambers, she showed him yet another door. "This passage leads beyond the walls. Only Smoke and Izzy and I know of it. There is another that some of the men do know of, leading below the armory and outside the orchard wall. Rivett will be watching the front gate. Tonight we'll use that tunnel to get most of the men outside the walls."

"I'll want to check both passages," Rafe said. His voice was hoarse and he forced a cough.

She nodded agreement. "We will spend today as normally as possible, as if Rosy had not confessed Rivett's involvement," Viv said. "I will send some men across during the day, and disperse them into their hideouts. Tonight the rest will use the tunnels to reach the river, and take the wherries across. Tadpole will keep track of Rivett. Jacob will be watching for my men, but he will take little note of Tadpole and his wrigglers. Rivett is a creature of the night—our best chance to kill him is after midnight."

Rafe leaned against the doorjamb of the tunnel space Viv had revealed, staring into the darkness. She placed a hand on his back and he felt the imprint like a brand. He tensed, hating her and hating himself for wanting her. Even more, he hated the unbidden tenderness that begged that she not be who she was.

"You're trembling," she said. "Are you afraid?"

Nothing would stop his vengeance. He did turn then, holding her tightly, not daring to let her see his face.

"Not fear. Desire." Not fear—fury. Fury and desire. He kissed her savagely.

❧

"You gave Marlowe quite a start last night," Burne said with an acid smile.

"He gave me a start as well. Vivian almost recognized the preacher. She has the wit to see past whiskers."

"He was not following you. We thought you were dead."

Rafe had wondered if Kit Marlowe had found out Viv was to attend Rosy's performance. But Marlowe had reason enough to come hear a play with another playwright.

"He did come to me after, and offered a tale filled with dramatic flourishes and little substance—since he was forced out of the theatre with the crowd," Burne said. "But Piper was found dead this morning.

Briefly, Rafe told him of Nick's death, and Vivian's revenge on Rosy. "He confessed Jacob Rivett had contrived the scheme. Vivian is planning a raid against Rivett."

"One rat has killed another rat, and looks to die in turn," Burne snapped at him. "It has nothing to do with your mission."

Rafe had no patience for Burne's condescension. Despite the bitter ache inside him, he told Burne why he had come. "The Swifts murdered Gabriel and sabotaged the guns."

"You have proof?"

"I saw something I had given Gabriel among Vivian's possessions. She herself showed me two cases of snaphances. I just spent an hour showing her guards the fine points of their use."

"She told you how she came by them?"

If he lied and it was discovered, it would be worse. "A country gentleman with gambling debts sold them to Chettle. My cousin is guilty of fraud, but his crime is against his own family. He has not committed sabotage or treason."

"The Crown will decide that," Burne said, but with little threat inherent in his tone. "What we must decide is the best means of attack."

"I can tell you that," Rafe said.

❧

"Where have you been?" Vivian demanded.

Her voice was sharp, but Rafe could tell the sharpness came from worry, not suspicion. He had not wanted to return, but it was necessary to the plan. If he had stayed with Burne, Vivian might have come looking for him. She must be kept here.

Rafe told the lie he had readied. "I checked the tunnels, then the safe houses, but nearing the Tower I felt I was being followed. So I led my stalkers on a unicorn hunt to misdirect their attention."

The words came easily. He felt like a hawk, hovering cold and distant over his prey. But there was a strange dark weight in his gut, one he knew would bring him crashing to earth at last.

Viv considered what he'd said. "Rivett's men—no one else would have cause."

"I only caught glimpses, but I thought I recognized one of Rivett's guards—the one at the theatre the other night."

Vivian nodded tersely, then took him to a meeting with Smoke and the henchmen who were to coordinate the attack with Maggot and the others against Rivett. Rafe sat at her right hand. She was fulfilling her promise to share her world with him. His nerves were strung tight with tension, yet he felt strangely detached as he discussed the strategy and tactics for the raid. His opinions were sound, but he conceded their better knowledge of the territories at stake. They listened, approving or disapproving details, accepting him as one of them. Tension, calculation—there was nothing in his demeanor at odds with tonight's work.

After the council, they went down to send out the penultimate wave. Viv talked to the men, rousing them for the attack, promising great rewards when it was accomplished. He watched, admiring her skill, her fervor, planning her destruction. Rafe shivered and shivered again, cold in the warm night. After that group embarked, only one other remained. Those Viv and Rafe were to lead after midnight. Small protection against the force Burne would bring.

She brought him back upstairs. They ate a late meal set on a small table in her bedchamber, sharing meat, bread, and fruit. He had to force himself to eat, and each bite seemed to clog his throat. She lifted her golden goblet and he followed suit, the metal ringing against his own. "To the future."

"To the future." He answered her toast. The finest red, smuggled from France. It tasted sour and metallic on his tongue.

Together, they talked of how to organize the territory after Rivett was defeated. Rafe watched her animated gestures—the defiant set of her shoulders, the quick emphasis of her hands. Her words shot like sparks. Viv knew she might die tonight, but the knowledge only intensified the vital force of life. She burned bright as a torch, beautifully, painfully bright in the darkness that shrouded Rafe. Would anyone ever seem as alive again? Her courage was poignant. Deliberately, he closed himself off to the protective tenderness it roused.

The clock on the mantel struck twelve, heralding the invasion. Burne would be punctual, he knew. In his mind's eye he saw the squadron approach the gates with a warrant. The plan was to draw the bulk of the remaining guards there, even as Burne and his men sneaked through the cellar tunnel and then up the secret passage into the salon, into the heart of Vivian's stronghold. Rafe's heart thudded, one beat of triumph, one beat of anger, one beat of guilt, one beat of regret. He wanted it to be over.

At the first noise, Viv frowned. Smoke and Izzy knew the secret passage, but they would have no reason to use it. She turned toward the door, listening intently. The sound was muffled, but he saw alarm quicken in her. "Trouble," she said to him, rising instantly.

Rafe rose with her, as if he would stand by her side. As she reached for her weapons, he seized her, lifting her. The first moment of shock was an advantage, then she yelled for her guards and struggled against his grasp. He was massive compared to her, but she was quick and supple as a ferret, fierce as a wildcat. Twisting in his grip, she bit, clawed, and kicked against his hold. He heard the two guards in the hall running into the salon, but Burne's men were waiting for them. Rafe listened to their fight, still grappling with Vivian as she wrenched furiously against his grip. Fury poured off of her, scorching him. He could barely control her seething energy, subdue it not at all.

Then the sounds of the scuffle stopped and Burne and two soldiers came through the door. Beyond it Rafe could see the bodies of Viv's men, and two more of Burne's, sprawled on the rushes. They all waited, a tense moment, but no more guards came to the rescue. The ploy had worked. The rest of Vivian's men were fighting elsewhere. Viv stilled, and Rafe lowered her so she could stand and face her enemies. At a nod from Burne, one of his soldiers took her away from Rafe. The man stripped her of her weapons, but he underestimated her enough to keep no watch on his own.

Viv seized the guard's knife from its scabbard and drove it up into his throat. Blood sprayed around them as she shoved the body against Burne, then leapt for Rafe, the blade raised, murderous fury glittering in her eyes. The knife slashed through the doublet above his heart, the point piercing his flesh, but Rafe caught her wrist before she drove it home. She went for his eyes with her free hand, her nails raking the side of his face as he grabbed that hand as well. Burne grabbed her and pulled her away, shocked at her power as she fought with vicious intensity. Viv cursed savagely as the other guard helped him subdue her, forcing the knife from her grip and tying her hands in front of her with leather thongs. Rafe did not interfere, only watched her, his heart leaden. The marks of her nails burned his cheek like a brand.

"Judas," she hissed, glaring at him. Tears streaked her face—rage, or grief, or both.

Rafe forced himself to hold her gaze, sure of the righteousness of his victory, but sickened by the method. The certainty of betrayal was a well of darkness in her eyes. He could see the knowledge of it poisoning her soul. He could feel it within, like black acid eating at his own.

Defiant, Viv squared her shoulders and set her jaw. "Will you come to my hanging, Fletcher? You'll want see the finish of what you've begun."

For an instant he dropped his gaze, unable to bear the image. Then he lifted it again, finding his own defiance in the memory of Gabriel's bloody death, of his helpless aunt and uncle slaughtered by her ilk on the highway, and of his innocent family left to rot in prison for her crimes. He would exact justice for them. But only for them.

Quietly, so only she could hear, Rafe said, "I gave you my word once. I have kept it."

I have not told them about Mortmain.

She knew what he meant at once, but he could see she did not believe it. Confusion mingled with her seething rage. "It takes little to slip a noose about a neck. You've done that well enough."

"Fletcher, make sure this area is secure, then take command of the men in the cellar," Burne snapped. "We'll take the prisoner back the way we came."

As they took her past Rafe, she said, "I hope they've paid you full worth."

"No one paid me anything," he told her.

"Then why—?"she asked.

But Burne signaled impatiently, and the man dragged her away, leading her out the door and back down through the secret passage that had been designed for her protection.

She was gone. Rafe had known it would be bad, but not how bad. He leaned on the mantel, the heavy weight of his heart sinking into oblivion. Blackness opened and swallowed him inside it. He had thought her a flame, and a quenched flame might be relit. But once the sun was gone there was only night.

24

Viv trembled with fury as they dragged her down the stairs of the secret passageway. She stoked the anger, letting the red blaze ward off the lurking shapes of fear and anguish. They hovered just beyond the flame, dark shadows emanating unfamiliar power in the wasteland of her heart. When they pushed her into the cellar, she saw other official invaders had broken open the storeroom and were carrying out the remaining snaphances. Alarm rang through her as she remembered the strange intensity with which Rafe had handled the guns this afternoon. But she could find no meaning in the cacophony of emotion and memory. The guns were important. But why? Her smuggling empire was based on the exchange of wine and wool. The weapons had been a singular coup. She could not imagine that they would arrest her for anything less than smuggling—or murder.

Her whole world was being stripped away. Her people would be arrested—or killed. All because of Rafe. Pain hollowed out her heart, filling it with a blackness that obscured all else. She fought it, forced herself to think. Rafe told her he had not broken his word, had not told them about Mortmain. Why not, if he meant to betray her anyway? Had he been working for the magistrates all along? But what profit could the greedy beaks have from tearing down her empire? There was far greater benefit in her bribes.

It must be some plan of Rivett's, who might have paid still greater bribes to destroy her, as he had destroyed Nicholas. Was Rafe working for Rivett? Was he involved in Nick's death after all? Pain and rage twisted in a fiery spiral. *No,* she thought. Rafe's eyes had shown guilt, but his grim defiance said he worked for the law, or thought he did. If Rivett controlled him, it was through others.

She glanced at the ostensible leader, tall and thin, with pale greenish eyes. *Like pond scum,* she thought. She hardened her look to a stare, quickly drawing his gaze. His expression was less conflicted than Rafe's, but of the same ilk. The cool eyes met her challenge and dismissed her with a smug contempt that infuriated her. She doubted he worked for Rivett. If so, Rivett had best beware.

On his order, four men left their work and headed through the tunnel with them, moving under the garden and outside the walls where another half dozen guards waited. They moved quickly, hustling her through the residential streets toward the river to the docks. Her arrest had been quick. People were just rousing to the sounds of gunfire and sword work behind them at her townhouse. Any arrest was noticed in the Clink, but everything that was to have worked against Rivett now worked against her—the late hour, the secrecy of the tunnel, the dispersal of her men.

They reached the docks, where there were more people, more curious glances. If anyone recognized the prisoner shielded by the guards as Viv Swift in masculine garb, she did not see it. Keeping her face straight ahead, she darted surreptitious glances down the familiar alleyways. Even with her hands tied, she could run. There were a hundred places in easy reach that would shelter her. But the guards had been warned and hemmed her close, blocking her from view and shutting off escape. She seethed with frustration and rage. At the river, they dumped her into a waiting boat and shoved off. Wise. The prisons in the Clink were well fattened on her bribes. Only four guards rode with her in the boat, more careless as they crossed the Thames. She could roll into the water, but knew she could not swim well enough with her hands bound. If they did not fish her out, the current would sweep her under the narrow arches of the bridge and drown her in the roiling water. *Better than hanging,* she thought.

But she wanted to live.

If she could survive, she would triumph. She would rebuild everything Rafe had taken from her.

Except her heart.

The boat bumped the north bank. The guards pulled her out, then marched her up the rise toward Newgate. As they approached the prison, a despairing darkness rose up within her, snuffing the fire of her anger. The only flame was external, as the torches of her captors cast twisting shadows against the buildings—the mocking dance of nightmare, like bodies flailing at the end of the rope.

But prison was a nightmare, as fearful as hanging. If they put her in the Hole . . .

Even the thought of it was like being buried alive, closing off her throat so she could barely breathe. She searched for her anger, desperate to lighten the darkness that wanted to swallow her whole. *Fight!* she raged at herself. She was neither coward nor fool. The jewels she had on would pay garnish to the jailers, buy a cell with some space, a window, candles. And from prison there would still be the chance of escape.

They came to Newgate and passed it. Confusion buffered the fear, as the guards led her higher up the street. They were taking her to the Fleet. The Fleet held prisoners condemned by the Star Chamber. It held heretics. It held traitors.

She projected her voice to the tall figure leading the guards. "The Fleet? That's much ado for simple smuggling."

The leader cast a scornful look over his shoulder. "Little enough for treason."

"Treason?" she said, shock hitting her like a blow. Disbelief was first. Then a wild intoxication rushed through her. *I am innocent.* But the moment of dizzy relief passed quickly, black mockery rolling in its wake. They had arrested her on false charges, but they would not waste the opportunity to hang her for smuggling. And till she could prove she was no more than a smuggler, they would guard a traitor closely, too close for escape.

The guns—it must be something about the guns. Well, she had not used those guns to commit treason—she had not used them at all. They waited in storage while she argued with Nick, who wanted to sell them abroad. Chettle had sold her the guns. She remembered how Rafe had probed about Chettle, how his questions had always circled back to the docks and smuggling. He had been skillful, but he had always been searching. She had not found the traps hidden in his words, or seen the lies hidden in his eyes. Had she been as blind to the lies in his touch? She thought of Nick, with the same sorrow and new compassion. Finally, she had been as foolish as he. She had chosen a love that led to death. To the gallows dance.

When the first rush of attackers came, Viv thought it was a rescue. The ambushers surged from the alley ahead and cut off retreat from the street behind, swarming over the guards. Steel glittered and clashed in the torchlight. Rafe had come to save her! The first bright flare of hope died, but another ignited. *No.* Rafe was her betrayer. But if Izzy was alive, he would try to save her. Bound, weaponless, Viv rammed the guard in front of her, kicked out at another, ruining his aim. A hole opened as the closest guards were cut down.

She did not recognize the burly man who grabbed her arm, but she went with his pull, running down the street, cutting across another, then zigzagging through a maze of alleys. Her balance was off and she stumbled, rolling on ground, then righting herself. She could still hear the cries of the guards, but not close.

"Cut me free," she demanded, but the man only jerked her harder, shoving her ahead of him. The clang of alarm sounded inside her again. She followed despite it. Wherever she was going, it was not to prison.

They dodged through a warren of back streets, veered down another narrow alley. At its end a cart waited, lumpen in the darkness. The man stopped there, glancing at her covertly as he panted for breath. Extending her wrists, she demanded, "Slice the rope."

He gave a derisive snort and spat.

Viv kneed him hard in the groin, then kicked him in the head when he fell to the ground. She planted her foot on his chest and pulled his dagger from the sheath. The grip was awkward, but once she found a safe cubby she could cut herself free. She turned to run back down the alley and saw two men emerge from the shadows. They rushed her. She tightened her grip on the knife, slashing at the one closing on her, but the other lunged from the side and grabbed her arm. The man she'd kicked struggled to his feet and closed a thick fist around her hair. She felt the pressure of his blade against her throat. Viv stilled. It made no sense to rescue her, then slit her throat—but she wasn't sure he had the brains to work that out, or the temper to hold to it.

"Take the knife away, Wedge." Pallid yellow light shone briefly on Jake Rivett as he opened a back door and stepped into the shadowed alley. He had not engineered her arrest, then. But why save her? Jacob had no reason to save her.

No reason you know of. It is not the same.

Viv did not want Rafe's earnest voice echoing in her mind, but the words were as true of Rivett as Rosy. There was a reason, hidden away. Her enmity with Rivett ran deep. She supposed he might want to savor her death, though he'd seemed a more efficient killer than that. He would enjoy contriving a personal revenge, but she doubted he would stage a rescue to achieve it. He might worry she could bribe herself free, even from a prison with so many guards on his payroll. Finally, this had to be about power, about control.

Standing in front of her, Rivett gazed at her intently. Even in the shadows, his eyes looked different. Something flickered there she was not used to seeing. A hint of fear? Uncertainty, at least. Squaring her shoulders, she gazed back boldly.

"Worried, Jake?" The question embraced a horde of possibilities.

He struck her, a sharp blow that knocked her back against the wall. Viv knew her life would run no longer than it took to pry forth the information he wanted—or to discover her ignorance. Perversely, a quick death from Rivett now seemed worse than the combined horrors of a dismal cell and the hangman's dance. She did not want him to triumph, to gloat on Nick's death and her own as he counted out his silver. Straightening, she gave him a sly smile, as if she possessed the knowledge he sought.

Rivett's eyes thinned to slits, glinting like knives in the darkness. Knives that wanted to dig the thoughts from her brain. He hit her again, hard, before he asked any questions, then pulled his dagger, tracing the old scar on her cheek. She had been expecting that and did not flinch. Rivett took hold of her doublet and jerked her forward. "What do you know? Who have you told?"

She only stared at him, letting silence draw him, hoping for a ploy to play back to him.

"You'll tell me what Rosy told you. Everything. Or I'll slice every word from your flesh."

No doubt Rivett would make her wish she was dead, but now her will to live was roused by the fight. Riptides of fury, vengeance, and curiosity raced over the dragging undertow of despair.

One of Rivett's men ran down the alley. "The Queen's men have turned this way."

"You picked an inconvenient night for this. But I'll get back to you soon enough," Rivett said to her, then motioned to his men. "You know where to take her."

The men moved up behind her. She heard the ominous swish of a sandbag. Pain stunned her skull. Darkness opened like the hangman's trap and she plunged through.

She woke in darkness, bound, with a thick gag jamming her mouth. Viv squirmed and felt wood pressing at all sides. For a second, panic overwhelmed her, and the darkness, the tight wood walls became her coffin. Then she heard muffled voices, scrabbling sounds, a sudden loud thump that rocked her where she lay. Awareness snapped into place. She remembered Rivett and the cart waiting in the alley. The noise might be Rivett's men, or it might be the Queen's guards searching. If so, she had not been unconscious long.

Weighing the hells of prison and Rivett's secret lair, Viv thought prison offered a better chance of staying alive to escape. But she was not to have her choice of hells. Even if it was the Queen's guards searching the cart, she was gagged too tightly to be heard, and tied too tightly to kick. After a moment, the cart lifted as someone leapt from the back, and the wheels rumbled forward. Viv did not know how long they traveled, but despite the gnawing fear, she knew it was not long.

Abruptly the cart halted. This time a panel was lifted and two men dragged her from the compartment under the seat. The stench of sewers was cloying thick in the air. With the gag almost choking her, she felt drowned in muck. One man pulled off the gag, then leered as he groped between her legs.

"Watch her knees, Blister. She's already jammed my bullocks," Wedge warned his companion.

"She's tied, and there's two of us now." Blister snickered lewdly, trading glances with Wedge. "Harder for her to kick. Let's flip her on her face and swive her before she goes inside."

Vivian could see them weighing the delight of raping her against the possible consequences. "Keep your pizzles for pissing or Rivett will cut them off and feed them to the pigs."

Blister snatched his hand back, and glared at her sullenly. But he would take her advice, at least until he clarified his orders. They cut the ropes that bound her legs and placed her on her feet. Her muscles were stiff but her stance held firm.

Deprived of rape, Wedge cuffed her ear. "I ought to stomp your kneecap."

Her head ringing from the blow, Viv glanced about, trying to get her bearings. It was only another alley, almost featureless in the gloom. A dim light shone at its mouth. Only the overwhelming stink gave a clue.

She wondered again if Rivett was keeping her alive. Was it revenge? Did he want to arrange some death more excruciating, more ignominious, than the Crown would condemn her to? Though if they judged her guilty of treason a death worse than hanging, drawing, and quartering, would be hard to devise. Whatever fate Rivett planned, he was not done with her yet. That meant escape was still possible.

Blister pushed her forward. When they reached the mouth of the alley, Viv could see London's torchlit walls silhouetted against the night sky. Bishopsgate, from the look of it. Seeing that confirmed where they were. Pinioned between two sewers, not far outside the northern wall, was St. Bethlehem's Hospital—Bedlam. Turning, she could see the walls of the old priory, the iron gateway lit by lantern light.

Blister laughed and shook her viciously, making a gibbering noise. Wedge chortled at his wit, then sneered. "Bedlam's the best place for a vicious bitch like you."

She knew the hospital took in perhaps twenty patients on charity, both feeble-minded fools and madmen. The rest were committed by their families or guardians. There was many a lord who had begged a fool for wardship, and so pillaged a rich estate. If Rivett had wardens in his pay, they could keep her locked up indefinitely. If he was using pure bribery to imprison her here, she could not outbid him. If he was using lies as well as money to keep her locked up, what good was the truth? It would sound like madness. And if she was believed, she would be arrested once more.

There was still escape. Her friends would search the prisons, but would they think to search the madhouse? She prayed Izzy was safe, and Smoke, but she could expect no help from them. And Rafe—yesterday, she would have sworn Rafe would search her out and rescue her, as she would have searched for him. Tears stung her eyes as pain and desperation merged. She drew a harsh breath, furious at her weakness. She clung to the fire of her anger.

They had not waited long when a man on horseback rode up from Bishopsgate to Bedlam's entrance and dismounted. Seeing him, Rivett's men hurried her up the street toward the dimly lit doorway. The stranger turned, watching them approach. He was tall, strong, of good figure for a man of middle years, and dressed in the long robe of a physician. The fine gray velvet glistening in the lamplight and the jeweled chain draped over his shoulders proclaimed his wealth. There was no doubt he was in authority, or that he was in Rivett's pay. Until they reached the door, the physician did not look at Rivett's henchmen but at her. The closer she came, the more her trepidation grew. A faint smile incised the edge of his lips. Large, wide-set eyes made him both compelling and sinister, their irises the opaque gray of a night fog. Beneath high, arched brows, and low, heavy lids, their expression was lazy, almost somnolent. But behind those eyes Viv sensed a cat waiting patiently at a mouse hole, musing torments for its prey.

"Here we are, Master Quarrell."

"Wedge. Blister." The tone of indolent courtesy was condescending. His deep voice rolled like a heavy unguent, smooth and oily.

"Here's one for your keeping, your worship." Blister shoved her forward a little, then performed his manic gibbering.

Master Quarrell turned his pale gaze from her onto Blister, watching him with the same bemused quiet until the man ceased his antics. Blister fidgeted uncomfortably under the physician's gaze. "I see fools enough daily," Quarrell said, then rang the bell at Bedlam's iron gate. After a moment, a door across the courtyard opened, and a matronly nurse and two colossal guards came to the gate.

"Good evening, Sister Mary. Cramer. Cross." The physician nodded to each of them with the same unctuous condescension.

"You received my message? This madwoman must be admitted tonight."

"Yes, your worship," Sister Mary answered quietly. Nuns no longer tended the sick, but the form of address remained.

"You can leave us, now," Quarrell said to Rivett's henchmen. "I have all the information I require."

With that, Master Quarrell took Viv's arm and guided her through the gateway. Instantly the guard stepped forward, his massive hand replacing the physician's hold, and the nurse shut the door on Wedge and Blister. Viv wanted desperately to fight, to kick and claw and rend them all, but she saw no chance of escape. Despite her fury, acting crazed was the worst thing she could do, especially if the others were not involved in Rivett's scheme. And if they were, struggle would only earn her mockery. She would save her strength and her wits.

They led her across the courtyard of the old priory and into the main building. Quarrell turned to the nurse. "Sister Mary, this woman's husband is placing her in our care. He has suffered greatly, but still has hope of her cure."

Viv gave a yelp of outraged laughter. Rivett, her husband?

Sister Mary looked at her with a mix of curiosity, compassion, and wariness.

Quarrell continued in his sonorous voice. "She has already attempted to kill him. She denies her true name, and her marriage, but suffers the delusion her husband is some notorious criminal bent on her destruction. As you can see from her garments, there are even times when she believes herself to be a man. For the moment, address her as Vivian, as it is the only name she accepts. This woman is violent, dangerous, and cunning. Be vigilant in her presence. Treat her in the usual manner until I decide on a course of treatment."

"Yes, sir," Sister Mary replied. She and the guards led Vivian to a small chamber. One man remained outside, locking the others within. The nurse drew a small curtain, giving some privacy, then said brusquely, "If you struggle, Cramer will undress you. Do you understand?"

"I understand perfectly," Viv said, meeting her gaze directly.

The nurse's manner was subdued and sensible. In the plain face, her brown eyes were watchful, but there was a kernel of kindness in them. Viv's mind raced, but she could find nothing to say that would not tangle her in incriminating lies or incriminating truth.

"Have you never known someone to be falsely imprisoned here, because their supposed madness would be more profitable than their sanity?"

The nurse regarded her steadily, then answered, "We have your husband's word that you are mad, Mistress Vivian. And Master Quarrell verifies it."

"And you trust Master Quarrell?"

The woman's gaze flickered. Finally she said, "No one would question his orders."

"Yes, I can see that would be difficult to do." Vivian nodded, building a sense of complicity, if nothing else.

"Your own behavior will be the best testimony," Sister Mary said. "Please undress."

Viv forced her hands to the task. After she had stripped off her garments and jewels, Sister Mary quietly unlocked a drawer and removed a pair of scissors, then turned back to Vivian. "I must cut your hair."

"No!" Vivian stepped back.

Sister Mary eyed her with the same calm sympathy and wariness. Without taking her gaze from Vivian, she nodded to the guarded and locked door. Viv's instinct was to fight them all, tooth and nail. But they would win, and she would prove Quarrell right in their eyes. She stood, naked and trembling with fury, while Sister Mary sheared her hair. The sudden lightness around her head felt strange, disorienting, and she loathed the humiliation of it. She understood how Samson might have felt, shorn of his strength. But she still had the will to fight.

Sister Mary handed her a loose gown of rough indigo cloth and tied the fastening after Viv had slipped it on. Dressed in the ugly uniform, she followed Sister Mary and the guards back into the hall of the old priory. From there they journeyed along dimly lit stone corridors and stairs worn smooth by three hundred years of foot-fall. More guards locked and unlocked the doors they passed through. Bedlam's night was filled with screeches and howls, whimpers and gibbering far more crazed than Blister's, chilling her spine. Viv knew little of real madmen, though there was a lucrative business for false ones. One of her forgers did an excellent business draw-ing up Bedlam licenses. Such a Tom or Bess O'Bedlam could wander from town to town at will, acting the lunatic to wring coins from fear or pity. But none of them had ever been inside the walls. The longer they walked, the louder the sounds that came from behind the closed doors.

I will go mad if he keeps me locked up here, Viv thought. *I will catch madness like the plague, except it will not kill me.*

At last Cramer unlocked a door and took Viv inside the cell, a bare room with filthy straw on the floor. The light of his candle showed a shuttered window high above. Sister Mary and Cross watched as he locked her ankle to chains in the wall. Cross handed him another set of loose manacles, and those he locked about her wrists, the long chain draping over her thighs. She wondered if any of the inmates had strangled themselves with it. If they'd throttled one of their keepers, no doubt the chains would be shortened. Sister Mary bade her good night, then they left her alone in the cell.

The August night was warm, but the stone walls were cold. Fear chilled from the inside out, marrow to skin. Viv gazed above her, searching out the rectangle of window, searching for a glimpse of starlight through a crack in the shutters. There was nothing but the darkness that pressed closer and closer. Vivian fought off the hideous claustrophobia. She would rather face Rivett, or Quarrell, and that itself was a kind of madness, for either would take pleasure in killing her, slowly and cruelly.

But it was easier to fight off fear when she was fighting for her life, lost in the fierce tumult of escape and fury. She'd always had raw physical courage. She could endure pain, though she did not pretend to know how much. She did not want to die, but she knew she could face death with a jest.

Now, alone with nothing but her fear, Viv felt the darkness play havoc with her senses. The straw stabbed at her like needles, and the strange gibberings and howls made the hair on the back of her neck rise in little prickles. Yet under the fear there was something worse. Something deeper, more all-devouring. Slowly, the solitude stripped her to the deepest anguish. Rafe . . .

She saw his face clearly, as he faced her across the room, with the Crown's soldiers surrounding them. There had been guilt in his eyes, but there had been defiance as well.

There had been self-loathing, and self-righteousness. There had been sorrow, but there had been triumph. He had done what he wanted.

She hated him.

She wanted him dead.

From prison she could have ordered it done—but she wanted to do it herself, as she had almost done tonight. Almost. With a burst of savage rage, she imagined the knife finding his heart, imagined stabbing into his body as he had pierced her with his calculating lust and treachery. Destroying his flesh was not enough.

Yet when she thought of him dead, the image shredded her heart and hollowed her belly with darkness, making her flesh the grave for her spirit. She cursed Rafe for the pain of his betrayal. Cursed him because she still cared. The hurt sapped her anger and her strength, sent her spiraling down into depths where she no longer cared. The blackness devoured rage and fear and even pain, leaving her utterly empty. Utterly alone.

I loved you, she thought. *I loved you.*

25

*R*eflections of torches and lantern light wriggled like yellow snakes on the surface of the Thames, water and sky the color of charcoal. Night was waning, and Rafe knew he should sleep. He also knew sleep was impossible.

He'd done what he should. Now he wanted it undone. With no mission on which to fix his purpose, the churning maelstrom within him flung memory after memory after memory to torment him—Vivian prowling like a tigress in the courtyard, her scarlet gown like a fire combusting from the heat of her flesh. Vivian laughing with excitement as she clambered over the rooftops in her doublet and hose. Vivian naked, leaping into his arms, passion alight in her eyes. Vivian in a fury, leaping to attack, her dagger aimed for his heart. He'd stayed her hand, but she stared down on him, eyes black with accusation. He did not blame her for wanting his death. The last image shifted, mutated, and Vivian stood at the gallows, her gaze searching him, still accusing as they slipped the noose around her neck.

A sound escaped him, a harsh breath of denial. Rafe quickened his pace, but he could not escape the furor in his mind. Walking along the edge of the river, he stared into the rush of black water under the bridge. Obliteration was strangely compelling, a craving he had never expected to feel. Life had always seemed too rich, too various, to be left unless forced. The water called, a cold blanket to cover him, oblivion deeper than sleep—equally impossible to surrender to. He did not want to die, he wanted life infused with the meaning his own betrayal had bled away.

Vivian Swift had committed treason, for which she should be punished. She had committed murder, for which she should be punished. Gabriel's death should be avenged, and it should be avenged by him. Rafe did not forgive her, but the flame of his rage had burned to ashen misery. Vengeance had not appeased his spirit, and the thought of her death opened the gallows trap in his soul, swallowing him in darkness.

Wearily, he leaned on the balustrade. The fighting was over, the Swifts' illegal empire destroyed, the townhouse seized by the Crown. Rafe knew that Izzy had escaped, and was glad. Smoke had been wounded during the attack, and arrested. After the battle, Rafe had accompanied the guns back to the Admiralty warehouse. Trusting no one, he had carefully recorded the number of weapons confiscated and had the document and a copy witnessed. He'd waited impatiently until a messenger arrived from Burne, but Rafe had received nothing but a terse dismissal for the night, and orders to meet with the intelligencer at noon. Burne's condescension rankled as always. Rafe had uncovered the source of the sabotage, now his grandfather and cousin must be freed.

At dawn he walked to the Fleet. It seemed bizarre that both his family and Vivian were now imprisoned here.

The desk sergeant recognized him, and a small bribe bought a visit to his grandfather and Peter. Rafe was relieved find his grandfather alert. Rafe told them the source of the sabotage had been discovered. They embraced, and at last Peter confessed that he had traded guns for the gambling notes. Chettle had been doing him a favor—or so he'd thought. Peter feared admitting the fraud would only implicate him further, and turn his grandfather against him. He swore again that he had not known the use for which the weapons were intended, and said he had traded only two cases to Chettle.

When he left them, Rafe decided he must see Vivian as well—if she would admit him. She was an unrepentant criminal who did not deserve his love or his loyalty, yet both clutched his heart obstinately. He must renounce the impossible passion that bound him to her still. Nothing good could come of it. But he wanted her to live. Once his family was released, he must contrive, somehow, that she escape. Resolution dispersed some of his melancholy humor, though new considerations rose. Viv would suspect that he was there again as a spy, to prevent just such a thing. But if he told her why he had betrayed her, she might hate him less, believe him more. If he could help her escape, perhaps she would forgive him. She was guilty, so her forgiveness should not matter. But it did.

If she forgave him. The dagger cut on his chest throbbed a warning. He ignored it.

But when he offered the sergeant another bribe to see her, the man denied any such prisoner had been recorded. At first Rafe was furious, convinced Burne had perceived his conflict and intended to deny him any access to Vivian. The sergeant gazed greedily at the silver Rafe offered, but shook his head. Yes, he'd been told to expect Vivian Swift, but he'd been on duty all night and the prisoner had not been delivered. He been hoping for it, as there were many like Rafe who'd pay to have a peek at the Queen of the Clink—perhaps she'd been taken elsewhere. The sergeant's information made no sense, but Rafe believed him. He spent the rest of the morning prowling the warren of London's prisons on a fruitless quest for Vivian.

Leaving the last of them, Rafe realized he was being followed. Doubling back, he observed Marlowe hunting for his lost quarry. It could only be on Burne's orders. It was close to noon, so Rafe went directly to the Tilted Jug to confront him. He opened the door to find the chief intelligencer waiting for him. Anger rose and subsided in the same instant. Burne's face was battered, eye and jaw swollen with purplish bruises.

"What happened?"

Burne simply stared at him, waiting.

"Did Viv do that?" Rafe asked. It was too good to be true—though such lovely clouts would cost her dear.

"Viv?" Burne queried acidly. "Not exactly. These mementos were left by friends of Mistress Swift when they rescued her last night—almost at the entrance to the Fleet."

Stunned, Rafe hoped his surge of elation would be mistaken for pure shock. Then he recalled his wrath and attacked in the same sarcastic tones. "I caught Marlowe following me. You must think I arranged her escape. Your logic confounds me."

"If you did not help her escape, then she knows full well you arranged her arrest," Burne countered. "Watch your back or you will find a knife in it."

Burne was right, but Rafe did not much care. Only one thing was important now. "You have the guns. Only the Swifts conspired with Chettle. I want my family released immediately."

"There is only your word to what Mistress Swift said about Chettle. Conveniently, she cannot confess."

Rafe slammed his fists on the table, and had the satisfaction of seeing Burne flinch. This man should be his ally, not his enemy. "Just what is in your mind? Do you think I engineered the escape to avoid Vivian implicating my family—or to save her life? Do you mean to provide victims for the gallows, even if you know they are innocent? Or are you just vindictive because you've lost the prisoner I caught for you?"

"Does it matter, Master Fletcher?" Burne returned, smoothing his collar. "Any of those will serve."

"My grandfather has done nothing but serve his Queen and country loyally. My cousin deserves a whipping for deceit, not disemboweling for treason," Rafe argued furiously, but that only made Burne more stubborn. And anything which sounded like a plea was greeted with utter scorn.

"Be grateful your work has assured you will not be charged with treason. Nothing else is proved."

"Question the men you've captured. Such sabotage must have been secret, but I cannot imagine Nicholas and Vivian sitting up all night exchanging every screw in the snaphances."

"They are being questioned. I will inform you if anything happens. For the time being, your usefulness is at an end. Unless, of course, you can find Mistress Swift." Burne gestured to the door, a summary dismissal.

Only concern for his family stopped Rafe from grabbing Burne and beating him to a pulp. The door shook as Rafe slammed it behind him and stormed out of the inn. Anger made him careless at first, but he quickly suspected he was being followed again. When he turned, there was always a shadow slipping away at the periphery of his vision—or perhaps it was only the expectation of retribution pricking his nerves. Not Marlowe again, surely? Some other intelligencer? Had Burne made him angry solely to try and keep him off guard? Better to have given false reassurances than warnings. For a time, Rafe deliberately ignored the stalker, then turned into an alley and waited. There was only the softest footfall, and it was not Marlowe but Izzy Cockayne who moved past.

Rafe grabbed him, twisting his arms behind him, holding him tightly. He dragged the pickpocket into a doorway, keeping his own back protected and securing a view of the street as well as Izzy. Rafe was more powerful than Izzy, but he knew the thief was slippery, and had every reason to fight viciously. He twisted Izzy's arm till the pain stilled him. "Don't make me break it."

Izzy cast a look over his shoulder, eyes blazing with

hatred. "Judas," Izzy hissed at him. "I'll break your balls open. What did they pay you?"

"There's no silver in my hand," Rafe said.

"So you did it for fun, then? Like Rosy?"

"Listen to me," Rafe snapped, squeezing his wrist. Izzy yelped. "It's true I betrayed Vivian to the Crown—but to save my own family. They're in the Fleet now, still under suspicion of treason because of the guns we seized."

Rafe could feel Izzy relax, listening. Izzy hesitated, then said, "Go on."

"I thought I had proved their innocence. Once they were free, I planned to help Vivian escape."

"Liar. I'll kill you and rescue her myself."

"You know where she is," Rafe surmised. "Tell me."

"Tell you? So you can have her arrested again?"

It was what Burne had just told him to do. It was what he should do. Viv's confession might be all that could free his family. But he could not woo her trust only to betray her again. He would find another way. "I swear to you—"

"You swear? You apple-peddling, honey-venomed, worm-souled Eden-serpent. Your word is filth."

"I keep my word," Rafe said. "Vivian said you were the only other one who knew she killed Mortmain. I haven't told them that. I won't."

Izzy stilled in his grasp. "Why not? They would hang her anyway, for thieving and smuggling. And you would get a rich reward for that."

"Because I gave her my word," he said. "Because she told me that in trust, without my seeking it, when all the rest was knowledge I sought."

"Like the tunnels?" Izzy mocked.

He nodded, sick with himself. Izzy tricked innocent people daily. Rafe should not care what he thought or felt. But he did. Izzy had a kind heart, and he loved Viv. Rafe gripped the thief with one hand and drew the snaphance Viv had given him. "I'll let you go now," he said, risking it. "Keep your hands away from your weapons."

Izzy stepped away quickly, rubbing his bruised wrist. Rafe leveled the gun at him. "I did betray her. But I do not want the Crown's blood money."

Izzy studied him. "You're no roguish fencing master then. Who are you?"

"My grandfather is George Easton," Rafe said, gesturing with the snaphance.

Knowledge brightened Izzy's eyes. "Easton Arms? Good weapons—they always fetch the best price."

"They cost me enough," Rafe answered bitterly. "Nicholas murdered my best friend, and framed my family for treason. Perhaps Vivian did as well. But even knowing that, I would have her free, as long as my family is free, too."

"I know Nick murdered nobody lately, and I know most things," Izzy said. "Neither he nor Viv kills without cause."

"Defending their empire would have been cause enough," Rafe retorted. "Profit would have been cause enough."

"Kings and queens would all say the same," Izzy remarked. Then, "Who was he, your friend?"

"His name was Sir Gabriel Darren, and he discovered Nick plotting with Chettle. Nick killed Gabriel and Scratch Jones when they discovered where the weapons were hidden."

"Not Scratch, he didn't. Nick and Viv were trying to find out who killed him. Chettle, too, for that matter."

Doubt chilled Rafe, but he insisted, "They hid it from you, then. Treason was too much to confide."

"I don't believe it." Izzy shook his head vehemently. "Nick hadn't much loyalty except to his own people, and only a few of those. But Viv always felt a kind of kinship with the Queen. One woman ruling in heaven, one in hell."

"A mirror to her power."

"If you will," Izzy said. "A bit of smuggling is one thing, but for all her daring and all her greed, Viv's not fool enough to draw the eye of the Crown by playing at treason. Just what makes you so sure Nick and Viv were involved?"

"Viv had a brooch that belonged to Gabriel—a golden dragon clasping a globe of amber."

"Viv likes such things, jeweled bugs and beasties, but I don't remember seeing her wear a dragon."

"Gabriel left wearing it the night he died. When he came back, it was gone." The memory struck Rafe again, carving into his gut. Gabriel had died trying to protect him from these very people.

"You loved him. That's something. I wasn't sure you had a heart," Izzy said reluctantly. "This friend died the same night as Scratch got his red throat?"

"Babington was captured the night before, the Queen of Scots arrested the day after."

"Memorable nights. So I can tell you for certain it was not Nicholas, for he and Rosy were drinking in the Lightning Bolt till the small hours. Rosy went to the theatre, and I put Nicholas to bed myself." When Rafe only studied him suspiciously, Izzy added, "Don't believe me, then."

"Viv had the brooch and two cases of snaphances from Easton Arms in the cellar," Rafe insisted. The two together had seemed beyond doubt. But Peter said he had traded only two cases to Chettle. Viv may have had nothing to do with the sabotage. The cold in Rafe's belly spread outward. His skin went clammy with dread.

"Someone's been playing us all for coneys," Izzy said. "The whole thing has the stink of Smelly Jakes Rivett."

Rivett had arranged Nick's death. He could have arranged more. Guilt and hope twisted within Rafe. Perhaps he was being a fool yet again, wanting to believe her innocent. But whatever else, he wanted to know the full truth. And he wanted Vivian to live.

"Tell me what has happened to her," Rafe pleaded. "This morning I searched the prisons, but I could not find her. If nothing else, I can see she escapes London. Perhaps to another city, or to France."

Izzy eyed him mistrustfully. "I've seen you look all innocence before, then learned you were lying through your teeth."

They were caught in the same dilemma. Drawing a breath, Rafe handed him the snaphance. Izzy eyed that dubiously as well, not bothering to point it at him. "This doesn't mean much. You weren't afraid to risk death before, to get what you wanted."

"I wanted to save my family—I still do—but not at the cost of her life," Rafe said. "If Viv needs rescuing, Izzy, you need help."

"Less than you'd think. The guards took Smoke to the Clink prison instead of the Fleet, and he'd bought himself an open door within the hour."

"Smoke was wounded."

"Yes," Izzy admitted. "But not in his gun arm. Viv's got friends all over. I've gathered enough for a raid."

"Where is she, Izzy?"

"Rivett put her away—someplace no one will look."

"Rivett?" The chill of doubt turned to icy fear. He remembered the scar Rivett had marked Viv with when she refused to whore for him, and the knife wound she said she'd left in turn. "He will kill her."

"Sooner or later. Rivett's tidy. Usually he prefers death to threats—but I think he'll enjoy the idea of her trapped for a bit, waiting on his whim for a bit of torture or rape."

"If he hurts her, I'll finish what she started," Rafe snarled. His own fury stunned him.

Izzy looked pleased. "Well, I don't know that there will be enough bits of him to go around, but we could split his bullocks."

"Where is she?" Rafe asked again.

"Bedlam."

Rafe stared at Izzy, stunned.

"That's where Rivett's got her," Izzy said. "His men grabbed her after the Queen's guards took her off. Tadpole was sent to track Smelly Jakes himself and saw them meet up. He followed Viv instead of Rivett after that."

"Bedlam," Rafe repeated, the horror of it creeping through him.

"They'll have her locked up, of course. But it'd be harder to get her out of Newgate or the Fleet," Izzy mused. "I know my way around Bedlam. My mother drank herself mad and died there, picking off the bugs that weren't instead of the ones that were. I'll go tonight, so as it's dark."

"We'll go."

Now Izzy lifted the snaphance, training it on him. "If I take you with me, I'm not letting you out of my sight. You'll get the gun back when we have to deal with the guards."

"I understand," Rafe answered. Izzy wanted no messages passed to the likes of Nigel Burne.

"I'm sure you do," Izzy said amiably. "If Vivian kills you, Fletcher, don't say I didn't warn you. I'll let you come along to give her the chance."

Izzy's voice was light, but Rafe knew full well he spoke the truth. His doublet still showed the scar of her knife. But there was no way to win her forgiveness except to face her rage. Rafe swallowed his apprehension and followed Izzy out of the alley.

26

When dawn came, Vivian at last saw a faint light seeping through the shutters. She slept fitfully then, lost in a dream even worse than her reality. In it Rafe embraced her, his arms so hard, so strong. She melted against him, but then could not escape their grip, locking around her like bands of iron. His lips covered hers, his tongue filled her mouth with poisoned kisses. The taste of him was a sweet poison, paralyzing her. She could not move. The Queen came and ordered her buried alive. Rafe gave her to the guards. They flung her into the same grave with Nick's rotting corpse and began shoveling dirt over her face. She woke with a cry, shuddering with horror.

No one came then. Her cry was puny compared to the screams of the mad. But a few minutes later, the door was unlocked by a brace of hulking guards and a wall-eyed nurse less kind than Sister Mary. One man kept watch while the other unbolted her chains from the wall. Despite protests that she could stand herself, the guard closed his hand about her arm, pulling her to her feet and then toward the door. Her wrists and ankles were chafed from the heavy irons, and their pressure weighted both limbs and spirit. Viv loathed the hobbled walk they inflicted, but she forced herself to alertness as they led her further down the hallway. Behind locked doors, other prisoners still groaned, other chains clattered. It was general knowledge that harmless, feeble-minded fools might roam freely about Bedlam during the day, but these precincts were for the dangerous madmen.

Viv tried to get her bearings. She remembered the layout of the buildings from the last night. Finding the way back to the front door would be easy enough, but she did not want to run that gauntlet without weapons. It was too well watched. The dangling chain of the wrist manacles slapped at her thighs. Weapon enough to fell one enemy, but the other would seize it if he had any wit and speed. The men turned down a new corridor. At its end, another guard saw them coming and unbarred the massive door.

"Behave, an' ye can stay out fer a bit o' time," the man holding her said with a smirk.

The door opened into a great common room filled with more of the lunatics of Bedlam. One man silently rubbed his forehead against the wall, leaving a trail of bloody patches in his wake. Another howled once like a dog, then curled into a ball and rocked back and forth. Yet another shambled about the room, waving his arms in strange patterns and chanting outlandish babble. An old woman rushed to greet them, lifting her skirts and performing a lewd dance for the guards, before pissing gleefully on the straw.

The guards crowded closer, as if they expected Viv to shrink away. Instead she walked forward into the chaos. Horrific as it was, she preferred this pandemonium to the suffocating blackness of the cell. Warily, she circled the room, her movement hampered by the leg irons. Others were chained only at the wrist, so perhaps she was considered among the most dangerous. She searched the faces of the patients. Of the thirty or so who were out, only three were not obviously demented or witless. Even these might prove to have no more than the semblance of sanity, but if she found someone else falsely imprisoned here, they could join forces. Viv knew she had little time.

There was a thin, dark woman who held herself apart from the others. She refused to meet Viv's glance, but that might be pure defense. No one here had reason to believe Viv sane. There was an older, thickset man who sat quietly, but his brooding seemed impenetrable. And another, younger man sat with his back to the wall in one corner. There was no one near him, as if he had surrounded himself with an invisible barrier. Even grimy and huddled, he possessed a fineness of feature and a composed grace that suggested a gentleman. The man met her gaze, then quickly looked down, denying the spark of interest. Roughly shorn, dirty hair only half concealed his face.

Apprehension made her wary, but she was never one to wait idly when action could be taken. She walked over to him, pausing when he lifted his head abruptly. His face was expressionless, the flat gaze warning her to approach no further—but he did not shrink back or try to attack her.

"My name is Vivian—" She halted. Her name was a danger to her. And the truth of her tale would sound more lunatic than any lie. She chose silence for the moment.

"Adrian." The exchange was equally abrupt, but he held her gaze, studying her as she studied him. Washed, she guessed his cropped hair to be a tawny shade. His face was elegant but gaunt, cheekbones and jaw angling sharply, the eye sockets hollowed. Under tilted brows, his eyes glinted like shards of colored glass, green and blue shot through with gold. Intense, disturbing even. But mad? She recognized the expressions that flashed within them well enough—hostility, curiosity, wariness, defensiveness.

"Why are you here?" she asked bluntly.

"Because I am mad," the man said, with a twist of a smile. The clarity of his eyes, the self-mockery, made Viv disbelieve him. Though his tone was harsh, his voice was beautiful, musical.

"Do the mad know they are?"

His smile turned bitter. "Often they do. And often they forget."

Bedlam might have thinned him, but he still looked strong. And despite what he said, his wits seemed clear enough. He was handsome, too, if not in the way she preferred. She found herself comparing him feature by feature to Rafe's brazen sensuality, and losing his face in the compelling memory of the one she had loved. Angrily she pushed Rafe's visage from her mind.

She crouched down at the rim of the stranger's invisible circle, but it was too close.

"Don't touch me!" His voice was pitched low as a whisper, but its ferocity was a shout.

Viv edged back, staring into eyes that gleamed now with what could be madness, or rage, or terror. Then the strange light in them faded, and he muttered, "Don't touch me."

"I had not meant to," she said sharply, more angry at her own fear than at him. No longer expecting a sane reply, she asked, "What would happen if I did?"

He leaned forward, pitching his voice to a deliberate threat. "Your touch will teach me your secrets. Leave me be."

Impossible as it was, the warning chilled Vivian. A madman after all. She wanted nothing to do with him. Frustrated, she rose and began searching the room again. The brooding man had barely moved. She looked over at the dark woman, who seemed the only other possibility. Viv watched her intently, until the scrutiny finally drew her gaze. Viv held it, searching the woman's eyes for some sense of connection before approaching her. But the woman could not endure to be looked at, much less touched. With a wild shriek, she flew at Vivian, her chained hands outstretched like talons.

Vivian retreated, but her feet were chained as well as her hands, and crippled her movement. Stumbling backward, she tripped. The woman was on her before Viv could lift her feet to kick. She only had time to ward off the raking claws with her arms, and her own chains swung down across her face, obscuring her vision. Then the woman gave another shriek of outrage as the enigmatic man from the corner leapt up and grasped her. He lifted the woman away, then with a wild cry flung her aside.

Quickly, Viv rolled to her feet, but the madwoman sprang up just as swiftly. Snarling, she rushed them again. This time the man only stood there shaking, his face pale as parchment. Vivian grasped the dangling chains with her hands and swung them hard, striking the woman's face. The woman staggered from the blow and fell, then crouched on her haunches. Slowly she crept toward them, snapping her teeth. Viv shuddered, gripping her chain. Then the guards arrived, hurling buckets of filthy water to leave them all drenched and gasping.

"Do it again, ye flipping flea-wits, and ye're all back in your cells," one guard threatened, cursing.

Viv didn't know if the madwoman understood, but the water had shocked her and she fled, cowering in a far corner. The fight caused a general uproar, sobs, manic laughter, and shrieks erupting from the inmates. The other guards moved among them, pelting them with water, curses, and blows.

"Move," the guard in front of them ordered. Viv began to back away from him, feigning submission. The guard turned on her rescuer, who was still standing there. "I said move!"

"Adrian," she whispered fiercely, remembering his name.

The man stayed where he was, staring at the madwoman huddled in the corner. The guard might have dragged him off that instant, but Viv grabbed his hand and tugged him toward the wall. A strange shock jolted through her and he jerked away as if scalded. He stared at her, but the dazed looked was gone. He cried out as the guard struck him from behind, whirling to face his attacker. This time it was anger that flared in his eyes, not fear, and he stepped forward. Viv was glad to see both the anger and the courage, yet he could do nothing against all these guards but earn himself a vicious beating.

"Back off, my lord," the guard jeered.

"Adrian," she called again.

Abruptly, he turned and walked back to his chosen corner, sinking down into the straw. This time he did not protest when she approached. The invisible circle still surrounded him, but the perimeter had diminished. He gave her a faint smile as she settled down, closer than the last time she had tried.

"Are you ill?" she asked. He still looked ghastly pale.

He nodded toward the madwoman who had attacked them. "She believes her husband killed her child—her lover's child—and had it baked up in a mincemeat pie. He made her eat it."

"What a ghastly tale. Worse as truth than madness." Vivian shuddered, but she did not understand why he seemed so stricken. Grotesque as it was, the story had nothing to do with him. Did he hate hurting a woman who might have been so wronged?

"I do not know if it is true." His voice was quiet, but edged with desperation. "But I can still taste the pie."

Then she remembered what he had said, that touch would tell him things. The madwoman had not told him this, he had felt it, seen it.

Imagined it—just imagined it. It was his own madness conjuring horrors.

Her first impulse was to move away. But he began to talk quietly, pointing out different prisoners, telling her who was safe and who was dangerous, who still had wits enough to converse. Viv sat tensely beside him, hoping to glean some information, but uncertain if she could trust a word he said. He indicated the heavyset man she had considered earlier. "The black humor fills him now, and he will not speak. But when the melancholy subsides he has wonderful tales to tell of journeys to the East."

Viv doubted she had time to wait. "What about the guards?"

"If you cause no trouble, this lot will let you be," he said. He drew a breath and leaned back wearily against the wall. "Their tempers are short, but none of those in the room now revels in inflicting pain."

Something in the way he phrased it made her skin prickle. "And the physician, Quarrell?"

"Quarrell is a monster. Do not even speak of him."

A shudder ran through him, palpable. He seemed to descend into himself, as though the circle around him filled with shadow, a dark well from which he looked out at her. She wondered if he would sink so deep he would cease to speak, like the brooding man.

She plucked at a topic. "The guard called you 'my lord.'"

The darkness retreated from his eyes, but he answered hesitantly. "I am Sir Adrian Thorne. My father is the baron, Lord Roadnight. I protested my rank overmuch when I first woke to find myself in Bedlam."

When she looked dubious, he said, "I did not expect you to believe me. After a time here, I expect I will no longer believe myself." He gave a harsh laugh. "My cousin apparently does not believe me. From the window

I watched him arrive and leave again, and I am still here. Perhaps my cousin was a delusion as well."

"I do not know if I believe you or not," she said simply. "If you speak truly, your cousin prefers your madness to your sanity, and looks to be lord in your stead?"

"So it seems. After he left, Master Quarrell said that Adrian Thorne is dead. I have no proof but my own memory—and the look in his eyes when he said it." His face closed. "Sometimes I wonder if I killed this Adrian Thorne. I wonder if his death spilled his memories into my brain."

Viv looked at him askance. Such strange talk made her wary. He must be mad, but his madness made him wretched. There was no one else to talk to, and perhaps he knew the things that could help her. He leaned back, watching her expectantly.

"An enemy imprisoned me—" Viv halted. What more likely for a madwoman to say? The truth could lock her in prison instead of the madhouse. She only wanted his help to escape, somehow. She said to him, "I'm not dangerous."

"Oh, you are dangerous, Vivian Swift," he answered, with his twist of a smile. "But I know you are not mad."

Her heart beat wildly. "You recognize me?"

Thorne said nothing, but lifted his hand, the one she had grasped. He looked at it and then at her, his eyes challenging. "Touching you was almost as much of a shock as the cold water. Except it was more like being burned," he said. "I could feel your anger, your pain, but it brought me back from the worst of the other."

He must be lying. He must have known who she was all along. He was neither madman nor lord, but was a spy placed here to trap her by Quarrell or Rivett. But if that were so, why play this bizarre game when he had far easier ways to win her confidence?

"I may be dangerous, but not to you," he said quietly. "And despite my threat, I do not know all your secrets."

"So what do you know?" She could hear the threat in her own voice.

"I know your name, and that Vivian Swift was the dark queen of Southwark. I saw you sitting before your mirror. You were thinking of the men who had poisoned your brother. One was dead, and one you still meant to kill. There was a man behind you—your lover, your betrayer."

"Rafe—" The memory cut her, watching him dress, watching him smile. But the shape of it was nothing Rivett might not have told him to say. What woman did not sit before her mirror? And Rafe's betrayal must be known by now.

"Rafe," Adrian repeated. "You gave him a gift, a brooch, because you saw him in the mirror, staring at it."

"A golden dragon," she whispered, suddenly amazed. Who but she and Rafe would know?

"You were reluctant. You did not know where it came from, but thought it might be the last thing your brother gave you. You delight in jewels fashioned so, birds, beasts, insects."

He could not fathom her thoughts unless he had been in her mind. But he knew more than she had known then. He must be a witch. She had always mocked such things, with just the sort of smile that curved his lips now. His strange pale eyes seemed like a mark now, a warning. Wonder and horror, anger and fear swarmed within her.

Then he added, "The dragon is important—I don't know why."

She fought her own fear. However bizarre this was, he had done nothing to harm her. "What else?"

"Nothing else. Sometimes I see a whole history, sometimes only scattered pieces of a mosaic. Sometimes there is meaning, sometimes not." He gave her his tilted smile again, full of sadness.

"When you touch someone? Anyone?"

"I never know. Most often it is through touch, but sometimes an object will reveal things."

She had guarded the secret of her past so long, yielded it only to Izzy and Rafe. But what would that secret matter when she was dead? Rivett would kill her as an enemy. The Crown would hang her for smuggling or murder. Staying alive was what was important.

"I have not told my keepers, for fear they would think me even madder than I seemed." He looked at her intently. "I am not sure why I told you—but now you hold my secret, as I hold yours."

"I will not tell them," Viv swore. She gave him her most audacious smile. "Tell me, Sir Adrian. Have you given much thought to escape?"

The smile he gave her was bright and charming. "A great deal, Mistress Swift."

"Tell me how to reach your cell from here. Perhaps together we can devise an escape," she said. "You must know the building, the movements of the guards better than I do. I can pick locks, if only I can find some sort of implement. Do you have aught I can use?"

"Nothing—"

Adrian paused as the guards opened the door, and Edward Quarrell appeared. He stood there for a moment, gloating quietly as he surveyed his kingdom. Looking over, Quarrell saw them together and crossed the room toward them. Adrian watched as if hypnotized, and Viv sensed fear coming off of him.

Quarrell is a monster.

The physician smiled down at him. "Sir Adrian, how are you today?"

"Well enough, Master Quarrell." His voice was barely audible.

"Mistress Vivian." He bowed slightly, then nodded to the guards. One pulled her up and held her, the other exchanged her manacles for ones with shorter chains. "Shall we go now? You have a visitor."

With one guard following, Quarrell led Vivian back to the cell. One of the sisters was waiting outside the door, holding a box which she handed to him. The door was unlocked. Walking in, Viv saw the shutters over the barred windows had been opened, and a quick surge of relief filled her. But, below them, the pale sunlight shone down on Jacob Rivett. Rivett said nothing as the guard locked her chains to the wall once again. Quarrell laid the wooden box on the straw.

"Leave us alone," the physician said when the guard was done. The man left.

Viv looked from one to the other, watching their cold gray eyes, Rivett's dark gray as pewter, Quarrell's like a night fog.

Two monsters now, she thought. And no weapons, except courage and defiance.

"I want to question her alone." Rivett nodded toward the door. Quarrell did not move.

"I've had no sleep," Rivett said sharply. "And I've little patience." He grabbed a fistful of her shorn hair, wrenching her head back.

"You should procure some," the physician said quietly. "The more you beat her, the more she will resist. You will spend a long time with little result."

"I'm good at getting results," Rivett said sharply, but his eyes were more assessing when they gazed into hers. He turned back to Quarrell. "Just what do you suggest?"

Moving close to her, the physician drew a fingertip down her cheek. "Our mutual acquaintance says you are not afraid of knives."

Viv held her tongue, despite her urge to rail at him. He was searching for weakness. His expression was dreamy again, the gaze under the heavy lids intent yet empty. He was waiting for her pain, her fear to fill him. After a moment he moved away, going to the box waiting on the straw. He took his keys and unlocked the box, looking at her over its open brim. She could not see inside.

"No," he said, at last. "I will not bother with knives."

From the box, Quarrell took out a hangman's noose. Approaching her silently, he slipped it around her neck. Watching her face, Quarrell drew the rope taut, slowly shutting off her breath. She glared at him till the noose closed, then resolution meant nothing against the primitive reactions of her body. Desperate for air, she gagged, choked, clawing at the rope with her manacled hands. Out of control, her body flailed like a crazed puppet. He loosened the noose and she drank air in ragged gulps. Then he tightened it again. Rage and terror swarmed as she jerked helplessly on rope. Blackness spun in a rising funnel, sucking the strength from her legs, spinning up through her chest and squeezing her heart. Her knees gave way and she sagged against him, her own weight pulling the noose tighter.

Quarrell loosened the noose and the blackness faded. Speckles of light danced hectically before her eyes. She gasped, her heart racing, her starved lungs greedy for every atom of air. Her larynx ached from the pressure of the noose, and her legs trembled violently. But fury consumed the fear. When he slid the rope back and forth, caressing her neck, Viv gathered enough spittle to spit in his face. His eyes lost their dreaminess, cold outrage sparking.

Rivett gave him a smug smile. "She resists you, too."

"I should think you would have more fear of the rope," Quarrell said to her. His voice was soft, chastising, as if she were a child who had disappointed him. "Surely you believed yourself destined to wear it?"

"I have a fine speech ready for the crowds, but I'd not waste it on such sewage-souled cowards as you." Her throat was raw, her voice was a hoarse rasp. Rivett slapped her, and she glared at him.

"Some other accoutrement?" Quarrell suggested, starting to remove the rope.

"She doesn't like the dark," Rivett said. "Or so her brother said."

No! It was a hideous blow. Nick had not told Rosy about Mortmain—but he had told him of their childhood fears.

Quarrell let the noose settle back in place. "Perhaps just one simple improvement?" Going back to the box, he took out a black hood, then came back. He drew the black hood over her head, blotting out the light. Her heart raced as he pulled the heavy cloth through the hemp. He ran his fingertips in a circle between her throat and the rope, then murmured, "Jacob, would you care to test her for a while?"

She sensed them changing places, forced herself to breath evenly, waiting. Then Rivett began on her, pulling the rope taut in a single tug and choking her ruthlessly. He loosened it, and she waited tensely for the next sharp tug, but this time he pulled noose tight slowly. And again. And again. Not three times, or six, but a dozen, taking her to the brink of consciousness. She did not know if it would be a quick hard jerk, or a long slow tightening like a snake squeezing a thick coil about her throat. Sometimes he spoke softly, asking solicitous questions about her comfort. Sometimes he waited in silence.

Finally he loosened the rope and Quarrell lifted off the hood. Fear made her shake, but it had not consumed her fury. She glared at them, willing them dead with a basilisk's gaze.

"She has a good deal of courage." Quarrell addressed Rivett, but his gaze was fixed on her. "I believe she is strongest facing an enemy. She needs to be alone with her fear."

"Leave me alone with her, I can break her."

"No doubt, but there will be more work than pleasure in it," Quarrell murmured. The lazy anticipation in his eyes gave her vertigo. "Go home and rest. Come back tonight, and she will be far more malleable."

Rivett started to protest, but Quarrell whispered in his ear and Rivett laughed. "You're right. I want to enjoy this."

"Back into the dark, my sweet," Rivett said as he forced her to kneel. He pulled the hood over her head, drew the noose snug about her neck, then tied the end of the rope taut to the ankle chain. There was little she could do without drawing it tighter. Short hard fingers gripped her face through the hood, squeezing her cheeks. "Tonight we'll be alone, and you'll dance on anything I choose."

She heard their footfalls on the straw, the sound of the lid closing, the key in the lock. He knocked at the door and the guard opened and closed it. She knelt, cold sweat drenching her skin, limbs trembling. The hood made a close suffocating world shrouding her head.

But for once, Vivian was grateful to be alone in the dark.

27

*H*ours. Hours and hours and hours Viv was alone in the close black world of the hood and the noose, alone with heartache, fear, and impotent hatred. Memories squirmed like maggots, eating at her will, her mind, her soul. It seemed the howls of the madmen were growing louder and louder and louder. So loud the cries should drown out even thought, but her abraded senses heard the footsteps, the sound of the bar being drawn, the key turning in the lock. She braced herself, gathering the shreds of her strength, wanting to deny Rivett what he wanted, however harsh the cost.

"Vivian."

Rafe.

The voice turned her body inside out, every nerve end exposed, her heart bare to the pain of betrayal, loss, and aching longing. Despite the terror, Viv thought she had kept her sanity through the ages in the suffocating dark. Now she feared it lost. Her mind had turned her worst enemy into her lover.

But who was the greater enemy, finally?

"Vivian," the lover's voice whispered again, caressing the syllables, its cadence echoing her pain. The man knelt beside her. Not Rivett. Someone big, like Rafe. It must be Quarrell, with his eyes like fog, stealing secrets from her heart and mind, then searching her out like an incubus in the darkness.

She pulled away from him convulsively, choking as the noose jerked taut around her neck. He caught her with powerful arms that felt like Rafe's. Even through the ugly miasma of odors in the cell, he smelled like Rafe, earth and spice and leather. Large hands loosened the noose, slipped off the hood, and it was Rafe kneeling before her, his face carved from shadow and flickering lantern light, his expression angry and distraught. He ran strong, warm fingers through her cropped hair. Her heart twisted again, a raw exposed thing.

"Your throat is bruised," he whispered, fingers stroking where the rope had pressed. "What happened?"

She did not answer. Emotion choked her as fiercely as the rope had done. She wanted to kill him. She wanted to cling to him.

Rafe unlocked the chains and raised her to her feet, but her stiff legs collapsed beneath her. He lifted her into his arms. "Put me down," she demanded, her voice still raw from the rope. Tears of humiliation, rage, and relief spilled from her eyes. She struck a fierce blow to his chest, fist thudding over his heart. There was a tear in the velvet, the slash of her dagger. His gaze met hers, held. Then his arms tightened, drawing her closer.

He carried her into the hall. Two guards lay by the door, bound, gagged, and unconscious, but Sister Mary stood quietly beside Izzy.

"Viv!" Izzy exclaimed happily.

"Put me down. I will walk," she commanded Rafe again. It hurt to talk.

Izzy's tone switched to indignation. "He behaved himself till we unlocked the door. Then he shoved me aside."

Viv did not know what to think of that, she only knew she must stand because she hungered for his arms so terribly.

Rafe set her on her feet, still supporting her, his arm locked about her waist. She pulled away from him and went to Izzy, grateful her quavering legs now carried her the half dozen steps. Izzy slipped an arm around her and kissed her cheek. Like Rafe, he rumpled her hair, then stroked her throat lightly with his knuckles.

"Rivett," she said tersely. She saw Rafe and Izzy exchange glances.

"Dog-hearted, bat-fouled, rat's pizzle," Izzy cursed.

"Yes, Rivett," she said, calling Izzy's attention back. "You vouch for Fletcher?"

It was hard to speak his name. *Rafe.*

"I was going to gut him for you, but he caught me first. We talked some." Izzy shrugged apologetically. "He said he wanted to help rescue you—and he did talk Sister Mary here into helping us. After we're free, you can settle the score as you will. But we've no time for more explanations."

Rafe said nothing, only stood ready, waiting. Viv held out her hand. "Give me your gun."

Everyone stilled. Silently, Rafe handed her the snaphance, then stood, making no move for his sword or dagger. The gun felt strangely heavy in her hand, but it would be easy enough to lift and fire. She could kill him here and now. It was what she wanted, to watch the bullet shatter his heart. Again, and again, and again. It was what he deserved. Except he had helped rescue her. Nothing made any sense.

Howls rose around them. Heavy thumpings and the metallic clanking of chains echoed as the lunatics locked within their cells clamored at the disruption.

"If you're not going to shoot him now, let's go before someone conscious interrupts us," Izzy said, starting down the hall.

Viv glimpsed two more sprawled in hallway beyond. Izzy pulled the two closest into the cell and locked the door. The cries of the inmates grew louder.

"Wait." Viv turned to Sister Mary, pointing the other way down the hall. "Adrian Thorne's cell is down there?"

"Adrian Thorne?" Rafe asked suspiciously.

"Is that wise?" Sister Mary asked her. "Adrian was violent when they first brought him here. I was a witness myself."

"Violent?" Izzy asked, his suspicion echoing Rafe's.

"He was not violent with me," Viv said.

"He is quiet now, if no one touches him," Sister Mary acknowledged.

"He helped me. I will take him with me," Viv commanded.

"Quickly then," Izzy said. He set his pistol at Sister Mary's back and she led them down to the next door and knocked. They stood to either side as the guard opened a peephole. "They're baying tonight, ain't they, Sister? You bringing me someone new?"

"There is someone with me, yes," she answered ambiguously. He opened the door and she moved through. Rafe grabbed the guard from behind, and Viv moved to point the gun at his heart. Izzy made sure the guard saw the pistol pointed at Sister Mary, then Rafe knocked him out with a blow from a small weighted sandbag and tied him up. Sister Mary opened Adrian's cell and unlocked his chains.

Adrian emerged looking bemused. "You are most resourceful, Mistress Vivian."

"I'm as surprised as you are," she said ruefully.

"And as grateful, then."

"Later," Izzy said. "Let's be out of here."

They made their way back through the hallways and down the stairs. To avoid suspicion falling on Sister Mary, they bound and gagged her carefully, and left her locked within the dressing room. They checked outside for guards, then fled through the courtyard and out the gate. In the same alleyway where Rivett's men had hidden, Smoke and Joan stood guard. Smoke gave Adrian a suspicious glance, but accepted him without question. The look he gave Rafe was pure rancor, but apparently, like Izzy, he left Vivian to decide their betrayer's fate. As they exchanged greetings in the alley, Tadpole and a wriggler clambered down from a nearby rooftop.

"Was Tadpole who found you," Izzy said. "Following after Rivett."

"Then I owe you my life," Viv said. She crouched beside him, clasping his hands in hers. He gave them a squeeze, proud of his skills, and smiled at his companion.

"Rivett is coming here tonight. Will you keep watch and follow him?" she asked them. "Be more careful than ever."

Tadpole nodded. "Smelly Jakes won't get by me."

"Nor me," the other declared. They nudged each other and winked. Izzy gave them a boost and they returned to their lookout.

Joan handed Vivian a bag stuffed with a long red wig and gaudy strumpet's clothes. "You'll need a disguise."

Viv stepped into the shadows of a doorway and stripped off the detested indigo gown. In the bag, she found wet rags wrapped in waxed paper, and quickly scrubbed off the dirt before pulling on the cheap satins. She tucked a knife into one boot, and the gun into the back waistband of the skirt, covering it with a shawl. She pressed a hand to her bruised throat. There was no ruff, but she looped a long strand of cheap beads about her neck to cover the bruises.

"You, take this," Izzy said to Adrian, holding out one of the bottles he'd taken from another bag.

"I do not need a drink," Adrian said quietly, refusing to reach for it.

"We need to look like revelers," Izzy said, pushing it toward him.

"Then I will sing," Adrian said.

Izzy stared at him, perplexed, then peered at the bottle. "It's not mucky, and you've no need to drink unless you will."

Just as she started to warn Izzy off, Adrian's expression firmed with resolution. He reached out and took the bottle. Viv tensed, but as far as she could perceive, nothing whatsoever happened. Adrian glanced at her, giving her one of his oblique smiles, and she released the breath she was holding.

Vivian wondered what life must be like when every object was potentially a knife, blade out to cut you.

"You'll need a disguise, Adrian," Viv said.

"He can have my cloak," Joan offered. "It's plain enough, and will hide that shirt."

Adrian accepted her cloak with the same gingerness, but nothing untoward happened. They made their way back along the street toward Bishopsgate, a disheveled and supposedly drunken party. Adrian trailed a little behind them, singing lewd ditties in an angel's voice. At the city gate, Izzy gave the night sergeant a full bottle of wine and a wink. That got them through easily enough. They hurried through the boisterous London night to the Thames, where two friendly wherries waited to carry them back to the Clink. It all went smoothly, and Rafe Fletcher fit in as he always had. Except that he was silent. He'd said not a word since she took his pistol in Bedlam, but she felt every breath he drew.

"Where are we going?" Viv asked as they made their way through the back alleys of the Clink.

"The Buzzing Hornet has a room or two, or Saucy Nan will take you. Your own house is under guard, and all the tunnels into it watched, too," Izzy explained as they approached the inn. He spared a glare for Rafe, then rapped at the back door.

Culpepper, the innkeeper, was pleased to see her, if nervous. "I've not rooms enough for you all, but Saucy Nan will put some of you up for a night."

"Rafe and I will go to Saucy Nan, if you can house the rest. Have you a room apart for my friend?" Viv asked, nodding to Adrian.

"Give him mine. Joan can show him where," Izzy said. "I'll go round the front way to Saucy Nan's. There's a girl there with some fine talents."

Viv did not doubt it, nor that Izzy wanted to be close by in case she needed help.

"Will you be all right tonight?" she asked Adrian. "Tomorrow someone will take you where you choose."

He nodded, following Joan up the stairs. Izzy went out the back door, heading for Saucy Nan's brothel. Culpepper led them down to the cellar and gave them a torch for the tunnel.

"I will repay you," Viv promised him.

"Call us even, Mistress Vivian. You've done enough for me," Culpepper said, then made his way back up the stairs.

Viv pressed the lever to open the entrance to the tunnel. She stepped inside, Rafe close behind her. With Bedlam so sharp in her mind, Viv thought the enclosing space would be horrific. Instead, after the black hours within the mask, the tunnel was almost luxurious. What disturbed her most was the memory of going through it, scarcely three weeks ago, with the man who followed her now.

The diminutive old bawd was waiting for them when they emerged, a wizened rose in her bedroom of pink and red tapestries and flowered plaster ceiling. She pinched Viv's cheek, a liberty Viv could only smile at. "It's good to see you back again, Mistress Vivian. Maggot's already paid me a visit, and One Eye Wallace, too. Both of 'em both eager to capture your realm."

"Rivett?" Viv asked.

"Smelly Jakes himself did a tour, though not as much of a one as you'd have thought, if he wanted to scare off the competition."

"I'll see him scared off," Viv said with quiet menace.

"You should finish the job you started," Nan said. "Every girl who's worked for him would fight for a jar of his pickled parts."

"That would be an event," Viv said.

"Wouldn't it? A penny for the show." Nan cackled gleefully. "Well, now, dearie, Izzy went upstairs. Bouncing Bess will keep him awake, in case there's trouble. But if there's trouble, you've got this big beauty to help." Nan nodded toward Rafe.

Viv looked at him. "Yes," she said. "Trouble."

Nan chattered on. "I've given you everything you need here for a night, wine and cold food, clean water and towels. So you lock the door and don't show yourselves. If you're seen, you best leave. You can trust me, dearling, and Bouncing Bess is sweet on Izzy—but I can't promise for all my girls, not with such fat rewards offered for you."

"You know you have my gratitude, Nan," Viv said.

"I know good value," Saucy Nan said with a wink, and slipped out the door.

As soon as the door closed, Viv had one hand in Rafe's hair, tugging his head back. The other laid her knife sharp across his throat. His whole body stiffened at the touch of the cold steel. His hands started to lift and Viv pressed the blade deeper, cutting a fine line into the flesh. Blood trickled down his neck. "Unbuckle your weapons." He did as she commanded, and his sword and dagger fell to the floor with a clatter of metal and leather. "Put your hands behind your back," she said, and he did. Then, "Don't move, not a fraction."

"I'm not moving," he said quietly. He swallowed hard.

She could feel the movement against the blade. Memories cut into her mind. "I should have let Garnet kill you, that first day. I should kill you now."

"Then why don't you?" he whispered.

"You rescued me."

"Izzy would have, if I had not."

"That's why I may still slit your throat." She did not move the knife. "You put yourself at risk to save me—but you betrayed me first. Why?"

"Two reasons."

"One for the rescue, and one for the betrayal?" she asked. "Give me both."

"I saved you because I love you." He stared at her with the strange desperation that she'd seen in his eyes before. "I love you, Vivian."

"So you say."

"Yes." His gaze held her, refusing to look away.

Her heart told her to believe the rough catch in his voice, to believe the blue eyes that held so much emotion. But with Rafe Fletcher, Viv had learned not to trust her heart.

She pressed close against him, close as a lover. She felt him harden against her, even with the knife at his throat. He closed his eyes, and a flush of embarrassment stained his cheeks. How tempting he had always been, with that mixture of innocence and brazen lust. She moved closer, blade and body, feeling all the exquisite maleness of him against her, the muscular planes of chest and thigh, the thrust of his sex against her belly. He throbbed, and she felt an answering pulse within her, sending flash fires along her nerves. Her heart pounded, a hollow ache. Furious at her own desire, her own longing, Viv pressed the edge deeper. She breathed the scent of his blood, hot and metallic. "The knife excites you? Did it excite you to dance on the edge of life and death with me?"

"You excite me," he whispered helplessly. "You burn in my blood, in my heart."

"Liar."

"You know I am not lying now."

"I know that you lie most excellently well."

"Vivian," he said softly, "there is one truth we share. We love each other. If not, I would have abandoned you. If not, you would have killed me already."

"Are you so certain?"

He drew a sharp breath as she pressed the edge deeper, then said, "Kill me in the morning, then. Give me one last night with you."

Viv could bear the closeness no longer. She moved back suddenly, across the room, leaning back against the wall. He stood where he was, blood still staining his throat. At last she said, "Did I ever lie to you? Did you ever tell me the truth?"

"I have never known you to lie to me," he answered. Then, drawing a breath, he said, "I swear I will never lie to you again."

"So—you love me? Why did you betray me?"

"I betrayed you to the Crown to save my grandfather and cousin from charges of treason. To avenge a friend."

"What has that to do with me?"

"Less than I believed, or I would not have betrayed you. But even when I thought you guilty, I wanted it undone."

"I don't understand—" she began, but he shook his head.

"Tomorrow," he said softly. "It is a long story. And the night is short."

Viv found she did not care why. Izzy would have the tale, and Smoke. They must have believed him. "Leave. I won't kill you, but I want you out of my life."

Rafe crossed the room, but not to the door—to her. He pulled her to him, kissing her deeply, desperately. Fire poured through Vivian, but she tensed against him, willing herself not to respond. He let her go abruptly. But he did not leave. He stepped back across the room and waited. His eyes looked huge, brimming with tears and burning with lust. Had anyone else ever matched her emotion? Vivian thought the air would explode from the heat quivering between them. It was impossible to love him, impossible not to.

She surged toward him, the knife slashing. Rafe gasped as the blade sought the rent in his doublet and linen, over his heart. The point ripped through the cloth and scored a red line down his chest. But he did not move, did not stop her, as the knife rose and descended, cutting his clothes away. He stood, panting, fear and arousal emanating in waves, until the fabric hung from him in scarlet-stained ribbons. More blood trickled from the shallow cuts. She would leave him scarred by the pain he had given her.

With a sob Viv lifted the knife again, but this time he reached up, grasping her wrist. "Let go." His fingers tightened, emphasizing the command, but not forcing her. He met her gaze. Not fear now, pure challenge. "Use your nails," he said. "Use your teeth."

Cursing, she dropped the knife and flung herself at him. Rafe lifted her up, carrying her to the bed. He kneed back the covers and dropped her onto the white sheets. Tugging and tearing, he stripped her of the lurid satins. Need was a blind haze. Only pure naked skin was enough for either of them. She kissed him, bit him, clawed him as he struggled to free himself of the rest of his clothes. She wanted every gasp and flinch of pain she managed to draw from him. They both cried out when the last garment was flung aside and he pressed her back on the bed, the full length of him hot against her. He moaned as she rubbed against him, feeling the hot expanse of his skin, the dark diamonds of hair at his chest and groin, the thin flow of his blood from the knife cuts. He pulled her closer, holding the pain between them, as if only the pain could heal them.

Aching, raging, wet with desire, Viv shoved against the power of his body. Rafe yielded to her, rolling onto his back. He gave a harsh cry as her hand grasped the hot tower of his cock. She mounted him, lifting her hips above the high thrust of his sex, then lunged down onto him. She cried out with him as her body sheathed his in one savage thrust, a blinding rush of pain and pleasure, joy and sorrow, rage and rapture. He filled her completely. Again she plunged down on him, driven by consuming need. Love was a wound and she took its hard blade within her again and again, for it hurt more to be without. She sobbed in fury as she drove her body onto his. His arms encircled her, urging the embracing vengeance of her flesh. With a low cry he arched up to her, his powerful cock pulsing wildly within her. He whispered over and over that he loved her. Confession. Defiance. Surrender.

Climax struck her like lightning, a bright obliterating ecstasy that scorched her soul and body, then flung her back to earth. Vivian lay still, aching and breathless, her heart pounding. She felt utterly naked, flayed by their passion. He whispered her name, as he had kneeling beside her in the cell in Bedlam. Suddenly all the long wretched hours alone came back with a rush. Sobs racked her. She turned away from him, but he pulled her back, held her close. Her tears poured with every breath. Too exhausted for pride, she wept as he stroked her, murmured to her. "Vivian . . ."

She cried for a long time, releasing all her unshed tears while his fingers caressed her shorn hair. When the storm subsided, Rafe rose and went to the dresser. He poured water into a bowl and brought it to the bed with a towel, settling beside her. First he tended her face, cleaning her tears, then the wet cloth moved over her body, wiping away the sweat and blood. She winced when Rafe touched her, as if it were the cuts on his own body that he cleansed. She trembled, every fiber aware of him. He murmured to her softly still, his hands gliding the cloth . . . touch cool and soothing.

"Vivian, I love you." He whispered the words with such passion, such tenderness, such sadness. She felt the force of his presence. He was the same as he'd always been. Yet more. Some barrier was gone, some new dimension manifest.

She shivered, though the summer night was hot. "You are a stranger."

"Not so strange," he murmured. "Truly. I was more myself with you than I wished to admit."

She drew him to her, holding him fiercely. Greedy for comfort from her enemy . . . her lover. His tenderness devastated her. She ached for him still, hollow with a need only he could fill. Slowly, he began to caress her, his hands, his lips moving over her. Her skin shimmered from his touches, her throat, her shoulders, her breasts, her belly. Soothing. Soft. His voice was soft, too, a whisper. "In the morning, the world will be the same. Tonight is ours."

Tonight. Only tonight. He was saying goodbye. Every touch treasured her as if were the last time. It made her weep again, but she saw he was weeping, too, his face glistening with tears. "Love me," he whispered. "I will love you forever."

This time it was she who yielded. He entered her, filled her. Irresistible. She was open, without protection, unbearably tender. Anger was burned away, her love exposed in hopeless sorrow and yearning sweetness. She had no defenses, yet he did not take her like a conqueror, but like a supplicant. Moaning, he gave himself up to her with the same vulnerability, trembling in abandon as their two bodies fused into one, endlessly destroyed and remade within each other. Pulsation after pulsation. There was no yesterday, no tomorrow, only the present, a moment that opened into eternity like an infinitely unfolding rose, its petals red as blood, soft as velvet, sweet as salvation.

The passion ebbed, but sweetness lingered. Laying beside her, Rafe drew the coverlet over them and gathered her in his arms. Vivian felt utterly safe, though she knew it was only an illusion. She lay cocooned within the golden afterglow, not wanting to move beyond the warm circle of his embrace, or look beyond its heart-easing comfort.

In the flickering candlelight, Rafe's smile was tender, holding sadness at bay. He stroked her hair. "Sleep, share this peace with me."

❦

Despite everything, Viv woke early. She sat in bed, watching Rafe sleep. His face was boyish under the tousled hair, his sensuous mouth soft, his long lashes curving against his cheek. She pushed aside the coverlet. The morning light spilled across his body, revealing the marks she'd left, thin cuts of the knife, tracks of raking nails, bite marks, bruises. She caressed him silently, not quite touching, her fingertips gliding over his skin. "You will always be mine," she whispered.

And I will always be yours.

Her ferocity had marked him. But his tenderness had opened places no one else had ever touched. Would ever touch.

For a while she watched him as he slept. Then, recognizing a simpler hunger than what Rafe stirred in her, Viv rose and went to the dresser to investigate the food Nan had set out. Bedlam served nothing but gruel. When she left the bed, he woke, so she carried the plates back and set them down in the center of the rumpled, bloodstained sheets. He grimaced slightly as he sat up, and gave her a rueful smile. They sat together on the bed, devouring bread and cheese until hunger eased, then fed each other morsels of the fruit. But neither spoke. Where to begin?

Abruptly, she asked him, "Who are you? What is your true name?"

"You have it already."

"Rafe Fletcher then. But not the son of a fencing master?"

"Son of an actor trained by the best fencers, grandson of the owner of Easton Arms."

"The Puritan grandfather who beat you till you ran away?"

"I ran, and he always came after. And when he beat me, he looked so miserable I felt guilty—not for my disobedience, but for his unhappiness. My grandparents loved me, for all their strictness. Or, finally, what they did not love I learned to hide."

"I love everything you are," she said, then wished she had not. "Or thought I did."

After a moment, Rafe said, "The reason I rescued you was love. Surely you know you have my whole heart. I told you the reason I betrayed you, but not the whole of it. There was so little time. I wanted our night, with the world shut away."

"But it is morning, and the world is still with us," she said to him.

"Yes." Rafe told her the tale then—his discovery of the sabotage, and his family's arrest. He told her how Gabriel had died in his arms, and the message that he'd given before he died. "Topaz and Silver, he said, and one other. We thought perhaps it was Garnet." She listened, quelling the urge to interrupt. Coming to the end, he said, "I did not expect to admire you, much less love you. It was like a fall from a cliff, the rush of it was like flying. Until I hit the bottom—when I saw the dragon brooch, and the guns."

"I did not recognize the dragon," Vivian said quietly. "But Nicholas often left me such trinkets. I thought the brooch might be his last gift, but I gave it to you."

"At first I told myself that Gabriel might have lost it. That one of your men found it and made it part of your tribute. But then you showed me the crates of snaphances."

"I told you then, I bought them from Chettle. Two cases just as you saw. I thought them a prize. Chettle always drove a hard bargain but he never cheated me."

Rafe could not help but laugh at something so preposterous. "The honorable customs conniver?"

Vivian smiled and shrugged. "In truth, Rafe, Nick wanted to sell the pistols in France, where we could have triple our profit, but I fought him. He did not care that they might be turned against our soldiers. But whatever else I may be, I am a loyal Englishwoman."

He leaned forward, clasping her hands. "They do not know about the Earl of Mortmain, and will never know from me. But they will not like that you have been arrested and escaped them. You are a far better scapegoat than my family. They have no reason to clear you of the treason charges, even if I bring them evidence of your innocence. You may not be able to rebuild your kingdom in the Clink."

"You would be surprised what money can buy."

"Yes, I am always surprised at greed and corruption."

"Then you will be eternally innocent. You cannot conquer them. Cut off the heads, and a hundred more will grow to spite you."

"I cannot change who I am," he said.

"Yet you expect me to."

"No, I do not expect you to change who you are," he whispered. Her heart plummeted. Looking into her eyes, he said, "I love you for your integrity, your loyalty, your unquenchable fire. I love you because you have survived and triumphed in your own right. I love you for your wanton joy—in life, as in love. But nothing changes the fact that you are a thief. You exploit the innocent however much you protect your own."

"Every lord and lady in this land protects their own and exploits the rest," she scoffed. "But they have fine titles to crown their thievery."

"It is more true than I wish, and less true than you would have me believe," he said. "There is honor among gentlemen as well as among thieves."

"It is just rarer," Viv responded sarcastically. She was afraid, and her fear made her angry.

There was an uncomfortable silence, then Rafe said, "Your smuggling connections in France must be extensive. You could rebuild your base from there, and so sustain power with the people you know in London and the port towns."

"What?" she laughed. "The Crown's minion instructs me in the craft of smuggling?"

"I am neither their minion, nor yours," he answered, stung. "I do not expect a queen to give up a kingdom, even such a one as you ruled. I do not believe you could."

She bristled, but said nothing.

"You are a good queen, Vivian, but it is a cruel kingdom."

"The world is cruel. And all its kingdoms."

"And you must have one." He smiled sadly, stroking her cropped hair.

She leaned into the stroke. "Rule my kingdom with me. You were happy at my side. I know you were not happy with your Puritans in Exeter."

"No," he admitted. "Not happy. Only busy. The tight Puritan shoe pinches my toes."

"You cannot tell me you do not love the wildness of the streets."

He did not deny it. "Yes, their wildness—your wildness—matches something deep within me. I cannot imagine another woman who will fire me so, or quench what you have roused. You have my heart as prisoner."

"I do not want to starve it behind bars. That is your choice," she accused. Then her voice softened, luring him. "There has never been anyone I've loved as I love you. Stay with me."

"It was easier before, half-living, half-playing the role. I wanted to protect you from those who were worse—creatures like Maggot and Rivett. But I would still protect those like my family from you." He shook his head. "Any life I try to imagine without you seems barren. I cannot ask you to change, but I cannot live as a thief. I could have been driven beyond the law, as you were. But I cannot choose your world, though I would choose you."

"Would you hide me in your world then? Squeeze onto my foot the tight Puritan shoe that you kicked off in London?"

"I would not destroy you, Vivian. You are what you have had to be. You breathe power like air. I cannot change that. You are a wild creature I trapped. Because I love you, I will set you free. But I serve the Queen and the law."

She eyed him skeptically. He was too idealistic for his own good. To offer loyalty to a sovereign was one thing. But the law played strumpet to the richest masters, tumbled on her back with her skirts flung up over her face. Yet there was something in his shiny innocence that touched her.

He saw her look of skepticism and returned one of exasperation. "I am not a child."

"You have proved that most admirably," she jested.

His gaze intensified, accusing her. "There are few things more childish than greed."

"Nor am I a child." She bristled, though she knew herself greedy. But not greedy as Rivett was, insatiable to fill a void of heart and spirit. Most men would disagree with Rafe, and fight fiercely for whatever wealth, glory, power, and passion they could seize. Viv's instinct was to battle them all for the choicest morsels, and revel in the victory.

"I do not want to quench your spirit," he said, as if he read her thought. "I know that battle too well."

She wanted to reclaim her kingdom. But without him beside her, the kingdom was hollow, the crown as heavy as Bedlam's shackles. She would struggle, she would triumph, and finally she would not care. She stroked back the dense black silk of his hair, admiration and tenderness tempering her pique. How curious he was, with his talent for deception, his love of honesty. What justice there was existed because such men as Rafe would fight for it. It was justice he loved, not her harlot sister, the law. Wondering if it was madness, she said, "And if I would try? If I would give up my kingdom and live in your heart?"

His gaze searched hers. Disbelief gave way slowly to hope. Very carefully he said, "I would sacrifice whatever you ask, till we find a way we can live together. Let us win what we will, earn what we will, but not steal it. We will build our lives, not destroy others'."

"I give you my word," she said. "What we build, we will build together, rule together."

"Together," he swore to her. "With no secrets."

They looked at each other, not knowing yet what they would do, only that they would try.

"There is still the world," Rafe said.

"I will not leave Jacob Rivett ruling in my stead."

"And I must finish what I started."

"I am a good scapegoat only if they can prosecute me, Rafe. So your family remains the best offering."

"Yes. Walsingham might be that ruthless, and Burne with him." He met her gaze. "I wanted justice, I wanted revenge, but now I want to know the answers as well. I will find whoever sabotaged the guns and killed Gabriel."

"You have the brooch?"

"Yes." He rose and got it from among his things.

"Perhaps I can give you part of the truth you seek," Viv said, staring at the amber bee. "Let me tell you about Adrian Thorne."

28

S ir Adrian, it's Vivian." Viv tapped lightly on the door.

Adrian Thorne opened it, looking far handsomer washed, she noted. His smile, welcoming and curious, faded when he saw her expression. The warm light in his eyes cooled, and his face became tight, shuttered. His hands curled into fists, and she saw that he wore gloves. "I should never have told you. But . . ."

But it did not matter in Bedlam, madman to madwoman. Now, he was free because of her, and because of Rafe. It was not a debt Viv had thought to claim, but now she would, even knowing it would cause Adrian pain. "You said objects would reveal things to you."

"Sometimes," he said, his voice a rough whisper. "Rarely—but it is as potent as touch when they do."

"Show him the brooch, Rafe," she said.

Rafe looked skeptical, apprehensive, but he opened his palm, revealing the dragon.

Adrian drew a soft breath.

"You recognize it? From your vision?" she asked.

"Yes," Adrian answered.

Rafe closed his hand protectively about the brooch, regarding Adrian with deep suspicion. Viv glanced from Rafe to Adrian Thorne and back again. "I want Rafe to believe you. I do not want him to think I have influenced you in anyway."

Adrian lifted his head and looked at Rafe. "I want you to believe I do not wish anyone harm."

"I don't know what I believe—yet," Rafe answered.

"There may be nothing for you to believe or disbelieve," Adrian said with a twist of a smile.

"But you will try?" Viv asked.

"I will not refuse you." He tugged off the gloves and laid them on the table, then held out his hand.

Rafe laid the dragon in his palm. Adrian's fingers closed around it in a spasmodic gesture and a visible shock rippled through his body. He stared, his skin blanched, his eyes fixated on some vision beyond them. Viv felt her own body tighten in response to the shock that gripped him. Adrian moaned, his fist tightening about the brooch. Another shudder swept through him. He staggered forward, gripping Rafe and sinking down to the floor. Rafe sank with him, his face almost the same bloodless white. Adrian stared up at him, beyond him, into death. He whispered one word. "Topaz." Then he shuddered violently, sagging in Rafe's arms. Rafe gasped, gripping him tightly, then laying him back on the floor.

"Adrian." Vivian pressed her fingers to his throat, feeling the pulse there, weak but steady. He gave a low moan. After a moment, he opened his eyes, his gaze going at once to Rafe. Raising himself, he held out his hand and uncurled his fingers to reveal the dragon. Blood trickled over his palm from where the pin had stabbed him. He offered the brooch to Rafe, who took it gingerly, trying not to touch Adrian's hand, wary once more.

"This was your gift to Gabriel, and before that your father's to you," Adrian said softly, intimately. He laid his hand on Rafe's shoulder.

Rafe pulled back, staring at him. Adrian drew back in turn, as if slapped.

"I do not know sometimes if my soul is my own," Adrian said, his voice sharpening to anger. "But it is not because I am a warlock who has bartered it to the Devil. I never asked for this curse. It has brought me nothing but grief and pain. I did not want to be locked in Bedlam, but that's where it brought me. I did not want to feel your friend's love for you—or his death."

"But you did," Rafe whispered. It was not a question.

"The images fragment, like pieces of a shattered mirror. There is too much pain to see clearly." He shuddered. "I can smell the docks—tar and pitch, beer, urine, refuse. My blood—his blood."

"Did he know his killer?" Rafe asked.

"Three men," Adrian answered. "He recognized them all."

"Names?" Vivian asked.

"Names of a sort." He frowned. "Agate. Silver. Topaz."

"If he recognized them, you must know their true names," Rafe said.

But Adrian shook his head. "That is all I can give you."

"Their faces? Can you describe them?" Vivian asked.

"I would know them. Agate had a pointed brown beard, a scar on his forehead." His hands sketched the air.

"Chettle," Vivian affirmed.

"Silver was short. His body, his face, square, like a child's blocks piled one atop the other."

"Gray eyes?" Vivian asked.

"Dark gray, cold. Like a reptile."

"Rivett," Rafe said. "And Topaz?"

"Thick yellow hair and brown eyes. Handsome in the bland way that is difficult to describe. Tall. Proud." Adrian shook his head. "I know him—Gabriel knew him—but I cannot find the name."

"It's all right," Viv said quietly.

"Silver and Agate held . . . your friend . . . while Topaz thrust in the blade." Adrian shivered, turning pale again. Viv wanted to take his hand, but touch would be another infliction.

There was silence for a minute, then Rafe asked, "Did Gabriel discover why the three men were meeting? Did they talk of sabotaging the guns?"

"Guns, yes. But I know nothing of sabotage." Adrian leaned his head back against the wall. "They plan to use the guns to free the Queen of Scots. That is what Gabriel died trying to tell you."

❧

"Smelly old Jakes was right raging when he came out o' Bedlam last night," Tadpole said. He pointed across the street, indicating the rooms on the second floor above an apothecary's shop. "He came right here, and caught the 'pothecary trying to leave, dragged him back inside and came out alone."

Rafe felt Vivian tense beside him. She said quietly, "This place belongs to Crabbe, one of the apothecaries Rosy summoned to treat him when he was ill."

"Maybe the one with the perfect antidote?" Izzy said. "Because he'd made the perfect poison."

Vivian nodded grimly, then nudged Tadpole to go on. "Smelly Jakes crept back here just before dawn, a dozen men with 'im, and hasn't come out since, though I've seen 'em moving about on the second floor. I think he must be waiting on something."

Waiting for Topaz' plan to succeed or fail, Rafe thought. He and Vivian had assembled a motley crew, Smoke, Izzy, one of Saucy Nan's guards, Viv's maid Joan, and Brick, the innkeeper of the Lightning Bolt. Adrian Thorne had been too exhausted to come with them. When he recovered, Viv would see to it that he had money and protection to get him wherever he needed to go.

"Look at this," Izzy whispered. "There's three of Rivett's men coming out."

They watched as the men made their way to the nearest inn for food. Quickly they formulated a plan of attack. Rafe and the others moved across to the alley, and grabbed the three on the way back with their stock of cold pies and beer. Rafe felt a thrill of triumph as they seized the snaphances the men carried. They were likely from the cache Gabriel had gone hunting. The three were questioned separately. Rivett held his men entirely through fear, and Rafe knew a little pain would soon yield the password, if threats did not. But it was the youngest and most stalwart who became outraged at talk of treason, declaring himself a good thief and a good Englishman like them. At his suggestion they took him with them, carrying as many pies as he could hold to the door of Rivett's lair.

He gave the password, and when the door opened, he tripped inside, flinging the pies into the air. In the midst of the distraction, the rest of the crew entered with their guns at the ready. With the element of surprise, the fight was quickly over. Vivian blasted a path to Rivett, his men toppling to either side. Rivett pulled his gun, but Rafe seized him. He struggled fiercely till Viv set the muzzle of her gun under his jaw. Within a few moments, the rest of Rivett's men lay dead or bound on the floor. Viv nodded for the youth who'd helped them to leave, but he attached himself stubbornly, declaring he'd always wanted to work for her. Viv was willing to take him on trial, and Izzy promptly dubbed him Pie.

Rafe didn't know who would be waiting at the Tilted Jug, if anyone, but he sent Joan with a message to summon Burne, alone, to where they were. He set Tadpole and Brick to keep watch to make sure it was so. An escort of Crown guards could be summoned later. He didn't trust Burne not to seize her again. Whatever other danger they shared, he wouldn't put Vivian in risk of arrest again.

She stood guard with a snaphance as Rafe searched Rivett meticulously for weapons—knives, guns, garrotes, or anything that might conceal poison. Rivett's hands were tied, but Rafe secured him to a chair as well. Finished, he backed away, and Viv moved to stand beside him. Rivett surveyed them in turn, his eyes dark as lead.

Smoke returned from searching the building. "Empty except for a corpse. The apothecary is in the cellar—or some bloody thing in an apothecary's robes."

"Good riddance," Vivian said.

"So you knew about Crabbe after all," Rivett said to her, livid with rage.

"He made the poison?" Viv asked archly, as if it were not a question. Rafe suspected she was leading Rivett.

"I was right to grab you," Rivett muttered, "for all the good it did."

"You were wrong to grab me," Viv said, her voice cold.

There was another mystery hidden here. Rafe shifted the pieces in his mind, searching for a fit. Leaving Viv to question Rivett, Rafe examined the crate of snaphances in the corner. The remaining weapons were perfect, not sabotaged but kept for their use.

"Crabbe said Rosy didn't know he'd distilled the poison," Rivett insisted, with the outrage of a man's who been lied to despite his best attempts at coercion. "He kept saying that Rosy only wanted a potion for his stomach."

Viv smiled. "I only knew that Rosy had summoned him with several others. I might have questioned him further, but Rosy told me you had given him the poison."

Rivett went very still, studying her through narrowed lids. When he spoke, his voice was menacing despite the bonds that kept him powerless. "If you did not know about Crabbe, then how did you find me here? No one followed me."

"Tadpole will be pleased," Izzy declared. "No higher praise than that."

The ripple of laughter from the others aggravated Rivett's rage. He glared at all of them.

"Tell me, Jacob, did the apothecary know you meant to poison Nick?"

Incensed, Rivett said nothing for a moment, then, "He guessed. He'd been hiding in a cupboard for days."

"You murdered Nicholas," Vivian accused. "That is what mattered to me."

Rivett looked both relieved and fearful. There was something else he was hiding. Rafe stepped forward, confronting him as well. "You murdered Sir Gabriel Darren."

The cold eyes did not blink as they shifted between them, calculating his chances. As Rafe expected, Rivett's gaze settled on him. There was no mercy to be had from Vivian. "Not directly, not in either case."

"Not directly?" Vivian backhanded him, hard. Rivett jolted against the ropes, and her blow left blood on his mouth. Rafe did not intervene, not after what she had told him of Bedlam.

"You framed my family for treason," Rafe said. "And I hold you as directly responsible for Gabriel's death as for Nick Swift's."

Vivian leaned closer to Rivett. "From my brief experience with the rope, Jacob, I can tell you it is an unpleasant way to die—or start to die. But you won't just hang, you'll be drawn and quartered."

"They've orders to draw it out as long as possible," Izzy added companionably from his corner. "The Queen's torturer finds great lechery in giving pain, so I've heard."

"I gave Rosy the choice of a quick death or a slow one," Viv said. "The only way I will forego the pleasure of killing you myself is to watch you executed as a traitor."

"A traitor?" Rivett turned to Rafe. "Where is your proof? Some smuggled guns I bought from a crooked customs official? The lady you seem to serve once more did the same."

"The guns are only corroboration of what we know already," Rafe said. Rafe would not tell him their information came from a dead man and a witch. The more Rivett thought they knew, the weaker his position became. The more Rafe learned from Rivett, the stronger his position when Burne arrived. "You are Silver. Chettle was Agate. Tell me who Topaz is."

Rafe could see the wheels of Rivet's mind turning like oiled clockworks, assessing and reassessing. Until Topaz was taken, Rivett's only value lay in negotiable information. Rivett's lips compressed, a line thin as wire. That piece was too valuable to give up so quickly.

Rafe pursued another line. "Why did you kill Sir Gabriel?"

"I didn't kill him," Rivett repeated.

"Like you didn't kill Nick?" Viv asked scornfully.

"Why?" Rafe insisted. The answer would test Rivett's veracity.

"He discovered us, recognized us," Rivett grated. "But it was Topaz who killed him."

Rafe ignored that. They were all guilty. "Gabriel discovered you had stolen the guns?"

"Yes."

"Discovered you had sabotaged them."

"Yes," he snapped.

"Discovered that you planned to use them to free the Queen of Scots."

Rivett stared at them, face pale as tallow. They were not supposed to know that. At last he grated out, "Yes."

"Was my family involved in any of this? Tell me the truth."

"No. Chettle got two crates from your cousin, and paid off his gambling debt. Those two boxes I had him sell to Nick and Vivian. A crew of my men sabotaged the guns in the warehouse, all but the ones we kept for ourselves. Chettle falsified the papers and shipped only part of the original order. We thought the damage would be mistaken for malfunction, but we'd already laid a false trail. If anyone came sniffing about, if we needed a diversion, we could point Walsingham to the Swifts—Chettle knew Viv planned to keep at least some of the snaphances."

"But Chettle was implicated. He dealt with Nick and with Rafe's cousin."

"As soon as anyone became suspicious of sabotage, Chettle was to sail for France." Rivett shrugged. "But he was reluctant to leave."

Rafe pressed him. "You were seen moving the guns. Tell us where they are bound."

In detail, Rivett revealed the arrangements to move the weapons north.

It was all unrolling too smoothly. Rafe regarded him with suspicion. "I don't believe you."

"What more can I tell you? You know the guns are traveling to Fotheringay, and that they left two nights ago. I can only tell you the routes, the places where they will be sheltered along the way. I've told you who knows their mission, and who knows only that his own pocket is richer. I've done all that. You can stop them before they reach Fotheringay." Rivett spoke with seeming frankness, but his eyes were still watchful, guarded. Even captured and bound, he was awaiting something.

Either the admission was false, Rafe thought, or he held some other secret close. It would take two days for the Queen's men to catch up with the weapons. Something else was to happen in that time. And Rivett hoped to live long enough for it to happen. "The guns are but part of the plot. Like Babington, you plan not to rescue the Queen of Scots, but to kill Queen Elizabeth."

Rivett gave a grimace that was to pass for a smile. "I know of no such plan."

"Everything you'd said about the movement of the weapons is suspect. It may all be a lie, or you may have revealed that plot in order to conceal the other. The Queen's torturer will pry the truth from you soon enough."

"Maybe not soon enough?" Izzy piped. "A new Queen means a new torturer—new victims, for that matter. He's hoping to wriggle away from us."

Rivett spared a glare in Izzy's direction, and received an impudent grin.

"You hope the Queen of Scots will set you free, Jacob? Well, the Queen of the Clink will make sure you don't escape." Smiling, Viv drew her knife and cut through Rivett's doublet to expose the pale belly beneath. Rafe backed away, crossing his arms across his chest. He would stop Vivian if she ventured much further, but he did not want Rivett to know that. He watched as she drew a fine cut in the tender skin. Blood seeped from the thin wound.

Terror flashed in Rivett's eyes. He turned to Rafe. "Stop her."

"In exchange for what?" Rafe asked, moving forward to grip her hand.

"No! He killed Nick," Vivian said furiously, twisting to face him. "There's no need to bargain with him. I will get him to tell us everything we need to know."

"Your vengeance will topple the Crown," Rivett broke in. "Every minute you waste could be the Queen's last."

No one spoke. Rafe could hear his heart pounding. Was the threat that imminent? He sought Vivian's gaze. She had loved Nicholas, but the Queen's life was at stake.

"I want my life," Rivett said. "I want a chance to run."

After a moment, Rafe answered. "I will give you my word. If your information saves Queen Elizabeth's life, you will have yours."

Rafe felt Vivian tense, but she did not intervene. For England's sake, he would forego his revenge for Gabriel, and she would forego her revenge for both Nick and Bedlam.

The promise within his reach, Rivett look even more desperate. "Why should I believe you?" he asked. "Why should I believe a betrayer?"

"I have acted as the Queen's agent." Rafe felt a flush of anger, a flush of guilt. He looked to Vivian. "And I have kept my bond to Vivian as best I might."

Vivian confronted Rivett. "Rafe Fletcher kept the oath he gave me. But you have a problem, Jake. A man who'd not keep his own word would never trust another's."

Rivett's eyes kept darting between them. Rafe knew Vivian was right. How could Rivett trust another soul when his own was consumed with greed? "You'll believe me, Rivett, because you've no other choice except Vivian's knife."

"You've never broken your word that I know of," Rivett said to Vivian, his voice thin and sharp with fear. "I want your word as well."

"My word will not stop the Crown from executing you."

"I want his word I will not be arrested. I want your word you will not kill me yourself."

"Tell Rafe what he wants to know, the whole of it. Do that and you have my word I will not kill you today. If you hold back even a crumb, I will slit you open slowly and save the executioners the trouble."

"Yes—everything," Rivett agreed tersely.

"Convince me, Rivett," Rafe challenged him. "Tell me how they plan to assassinate the Queen. Tell me who Topaz is. And tell me quickly."

Three sharp raps sounded at the door. Izzy let in Joan,

followed by Nigel Burne. His pale eyes glinted with hostility as he surveyed the room.

Tadpole appeared soon after and said, "He's not alone. There are two out on the street, holding horses."

Rafe glared at Burne. "You were told to come alone."

"I come as I wish, Fletcher, not as you would summon me."

"Oh, we led 'em in circles," Tadpole said cheerily. "They don't know where this one is."

Rafe spared a grin for Tadpole.

"So you've trapped a rat, Fletcher." Burne indicated Rivett, then surveyed Vivian coldly. "And helped another escape."

It took every ounce of willpower for Rafe not to strike him.

Viv placed her hand on his arm, and addressed Burne boldly. "It was the rat Rivett who first set me free, if only to trap me in another cage—in Bedlam."

For once, Burne looked shocked, Rafe thought with satisfaction. The spymaster looked back and forth from Rivett to Vivian.

"Rafe rescued me from that bondage," Viv continued. "In turn I have helped trap Rivett. For such a proud piece, Sir Nigel, you have missed many moves of the game."

Burne turned back to Rafe. "Why is the rat of any interest to me?"

Quickly, Rafe told him what they had learned. His family was innocent of the sabotage. More guns were en route to Fotheringay. "It is all part of a plot to assassinate the Queen."

Burne stilled, more quiet and intent than Rafe had never seen him before. Cold hatred gleamed in his eyes as he looked at Rivett.

"We've given our word he goes free," Rafe told him.

"Have you?" Burne said.

"Yes. Rivett is buying his life with the Queen's—if he speaks the truth and what he tells us can prevent her death. Surely, that is worth the price."

Burne moved forward purposefully, but Rafe blocked his way, shaking his head slightly. Burne stared at him with cold fury, but had sense enough to step back and let Rafe continue the interrogation he had started. Rafe swerved back to Rivett. He had evaded long enough. "Who is Topaz?"

"His name is Oliver Haughton, the Earl of Mortmain."

"Recusant Catholic," Burne whispered, like a curse.

Viv inhaled sharply, and Rafe turned to her, equally stunned. When Burne looked to them, Rafe said quickly, "I know Mortmain. I fought a duel with him once. He lost."

Rivett gave a snort of laughter.

Rafe turned on him. "You knew? Then you must have known I was George Easton's grandson."

"Not at first," Rivett answered. "You were recognized at Court. Topaz wanted me to kill you. But you suspected the Swifts, not me."

"Oh, I suspected you," Rafe said.

Rivett shrugged. "I thought you might be useful where you were."

"The knowledge gave him an extra pawn in his game against Nick and me," Viv said to Rafe, and then to

Rivett, "You must have given Rosy the brooch to hide among my jewels, to see what mischief it might cause."

"Mischief enough," Rivett sneered.

Vivian regarded him scornfully. "It has been your undoing, not mine."

"I undid Nick well enough."

Viv lunged at him, but Rafe grabbed her arm, drawing her back. He wanted Rivett to keep talking. "And the assassination?"

"The poison," Vivian said suddenly. "Rivett was afraid of what I might have learned about the apothecary from Rosy. That's why he grabbed me away from Burne's guards."

"Yes, poison," Rivett broke in quickly. "It is the same essence of monkshood that Rosy used. A single drop will kill. It is to be put in her new perfume, some fancy scent from France."

"Her perfume?" Viv breathed, seeing the danger as Rafe did. The Queen might well be dead already.

Rafe prodded Rivett with questions. "Mortmain would not have that kind of access. Who has he bribed? Who else is conspiring?"

"One of the ladies-in-waiting to the Queen," Rivett answered. "I do not know her name or what she looks like. I only know that she has the poison, and that she will use it. Her secret lover is a friend of Babington, and will suffer his fate unless she kills the Queen."

"What else?"

"That is all I know. You have Mortmain, the location of the guns. You have the method that will be used against Elizabeth. If you are a man of your word, let me go," Rivett demanded, but it was bravado. He was pale and sweating, fear drawn to the surface at last.

"No. You go free only if the Queen lives," Rafe decreed. "Smoke, Izzy, hold Rivett here until we have captured the conspirators. Once we know he's told the truth, escort him down to the docks. Let him take ship with what money and jewels he has on him."

Rivett cursed him briefly.

"No," Burne said.

"Yes," Rafe countered. If Vivian could forgo revenge, so could Burne. "He is scum, but you will have the true instigator of the plot, Mortmain."

"Rivett goes to the Fleet, like all traitors," Burne said. "And then to the hangman."

"He goes free. With luck you can catch him for some other crime."

Burne looked from Rafe to Vivian's men gathered close by, and saw he could not assert his authority over them. Turning back, Rafe nodded to Izzy to untie Rivett. Before he could reach him, Burne stepped forward, pulled a gun from beneath his cape and fired it straight at Rivett. The sound and scent of gunpowder burst in the air. The force of the bullet toppled Rivett over backward, a bloody hole in his chest. The corpse stared up at the ceiling with unblinking eyes, looking startled and ludicrous still bound to the chair.

There was a moment's stunned silence, then Rafe turned to Burne, appalled. "I gave him my word as the Queen's agent."

"My word, too," Viv added grimly, though Rafe knew she wanted Rivett dead.

"I did not give him mine," Burne said, replacing his pistol. "And I had no intention of arguing my decision with you."

Not when Burne would lose the argument, Rafe thought. "What would your word be worth if you did give it?"

Burne's eyes narrowed. "I give you my word I will let no traitors escape. If his information is true, I will testify for your family. For their sake, you had best pray Rivett did not play you false."

"We can get neither truth nor lies from him now," Viv said.

Rafe stepped protectively closer to Viv, glad that Burne had no troops at his command. Burne looked at him contemptuously. "If Mistress Swift had no part in the sabotage, I do not care if she lives or dies."

"There is no time for this," Viv broke in. "The Queen must be warned."

"Yes," Rafe agreed. "And Topaz must be taken before he can escape."

"It is best I go with you to take the Earl, but I am the only one who can warn the Queen," Burne said.

"Vivian can go," Rafe said.

"I cannot entrust such a mission to her," Burne snapped.

"I give you my word, I will carry it out faithfully," Vivian said.

Burne's head snapped back as if struck. "Impossible."

"It is possible," Rafe insisted. His eyes met Vivian's, and he knew she had already decided to go. It was a great risk, but it was a chance to save Queen Elizabeth from death, and England from chaos. He prayed it was a chance at salvation for herself. "Vivian can take a message to Claire Darren, and Lady Claire can approach the Queen."

"Is she not one of the Queen's ladies-in-waiting?" Viv asked.

"Yes." Rafe did not understand her at first. Then he shook his head. "No, you can trust Claire."

"I have had her followed since Sir Gabriel's murder," Burne said. At Rafe's angry glance, he added, "For her own protection. She has met with no one untoward."

"She would have no part in treason, or in her brother's death," Rafe affirmed.

"Give me the message then," Vivian said, accepting Rafe's friend as her own.

"No," Burne insisted. "The peril is too great. I must go directly to the Queen."

"You speak of peril," Vivian said sharply, but with less rancor than before. "Your presence alone is enough to alert the poisoner. You and a squad of armed men rushing to the Queen's chambers could bring disaster. This woman has nothing to lose, everything to gain, and the potion needs only one drop to kill. I have seen it at work. Let me approach the Queen quietly, through someone she trusts."

Burne wavered for a moment, but reason took precedence over pride. "Take one of my horses," he said grudgingly, accepting the sense of her argument without giving it a direct acknowledgement. He turned to Rafe. "You and I will take the other two, and my men will go to the palace separately and summon others to help us. That can be done without causing alarm. If Mistress Swift is successful, still more can be sent as reinforcements."

Rafe handed Viv the dragon brooch, closing her hand about it tightly. "I promised this token to Claire, if I recovered it. Give it to her, then tell the tale yourself—whatever you think the Queen should know."

"You will not be admitted to the palace dressed like that." Burne nodded disdainfully at the groom's clothes. "You'd best steal a gown quickly."

"For a visit to the Queen, I will be proper and borrow one," Viv returned with acid sweetness.

29

The four octagonal towers of the palace gate rose as Vivian approached Whitehall. Beneath crenellated gables and checkered walls of stone and flint, two guards stood on duty, long pikes firmly in their grasps. Admittance to the palace grounds was not impossible to get—for law-abiding citizens with known business. She looked respectable and prosperous in amber satin draped with a rope of dusky pearls. A lace-edged ruff hid the bruises on her throat and a velvet cap covered her cropped hair. The clothes were lent to her quickly and without question by the wife of a merchant she had once protected from Rivett. But it was the sentries' duty to shelter the palace residents from uninvited favor-seekers as well as from danger. Dismounting, she found a boy to hold her horse, and approached the guards on foot.

If either of them recognized her, of course, the game was up. Many men slipped over to the Clink to indulge in bear-baiting, gambling, and whoring. They would never let the Queen of the Clink within the same walls as the Queen of England. They might even seize her, and she did not have time for that. Neither did Queen Elizabeth. Squaring her shoulders, Vivian approached with a light, confident step.

"Your business?" one of the guards asked in a curt snap.

Clearly, he had been chosen for his size and military bearing, a ruddy young bullock with a flat, proud face.

"I have a message awaited by one of the Queen's attendants, Lady Claire Darren."

"We've been told to expect no such thing," the ruddy beef dismissed the notion.

"Your name?" the other ordered. He was taller, with a rancorous curl to his lip. She did not like the closeness with which he studied her.

"Mistress Anne Grey." She chose a name too common for an outright claim to power, but anyone named Grey might have connections too high for an ambitious soldier to antagonize. Before they could ask further, she went on, "My name is less important to Lady Claire than my message. She does not expect it today, but mark you, she wants to hear it. Delay would not please her." Stepping closer, she lifted the purse hanging from her waist. Taking from it the handkerchief she had put there, she allowed the guards a glimpse of the silver beneath.

"Well, if that be so," the beef began, but the other seized her arm. Vivian tensed, forcing herself not to resist further.

"A message from the lady's lover, is it? The Queen doesn't hold with lewdness in her ladies-in-waiting." With his thumb he traced the scar on her face, not quite touching it. So that was it. He thought she was a drab picking up wages as a go-between. He did not recognize her after all.

Vivian smiled, dropping her voice to a huskier, more seductive note. "What, do you wish to hear all about it afterward?"

The insolent mouth twisted in a smirk. "That bargain might do. Give me your pearls—for security. You can redeem them for their worth."

Which was far more than a single night's tumble. Greedy fool. She would redeem them, all right, and he would find the bargain more than he had asked for. Quickly she unclasped the necklace and handed over her purse, shielding the transaction from the sight of the street with her skirts. The guard whistled. A page appeared from within, and took his direction to conduct her to the Lady Claire Darren.

Vivian passed through the massive gates, entering the palace at last, after all these years of exile from the possibilities that had once been hers. She kept a sharp eye for the people she saw there, verifying the arrangement of the guards, the layout within the walls, any details that might come in handy in the uncertain future. But the crisis pressed sharply and she moved swiftly through the sweeping lawns, cloistered courtyards, and rambling buildings. The page brought her through an imposing doorway, along a gallery with tall, narrow windows and rich tapestries, and through other corridors, at last stopping before a door of carved oak.

"Tell the Lady Claire it is an urgent message from Rafe Fletcher."

Without reply he rapped quietly. The door was opened and the boy stepped in.

Viv shifted restlessly from one softly slippered foot to the other, chewing her lip. *Hurry, fools.*

To her relief, the page came out and motioned Vivian through the door. She would not have to force an entrance.

He closed it behind her. The antechamber was surprisingly small, but comfortably furnished. Tapestries of elegant needlework covered the walls and table. Viv knew the Queen's attendants shared quarters, but only one lady stood facing her, slender and assured. Viv felt a pang of jealousy, for the woman was exquisite, with fine features and a tender mouth, her hair gleaming rich chestnut under her coif. Claire Darren was sister of the friend dear to Rafe. She shared a mutual love and loss with him that Viv did not. But beautiful as she was, Rafe had spoken of Claire Darren as a brother might. Viv wondered if the Lady Claire was equally immune to Rafe's beauty.

Regarding her in return, the woman's eyes widened slightly. Her bearing changed, tense and on guard. Vivian knew the lady had recognized her. At some public gathering, a palace gossip, or her brother, had pointed her out.

"I am Vivian Swift." She confronted the suspicion directly even as she dropped the required curtsy. Luckily, Lady Claire was too sensible and self-possessed to shriek at the sight of a notorious criminal in her apartments. "I spoke the truth. I bring urgent news from Rafe."

Both registered, the use of his first name and that she, who did not run errands for anyone, did so for Rafe. Seizing the advantage, Viv took the brooch from within her bodice and placed it in Claire Darren's hand. "He gave me this token to bring you, as he promised."

Claire gazed at the enameled dragon only a moment. Her hand closed over it. Hazel eyes met Vivian's gaze directly, filled with intelligence and resolve. "If he trusts you, so shall I. Tell me what has happened."

"Rafe's family is cleared, and your brother's murder half avenged." Viv stopped any questions with a quick gesture. "The Queen's life is in danger even as we speak. Your brother died because he learned too much of a plot to assassinate Her Majesty and set the Scottish queen on the throne. Our source of information said the Queen will be presented with a gift of perfume from the King of France. Has this happened yet?"

"This morning she received the French ambassador. I was not on duty, but this afternoon one of Her Majesty's favorite perfume bottles was brought to her apartments newly filled."

"Have her ladies-in-waiting had access to it? One of them plans to add a poison so deadly a drop on the skin will kill."

"Each of us has her responsibilities over the Queen's wardrobe, jewelry, and toiletries. We all enter her dressing room a dozen times a day," Lady Claire answered in growing alarm.

"Take me to the Queen," Viv said. *"Now."*

They presented only the familiar figures of a lady-in-waiting and a small, seemingly respectable woman with her eyes cast modestly down. The guards at the door did not question Claire Darren's offhand remark that her companion was the lacemaker the Queen had sent for. Viv was glad the light was not bright enough to reveal the distinctive scar on her cheek. Within, four ladies-in-waiting sat at their needlework, clustered around a window to make the most of the late afternoon light. Three were young, the other only in her middle years, but her face was foully disfigured by smallpox. The older woman glanced sharply at them as if she had eyes in the back of her head.

"Here is the lacemaker from York," Claire beamed as if proud of herself. "I have found her at last."

"Lady Claire! You know the Queen is resting," the older woman sternly forbade.

"At once, Her Majesty commanded," Claire replied mildly, and kept moving toward the inner door. The lady's annoyance increased, but she kept silent. The Queen's ladies were too perfectly trained to flout the rules, so Elizabeth must indeed have made some such request of Claire. The surreptitious grimace shared by the three younger women told Viv what a dragon the pock-face could be. One was a plump girl with carefully curled brown hair and brown eyes, the second flaxen blonde, her fair brows and lashes making her sapphire eyes all the deeper, the third ginger-haired. *Is the killer one of these?* Vivian wondered, studying them freely since they ignored her. But she did not expect to see murder in the assassin's eyes. She knew all too well how much could go cloaked in secret, and for how long. And what the cost could be.

Claire Darren tapped lightly at the inner door.

"Enter," commanded a voice that did not sound sleepy. Lady Claire opened the door, motioning Vivian to follow.

The bedchamber was surprisingly dark and airless compared with Viv's own bedroom. The air was warm and stale, and no wonder, for there was only one window. Yet the ceiling was entirely gilt, and a magnificent and curious bed of woods of different colors was hung with painted Indian silk, and draped with quilts of silk and velvet thick with glittering metallic embroidery. Viv had a glimpse of a table overlaid with silver, a chair built up from the floor entirely of rich cushions, and through a further door a luxuriously appointed bathroom glinted with mirrored walls, but all this was the whirling impression of a moment. At once her attention was caught and held by the woman standing by the window.

For despite the power, the legend, the more than human figure she made at public appearances with her puffed sleeves and stiff farthingale skirts embroidered and bejeweled, with the gigantic white bloom of lace framing her head, the woman gazing out the window at the river and its multitude of barges was neither inhuman nor larger than life. She wore a silk dressing gown, and her light red hair, mingled with dulling gray, frizzed in a cloud. Her pale skin bore a few faint scars of the pox she had survived nearly a decade ago. But her large eyes, pale lashed and deep lidded, were as dark and vivid as a falcon's. The eyes of a bird of prey, fierce and ruthless, and the most intelligent eyes Vivian had ever faced. As she dropped a low curtsey beside Lady Claire, Viv had the unsettling impression that perhaps, at last, she had encountered a woman who might best her at her own game.

"Who is this?" Elizabeth's voice was harsh with irritation.

"One who risks her life for your safety, and to reveal a traitor, Your Majesty!"

"Rise."

Vivian straightened, raising her head. The Queen's hand was clenched, the dark, glowing eyes dangerously piercing Viv's. "You may speak. What is this tale you bear?" The eyes hardened. "And mind your accusation is truthful, or the penalty will be yours."

Vivian nodded acknowledgment. "The new perfume, Your Majesty must not wear it! It is most deadly."

"The gazelle's musk and amber scent from France?" One delicate brow rose. "I already have."

"What?" Viv burst out before she could help it.

Elizabeth's mouth curved ironically. "More than six hours ago. So you see your errand is not so urgent. Nevertheless, for Our safety, repeat whatever gossip you have heard. But think twice before accusing any of my court, Mistress Importunate."

"My name is Vivian Swift."

The Queen regarded her silently, brow arching higher. At last she said with quiet menace, "You do indeed risk your life, coming here."

"Yet Your Majesty no longer thinks I bear mere foolish gossip."

Elizabeth's thin lips quirked slightly. "You are right. Whatever I do with you, I shall listen to you first. Who gave you this tale?"

"Master Rafe Fletcher uncovered the conspiracy, Your Majesty," Vivian said with fierce pride.

"Ah, my Centaur claims to have triumphed on his quest." The Queen smiled slightly. "But from what I have learned of him, he has reason to lie."

"Sir Nigel Burne will verify the truth of what I say," Vivian added, and hoped it was so.

"Yet the truth is that I have sampled the perfume and live."

"If the scent came from the hands of the French ambassador, straight from the flask in which he brought it, there would be no danger, Your Majesty. But Lady Claire tells me some has been measured into a favorite bottle in Your Majesty's dressing room. Do not touch a drop of that! The poison was to be added to that bottle."

"By whom?"

"One of Your Majesty's ladies-in-waiting. I do not know which, except there are good reasons why it cannot be Lady Claire."

"Because Sir Gabriel was dear to her?" The Queen's voice was gentle, but her eyes asked for more proof. Someone contemplating regicide might commit fratricide as well.

"To safeguard her after her brother's death, Sir Nigel Burne has had her watched. He is satisfied of her innocence, Your Grace."

"A man difficult to please," the Queen murmured.

Lady Claire flushed slightly, but she held her chin high. "Like my brother, I would die to protect Your Majesty."

Vivian ventured to speak. "I do know who planned the scheme and gave the lady the poison, Your Grace. He is Oliver Haughton, Lord Mortmain."

"Lord Mortmain," Elizabeth repeated doubtfully. "He has served me for a decade with no hint of unfaithfulness." But Vivian sensed that along with any motives the Queen of the Clink might have for bringing about the Earl's downfall, Mortmain's character and actions were also being reassessed. "This is yet another plot to put the Queen of Scots upon my throne?"

"Yes, Your Majesty. That is Lord Mortmain's plan. The lady-in-waiting who has betrayed you hopes to save her lover, who was arrested with Babington."

"She will die with him instead," the Queen said coldly. "Mistress Swift, you are certain the tampering was not to take place until it reached my apartments?"

"Yes, that was the plan, Your Majesty," Vivian answered.

The Queen turned to Lady Claire. "Fetch one of my bottles matching the one containing the new scent. In absolute secrecy have it filled with more of the scent from France."

"Yes, Your Majesty," Claire agreed.

While Lady Claire was gone, the Queen paced restlessly. Even lost in thought she held her head erect, her shoulders thrown back. Her hands clenched, and occasionally she muttered a fierce oath. Though she did not show it, Vivian sensed the ceaselessness of the fear gnawing her, too. As she turned, her glance fell on Viv, and she paused. In mild surprise she acknowledged, "You know what it is to feel as I feel now. I see it in your face."

The Queen's gaze turned inward, recalling tales of the roguish spiritedness of a youth spent in fear for her life, and the legendary mischievous smile of her mother, Anne Boleyn, who had gambled all for a crown and won, and then lost the next gamble, and with it her life. Elizabeth's control over her domain, her very existence, had been as precarious as Viv's own. The moment of reverie was brief, and her glance returned to Viv. The two exchanged a brief smile, comrades in the victories and terrors of the battle against fate. Then the Queen turned back to the window, and as she watched the river flow her face only looked weary, old beyond her years. "Yes," she repeated. "You know the full weight, I'll wager."

In the shadows of the room Viv felt it pressing down, too. If she got out of this, and got Rafe out of it, little matter that Jake Rivett was dead. Oh, she could carve a bigger territory from his, but others would profit, too, to become threats in their turn. Would there ever be a moment she did not have to watch her back, a day free of the fear in the deepest pit of her soul? No. Sooner or later her secret would be discovered. It was only a matter of time. Like the Queen, she was too proud to give up, but she was weary. She wanted only peace, and Rafe.

Lady Claire entered and presented a small bottle of gold set with rubies. "The unpoisoned duplicate, Your Majesty."

"Good. Send for my ladies—not Mary Sydney. I refuse to test her." The Queen glanced at Viv. "You saw her in the antechamber. She nursed me through the smallpox when my other ladies fled for fear of contagion." Hand going to her own unravaged cheek, Elizabeth said bitterly, "Heaven rewarded her thus for her faithfulness." To Claire she added, "Summon the rest one by one, privately. Tell each only that a whim has taken me. Be merry, understand?"

"Yes, Your Majesty." Despite the danger, Lady Claire smiled slightly at the incongruity of the last command.

Vivian saw the glint of grim humor in the Queen's eye. She handled her people with masterful skill. "You," Elizabeth addressed Viv, "withdraw into the shadows. Keep your eye on their faces."

As Elizabeth took a seat in her many-cushioned chair, Viv found a place to stand by the head of the bed, where the light of the single window did not reach and the curtains partly hid her. Claire brought in the first of the attendants, quiet laughter from the outer room signaling that the ladies-in-waiting were gathering as the time approached for the Queen to dress. The laughter also meant no suspicion of the plot had escaped beyond this chamber. The young woman who curtsied to Elizabeth had nut-brown hair and gentle eyes. From her corner Vivian detected no deviousness, no strong fire or coldness beneath the graceful self-possession conferred by pride of breeding and rigorous training.

"Well, Lady Katherine, I have decided the new scent is too outlandish. It does not suit me. I will stay with my old marjoram mixture." Elizabeth turned the small jeweled bottle idly in her long fingers.

"I shall see the marjoram is brought when Your Majesty dresses." No trace of frustration clouded the calm features.

"It seems a shame to waste such a costly gift. I am thinking perhaps the scent might suit you." Elizabeth held out the bottle. "Come, try some."

The lady came forward. Without hesitation she took the proffered bottle and dabbed some of the scented oil on each wrist. The Queen sniffed her, considered, and frowned. "No. Not a good match after all."

Katherine held her wrist to her own nose, looking disappointed. "No, Your Majesty, I suppose not." Clearly she wished with all her heart people would think her the type to wear exotic scent.

"Never mind." Elizabeth smiled warmly. "I value an honest English rose above all other flowers—and so does a certain young knight who excels with the bow, I hear. Have a care for his arrows."

The next trial went much as the first, except that the lady rubbed in the perfume with such vigor that if it had indeed been poisoned, she would have died before she could stopper the bottle. The third was the flaxen-haired beauty oppressed by Mary Sydney's strictness in the antechamber.

The Queen began with the same gambit, but even before she had finished speaking Viv saw the blond woman's eyes search out the small bottle peeking from her hand. Elizabeth noticed, too, but after the merest fractional pause, continued in the same indulgent tone as before. "I think this new scent might suit you. Come, try it on."

Lady Barbara's sapphire eyes lowered until the fair lashes hid them. "I could not presume, Your Majesty. Surely such perfume is a rare and princely gift from one sovereign to another?"

Elizabeth smiled. "Yet I begin to think your service has deserved such a gift." She held out the bottle. "Put some on, Lady Barbara. I am most curious as to the effect."

The girl took the jeweled bottle in shaking fingers. She hesitated, looking from the bottle to the Queen like a trapped hare. Suddenly pulling the stopper, she flung the perfume at the Queen, splattering the dressing gown and the bare skin of Elizabeth's face and hands.

"God's death!" Elizabeth roared, rising from her chair. "You dare? Guards!"

Even as they burst in and seized her, Lady Barbara grinned savagely. "Maybe the new queen will pardon me, maybe not, but I've saved one life, and avenged a wrong, too! Soon you'll be writhing and screaming, and no antidote can help you!"

"I think not," Elizabeth said calmly. "Your poison dram is still in my dressing room. This dousing is harmless, save for the reek."

Shrieking, the fair girl lunged for the Queen with her fingernails, but the guards held her back easily. Relieved as she was, Vivian could not help a pitying contempt for the young woman's ineptness. Any nimble street urchin could have slipped that grip ten different ways.

"Take her to the Tower. Cover her mouth and be as secret as you can, but send for my guard commanders," Elizabeth commanded, and the guards took Lady Barbara away.

"I should have known." Claire addressed the Queen and Viv equally in her consternation. "Lady Barbara has been withdrawn and moody ever since Sir Anthony Babington's arrest."

"My death might place the Queen of Scots on the throne and save her lover—but not her own. Few rulers forgive a regicide, even one who placed them on the throne. Of all these conspirators, Lady Barbara was the one most like to die. She was a fool for love."

"A pawn, Your Majesty," Vivian said.

"There is no doubt of that," the Queen said. "Despite precautions, Lady Barbara's arrest will soon be known. We must work fast to apprehend Lord Mortmain. Whether he is behind this or not can be determined at Our leisure—once We have him. Until then, Our life is in peril. See what the Devil is keeping my commanders, Claire, and send for Walsingham."

"Yes, Your Majesty." Lady Claire dropped a hasty curtsey and hurried out.

In a grim undertone, the Queen added, "Cousin or not, it is time to do something about Mary."

Her tone made Vivian shiver.

Queen Elizabeth turned to Viv, regarding her closely. When she spoke her tone was more familiar, but equally compelling. "Well, Mistress Nefarious, now I must play a waiting game. While I wait, I would learn just who has saved my life."

30

*A*s they rode, Burne pointed out the roof of Mortmain's townhouse rising in numerous peaks more massive than any of those around it. "By his own lights, his family has been slighted for their Catholic leanings, and not received its due from the Crown. But he still commands an extravagant household, including a large number of men at arms. Be on your guard."

Rafe could have said the same. Against an army of retainers, they were only two. "He will recognize us both."

"Not too soon, let's hope."

As they drew rein before the gate, the two armed men there were joined by four more, all of them alert. Perhaps even a force of two was too large to gain admittance.

"His lordship is occupied," a guard told them brusquely. "No one is allowed within."

Burne answered, "Tell him we come from Silver to Topaz."

"What cryptic words are those?" At his nod two others seized their reins.

Burne ignored the aggressive move, dismounting as if the guard were a mere groom holding their reins for courtesy. Rafe followed suit, keeping his hands away from his sword and snaphance. "Not words to be understood by you, clearly," Burne replied. "Just send the message and see what happens."

The leader of the guards considered, fearing to be wrong. Then he decided. "Keep them here," he commanded the others, and strode toward the house.

He returned with even more speed, nodding them through the gate, but staying with his men there. They entered the door a servant held open, and past more guards, into the dragon's very mouth. As they did so, Burne fell back a pace. Probably Burne wanted Rafe occupying the Earl's attention for the first moment. He meant to move at once, then. "Be ready," spoken quietly through Burne's closed teeth, confirmed it as they were ushered up a carved stairway.

"I have been nothing else," Rafe retorted. The man's habit of behaving as if all the accomplishments so far were his and Rafe only dead weight was irksome in the extreme. Remembering the intuitive ease with which he and Gabriel confronted a foe together, Rafe bristled at Burne's condescension.

The servant showed them along a paneled gallery, then into a luxurious library rich with books and richer still with tapestries. Bowing, he asked them to wait. As far as they could tell, they were alone. Entrances at either end of the long gallery outside could admit household guards, trapping them here. From the library, tall, narrow windows looked down into a formal garden, enclosed on all sides by high walls. No way out there, if they needed it. The tapestries opposite did not reach to the floor and could conceal no hidden guards, but a house such as this might have listening closets. The hangings bespoke power, pride, and strife, displaying the Mortmain coat of arms and ancient scenes of the Earl's ancestors in the crusades. Rafe supposed that was what Oliver Haughton of Mortmain thought he was fighting now, a new crusade against a new infidel. The family would have done better to control its own hubris and depravity. •

Such a crusader, blind to his own sins and fanatic against others', a man who would kill his queen, would not hesitate to kill them. Rafe did not like the odds against them unless he got one thing straight with Burne. Moving closer to the other man, he phrased his question carefully in case of eavesdroppers. "You have got thus far because of me, yet you still behave as if my effort and judgment were unworthy. Merely laying the groundwork for taking the credit yourself, or do you have deeper doubts of me?"

Burne looked at him directly. "You are unpredictable. I do not like that."

"And I thought you disliked me for speaking my mind." Rafe smiled bitterly. "You equate unpredictable with untrustworthy, yet I keep my word. You broke my word to Rivett, and enjoyed it."

Burne looked at him as if he were a fool, or a child. "That was your word. I am not bound by it." Seeing Rafe's mounting anger, he added coldly, "As for trusting your judgment, consider whom you are bedding."

The accusation sobered Rafe, but for a different reason than Burne intended. Indeed, he had learned much about loyalty and honor from an outlaw. He knew now beyond doubt that he was right in loving and trusting Viv. The future was uncertain, but at last he was at peace, his heart whole. He smiled at Burne, and was amused at his narrow, suspicious look.

Amused, but not at ease. Rafe would much prefer to survive this encounter. He could count on Burne only so far in this situation. At least Burne had revealed that beyond doubt.

Steps echoed from the gallery outside, one man approaching with rapid strides. As Rafe had hoped, Mortmain came alone, thinking this matter too secret to allow his servants within earshot. Together, he and Burne moved to stand with the light of the windows behind them. In accord for once, Rafe thought grimly. The Earl entered, the same light that fell on his face obscuring them as they stood before the window. Rafe saw that Mortmain was older now. The golden hair framed a thinner face and hard lines carved either side of his mouth, but it was still the overbearing Midas Man of their long-ago duel, a man who believed himself entitled to do whatever he pleased. He moved toward them, fuming.

"What fool has Rivett sent me now? Why did he have you give those words to my guard?"

Rafe stepped forward, obscuring Burne and confronting his enemy.

Mortmain checked abruptly, his wrath erased by shock. "You!"

Burne moved forward to stand beside Rafe. Mortmain's expression congealed to a blank mask. "Yes, Topaz," Burne said. "We have indeed come from Silver. He talked before he died, and now we wish to continue the conversation with you. A dialogue on monkshood and ladies-in-waiting."

Mortmain pondered, then his smile seeped back. "If you know that much, you know your master Walsingham may already have no Elizabeth behind him. Our positions may already be reversed. I, Queen Mary's man, and you, the traitor."

Burne nodded acknowledgement. "In that case, count my curiosity as theoretical, but nonetheless fervent. Tell us about the poison, my lord."

He was playing for time, Rafe knew, hoping to delay Mortmain until the royal troops arrived. Though the Earl was right. Perhaps there already was no Queen Elizabeth, and the troops that arrived would be baying for Burne's blood and his.

Mortmain's smile quirked. "I know your game. The direction of the tide being so uncertain, why shouldn't I just kill you and this lackey of yours now? Whichever queen the palace guards serve, mine are much closer."

"You have miscalculated," Burne said in a level voice. "My job is not to stay alive. It is to stop traitors." Pulling out his snaphance, he pointed it at Mortmain. Rafe drew his as well.

"Oh, look at this, more Eastons," Mortmain taunted them. "Do those work any better than the rest?"

"Perfectly." Rafe wanted to drop the gun and pound him to a pulp. "Eastons are the finest guns in England. It is you who ruined the soldiers' weapons in Holland. And the soldiers bearing them. You and your family are fit for nothing but ruination."

"I knew this lout at college," Mortmain remarked to Burne. "He always was so. Insolent, rash, and careless. Family traits, no doubt." He shifted his weight casually to his left leg, apparently unafraid of the guns pointed at him. "It was I who insisted the stolen weapons should be Easton. Why weren't you arrested with your family, Fletcher?"

"I was in the Netherlands, Mortmain. I uncovered your sabotage."

"I was careless, I admit," the Earl said. "You were so unimportant."

"You framed my family as you framed Vivian Swift."

"Yes—doubling my vengeance has proved more costly than I planned."

Rafe tensed; Vivian was now included in Mortmain's vengeance. Or had she always been a target?

"One decade, two—I avenge my family's honor. The heretic Queen promised my father estates to the north rich with topaz mines—and gave him instead a paltry estate in Kent. He died there." Mortmain gave him a cold smile.

"So you took the name Topaz," Rafe said, deflecting Mortmain from talk of his father's death.

"And the others followed suit. Silver's choice has proved accurate, for a Judas."

"Your treason with the guns is known, Mortmain. Now we would like to know what you plan to do with the stolen crates," Burne interrupted, playing Mortmain out, as if Rivett had not revealed all.

"There are numerous possibilities," the Earl returned. "Perhaps I will use them to save Babington's friends.

Perhaps I have armed every loyal Catholic in London. Even if I die, the heretic bastard will be struck down, and Queen Mary put in her rightful place." Mortmain's smile thinned as he spoke, and he gradually shifted toward the wall. Hanging alongside the tapestry Rafe saw a draw cord.

"Stop!" Rafe ordered and Burne stepped closer.

Mortmain smoothly checked his momentum, smiled, and stepped back from the cord, turning slightly toward the bookcase.

"You won't permit me to summon my guard, but what if I cry out?" Mortmain asked.

"Then you die that instant," Burne assured him, "though I'd prefer to see the ax take your head. Either way it will decorate a pike on the Tower."

"No doubt you would blunt the ax yourself, if you could. But how do you propose to get me out of here?" Mortmain replied, sweeping his left hand up to indicate his grand house containing them. "Even if you have stopped the monkshood, perhaps I'll be off to friends at the Spanish court." As his left hand drifted even higher in emphasis, Mortmain suddenly reached among the books beside him, then wheeled about with a gun in his hand.

"No," Rafe commanded. Lunging forward, he grabbed the muzzle of the snaphance, jamming his hand into the space where the cock would fall, preventing it from firing. Mortmain tried to jerk it free, but Rafe held on tightly and stepped closer, bringing his gun up against the Earl's chest. As Mortmain realized he could not shoot, his false smile froze into a raging grimace.

Through gritted teeth, Mortmain whispered, "Anne Rive." Seeing Rafe's eyes widen in recognition, he said, "The Crown may send me to the grave, but I will take her with me."

"What?" Burne demanded.

Mortmain knew Vivian had killed his father.

If Rafe knew nothing else, he knew Burne could not be trusted with Viv's secret. He glanced over his shoulder to judge what Burne could have heard. Rafe's grip faltered for only a heartbeat, but Mortmain seized it, twisting the gun partly free. Rafe snapped his head back toward the Earl. Suddenly everything seemed to slow. The barrel of gun was coming around toward him. The web of flesh between Rafe's thumb and forefinger was still almost where it could jam the mechanism. He had only to turn his hand slightly, if he could, and grab the gun again. The barrel was still swinging around. The time in which to choose between grabbing or firing had narrowed almost to nothing when Rafe suddenly pulled the trigger of his own weapon.

Mortmain jerked back, screamed, and fell to the floor, trying to call out. Rafe knelt beside him and clapped his hand over the gaping mouth to keep a dying word from destroying Vivian. He watched the blood of a monstrous traitor spurt out, avenging Gabriel, obliterating his grandfather's dishonor, and annihilating the pain this man and his father had caused Vivian.

Burne rushed to him and pulled Rafe off Mortmain "Speak, damn you," he cried.

Mortmain jerked in a violent spasm, then lay still.

Burne turned to Rafe. "What did he say to you? What was it?"

"Nothing," Rafe replied defiantly. "A curse."

"Give me your word it was nothing," Burne demanded.

"I cannot imagine ever giving you my word about anything," Rafe smiled scornfully. "But I assure you the Queen's life is safe."

A rush of footsteps came from the hall. Voices cried out. Then the library door was opened by a servant who saw Mortmain on the floor and shouted out, "Murder! The Earl is murdered!" More footfalls sounded and then armed men rushed through the door.

Burne and Rafe lowered their guns as they were surrounded.

"I am Nigel Burne, agent of Her Majesty, Queen Elizabeth," he said calmly. "Your master was a traitor to the Crown." His pale green gaze took in the armed men at one end of the gallery, then the other. "Do you love this dead traitor's memory enough to raise your hands against the Queen's men, or will you choose a gentleman from among yourselves to return with us to the palace and satisfy yourself as to the justice of this death?"

They exchanged looks, different emotions reflected in their faces. But even if they too were Catholic, the Earl had not inspired the loyalty for revenge out of hand. At last one stepped forward. "I was the Earl's secretary. I will go with you."

Dark flecks filled Rafe's sight as he slowly rose, dizzy with relief and exhaustion. It was over. Mortmain was dead, his treason exposed. Drained, he followed Burne through the opening the servants made for them. They made their way back through the house and out to the courtyard, where they mounted. Even as they set out, Burne's personal guards met up with them, and halfway to the palace, the Queen's troops as well. Burne's men came with them. All but one of the Queen's troops went on to seize Mortmain's estate.

It was not until they entered Whitehall that the lethargy that enveloped him lifted, and hope filled him, clear and sweet as rain water. They were summoned to the reception room, and there his grandfather and Peter waited. They were a curious and bedraggled pair amid the splendor of the court, but his grandfather stood proudly, his eyes clear, and Peter's smile was warm and welcoming. Rafe went to them and embraced them fiercely, tears of relief springing to his eyes. The Queen was announced, and they all knelt as she made her entrance. She bade them rise, and when Rafe stood, he saw Claire amid the Queen's ladies-in-waiting. And beside her stood the Queen of the Clink.

Meeting his gaze, Vivian gave him a triumphant smile.

31

Beckoned forward, Vivian and Rafe knelt before their sovereign. It was a private audience, only the three of them within the small elegant receiving room. With the Eastons freed, only her own fate remained undecided. Seconds ticked by as the Queen surveyed them. Viv retained her composure, her gaze fixed on the red satin skirts spilling about her knees. Fiery red for courage. But the Queen's icy silence sent chill flurries racing up and down Viv's spine, fear playing havoc with hope.

Elizabeth was a snow queen, cold and silent, her gown of white satin embroidered with silver thread and studded with diamonds, moonstones, and cold blue sapphires. Heavy ropes of pearls hung beneath the layers of starched lace that circled her neck like a ruff of snowflakes. Diamond crescents ornamented the tight curls of her wig. Her face was powered to a white mask. Painted eyes measured them each in turn, painted lips pressed to a grim line.

At last the Queen spoke. "From diverse sources, We have come to believe that the Mortmain line was corrupt, and it is well that it has died out. The son was traitor to Ourself, an unpardonable crime. The father proved himself unworthy of his title, exploiting rather than protecting those subject to his rule." She paused significantly, and Vivian shivered. "Even so, the murder of a peer cannot be taken lightly. Such a crime is an act of rebellion, rebellion an act against country, queen, and God."

Vivian held herself in firm control, feeling Rafe tense beside her. This would not be a sentence of death, not with only the three of them in the room. However uncertain her future, if Elizabeth meant to condemn Vivian for Mortmain's murder, she would condemn her openly, dismissing their personal connection in the midst of public censure. So Viv remained silent. The Queen, she suspected, enjoyed her dramas.

"Some mysteries will never be solved. And there are limits to Our tolerance. Though in imagination We can sympathize with the unknown fate of Anne Rive and her brother, England could not pardon the murder of an earl. Though We shall not look for them, it is best that they never be found." Elizabeth paused once again, smiling down at Vivian. "However, in gratitude to her valor in Our service, the crimes of Vivian Swift can and will be pardoned—providing, of course, that such wit and knowledge she possesses be put to use in service of Our interests rather than her own. Few would have such intimate knowledge of the criminal world, and how the Crown might protect itself from such swindles as corrupt and treasonous customs officers might perpetrate."

"Your Majesty is compassionate and generous," Vivian murmured, a warm flood of relief melting the ice. It was not absolution, but it was as much freedom as Vivian could ever have. The Queen would not pardon Anne

Rive, but few would dare question the favor Elizabeth chose to bestow on Vivian Swift, however nefarious her past.

The Queen's posture relaxed slightly, and her tone was warmer as she said, "Mistress Swift, to insure your good behavior, it is Our decree you shall have not only a new mistress, but a new master." Shock raced cold then hot along Viv's spine. For a moment she was speechless. The Queen turned to Rafe. "Master Fletcher, it is Our wish that you marry. I trust you will keep faith, and see your wayward lady cleaves to you."

"Yes, Your Majesty," Rafe responded, a rough catch in his voice. Viv could hear his breathing quicken, and the answering pulses of her heart, warm and swift.

"Your service to the Crown has been invaluable and intrepid. In reward, you will receive a knighthood, and the property of Hawkfields, in the county of Kent, which most recently reverted to Our hands. Use your talents well in Our service, and see your wife does likewise. I believe it may take a creature as noble and powerful as a Centaur to tame such a determined hellcat."

Hawkfields, Viv thought, her heart swelling as if it would burst. Her home returned.

"Yes, Your Majesty," Rafe murmured again. From beneath her lashes, Vivian could see his lips quirking in a smile.

"You may rise."

They rose of one accord, as if their buoyant happiness lifted them to their feet. Viv wanted to throw her arms about him and kiss him, to dance on the rushes.

But the Queen sat in her canopied chair and gestured for them to bring stools and sit beside her. Now her eyes glinted with mischief, and her tone was conspiratorial. "Before you leave, Mistress Swift, I require you and Master Fletcher to entertain me with more tales of the dockside. Rude tales they may be, but there is mirth in them as might make a goodly comedy—tales of Saucy Nan and Maggot Crutcher—if there could be found an apt playmaker."

&

The audience over, they made their way through the green gardens and gilded corridors of Whitehall to the guest room they'd been granted. As soon as they crossed the threshold, Vivian yielded to her impulse and flung her arms about Rafe's neck, covering his face with kisses. His lips tasted tangy and sweet from the mead the Queen had offered them, and the rush of relief was as intoxicating as the honey wine. Laughing, Rafe picked her up and carried her to the bed. He fell backward onto the mattress, bearing her with him. Sunshine poured over them like a golden syrup, and the warm breeze carried the poignant fragrance of late summer roses. With the light slanting across his face, Rafe's eyes burned pale blue as the tips of flame, as if the sky had caught fire. He was so beautiful, her breath caught, then rushed forth in giddy laughter. He answered with the same mirth. Between laughter, sighs, and kisses they pushed aside the covers, then plucked at hooks, points, and pins on the rich garments they had worn to their audience.

Desire urged, but delight led. He untied her sleeves and slowly pulled them down her arms. Taking one hand, he pressed his lips to the center of her palm, teasing the ticklish hollow with his tongue tip, then stroking the length of her fingers and nipping the pads. He kissed her wrist, then traced his tongue up the length of her forearm to the hollow of her elbow, a spot as sensitive as her palm. Viv loved the moist, cushioned touch of his full lower lip, which licked her like another tongue. He had the most lush, beautiful mouth—exquisite to look at, to kiss, and to feel against her skin.

She divested Rafe of the black velvet doublet and trunk hose. He peeled away her crimson bodice, stomacher, skirt, and forepart. Rafe lingered, kissing every bit of her he uncovered, leaving her in the cool softness of her linen shift. He teased her, cupping her breasts and suckling the peaks through the fabric till they drew up taut and aching. The moisture of his mouth left the fine cloth transparent, and her nipples poked at it, dark, hard points. He bit at them softly, sending bright sparks along her nerves. His hands drifted down, edging the hem of the shift up to her hips. One hand slid over the curve of her hip, descending to mold itself to the mound of her sex. His palm rubbed there with seductive pressure, while his fingertips caressed her swollen lips, then dipped into the welling moisture. Each touch enticed a brighter shimmer from her nerves, his fingertips stroking through her slick heat till they found the small pearl of flesh at the crest. They circled on that sweet pinnacle, spinning a vortex of sensation till she writhed beneath him. When it seemed she would fly over the crest, Rafe stopped, giving her a smile wicked in its sweetness, then eased the shift up over her head so that she was naked at last.

Sitting up, she tugged furiously at his remaining garments. He rid himself of the shirt, tossing it amid the satin, velvet, and linen that lay scattered on the floor. His skin gleamed in the sunlight, chest and arms scored with the half-healed cuts her knife had left in his skin. She felt a tinge of remorse, a fiercer rush of possessiveness. He was hers. They had claimed each other in both pain and delight. He was lover and husband, knight and king. Reaching out, she drew him closer, licking at the marks on his chest. Rafe shivered and moaned, his hands gripping her arms, pulling her closer.

"You are mine," she murmured.

"Yes. Yours," he answered, not rebuking her possessiveness, but tightening his grasp, claiming her in turn. "As you are mine."

"Yes," she whispered. "Yours."

Moving to his nipples, she mimicked his touches, tormenting the rose-bronze disks with sweet moist tugs of her mouth, sharp little bites of her teeth. They were as sensitive as her own, the points drawing taut against her tongue. She licked and nipped them till he gasped and twisted beneath her. Reaching down, she could feel his arousal straining against the silk hose, and quickly loosened the cord at his waist. Sliding off the bed to kneel between his legs, she peeled the fabric down over the dense muscle of his thighs, the strong shapely calves, and off the big feet with their long, endearingly crooked toes.

He pushed up to sit on the edge of the bed, and gazed down at her. Viv returned his wicked smile, her view distracted by the sway of his manhood, flushed scarlet with lust. She pushed his legs wide, her fingernails sketching sinuous patterns on his thighs. The muscles of his thighs quivered, and she delighted in the power and vulnerability she commanded with her touch. With one fingertip she traced the blue pattern of the veins, like secret rivers running beneath his skin, and felt him surge at the touch. She blew lightly on the heavy roundness of his balls and watched them draw up tighter. He exhaled a breath, half laughter, half plea as she nuzzled them, breathing his musky scent. She licked a path from the base of the shaft, over the blue veins, up to the slit that wept a hot bright tear of desire. She kissed the tip, her tongue flicking there lightly. He murmured her name, urging her, hungry for more. Still teasing, she parted her lips, stroking the satin crown with their inner moistness. He thrust toward her and she seized him, wrapping her hands about the shaft while she swirled her tongue about the head. She loved the searing heat and magnificent size of him.

Opening her mouth, she took him deeper, exploring all the subtle shapes and textures with her tongue. He watched her, fascinated, his chest rising and falling with his panting breath as her tongue laved the hot column. When she tightened her mouth around him, he gave a low groan and slumped back on bed, prisoner of her skill. Viv suckled him with ferocious pleasure, drawing him to the edge of quivering need, then easing back. He moaned and shivered as the cool air licked him in place of her tongue.

"Greedy," she chided him, her lips quivering.

"I learned from a master," he retorted, reaching down and pulling her back onto the bed.

They tumbled on the sheets, lips and tongue at play, laughing and gasping as they kissed. She pressed close, reveling in the naked sweetness of skin on skin. Her body glowed where they touched, breasts and belly and thighs. His hands flowed over her, shaping the curves of her hips, then turned her over to caress her back. Warm fingers ruffled her cropped hair, warm lips nuzzled the nape of her neck. His mouth laid a line of kisses along her shoulders, then moved down her spine, the tip of his tongue weaving a path around each vertebrae. Mock growling, he nipped the sensitive mounds of her buttocks till she squirmed. She lifted her hips and he nudged between her legs to lick her sex from behind, his hot tongue coaxing the flow of honey. She pressed back for more and his tongue lashed till she was frantic with desire.

Excitement urged her to soar to completion, but Viv wanted to see his face. She squirmed away from him, then seized his shoulders and rolled him onto his back. His eyes glittered as she straddled his hips, and his tongue tip emerged to lick the hot liquor of her sex from his lips. Leaning down she gave him a long, avid kiss, drinking his taste and her own. His manhood swelled against her, and she nestled the long length of him in the wet cleft of her nether lips, stroking him with the wet heat of her sex. He sighed and shivered with bliss, flinging his arms wide and gathering soft fistfuls of the covers. She teased him so, slickness stroking hardness, till his head thrashed slowly from side to side.

Rising, she felt the surge of him lifting beneath her, seeking her. She poised over him, centering herself, feeling the tender resilience of the crown and the pulsing vigor of the shaft. She held herself there, waiting till he met her gaze. His eyes were bright, the irises luminous blue in the sunlight. She inhaled sharply as she felt him nudge inside her. She held his gaze as she sank down, bringing him within her in a long exquisite slide. They cried out wordlessly to each other. The moment of entry was so exciting, so compelling, her body opening to embrace his power, capturing him even as he conquered. Pleasure suffused her, radiating out from their shared center. He gave a low, almost inaudible cry, arching to fill her completely. His head tilted back and his eyes almost closed—almost but not quite. Shaded under the dark lashes, they were smoke blue now, the fire deep within. He watched her as she lifted and lowered, riding the smooth hard thrust of his hips, his sex.

"Viv," he whispered, his voice hoarse with pleasure.

"Rafe," she answered, clasping him tightly within her, every inch of him. The wet silk of her sex squeezed as her hands might, wringing spasms of pleasure from them both—holding him as if she would never let go. "I love you . . . love you . . . love you."

He gave a low groan, and she could feel him swelling, larger still, overwhelming her with pleasure, with awe. Emotion fused with passion and she contracted around him suddenly, deep pulsations releasing a climax of utter joy and wonder. He cried out, filling her with the pulsing seed of his passion. Shudders rippled outward from the hot core they shared, quivering through every particle with fierce delight, expanding her entire being. Flesh and bone melted, spirit dissolved from flesh, and at last even spirit evaporated into purest rapture.

She lay beside him, sated, yet vibrantly aware, brimming with life. Free beyond any known freedom. Home. A cool breeze skimmed their bodies. Beside her, Rafe curved to fit her, one warm hand cupping her breast, the other and sliding smooth over her belly. Her womb glowed as if it held the sun. She felt certain his seed had quickened within her, that there would be a child—its life beginning with their new life together.

Lying beside her, he whispered, "I love you. Forever."

Epilogue

Kent, 1592

The chestnut trees spread their branches overhead, yellow leaves rustling as if laughing at tales told by the breeze. On the blue cloth, platters held scraps of bread and cold meats, the rind of a cheese, what remained of a bounteous bowl of pears, apples, and grapes. The hills stretched away in verdant swells, each shape familiar, their crowning copse bright with an autumn largesse of gold. After six years of tender care, the neglected estate of Hawkfields looked as it should once more, its gabled roofs and mullioned windows gleaming in the sun, its gardens and orchards abundant with blossoms and fruit.

Lazily Vivian watched Rafe's grandfather explain to little Elizabeth the wooden gun he had made for her. It was a replica of Easton Arms' latest model. He had painstakingly carved the flint in its screw, the pan, even wooden bullets to go in the chamber, and Bess followed his explanation with attention punctuated by observant questions and pokes of her sticky fingers. The old man's pleasure was as evident as the child's.

Stretched out on the grass, Rafe looked dubious. Delight in his daughter alternated with alarm. Though the wooden gun would not fire, Viv knew he did not entirely approve. Soon Elizabeth would demand one that did—and a fine sword as well. Viv had already determined that no one but Rafe would teach Elizabeth to fence. He would do it, she knew, with but a little cajoling, though he had asked Viv what need had the daughter of a respectable knight for such skills? Better Elizabeth learn the graces of well-read conversation and music, the responsibilities of managing a manor, the pleasures of hawking and hunting. And so she would. Even now, she could stick on a horse like a cocklebur and dance with the beginnings of quick grace. As for books, if she hungered for them she would have them in the abundance Viv had once craved. Rafe not only understood that longing in a girl, but approved of it. In truth, he doted on Elizabeth's every talent, but spread warm protective wings over her whenever she rushed toward danger. In her joyous charge, Bess could neatly dodge every feather, yet nestled there readily enough when she tumbled.

Smiling amorously, Viv selected an especially plump grape, dark and purple, from the bowl. Leaning over Rafe, she teased his lips with it. He took the offering she urged, then caught her wrist and bit her finger. "Guns indeed," he murmured.

"One never knows what may come in handy," Viv murmured back. He frowned uneasily, but she stroked his cheek with her finger. "Should she not develop every strength as well as every grace?"

"Yes," he whispered, his voice husky. "Like her mother."

She smiled at him. Leaving her old ways behind had not been easy, especially when the Queen had placed so much potential for empire building in her reach. But Rafe had meant it when he asked for her promise that she would use her skills within the boundaries of legality, and Viv had given him her word. Such boundaries were supple, but she was true to Rafe's intent. He would pit all his deviousness against an enemy, but by choice he was honest and generous. As much as she loved the fire and the darkness they'd shared, she loved the open-hearted goodness that was larger than her own passionate but narrow loyalties.

The rewards had proved worth her promise. Her old territory prospered. Smoke was now King of the Clink. He'd cleaned up Maggot's foundering territory and taken over a goodly piece of Rivett's. The wider holdings were profitable enough that he abandoned smuggling, at least directly, to insure his interests did not come in conflict with hers. Taking the pardon that Smoke had scorned, Izzy now ran a successful inn where news of every venture in London reached his ears, and so Viv's. She and Rafe spent part of their time here at Hawkfields, and part in London or Dover on the Queen's business. Peter had married and tended conscientiously to Easton Arms. Viv had her own ideas on the development of the pistols, which Rafe presented along with his own, much to his family's chagrin. Grandfather Easton was quite convinced Vivian was going to hell, but he thought it a great pity, for he was very fond of her.

Viv smoothed Rafe's wayward forelock, an innocent caress even the Puritan old man could not disapprove. She understood Rafe's bite well enough, and the flick of his tongue on the sensitive pad of her finger. She met his eyes, anticipating the hour when the others were tucked safely in their beds. Then bright fire would burn in the midst of the dark. However much she had yielded to his goodness, there were times when she drew forth all the sweet wickedness of his soul.

Smiling, Rafe shaped his big hand to the rising curve of her belly, the warmth of his touch penetrating to her womb and the life within. Only the smallest swell yet, but Viv was certain this child would be a boy. The splay of Rafe's long fingers, protective and sensuous, so strong and yet so gentle, roused all her love for him.

Yes, she mused, *I will honor this bargain. I will protect it with all my will, and all my heart. For all I have lost, I have won more. Far, far more.*